**Praise for the novels of *New York Times*
bestselling author Jo Beverley**

"A delightful, intricately plotted, and sexy romp."
—*Library Journal*

"Storytelling at its best!"   —*Rendezvous*

"A well-crafted story and an ultimately very satisfying
romance."   —*The Romance Reader*

"Jo [Beverley] has truly brought to life a fascinating,
glittering, and sometimes dangerous world."
—Mary Jo Putney

"Another triumph."   —*Affaire de Coeur*

"Wickedly delicious. Jo Beverley weaves a spell of sensual delight with her usual grace and flair."
—Teresa Medeiros

"Delightful . . . thrilling . . . with a generous touch of
magic . . . an enchanting read."   —*Booklist*

"A stunning medieval romance of loss and
redemption. . . . Sizzling."
—*Publishers Weekly* (starred review)

"A fast-paced adventure with strong, vividly portrayed
characters . . . wickedly, wonderfully sensual and glori-
ously romantic."   —Mary Balogh

"Deliciously sinful. . . . Beverley evokes with devastating
precision the decadent splendor of the English country
estate in all its hellish debauchery. . . . A crafty tale of
sensuality and suspense."   —*BookPage*

ALSO BY JO BEVERLEY

The Rogue's Return

Jo Beverley

A SIGNET BOOK

SIGNET
Published by New American Library, a division of
Penguin Group (USA) Inc., 375 Hudson Street,
New York, New York 10014, USA
Penguin Group (Canada), 90 Eglinton Avenue East, Suite 700, Toronto,
Ontario M4P 2Y3, Canada (a division of Pearson Penguin Canada Inc.)
Penguin Books Ltd., 80 Strand, London WC2R 0RL, England
Penguin Ireland, 25 St. Stephen's Green, Dublin 2,
Ireland (a division of Penguin Books Ltd.)
Penguin Group (Australia), 250 Camberwell Road, Camberwell, Victoria 3124,
Australia (a division of Pearson Australia Group Pty. Ltd.)
Penguin Books India Pvt. Ltd., 11 Community Centre, Panchsheel Park,
New Delhi - 110 017, India
Penguin Group (NZ), cnr Airborne and Rosedale Roads, Albany,
Auckland 1310, New Zealand (a division of Pearson New Zealand Ltd.)
Penguin Books (South Africa) (Pty.) Ltd., 24 Sturdee Avenue,
Rosebank, Johannesburg 2196, South Africa

Penguin Books Ltd., Registered Offices:
80 Strand, London WC2R 0RL, England

First published by Signet, an imprint of New American Library,
a division of Penguin Group (USA) Inc.

First Printing, March 2006
10 9 8 7 6 5

Acknowledgments

So many threads come together as I weave a book, but in preparing to write *The Rogue's Return* I made heavy use of ECO (Early Canadiana Online), a Web service of Heritage Canada, part of the federal government. One text was particularly useful: *The Ridout Letters— Ten Years of Upper Canada in Peace and War, 1815–1815*. It was poignant to read in there about young John Ridout, playing a gallant part in the War of 1812 at only fourteen, knowing his tragic end. There's more about that in my author's note at the end.

Reader Judy Dawe very kindly did some leg work for me on a trip to Carlisle and settled a couple of questions, principally the one of where the Otterburns lived.

At just the right moment (it often happens), my friend Jennifer Taylor decided to declutter and give me her copy of *The British Code of Duel* from 1824.

I gathered most of my medical information from the facsimile copy of the 1771 *Encyclopedia Britannica*, with some later sources as confirmation. My fellow author, one-time emergency room nurse Eileen Dreyer, helped me make sense of what I'd learned.

Thanks to all, and to the many others whose brains I ruthlessly picked along the way. As always, any errors are my fault alone.

Chapter One

York, Upper Canada, September 1816

*W*hen silence settles raggedly on a group of drinking men, it's wise to brace for trouble.

Simon St. Bride was playing whist in D'Arcy Boulton's house and had been as unaware of the noise of voices as of the smoke from clay pipes and cigarillos. As the last few careless voices stopped, however, he came alert. The back of his neck prickled—especially when Boulton, his card partner, glanced sharply beyond him.

He was about to turn when he heard: "Damned peculiar if you ask me."

Lancelot McArthur.

Simon could envision the Indian Affairs officer—fleshy, high-colored, with abundant dark curls glossy with pomade and sharp dark eyes set a bit too close. His collar would be too high, his waistcoat too loud, his brass buttons too big, but he'd think himself the very picture of a man of fashion.

Simon wouldn't give a fig about that if the funds for McArthur's tasteless excesses weren't stolen. For years, the man had been using tricks and lies to embezzle money and goods sent to reward the Indian tribes for fighting for the British in the recent war.

Simon had lingered here in Upper Canada to dig out evidence that would bring the man down. He was ready to leave but had been warned only days ago that

McArthur had caught wind of his work. Beneath the friendly warning, he'd heard another message.

Go back to aristocratic England, where you belong.

So now McArthur was openly stirring trouble. With what purpose, and how to react?

Most of the gentlemen in this room were casual friends, but most would also be in favor of anything that drove the Indians west into wilder lands, freeing up land for settlement and prosperity.

"My lead, I think," Simon said and put down the five of clubs. Captain Farleigh to his left played to it and the game went on. Conversation shook itself and revived, but half of Boulton's attention was still on matters behind Simon's back.

Simon knew McArthur would love to stick a knife into him, but he wouldn't. Not here, in a gentleman's house. Not even in the street on a dark night.

There were others attempting to redress wrongs, principally the Quakers, but they didn't have, as people put it, "the clout" back in England. He, however, did. He was a St. Bride of Brideswell, closely related to the Earl of Marlowe and distantly to nearly every titled family in Britain. He also had powerful friends, and in the cause had let names drop. The Earl of Charrington. Viscounts Amleigh and Middlethorpe. The Marquess of Arden, heir to the dukedom of Belcraven.

He was simply too wellborn and well connected to be murdered without causing trouble for the people of York.

He hoped.

The moment seemed to have passed, but then someone chided, "Lady's name, McArthur."

"Of course, of course," McArthur drawled—louder. He wanted to be heard. "But damned strange, wouldn't you say? A pretty young lady who won't dance at a ball or even attend a musical evening?"

"Simon?"

Boulton's vocal nudge made Simon aware that he'd halted play. He discarded, but now his senses were all focused behind. That sneering reference had to be to Jane Otterburn, but what scandal could McArthur make of her?

Jane Otterburn was the niece of Simon's friend and mentor, Isaiah Trewitt. Last year she'd been orphaned and crossed the Atlantic to live here with her uncle. She was eighteen and of a Puritan disposition, dressing soberly and keeping to herself. She was the antithesis of scandal. Simon should know. When in York he lived in Isaiah's house.

"Mourning, aye," McArthur said, obviously in response to a comment. "But her year's over now. Was over in August, I understand."

"Quiet gal. Nothing wrong with that."

Simon recognized the protester as Major Turnbull, a good-hearted man with daughters of his own. He had spoken as loudly as McArthur, trying to head off trouble. "Wish my daughters were as dutiful and quietly behaved."

"Perhaps the charming Misses Turnbull could coax Miss Otterburn out," McArthur suggested.

"Tried. Sweet-natured girls. But Miss Otterburn won't have it. Nothing wrong with that," the major added firmly.

"But is it *natural*?" McArthur persisted, and the room fell silent. "To show no interest in innocent pleasures? In handsome young officers and other gallant gentlemen who wish to pay her honorable attentions?"

Simon's jaw tensed. No man of honor could let such words go unchallenged—unless they were true. *Hell almighty*. Typical of a cur like McArthur to work his spite on an innocent, but to react would only draw closer attention to it.

"Perhaps it's as well that Miss Otterburn didn't take up your innocent daughters' offers, Major. After all, what do we know of the young lady except what Trewitt has told us? Has he offered us honest coin, or is she not precisely his niece . . . ."

Simon surged to his feet and turned, his chair clattering to the floor behind him. "What the devil are you insinuating, McArthur?"

"My dear St. Bride, what could I be insinuating to cause such a rage?"

Simon heard mutters directed against McArthur, but the wrong move here could throw Jane's reputation on the dung heap.

He matched McArthur's lazy malice. "Why, honest coin, of course. How dare you accuse Isaiah Trewitt of theft or embezzlement, sir? Though I'm sure that's a touchy subject in the Indian office."

McArthur stood, his naturally high color deepening to purple. "And what the devil do you mean by *that*, sir?"

Simon saw disaster ahead, but by God it felt good to turn the tables on the man. And to bring the stink into the open.

"Quite a lot of honest coin arrives in the Indian office but never reaches the tribes. Strange, wouldn't you say, especially when some people in the department live surprisingly well, given their salaries."

The silence became total. To nail the business shut, Simon added, "Fine new house you have, McArthur."

McArthur went from puce to white, and if it were possible his eyes grew closer together. "You lie, sir."

"You *don't* have a fine new house? My sincere apologies. Blame the architect—"

"About my honesty, damn you!" McArthur roared. "Name your seconds."

Simon had to fight a grin of insane satisfaction. Perhaps McArthur had wanted a duel all along, in which case he hoped to kill his enemy that way. But he'd intended it to be over Jane Otterburn's virtue, and now they would exchange shots over his nonexistent honesty.

Too late, McArthur was realizing it.

He looked like someone striding boldly down a street who finds himself neck-deep in a bog. No matter how the duel turned out, close attention would soon be paid to the treatment of Indians in Upper Canada. And Simon's evidence would make its way back to London, with or without him.

He needed a second. Boulton's family was rooted here, so taking sides in this issue could put him in a difficult situation. Farleigh was married. Captain Norton, the other man at the table, was a steady fellow with no long-term interest in Canada.

"May I call on you, Norton?" Simon asked

The man looked taken aback but nodded. "Honor."

"Delahaye?" McArthur rigidly asked of the man beside him.

Lieutenant Delahaye, one of McArthur's closest friends, agreed.

Conversation picked up again, quiet, speculative, even furtive.

Simon stepped aside with Norton, who said, "If he takes back his words about Miss Otterburn . . ."

"This is not about Jane Otterburn."

The man grimaced. "Quite, quite. Then will you retract your implications? Say you were misunderstood?"

"No. If he wishes to retract his challenge, I will not pursue it."

Norton sighed. "Pistols? Twelve paces?"

Fists would suit Simon's mood, but he agreed. He'd never fought a duel, but he knew the code.

He was a good shot, but presumably McArthur was, too, since he'd needled for a meeting. He shrugged that aside and turned to leave, but McArthur was already at the door. Simon had no wish to walk the streets with him, so he strolled to the fire for a moment, aware of the space forming around him. He'd enjoyed his four years in Upper Canada and made some good friends, but his recent activities had created divisions.

Men were drifting out, anxious to leave and also to

carry the news home. Within a half hour everyone still awake would know about the duel and the overt reason for it—McArthur's embezzlement. They'd be chewing over the implications for McArthur, for the Indians, for local politics and settlement, for profits and prospects. And doubtless cursing meddlesome Simon St. Bride.

But they'd also be speculating on McArthur's insinuations. Surely no one would believe that Jane was Isaiah's lover? Incestuous lover, even.

Damn McArthur, Simon thought, looking into flames, but damn Jane Otterburn, too, for being so peculiar.

True enough, she'd arrived here worn out from a difficult journey and grief. She'd lost not only her mother before leaving England but also a cousin on the voyage—a cousin who'd been raised with her like a sister. To seal her misery, she'd arrived in November during the first bitter spell of what was to be a severe winter.

Perhaps it wasn't surprising that she'd refused sleigh rides and skating, and mourning was reason to avoid assemblies and balls. By Easter, however, both she and the weather had recovered, and still she'd refused all invitations.

Isaiah would have loved to dress her in fashionable clothes and introduce her to fine society. He might have started life as a ship's carpenter, but he'd done well and was accepted here. Such a pretty girl could have made a grand match. Even though York was in the wilds and had a population of only a thousand, it was the capital of Upper Canada and a major garrison. It was bursting with young men of good family.

But Jane had insisted on living like a nun. She even dressed like a nun, in plain dark gowns and close white caps. A radiant nun, because dismal clothes couldn't hide an excellent figure, clear Celtic skin, fine blue eyes, and soft, sensual lips. And try as she might, tendrils of red-gold hair constantly escaped her caps.

No man could help noticing these things—and occasionally imagining. Which was presumably what every other normal man in York had been doing, making fertile ground for McArthur's mischief.

Norton came over. "Dawn tomorrow. Elmsley's Farm."

Simon nodded, thanked him, and left the almost empty room.

Norton, Farleigh, and Major Turnbull came out with him. "Keep you company, St. Bride."

Simon knew that if McArthur thought shooting him on a dark road feasible, he wouldn't be about to face him in daylight, but he didn't argue. There were certainly plenty of ambush spots on the arrow-straight street dotted with wooden houses on large, treed lots. Wood and land were cheap here.

They chatted about the terrible weather and the probable early freeze of the Saint Lawrence River, which annually cut York off from the Atlantic and Britain for four or more months. They discussed the wedding of Princess Charlotte and the future of the Crown. Anything except the duel.

Within sight of the doorway, Simon thanked the officers for their company and added to Norton, "Can you persuade Playter to be the doctor in attendance?"

Norton nodded. "Already thought of that."

Simon went into the house, somewhat chilled by that practical detail. The army surgeon was the physician with the most experience with gunshot wounds.

And with amputations.

More than death he feared maiming. It was folly, but he couldn't help it. The fear had come upon him when a friend, Major Hal Beaumont, had lost his arm after a battle near York two years ago. Simon had done everything he could for Hal, but he hadn't been able to overcome a squeamish, shameful horror.

Some officers carried on after such injuries, but the

war had seemed over, so Hal had sold his commission. True, he had independent income left him by an uncle, but perhaps he'd felt unable to do the job.

The house was silent apart from the ticking of the clock. Though Isaiah was a prosperous merchant and Trewitt House handsome by York standards, servants, especially male ones, were hard to find and keep here, surrounded by the siren song of available land.

Isaiah made do with two young maids who came in daily, an ancient cook-housekeeper, Mrs. Gunn, plus a lad, Tom, who took care of the horses. An old friend, a one-eyed rascal called Saul Prithy, lived over the stables and tended the gardens when he'd a mind to.

Tom and the young maids lived at their own homes. Mrs. Gunn lived over the kitchen, which sat behind the house but was joined by a walkway—a sensible defense against fire in a town almost entirely built of wood. Isaiah had given up trying to find a valet worth the hiring, and even his clerk, Salter, had gone off to carve an "estate" out of the bush.

Simon knew it was unfair to sneer when he was heir to an estate back home, but so many of these hopeful empire builders failed and then blamed the Indians for it.

His mind turned to beautiful Brideswell, a rambling stone manor house four hundred years old in parts, set amid rolling Lincolnshire countryside. It sat close to the village of Monkton St. Brides, where houses and cottages snuggled together and streets wound about as fancy took them. Neither place could be less like raw, squared-off York, and it was so long since he'd been home.

Simon stood in the silent hall, breathless at the thought that he might not see Brideswell again. He'd been away four years and he'd missed it frequently, but he'd never—not even when fighting off the invading Americans—imagined that he would not return.

Was this a premonition?

He shook that off and sat to remove his boots with the jack. Then he picked up the candle that stood waiting for him, glowing steadily within a glass storm lantern. Jane's work. Whatever her peculiarities, she was an excellent housekeeper. In the past year the bachelor residence had taken on little graces—flowers in season, potpourri, and a change in the polish used on the wooden floors so that they gleamed brighter. Simon could smell it as he went upstairs, subtle but reminiscent of an English spring.

He turned his mind to things he must do. A will. Letters—to Isaiah, to his parents.

God.

The nearest door opened.

Jane Otterburn stood there, wearing a nightcap that tied beneath her chin and a long green robe that showed her nightgown only by frills of white at the high neck and wrists.

How could she look so *undressed*?

"Yes?" he asked, hearing irritation in his voice. "Is something the matter?"

Oh, Lord. Has she heard?

She looked as awkward as he felt. "Isaiah isn't well," she whispered. "Another attack of the ague, but he refused to send for Dr. Baldwin." She bit her lip. "I'm sorry. There was no need to interrupt you. I'm sorry."

He reminded himself she was only eighteen. "If he's no better in the morning, we'll deal with it." *If I'm alive.*

"Yes, of course. Did you have a pleasant evening?"

What could he say? "Tolerable. Good night, Jane."

"Good night, Simon."

Simon carried on quietly past Isaiah's door to his own large room at the back of the house. The bed sat in an alcove concealed by a curtain during the day, which gave the room the look of a parlor. Sometimes Simon entertained friends here, though mostly he used the downstairs parlor. Isaiah enjoyed young company.

He looked around at the welcoming fire with the jug of water nearby, covered to keep it warm. Strange to think that this might be the last night he'd sleep here, the last night he'd wash his face and clean his teeth.

He shook himself.

He poured himself a glass of brandy and drank half, and then sat at his desk to write his will. There was little to it, for though he was heir to Brideswell, at the moment he owned only his personal possessions and a modest amount of cash left from the income his father provided.

The letter to Isaiah was more difficult, for sooner or later he'd learn the cause of the duel and feel responsible. Simon couldn't see how to avoid that, so he wrote a grateful, affectionate farewell, emphasizing that he'd chosen the duel as a way to expose the festering sore of corruption here.

The most painful task was the letter to his parents, and for a while he couldn't bring himself to write it.

They'd tried so hard to keep him safe. It was the Brideswell way. St. Brides of Brideswell stayed close to home. They served their country but in quiet ways from Lincolnshire. For generations they'd flourished there, with large, healthy families, but like a hive.

He'd wanted to follow his friends Hal Beaumont, Con Somerford, and Roger Merrihew into the fight against Napoleon, but his mother had thrown fits, and his father had talked of Simon's responsibilities as the oldest son. As if his younger brothers, Rupert and Benji, didn't exist.

In the end, they'd allowed him to take a post as secretary to Lord Shepstone, who was traveling to Canada to make inquiries into discord with America. It had involved a somewhat risky sea voyage, but even he hadn't expected to land in a war.

When the Americans had invaded, however, duty had required him to fight. Despite the inevitable horrors of war, he'd reveled in it, and by the time the invasion was repulsed, he'd been outraged by the treatment of Britain's Indian allies. He'd stayed to fight new battles. . . .

He realized he was trying to excuse himself to his parents and dipped his pen. Though he could imagine all too well their agony and tears if he died tomorrow, surely reading something from him would be a comfort.

In the end the letter was brief. What was there to say that would help? He simply told them how much he loved them and how much he appreciated their guidance and care. He ended it:

> *All I am that is good I have from you, my dearest parents. Any follies can doubtless be ascribed to Black Ademar's hair.*

He wondered if a family joke was the wrong tone, but how could there be a right tone in such a damnable letter? And it was true.

Most St. Brides of Brideswell saw no pleasure in adventure, but far back on the family tree lurked Ademar de Braque.

Ademar had been born a younger son of a poor knight of the thirteenth century and made his fame and fortune through violence—on crusade, on the battlefield, and especially in tournaments. He had doubtless deserved to be called Black Ademar for many vile reasons, but it was said his other nickname, Diable, came from Tête du Diable because he had black hair shot through with red.

The same devil's hair Simon saw in a mirror.

It was an attribute that lurked for generations, but whenever it popped up, the parents knew they had a cuckoo in the nest—a St. Bride who at best would want to wander and at worst would be a fiery hothead best suited to war. His poor parents had two. When a baby girl had arrived with the hair, they'd stared down fate and called her Ademara. Mara hadn't run wild yet, but then she was only eighteen.

He left the joke, signed the letter, folded it, and sealed it. As he placed the three documents on top of the desk, he realized there was something else to take care of—the evidence he'd collected here.

Not all of it was irreplaceable. Evidence of the sufferings of the Indians—of promises broken, tricks played, and vast lands purchased for a pittance—was all too easy to find. Others, especially the Quakers, were working hard for reparation.

However, he also had evidence of trickery and even crimes committed by McArthur and his associates. Some documents were signed and witnessed testimony from people now suspiciously dead. Others were copies of cryptic messages that needed to be studied exactly as they were. He'd become sure that references to "coin" and "land" were actually codes for individuals in the administration or the military, but he couldn't break them.

If he died, the papers must go safely to England. But who could he trust? Isaiah was unwell. Friends here could have divided allegiances or even be hand in glove with McArthur. Lieutenant Governor Gore, the chief administrator, was an honest man, but even he might be tempted to bury trouble.

Simon thought of Jane—but it was too weighty a burden to place on an unworldly girl. In the end he unsealed the letter to Isaiah and asked him to take care of things. Even ill, he'd know what to do.

He then took out his pistols to clean and check them. They weren't dueling pistols, but they were excellent guns. He hoped to able to use them, but if McArthur had a matched pair, they'd toss for it.

Then he poured himself a little more brandy and sat before the dying fire, trying to think profound thoughts. It didn't work, so he went to bed.

Chapter Two

*W*hy the devil did people duel at dawn? In great-coat, hat, and gloves, Simon paced to keep warm. He glanced to where heavy clouds seemed to be weighing down the rising sun, wondering if rain or even sleet would halt the affair entirely. No one could risk damp powder.

No birds sang. Not even a dog barked. The only sound was the constant muffled moan of the great forest. Simon didn't usually notice it anymore, but he remembered how it had struck him when first here. White men found it foreboding, but for the Indians it was the music of home.

He supposed the early hour was to avoid the authorities. Pointless here, where lawyers and military officers were as likely to duel as anyone.

No wonder McArthur had hit upon this way of getting rid of him. A sprig of the aristocracy shot in a duel over a woman. Unfortunate, but not outrageous. It gave Simon satisfaction to know that whatever happened, a duel over embezzlement would never be seen as trivial.

And he hoped McArthur was choking on that.

He looked to where his opponent was also pacing and couldn't read any expression. The man was brave and bold enough—he'd grant him that. But a villain. Greed had driven him to fraud, theft, and, though Simon couldn't prove it, murder.

Delahaye and Norton were meticulously settling the last details. At a distance, Playter, the garrison surgeon, stood hunched and disapproving, his wide-brimmed hat pulled well down, a woolen muffler wrapped twice around his neck. He'd greeted everyone with a curt "Damn folly!" and then taken himself and his ominous dark bag aside.

The seconds paced off the distance and then marked the firing lines with short lengths of rope. *Come on, come on,* Simon thought. *Let's get it over, live or die.* But the proper procedures were important or someone might hang for murder, even including the seconds.

Norton and Delahaye went to one side to inspect and load the pistols. In the end they'd agreed to use a set of dueling pistols borrowed from someone else. No advantage to either and theoretically more accurate, but guns were unpredictable. Norton was loading Simon's. He hoped the man would take sufficient care.

Seeking calm, Simon turned to face the distant grayness of Lake Ontario. It didn't help. The lake was so huge that it could be the sea—it even had its own navy. But it wasn't. Abruptly it mattered that he might die so far from the North Sea, which he'd been able to look out on from his bedroom window at Brideswell. Where he'd spent idyllic summers out in boats. That smelled of salt, which this freshwater lake did not.

In wartime, caught up in urgent purpose, he'd not pined about where and how he'd die, but now it threatened to distress him.

Come on, come on. Get on with it.

He heard someone approach and turned. Norton with the pistol in his hand. Simon's heart started to pound as it had before facing an onslaught, so as he stripped off his gloves and coat, he did as he'd learned to do and took steadying breaths.

His heart rate wasn't fast from fear, but its intensity could make the hands shake.

He handed his clothing to Norton, taking the pistol in

exchange. Steadiness returned. He walked to take his place, concentrating on the justice of his cause and on the absolute necessity of returning safely to his family.

Would McArthur shoot to kill?

Almost certainly.

Which meant he should.

But he knew he couldn't. He'd aim high, hoping to hit the shoulder and put an end to it that way.

He presented his side, the narrowest target, murmuring under his breath, "Ademar, *aidez-moi*." It was a habit he'd formed during the war, and as always it brought the cool detachment he needed.

Delahaye was to give the count—one, two, three—and then drop a handkerchief. That was so that the duelists would have to watch him, not concentrate on aim.

"One."

Simon cocked the pistol and raised it.

"Two."

He took steady aim on McArthur's upper torso.

"Three."

He looked to Delahaye. . . .

"*Stop!* Stop, I say!"

McArthur fired.

Simon whirled to the voice, feeling the ball whistle by him.

With the noise still shaking the air and smoke curling from McArthur's gun, everyone turned shocked fury on Jane Otterburn, running across the frosty field, skirts hiked up to her knees, hair flying loose.

Simon was tempted to shoot her out of pure fury. "Jane, go home."

"No! Uncle Isaiah—" She stopped to heave in a breath. "An accident. He's *dying,* Simon. He wants you."

She wore her usual dark dress and cloak, but her red-gold hair rioted loose down to her waist, shocking in its magnificent abundance.

She sucked in more breaths. "Come on. You men can kill each other tomorrow!"

After a numb moment, Simon gave his pistol to Norton and strode off.

"My God," McArthur protested, "you shan't slide out of it like this, you coward. I'll have you horsewhipped!"

Simon wheeled on him. "I'll fight you tomorrow, McArthur, and kill you tomorrow. With pleasure. Now, I attend my friend."

He began to run toward his horse. He became aware of Jane only from gasping breaths and slowed. "What happened?"

"He . . . shot himself." She was still breathing hard, a hand on her side. "He heard about the duel. . . . Wanted to fight in your place. A pistol. Something went wrong."

"Old fool." Simon wanted to howl it. Damn it all to Hades!

He could hardly pick out his horse from the others because tears were blurring his vision. Isaiah couldn't be dying. He turned to glare at Jane, loathing the bearer of bad news, but he couldn't abandon her here. "Can you ride behind?"

She looked up at the horse. "I never have." But then she firmly added, "Of course."

He mounted and then helped her up behind him. With a struggle, she got a leg over to sit astride, not seeming to care that she was showing her knees. But then, she'd not cared about that as she ran across the field to stop the duel.

What had happened to the quiet nun?

He felt her hesitation before she put her arms around him, but when she did, she held on tight. Once she was secure he urged the horse to speed toward the town. They'd be there in minutes, but had Jane run all the way, skirts up, hair down?

And why her? Why had she brought the news?

He felt as if his entire world had been shaken up and spilled in pieces. Was the duel over? Was he shot and hallucinating? But everything—sharp air, pounding hooves, arms clutching—was absolutely real.

He drew up in front of Trewitt House, swung off, and helped Jane down. Abandoning the horse to the gathering crowd, he ran into the building, only realizing as they entered that he was hand in hand with her.

He let her go.

There were people inside the house, too—probably anyone who thought they had an excuse to get close to the drama—so he had to push his way through. As he was recognized, a way parted and he was soon in Isaiah's office. It stank of blood.

His friend lay on the floor, perhaps where he'd been found, his head on a pillow, his rawboned body covered by a blood-drenched blanket. The wound was clearly somewhere in the lower torso, and that demolished hope. No one survived a belly wound.

Dr. Baldwin, Isaiah's neighbor and friend, was kneeling by his side. He looked up and shook his head before Simon could ask the hopeless question. Simon fell to his knees on the other side. Isaiah was conscious but his eyes looked glazed.

"I've given him opium," Baldwin said quietly. "It's all I can do. Blood loss will get him soon and it'll be a mercy."

Simon knew about belly wounds, how they could take days to bring an excruciating death from infection. He took his friend's big hand; the hand of a sea carpenter, trapper, and adventurer that hadn't been softened by a decade as a merchant.

"I'm very angry with you," he said.

"Angry with you. My fight. Dying now," he added without apparent concern. Opium could be a blessing. But then he frowned. "Need to take care of Jane."

Simon squeezed his hand. "I'll do that. Don't worry."

"Marry her?"

Simon's mind froze.

"No!" Jane knelt beside the doctor. "Uncle Isaiah—"

"Got no one," Isaiah said, his eyes on Simon and obviously staying open only with effort. "And this trouble . . . can't die easy, Simon."

It was pure blackmail. Isaiah Trewitt had always gone after what he wanted, using every weapon, legal and illegal, and a drift toward an opium-veiled death hadn't changed that. Simon knew that if he debated and delayed Isaiah might die before he made the promise, but what sort of gratitude was that to a man whose guidance had probably saved Simon's life many times over?

"Of course." For the listeners he added, "Jane and I were intending to ask your blessing anyway."

He flashed her a look, commanding that she not argue. Her eyes were huge and dark with shock, but then she lowered her head to look at her uncle. Tears leaked down her cheeks to splash darkly on her gray bodice. Her hair trailed loose around her and she still wore her dark blue cloak.

She resembled a mourning Madonna.

Painted by Raphael, perhaps.

"Now."

Simon jerked out of tangled thoughts and met Isaiah's eyes. They were attempting a ferocious glare but looked only piteous.

"Now, Simon. Want . . . want to witness it." His eyelids conquered his will and closed, but he whispered again, "Now."

Simon stood and gestured for Baldwin to step aside with him. People moved courteously away, though he was sure they were stretching their ears. Someone put a cup of hot tea into his hands and he was deeply grateful, especially when he tasted the sugar and brandy in it.

"How long?" he asked.

"Hard to say. Even with blood loss, willpower can hold a man to life for an astonishing length of time. Is McArthur dead then?"

"She stopped it." Simon glanced back at Jane, who still knelt. "Why was she sent?"

"Good God, of course she wasn't, but the men were dithering. Shouldn't interfere with an affair of honor. He'd probably be dead before you got here. That sort of thing. She just took off."

Jane had always retreated into the background, but what sort of woman was she really? Simon hadn't bothered much about it before. But now, when she was to be his wife? A wife he'd have to take home to Brideswell, God help him.

McArthur's words came back like vomit rising in the throat. What did any of them really know about Jane Otterburn? What, even, did Isaiah know? He'd left England at sixteen and returned only once, when Jane had been an infant. All the rest had been from letters.

Simon pushed such poisoned thoughts away. Here, Jane had been nothing but industrious and virtuous, and Isaiah was correct that she'd be alone in the world. Her father had died years ago, her mother last year. If there was any closeness with either family apart from Isaiah, he didn't know of it. At only eighteen she'd be alone in a frontier world still new to her.

But he didn't love Jane Otterburn.

What a time to realize that he had a romantic view of marriage. That he'd been waiting for some blinding attraction to one special person, for the delirious love of the poets.

And could Jane fit into his world? She certainly wasn't of it.

Isaiah's parents had worked their way up from farm laborers to shopkeepers. They'd had their children taught trades—a carpenter, a butcher, and a seamstress. Martha Otterburn had done very well for herself in marrying a schoolmaster, and her daughter had been raised a lady, but when widowed, Martha had had to keep a small haberdasher's shop to support her family.

He'd be marrying a shopkeeper's daughter.

He looked at the dying man again and saw a slit of filmy eye. Isaiah was doing his best to command him. With an internal shrug Simon surrendered. At least this would save him from the parade of suitable young ladies who apparently waited for him back home. His mother wrote of a new one in every letter.

> *You must remember Alicia Pugh-Mattingly, dearest. Such a pretty girl she's become, and with the sweetest nature. Plays the harp beautifully. With twenty thousand as her portion, too. If you come home quickly . . .*

What would his mother make of penniless, Puritan Jane Otterburn?

He looked around the room and approached the first man he recognized. "Could I bother you to find Reverend Strachan, Mason?"

The plump man nodded and hurried out.

Norton entered and came over.

"How do things stand?" Simon asked him.

"McArthur blustered, but his friends persuaded him to act like a gentleman. He'll want a rematch."

"He shall have it. You are in time for my wedding."

"Wedding?"

For Jane's sake he must express his doubts to no one. "Miss Otterburn and I have been planning to wed, and Trewitt wishes to see it done before he dies. It'll be irregular but things often are here."

Norton's brows twitched. Was he, too, thinking what a mismatch this was? He came from a cadet branch of the aristocratic Peel family, and his brother had been at Harrow School with Simon.

Simon drained the brandied tea, trying to pull his mind into order, make decisions, make plans. It was like trying to catch water. He looked at Jane and was struck again by the stunning beauty of her wavy red-gold hair.

Then he recognized hair recently unplaited.

As the only other person in the main house, she would have been the one to hear the shot, probably as she was loosing her hair from a nighttime plait. She must have found Isaiah, poor girl. Probably some of the dark spots on her gown were blood. By rights she should be lying down with female attendants and a soothing draft.

As if feeling his gaze on her, she looked at him, eyes glistening with tears. Freckles stood boldly on her cheeks because her naturally pale skin was as white as the linen ruffle at her neck.

His protective instincts took over. And really, they had no choice. If he didn't go through with the marriage now, it would be seen as a rejection of her and thus confirmation of McArthur's slander. Then there was his impulsive lie about a prior arrangement. He'd meant well, but that cut off escape.

If it must be done, it should be done well. He went to her. "We need to talk, my love."

He raised her and led her from the room. Again people parted, but avidly, as if sucking up every detail. That was another problem. York was as bad about gossip as any small English town. Worse, in fact. The isolation here magnified everything, and the magnified gossip traveled.

York was less than thirty years old, so everyone had ties elsewhere. Many, military and civilian alike, were recently come from Britain. Letters home might take months, but they left weekly. By the time Simon arrived back in England with his bride, everything that happened here today would be there to greet them.

He took her into the parlor at the back of the house but was instantly frozen by the familiar smell of snuff, tobacco, and leather. In this comfortable, worn room Isaiah had delighted to host his friends, drinking claret, port, and brandy, playing cards, backgammon, or sometimes his favorite old game, dominoes.

Simon had come here to talk over their situation, but

however it happened he and Jane moved into each other's arms, silently comforting and being comforted. Her hair flowed over and under his hands, and she smelled of blood and herbs. She must use herbs in her soap or creams as well as in potpourri and polish. How did that fit with her sober clothes and reserved manner? Marriage should provide answers, and he wouldn't object to a sweet-smelling house—or a sweet-smelling wife.

Or a soft, warm, sweetly curved one. He held her a little closer.

She tensed and then eased apart. "Simon, we can't do this."

"I see no choice."

"Uncle Isaiah can't last long—" She covered her mouth with a hand. "I don't mean it that way. But it's not fair to trap you into this!"

"I don't mind." How inadequate. He sought better words. "It's time I wed, Jane. I'm twenty-five and my mother nags me in every letter."

"Of *course* she wants you to marry, but to marry someone suitable! Not"—she seemed to have to gather herself to say the words—"not a girl who served in a shop."

"Hardly that."

"Exactly that. My mother kept a shop and I helped there."

He hadn't known that she'd actually worked in the shop. He tried to tell himself that he minded only because his family and circle would mind, but it bothered him, too.

"Your father belonged to a good family."

"Minor Scottish gentry with very little money attached. And the Trewitts were farm laborers before they became shopkeepers."

She was throwing these things like missiles to drive him off and they might have worked if they had any choice. Gads, his mother would have a fit.

"Isaiah isn't ashamed of his background. He's proud of what he's made of himself and so should you be."

"Made?" She stared at him. "What do you mean? I've made nothing of myself."

She was distraught and it wasn't surprising. He was an idiot for attempting rational conversation, but then he was distraught, too. Or numb. Yes, that was it. Somehow he'd erected a wall between himself and reality, but it was a wall of sand, already crumbling under the pressure of grief behind it.

"Unless you're willing to refuse Isaiah," he said, "we must marry. I promise to be a good husband and I have no doubt that you will be a good wife."

She looked up at him, those blue eyes huge and stark. "What does that mean? Good."

Why the devil press him on a word? "I will be kind, dependable, and faithful. You may define your goodness as you wish."

She flinched at his sharp tone. "I'm sorry. You're being kind, dependable, and faithful now. Faithful to Uncle Isaiah. But is it really worth shackling yourself in this way to satisfy his whim before he dies?"

A good question, but Simon meant it when he said, "Yes."

"And if he's dead already?"

"Still yes." To persuade her, he'd have to sully her with the truth. "Perhaps you don't know the cause of the duel."

She became wary. Strangely, he saw the instincts of a wild thing, fearful of predators. It had to be a figment of his scattered mind.

"At the end the duel was over McArthur's abuse of funds intended for the Indians. However, the initial cause was comments he made to imply that you are not what you seem."

She went deathly white.

He hurried on. "That you are—I'm sorry—Isaiah's

mistress. That you live together here in that relationship."

Red flooded white. "*What?* The swine!"

"Quite. But . . ." He couldn't think how to say the next part. "He's not the only one to speculate. I'm sure no one else thinks the worst, but people wonder why you act as you do. They wonder why you have turned down all invitations—"

"I was in mourning!"

"Even a lady in mourning could attend a concert or go on a boating expedition. Especially nine months after the event."

"And if I simply didn't choose to? There's a rule about it here, is there?"

He'd snapped and she'd snapped back.

"People simply wonder," he said as calmly as he could. "And some will always move from wondering to a scandalous explanation. You have to know that healthy single women are in short supply here, yet you've ignored all suitors. Why?"

"Do I have to answer that?" She looked and sounded like a prisoner in the dock.

He rubbed his hand down his face. "No. I'm sorry. It was rhetorical. I simply mean that you'd have been better off to flirt with dozens."

She bit her lip, rubbing her hands together anxiously. "I could leave. Go somewhere else."

"Where, young and penniless?" They had no time for this. "Come, we must do this thing. We can talk about the future later."

She ignored his offered hand. "I won't be penniless. Uncle Isaiah made me his heiress."

Of course, he must have. Was there enough to make her independent? If so, perhaps he shouldn't compel her to this marriage. Surely even a dying friend's wish shouldn't have that power.

"Do you know how much?" he asked bluntly.

A shift in her expression showed her reluctance to answer. "Enough to get by on. And I can work. As a seamstress. Or open a shop. I know that business."

"Am I truly such a bitter pill to swallow?"

She looked stricken. "No. Oh, no! But I don't know what to do for the best."

Her hands went over her mouth again. He pulled them down and held them. "This *is* for the best. Consider Isaiah's reputation. It as well as yours will always be under a cloud unless we marry."

She swayed and he took her into his arms again, where she lay limp against his chest, held up only by his strength. He didn't want to bludgeon her, but he must.

"Consider, Jane. Unless we straighten out everything now, you will be in a sorry state. People will say I refused to marry you because the stories were true. Doesn't even a shopkeeper need a sound reputation? And really, you are too young for business yet."

A knock at the door interrupted them. Simon gently disengaged and went to answer it.

Reverend Strachan stood there. The stocky, dark-haired man wore his stole around his neck and had his prayer book in hand. "If you wish to fulfill Trewitt's wishes while he is still alive, St. Bride, it must be soon."

Simon turned to Jane. "It's in your hands, my dear."

Her set face spoke of how much she didn't want to do this, but she straightened her shoulders and walked with him out of the room.

Isaiah lay as before, but bloodlessly pale, sunken cheeked, and visibly sliding toward death. Baldwin looked up with a clear message.

Simon said, "We're ready."

Isaiah's eyes opened a little and might even have filled with tears of joy. Or relief. It didn't matter which. It was enough.

The reverend read the marriage service at a fast clip, an eye on the patient, so that they hurtled to the vows with no time for second thoughts. Simon spoke his part quickly. Jane started more slowly, but then she finished in a breathy rush.

They needed a ring. Simon took off his signet. It was too big, but it served for the ceremony.

"I now pronounce you man and wife."

And thus, Simon thought, feeling as if a hurricane had suddenly stilled, it was done.

Isaiah even smiled a little, nodded a little, and Simon knew they had done the right thing. He and Jane went to kneel by him, one on either side.

"Thank you." It was hardly more than a whisper. "Be good to her," Isaiah said, each word seeming to need a breath. "And you, Jane, be a good wife. . . ."

He hadn't the strength to turn his head toward her, but she took his hand and squeezed it. "I'll to do everything in my power to make him happy, Uncle. Everything."

"I know. Good girl. Proud. Take care of her, Simon. Take good care. . . ."

A second later, Isaiah Trewitt was dead.

Simon felt almost as if the breath left his own body. This day had been as wild as a battle. The battle was over now, leaving its dead and its wounded and the future to be faced.

Had Isaiah known that Simon might not be able to obey that final order? He wouldn't be able to take care of Jane if McArthur killed him, and there was no one here he trusted enough to do it for him.

Chapter Three

*B*aldwin closed his bag. The friends and neighbors began to leave, murmuring condolences. Simon and Jane signed the marriage register that Reverend Strachan had brought with him. Baldwin and Norton signed as witnesses.

The marriage was definitely official now.

Jane returned to kneel at her uncle's side. Simon saw her fingers curled to keep his ring on and wondered where the devil one bought a wedding ring in York. There were other necessities—coffin, burial, mourning bands. How was all this managed here? His head felt empty. Someone cleared his throat, and Simon realized that Baldwin was still in the room.

"I was Trewitt's solicitor." Simon remembered that the doctor served both functions. "His will should be in his desk, but I have a copy."

"I understand he left everything to Jane."

"Apart from a few bequests, yes. But it won't amount to much by St. Bride standards."

"I didn't marry her for her money." Color touched Baldwin's cheeks and Simon quickly added, "I'm sorry. Of course you didn't imply that."

"No one could suspect a St. Bride of being a fortune hunter. His affairs have to be tidied up, however." Baldwin rubbed his nose. "The thing is, you're his executor."

Simon swallowed a curse.

"You can refuse the responsibility."

"If what's left is Jane's property, then I should deal with it. Can it be done quickly? I have passage booked at the end of October."

"It'll mostly be a matter of paying his debts and tidying up business ventures. There are people who—"

Simon had reached the end of his endurance. "This can all wait. Thank you for your care of him, Baldwin."

Baldwin nodded and left. Simon simply breathed and tried to think. Jane still knelt beside the body, tears leaking steadily to fall onto a gray bosom already dark with them. No one could doubt her grief. She had truly loved Isaiah, and she had lost so many in her life—father, mother, cousin, now uncle.

She had no one except him and was now his to take care of. It seemed that everything was his to take care of. Where to start? He heard a footstep and turned, ready to drive the intruder away.

A brown-haired man in a dark suit stood in the doorway. Simon recognized John Ross, York's undertaker, come like a crow to the feast. That was unfair, but he even hated that Ross must know how he felt. The damned understanding in his eyes was intolerable.

As if respecting even that, Ross looked down as he bowed. "Mr. Trewitt's death is a great loss for us all, sir. It will be my honor to take care of him."

"Thank you. I have no idea . . ."

"You may leave everything in my hands, sir. If we could just settle a few details. . . ." He opened a leather-bound record book and began gentle questions.

They agreed on a coffin, that the body would rest overnight in the home—"The dining room, sir?"—as was the custom, and that the ceremony would also take place here before the coffin was carried to the churchyard.

"Some people choose to be buried on their own property. . . ."

"No. The churchyard."

Part of Simon raged at these details, but another part realized that working through them was soothing.

Ross closed his book. "Now, sir, may I suggest that the lady would be better elsewhere for a little while?"

Simon went to Jane and raised her to her feet. "Come away. Mr. Ross is here to take care of your uncle."

She looked at the undertaker with the same flash of resentment Simon had felt but then let Simon draw her from the room. His wife. Trusting him, leaning on his strength.

Which felt almost nonexistent.

"Do you want someone to sit with you?" he asked. "One of the maids?"

For I have no idea what to do for you.

She shook her head, leaving him at a loss. But then he saw wizened little Mrs. Gunn, cheeks sunken farther with sorrow, waiting in the hall.

"Best you both come to the kitchens and get some food in you," the cook said. "Come along."

Following an order was a relief, so Simon steered Jane that way. He had no appetite, but he'd not eaten before the duel and it was going to be a long day. If Isaiah's accident had happened as Jane was getting dressed, she might not have breakfasted, either.

As soon as they left the house and entered the open-sided walkway, Simon felt better, perhaps just from the cold, crisp air. Jane must have felt the same, for she eased out from under his arm.

At the kitchen door she held out his ring. "You should take this back."

"No—"

"I'll only lose it."

He took it. "I'll find you a better." He guided her through the doorway.

Sal and Izzy, twelve and thirteen, and both stick thin, were sitting at the deal table, eyes huge.

"Aye," Mrs. Gunn said, "the master's dead, but life goes on. Now we've breakfast to make, and then plenty of work to get ready for the rites." She said to Simon and Jane, "I'd better bring in my granddaughters. There's cleaning and funeral cakes."

Jane straightened and reached for an apron hanging on the wall. "Of course. I'll help, too. But first we must provide breakfast for Mr. St. Bride."

Simon need food, but he couldn't abide this bizarre female bustle. He retreated. "I have things to do."

"Don't be foolish." Jane uncovered a loaf and cut two slices. She buttered them and added thick pieces of cheese and then wrapped it all in a white cloth and put it into his hands.

"I see I'm to be under the cat's paw."

She flushed pink and not with pleasure. "If that means I won't let a husband starve, then yes."

Her gaze was direct, her tone crisp. Again he wanted to ask, *Who are you, Jane Otterburn?* No, Jane St. Bride now.

At the door he paused to look back. She'd already pinned the apron around herself and was tying her hair back with what seemed to be a piece of string. She looked like a countrywoman, but as wholesome as bread and cheese.

"Eat something yourself," he instructed and then left.

Once outside he wondered what right he had to tell her what to do. Strange but true, he had every right conceivable, simply because of a hasty service and some signatures.

Instead of taking the walkway back to the clapboard house, he crossed the garden, seeking a moment's peace. Isaiah had not been a garden enthusiast, and if Jane was, she'd made little headway here. Saul Prithy was most interested in the vegetables and there wasn't much left of those at this time of year. Soon winter would seal everything under snow and ice for long months.

This year he'd be gone by then. If he lived.

He had to live. For Jane's sake now, as well as every other reason.

Hell. This time yesterday his only problem had been what to take back to England. Now he had a dead friend to bury, a wife to cherish, and a duel to complete.

And a wedding ring to find.

He seized on the simple, solvable task.

He'd abandoned his greatcoat on the dueling field and went into the house to find a warmer jacket, but he found his coat neatly arranged on a hall chair. Norton must have brought it. Then he noticed the wrapped sandwich he still held in his hand and hunger growled.

He went into the parlor and took a bite. It seemed almost heartless to be eating at such a time, but it tasted delicious. Isaiah kept decanters of wine and spirits here, and so he poured a glass of his friend's favorite claret and toasted him.

"I hope heaven really is a happy hunting ground, Isaiah, with jolly companions, fast rivers, and new lands to explore."

"Do I intrude?"

Simon turned, flushing to be caught talking to air. Then he said, *"Hal?"*

For the tall, dark man in the doorway, his empty left sleeve pinned neatly across his chest, was, impossibly, Major Hal Beaumont.

"In the flesh, and come at an interesting time, I gather."

Laughing, Simon went to grasp his friend's hand. "My God! I'm speechless. Why? How? What the *devil* are you doing back here?" He looked at the glass in his other hand. "Claret?"

"For breakfast?" But then Hal sobered. "I gather condolences are in order."

Simon nodded. "Isaiah Trewitt. A good man, a good friend. I'm not sure you met him."

"No, but you spoke of him. You used to call him a Rogue."

Simon smiled at the memory. "With relish."

He and Hal had been part of a schoolboy band that

called themselves the Company of Rogues. The best of friends, scattered now. Some dead in the past war—Roger Merrihew, Allan Ingram, Dare Debenham. That was the most recent, most painful loss, for Dare had been Simon's closest friend.

"I think I'll have claret after all," Hal said. When Simon gave him the glass, he asked, "What happened?"

"Shot himself by accident. He's been plagued by a malarial ague for years. His hands shook, I assume." Simon gestured helplessly. "The rest is more complicated. But by God, Hal, whatever's brought you here, I'm glad of it. Have you eaten? We're at sixes and sevens, as you can imagine."

"I've breakfasted. I've rooms at Brown's Hotel. I only arrived last night and was preparing to call at a decent hour when I heard the news. How can I help?"

The simple words were an immense relief.

"Prop me up. Look, let me offer you tea. I should drink something other than wine, and I'm sure the kitchen can manage that."

Ross had brought assistants and a young lad sat in the hall clearly waiting to run errands. Simon sent him with the message, and then they both sat by the fire. "How do you come to be here? What news of home? When did you leave? My head's spinning."

"That's what you get for drinking wine for breakfast. I am here because I agreed to escort a Gresham pup to a posting in Kingston."

"Why?" No one traveled six weeks or more across the ocean for such a reason.

Hal's lips twitched more in grimace than humor. "It suited me. It also suited me to see what you were up to. It's been four years, Simon."

"Time can slip by like oil. But you could have been spared the trip. I'm booked for home. All being well. What news? Has Luce's child been born?"

"A son."

"And there was much celebration. And Francis's?"

"Not when I left. Simon—"

"I've been thinking how strange it is that Rogues are marrying, and now—"

"Simon."

Simon gathered his wits and paid attention. More tragedy?

"Dare's alive."

Simon stared, his mind suddenly a blank.

"It's true," Hal said, "but attached to a complicated tale. He was badly injured at Waterloo and given opium—too much and for too long. He's a slave to the drug, but he's alive."

"God be praised." Simon couldn't stay seated. "God be praised! Is he"—he stopped himself from saying *maimed*—"recovered? Physically."

"I left shortly after his discovery and he was very frail. But it seemed his original injuries had healed, yes. I gather there's hope he can free himself of the drug. Those who use it for pain, not mental support, have more success once their pain is over."

Opium addiction seemed like an irrelevant detail. "Thank you! For bringing good news. Today of all days."

The door opened and Jane entered, the tray on her hip as she managed the door.

Simon hurried to assist her, noting that she'd removed the apron and found a ribbon to replace the string tying her hair. She still, however, looked like a servant. He'd not yet told Hal that he was married, which would look peculiar. As if he was ashamed of her. And she had no ring.

He placed the tray on a table. "Jane, may I introduce an old friend of mine arrived like a genie from a bottle in our hour of need. Major Hal Beaumont. Hal, this is my wife, Jane."

Hal had risen to bow, but both he and Jane were momentarily frozen—he by the news, she by his empty sleeve.

She recovered and curtsied. "You are well come, Major. It's a blessing for Simon to have a friend here now."

"And for him to have a wife, Mrs. St. Bride. Delighted to make your acquaintance."

However, Simon saw Hal note Jane's lack of ring.

"We were compelled by circumstances to wed this morning without proper planning," Simon explained.

"Then I am definitely de trop."

"No."

Simon and Jane spoke together and then laughed nervously.

"Jane, Hal brings excellent news. You must have heard me speak of Lord Darius Debenham, who was assumed dead at Waterloo? He lives."

"Oh, excellent indeed! And well?"

She'd phrased it more neatly than he.

"Addicted to opium, but there's hope of a full recovery. By the time we reach home, he might already be his old self." He turned to Hal. "He's at Long Chart, I assume?"

"He was going there."

At Hal's expression, Simon grinned. "I'm spinning like a top, aren't I? Perhaps great news after abysmal is too much for the mind. But it will make sense to disembark at Plymouth or Portsmouth and visit." To Jane, he said, "Long Chart is his family home, seat of the Duke of Yeovil."

Jane was pouring tea, and she handed them both cups. "Simon, I'm truly happy that your friend is alive, and we must certainly visit him. Now I must return to the kitchen. Death, it seems, requires immense amounts of food, and I welcome the work. May I hope you will join us for dinner, Major?"

Hal accepted, and with a vague smile at Simon, Jane left.

Hal said, "Congratulations, Simon. She's delightful."

Of course he had to say something of the sort, but it

sounded sincere. There was a lot to be said for having a wife other men found appealing, and she'd handled the awkward situation with sublime grace.

"Yes, she is," he agreed. "Now tell me more about Dare's revival."

They moved from there to Simon's affairs. At least he didn't have to explain or justify his intent about the Indians. Hal had fought alongside them. He had known and admired Tecumseh, who'd been a brigadier general in the British army. He knew the promises that had been made.

But he commented, "You can't be the most popular man in York."

"Most people are at least courteous."

"Of course they are. You being who you are."

"Idiotic, isn't it? But you're right, Brideswell and Marlowe do impress those who care about such things, and I've used that in the cause." He poured Hal more tea. "If anything goes amiss, however, Jane can't stay here. You'll get her back to England, won't you?"

"Amiss?"

"I still have to meet McArthur."

"Dammit." Then Hal said, "If he fired, precise adherence to the code gives you a shot."

"I couldn't demand such a thing. It's a wonder my pistol didn't go off, too. So, you'll take care of Jane?"

"Of course, but I'll be annoyed to do so without you along. Where do I take her?"

"To Brideswell, of course."

"Will she, nill she?"

"There's nowhere else. She has no family I know of other than a brother of Isaiah's who's a butcher. That's hardly suitable for my widow. I know it'll be awkward. . . ."

"An understatement."

"But I need to know she'll be safe."

"I'll see to her comfort."

Simon understood that Hal was reserving the right to

make his own judgment and appreciated it. "Thank you. There's something else."

"Just as long as it isn't another woman."

Simon laughed. "No, but perhaps trickier. My papers." He explained what he had and what he hoped to do with them. "If McArthur knows enough to want to kill me, he'll want to destroy the evidence as well."

"Then I'll make very sure they get into the right hands. Stephen will know the best people."

Simon nodded. He'd followed from afar their friend Sir Stephen Ball's rise in politics.

Hal put down his teacup. "So, what needs doing now? I travel with two servants. Reliable men. Ex-soldiers. It looks as if extra hands will be useful."

Simon wondered if the phrase "extra hands" had been used deliberately. There must be many things Hal could no longer do for himself. "It feels as if everything needs doing. Right now, I need to buy my wife a wedding ring, but I don't care to leave the house unguarded."

"Then I'll stay. Is there nothing useful I can do while on guard duty?"

Simon looked around the room. "Would you go through the drawers here? Isaiah tossed anything and everything into them, but there might be money or important items."

"Very well." Hal rose and walked closer to the framed picture that hung over the fireplace. "This is a rather a good drawing, and that's your wife, isn't it, when younger? With her mother?"

"Yes."

Simon had grown used to the picture, but he studied it anew. It had probably been drawn about three years ago, which was a long time at Jane's age.

In the picture, her breasts were smaller, but her cheeks rounder. Her pale dress had a girlish simplicity but enough ribbons and frills to make it completely unlike the clothes she wore here. She wore her hair as she did today, simply tied back.

She stood by the chair in which Martha Otterburn sat in widow's clothing, looking a lot like Isaiah. His strength and kindness showed there, but also a stiffness he'd never had. From all accounts, Martha Otterburn had been a conventional woman. She'd refused to travel to Canada when widowed, even though Isaiah had urged her to, promising her a grand life here. She'd replied that her daughter was a lady and she wasn't bringing her to live among savages in a forest.

It was hard to see any resemblance between mother and daughter, but then Jane strongly resembled her Scottish father. She had brought an oil portrait of Archibald Otterburn, which hung in her bedroom. It showed similar features and identical coloring, though his hair was thin and receding.

"Drawn by Jane's cousin," Simon said. "Nan, I think the name was. Some orphan connection of Jane's father who was adopted by Martha as a child. She took ill and died on the way over. Sad case, for she and Jane were almost the same age and like sisters."

"She had a remarkable gift."

"Especially as she could only have been fifteen or so when she drew that."

Hal turned from the picture. "Too much thought of wasteful death. Off you go. I'll ransack the drawers while keeping any other pillagers at bay."

Simon knew it was a pledge of all-encompassing help and support and gripped Hal's arm briefly before leaving.

He went to Klengenboomer, York's only jeweler, but the portly man was apologetic. "Wedding rings are generally made to order, sir, or sent for from Montreal. I could make one by tomorrow afternoon. . . ."

"My wife needs one before the funeral."

"I see, sir. Excuse me a moment."

Klengenboomer went into a back room and returned with a small tray containing six rings. "Sometimes people find it necessary to sell."

"A pawned wedding ring?" Simon asked in revulsion.

The jeweler shrugged. "Perhaps a loan until I can make a better, sir?"

For some reason switching about revolted Simon even more.

He'd wanted a grand ring to counterbalance the unfortunate situation, but these were all thin and worn. Only a desperate woman would part with her wedding ring, or a desperate man sell that of his dead wife. Some ring was better than none, however, so he chose the one most likely to fit.

What, however, could be more ill-omened than this wedding day?

Except for the news about Dare. That could outweigh all the rest.

He paused to consider other jewelry. He'd never seen Jane wear anything other than plain hoops in her ears and a gold cross around her neck, but his wife should have more than that. Unfortunately, he had little money in hand. He'd been spending heavily on gathering evidence and assisting those Indians who were in the worst state.

Hoping Hal had cash to lend, he bought a pretty silver brooch set with amethysts and a pair of pearl earrings. Sober ornaments, but even so, this wasn't a day for gifts. He'd give them to her at the right moment.

He returned to Trewitt House, preparing for an encounter with his wife.

In many ways he was pleased with Jane, but neither of them had wanted this marriage, and she did not have the background his family and friends—his world— would expect. He could see how it shouldn't matter, but facts don't dissolve because we wish them to. Even in America, with its republican principles and its declaration that all men are born equal, many families wouldn't welcome a girl from a shop.

But Jane was his wife now. Till death did them part. Presumably at some point they must share a bed, join their bodies, attempt to produce children. That was the purpose of marriage, after all. It created a painful band of tension around his head.

The kitchen only made that worse. It was hot, crowded, and full of the aroma of the baked goods piling up on every surface. The two buxom young women must be Mrs. Gunn's granddaughters. One was very clearly with child.

There were biscuits, tarts, and pies enough for a hungry army.

Jane was lifting small cakes onto a wire rack. Despite the ribbon, hair straggled over her red face and she looked glazed with exhaustion, grief, or both.

His to take care of.

But also as earthy as baking bread . . .

As soon as she'd dealt with the last cake, he said, "Come with me, please, Jane."

Because he was fighting improper thoughts, he spoke harshly. Her eyes turned wary, which struck him like ice water.

He was careful to speak softly and gently. "You will want to tidy yourself and sit with your uncle for a while, I think."

He saw her almost sag with relief. "Oh, yes."

Had she thought he was going to drag her off to the marriage bed?

As she unpinned her apron, he took her dark blue cloak off a hook. When she was ready, he put it around her shoulders and escorted her out. Her cheeks were still rosy, her hair still wild. Was it only his imagination that she smelled like a sweet, spiced bun? Shamefully, he wanted to lick her.

He produced the ring. "It's not as fine as I would like, and it may not fit . . ."

She looked down at her left hand and dusted off flour and crumbs. "I should have washed."

He hesitated between giving her the wedding ring and putting it on her finger as he had his signet during the ceremony. Clearly it had to be the latter. He took her left hand and slid the ring on. "A little loose, I'm afraid."

She touched it, sliding it up and down as if it were a puzzle. "String beneath will hold it snug. And perhaps I'll grow plump, eating all those funeral cakes."

They shared a smile that seemed remarkable, for it did not deny a jot of their shared grief while affirming the universal truth that life goes on.

"This is a strange situation, Jane, but we must give the appearance that we intended this and that Isaiah merely hastened it."

"I suppose so."

There had to be words to ease this moment. "I'm not unhappy with our marriage. I admire much about you." How feeble.

She looked neither disappointed nor amused, but rather stricken. That looming marriage bed.

"Jane, you mustn't imagine that I wish to rush." This was a damnably awkward subject to discuss with an innocent young lady. "What I mean is, there will be no need for us to share a bed for a while."

Her brow wrinkled. "Won't people think that strange?"

"How are they to know?"

"Two sets of sheets sent to the laundry woman. Two rooms still in use."

He wanted to say that was no one's business, but he knew that such things were talked of. "Many married couples use separate bedchambers."

"Do they? And surely not rooms at either end of the house."

What was she saying? That she *wanted* to share his bed tonight? Despite his awareness of her as a woman, he couldn't bear the thought.

Then she added, "At least no one will think it strange for us to keep to our usual arrangement tonight." She spoke so calmly, he wondered if she understood the physical implications of marriage at all.

But he knew she did. By some instinct he was sure she wasn't that kind of protected innocent, and he was grateful for it. Remembering the comfort they'd found in each other's arms, he drew her close. She tensed for a moment, perhaps thinking he meant to kiss her, but then relaxed.

He had meant only to comfort her, but he found comfort for himself. She was a sweet armful, neither too angular nor too soft, too large or too small, and she carried the soothing aroma of a bakery.

He rested his head against her hair, more at ease now with his mild stirrings of desire. They offered hope that when the time was right, their marriage bed would be natural and pleasurable for both of them.

Chapter Four

*T*he new Mrs. Simon St. Bride rested against her husband's chest thinking miserably that one should be careful what one wished for.

How many nights had she dreamed of being in Simon's arms? Dreamed even of becoming Simon's bride, bride to the most wonderful man she'd ever met.

To her, he was perfectly handsome, with his lean, vigorous body, his ready smile, and his deep-set hazel eyes that came alive with every vivid emotion. She had often had to resist an urge to touch his thick dark hair that shot fire in the light.

Presumably a wife was allowed to do that. But not an unwanted wife. Simon hadn't wanted to marry her, which was hardly surprising. And she hadn't wanted to marry him. Because if he ever learned the truth about her, he would hate her.

Oh, Lord, what was she to do?

Move, for a start, so she did, separating them.

He adjusted her cloak, a slight smile in his eyes, or at least a look of pleasure.

If only, if only . . .

She pushed straggling hair off her face. "I must look a mess."

"Somewhat, but it's a pleasure to see your hair. It's lovely."

For some reason that seemed threatening. She turned

quickly to lead the way into the house. She didn't want him to come upstairs with her—to the bedrooms—so in the hall she said, "I believe I can make my way to my room without help."

"If you wish to lie down for a while, it will be all right."

"No, I'll be back soon."

As she climbed the stairs she reflected on how easy it was to act a part. Once in her room, however, she collapsed back against the door, her knuckles in her mouth.

This was her first real solitude since she'd heard the *boom* of the shot. The memory of finding Isaiah on the floor, clutching his belly, blood already welling between his fingers, made her bite down to conquer a howl.

She hadn't screamed then, however, and she would not do so now. Life, dreadful life, must go on.

Her hair. She hurried to her dressing table, but as soon as she saw herself she groaned. It clung tangled to her forehead and cheeks, and flour and mud marked her gown. She looked like a vagrant.

Like a Haskett.

She ripped off the ribbon and attacked the mess, looking anywhere but at her reflection as she untangled and brushed. Her image stayed in her mind, however. She'd looked like that for her wedding!

So many times she had imagined the perfect wedding. It would be summer. She'd walk to the church in the company of friends and family. There would be flowers and a handsome groom. . . .

She opened her eyes and inhaled. She had the handsome groom, that was for sure, but he thought he'd married Jane Otterburn, and he hadn't.

She was an impostor. She was Nan Otterburn, Archibald Otterburn's misbegotten child taken in by his widow out of charity and raised as Jane Otterburn's foster sister.

She turned to the mirror again, seeing swollen eyes that at least were honest. She'd come to love Isaiah

Trewitt, even if he was no true uncle of hers. That had led her to agree to this terrible situation, but what was she to do?

It was as if two parts of her argued.

You truly are Jane St. Bride. You married Simon.

In a lie. It's probably not even legal.

You were married as Jane Anne Otterburn, daughter of Archibald Otterburn, deceased schoolmaster. That's all true, isn't it?

It was. Martha Otterburn had made sure that Jane Anne Otterburn was her legal name. But she'd been the result of an encounter between Archibald Otterburn and Tillie Haskett and had spent the first nine years of her life as Jancy Haskett, part of a tribe of itinerant farm laborers. In Cumberland, "Haskett" was a byword for sinners and petty thieves. She'd sometimes heard people say, "He's as bad as a Haskett."

They'd had a home of sorts—a run-down farm on the bleak edge of Carrock Fell—but if anyone had ever been able to survive on that land, the Hasketts couldn't, so from spring to autumn they wandered like Gypsies. They worked where they could, begged when they dared, and stole whenever they could get away with it.

The women weren't whores, but there'd been nothing strange about Jancy being an outsider's child. Jancy hadn't given a thought about who her true father might be, but when the Hasketts arrived in Carlisle for the annual horse fair in 1806, her bold, brown-haired mother had told her.

"Archibald Otterburn, our Jancy, a gentleman born. A schoolmaster, no less, here in Carlisle. But I hear he's dead, so we're going to see his widow."

"Why, Ma?"

"Because you're the very image of yer da, ma pretty. You wait and see. There'll be caylo in this at least."

Later, Jancy had remembered that "at least."

The next day, Tillie had led Jancy down Abbey Street,

the sort of quiet, respectable street Hasketts avoided. She'd enjoyed the new experience and looked forward to earning "caylo," or money, for the family. She was already good for pennies at a market because her pale skin and red-gold hair made her stand out among the swarthy Hasketts.

Her "Can you spare a penny, kind sir?" often produced one. It sometimes produced questions, too.

"Who are your parents, dear?"

"Have you always lived with these people?"

"Are you happy?"

"Do you need help?"

This had puzzled her, but Tillie had explained that people thought she might have been stolen. "Though why, I can't imagine, chick, babbies being easy enough to come by."

Hasketts didn't steal babies, but they'd steal just about anything else and didn't like people paying them too much attention. Jancy had thought later that might have had something to do with Tillie's taking her to Martha Trewitt's house.

That and Uncle Lemuel Haskett. He'd taken to treating Jancy in a funny way. Liking to take her on his knee when she was too old for that. Asking her to kiss him on the mouth. Tillie had warned her not to be alone with him.

These thoughts had come later, however. That September day, she'd skipped along, seeing the outing as a treat. She'd approached the green-painted door of the small house ready to do her begging act to earn some caylo and please her mother.

It hadn't been like that. When the stern woman dressed in deepest black opened the door, Tillie said, "I've come t'talk to you about me daughter, ma'am." There'd been none of the usual cheek or whine.

The woman had looked at Jancy almost without expression, but all the same Jancy had wanted to slide behind her mother. But then they were in the house, in a narrow corridor that seemed frighteningly tight and smelled awful.

She'd come to know the smells as the ones considered clean—vinegar, camphor, lavender, and beeswax—but on that day they'd wrinkled her nose. She'd also been terrified of spoiling something. The polished floor looked too clean to walk on, especially in the boots that felt heavy because she went barefoot most of the time.

Martha Otterburn had listened in silence, glancing at Jancy now and then but asking no questions. Jancy understood why when a girl her own age came into the corridor. Tillie had a mirror, and the girl in a pretty white dress with a black sash, a black ribbon in her hair, could almost have been herself.

"What is it, Mama?" the girl asked.

"Go back to the kitchen, Jane, dear."

After one wide-eyed look, Jane Otterburn had obeyed, but that look had fixed in astonishment on Jancy, clearly seeing the same resemblance.

"Well, now, ma'am," Tillie said. "You see how it is, and me and me family come often to Carlisle. I'm afeared people might notice me daughter's resemblance—to your husband, and to your own child. Takes after him, don't they? Both of them."

With a beggar's fine instinct, she'd waited.

Jancy had felt as she did when a magistrate or beadle questioned the Hasketts about missing tools and missing sheep. She'd wanted to curl into a ball like a hedgehog and pretend she wasn't there.

Then Martha said, "If my husband had known, he would have wanted the child to be raised in a decent home. Leave her with me and she will be treated as my daughter. But there must be no further contact with you and your family."

Jancy had still been trying to take this in when Tillie turned to her. "There, chick. That's a fine offer. You're a very lucky girl." She kissed her and gave her the wink that said this was a plan that would do the Hasketts proud. "You be good, our Jancy."

Then Jancy had been alone in the stinky corridor with the dark, stern woman, who'd said, "First, a bath."

She shuddered now to think that she'd been infested. Her hair had been so full of lice that Martha had cut it short, apologizing and promising it would grow again, prettier than ever. Jancy supposed she'd been crying or even screaming, but she couldn't remember. She remembered crying a lot in the next days and weeks, desperately missing the rough-and-tumble of Haskett life and wishing her mother would hurry up and come back for her.

Even her name had to change.

"Such a common name," Martha said. "And of course you can't be Jane. You will be Nan. And you will forget all about Hasketts, child. Never mention them again. When you're fit for polite company we will say you are an orphan from Mr. Otterburn's family. From Argyll. That's a wild enough place to explain some of your flaws, but if anyone asks, try to be vague. Say you lived in many places. That you passed from person to person. We can only pray that it will hold.

"Haskett," she'd added with a shudder, and perhaps that had been the greatest force in getting Martha Otterburn to take her husband's bastard into her house. Bad enough for anyone to discover that Archibald Otterburn had sinned. But with a *Haskett*?

So what was Simon St. Bride going to think if he ever discovered he'd married a Haskett?

She should tell him the truth before this went any further.

But a little voice counseled against that in tones that reminded Jancy of her mother.

It wouldn't be right to do anything now, though, would it, chick? This is the time for mourning that good man Isaiah Trewitt and seeing him decently into his grave.

Right or not, she couldn't face anything else.

Her dirty dress was easy to remove. She'd arrived with a few gowns hastily dyed black, which were beyond hope after the voyage. As she wasn't used to servants she'd made new ones in a crossover design that let her dress without help. Beneath she wore a soft bodice instead of a corset.

She still had her best black, however; the one made for Martha's funeral. She'd worn it here for church a few times in the early days. She took it out of the clothespress and shook it. She'd stopped wearing it because it had become tight in the chest and deep black hadn't been necessary. She wanted to wear full mourning for Isaiah, however, so prayed she could still fit into it.

Fortunately it was a simple design with a drawstring waist, and her soft bodice allowed her breasts to squash. It was long sleeved and high necked, and when she faced the mirror again she nodded. That was more like it. Funereal propriety.

She dragged her thick wavy hair back, twisted it, and then pinned it up. When she put on the black cap, the one with the mourning drapes on either side, it hid all her hair.

She was Jane St. Bride, grieving lady.

Nothing else.

Simon watched Jane go upstairs, but then Ross came to say that all was ready. He went with some reluctance to the dining room, made gloomy by drawn curtains. The glossy coffin sat on a heavy black cloth. The lid was off, so he went to look at Isaiah, still hardly able to believe that he was dead.

Perhaps undertakers used pads in the cheeks or some other trick, because Isaiah looked much as he had the last time Simon had seen him alive. But he was undeniably dead, spirit gone, hopefully to a place where he was young and healthy again.

Ross was standing by, so Simon said, "Excellent. Thank you."

"You will want mourning bands, sir." He gestured to an assistant, who came forward to put one around Simon's sleeve.

"I will put one around your hat, sir," the young man said before he and Ross left Simon with the corpse.

"This marriage is your doing, you old Rogue, so be our guardian angel." He couldn't help but smile. "No matter how unlikely an image that is."

He stood there, trying to pray, but he didn't think Isaiah needed many prayers. Instead he let his mind turn to the practicalities of traveling home, which seemed particularly precious now. He had passage booked but had not expected to take much with him. Would Jane want to take many of Isaiah's possessions? He doubted there was much worth the cost, but if she wished to . . .

He heard footsteps and turned as Jane entered the room.

How different she seemed from when he'd seen her last. Different, too, from the Jane he'd grown accustomed to. That Jane had been sober. This one was severe.

He vaguely remembered the long-sleeved, high-necked plain black dress from her early days here. He didn't think he'd seen the nunlike black headdress before. Despite newly reddened eyes, in this frame her delicate pallor glowed like lamplit alabaster, illuminating sky-blue eyes and rose-pink lips. The effect was as shocking as a work of art suddenly lit by a shaft of sunlight. He wished it shadowed again.

He wanted her back in her ordinary clothes. No, in fashionable ones. If she was dressed in a flounced gown of yellow or green with a beribboned bonnet on her head, surely she'd be just another pretty girl. He could deal with pretty girls.

She walked to the coffin and bowed her head.

"Would you like me to stay with you?" he asked. "Or would you rather be alone?"

She didn't look up. "Alone, thank you."

Perhaps he should stay anyway, but he took her at her word. There was a great deal to be done and not much time in which to do it.

When he went to the parlor, Hal said, "I found some coins and these snuffboxes and miniatures. A few old letters, as well. Nothing else, unless you treasure broken clay pipes, assorted buttons, and balls of string."

"Isaiah thought anything might come in useful. Probably because of his early years. He arrived in Canada with hardly a penny. The snuffboxes might be left to someone. I need to read the will."

He unfolded a letter to find it dated 1809. "I hope he answered these."

The three miniatures showed a heavy-jawed officer, a solemn young woman with dark hair, and an infant. "I don't even know who these people are. Jane might, but from the fashions, they look decades old."

"I think the woman might be the one in the drawing. Her mother."

Simon compared the miniature to the sketch. "You could be right. I wonder if the child is Jane. The coloring's right, but she looks so . . . reserved. Of course, yesterday that wouldn't have struck me as strange." He put them down. "I need to start on the business papers, though I don't relish returning to the office."

"I'll come with you."

As they crossed the hall, Simon asked, "When do you plan to leave?"

"When you do."

Simon stopped. "Thank you. I apologize for this mess, but by God, Hal, you're a godsend."

He was uncomfortably aware that some of his relief was because Hal being here meant less time alone with Jane. And that would extend to the six weeks or more it would take to travel back to England.

"Onward to the paperwork," Hal said, "though I warn you, it's not my forte."

"It's not mine, either. I've had nothing to do with Isaiah's business dealings."

Simon entered the office braced for unpleasantness, but Ross and his people had done their work well. It looked as always except that the carpet had been taken away. And that a small stain on the wood showed where blood had seeped through.

Perhaps his nose detected blood and other odors of death, but the fire crackled merrily, filling the room with that pleasant, tangy smell, and someone had uncovered Jane's potpourri.

Looked at with an executor's eye, the room was a daunting jumble. Shelves were crammed with books, ledgers, and boxes, but he also saw a riding whip, a saber, and more pipes. Drawers doubtless concealed yet more chaos. Isaiah had known where things were, but he'd not been the most organized of men.

"I'll start on the desk," Simon said. "Perhaps you can flip through the books. He was always tucking papers and even money into them."

Too late, he wondered if Hal could do such a thing, but he could hardly imply now that he couldn't. *Damnation,* he thought, gathering the papers on top of the desk into one pile, *why is everything so complicated today?*

He saw Hal pull a book off a shelf, put it down, and riffle through it. So that was all right. It was over two years since the amputation, so he must have learned to cope, and surely they were friends enough that he'd say if he couldn't.

Simon settled to an orderly investigation of the papers. He'd deliberately left the door open so he'd see if Jane left the dining room or hear if she called for him.

He found Isaiah's will, and it was exactly as Baldwin had said. Apart from a few specific bequests—he'd left Simon his guns and some Indian artifacts—everything went to "my dear niece, Jane Anne Otterburn, who has brought such pleasure to my life."

How much would it amount to? Baldwin didn't consider it much, but Jane thought it enough to live on. A substantial sum, a few thousand even, would make her more acceptable to his family.

He found a number of invoices and bills and a hodge-podge of recent letters. Presumably these people should receive an announcement of the death, but Simon knew few of them. Who should get a personal letter? And what did one say?

He dug his fingers into his brow.

Chapter Five

"*C*an I do anything to help?"

Simon looked up to see Jane in the doorway.

She said, "I can imagine Uncle Isaiah's opinion of my sitting watch over his earthly remains when I could be doing something useful. Ross has supplied a professional mourner."

Simon rose. "If you feel able, I would be very grateful. I find I don't know most of his correspondents or the context of most of his business documents."

"I probably do. You're pressed into service, too, Major."

"Willingly, ma'am."

She looked between the two of them and settled her gaze on Simon. "Would it be inappropriate for Major Beaumont to call me Jane, and for me to use his first name? I'm afraid I can't start calling you Mr. St. Bride, Simon."

"I would be honored and delighted," Hal said, "as long as your tyrannical husband does not object."

"I'll give you tyrannical. . . ." But Simon smiled at Jane, grateful for her practical good sense and the way she'd lightened the mood without being flippant.

"Hal plans to travel back with us," he said.

"Oh, excellent news."

Simon wondered if her sincerity rose from the same

cause as his. He probably should have another forthright talk with her about the marriage bed.

Whatever her nervousness about that, here, with the three of them together, she seemed comfortable. She sat beside Simon and went through the letters, sorting them into acquaintances and friends, giving him details about people he didn't know. Together, they composed an announcement and she offered to write them all.

"That would be an imposition," he said.

"I'll be glad to do it. I've been acting as Uncle Isaiah's secretary since Salter left."

Simon had been aware that she'd assisted in some way, but not so formally. "Dare I hope that you understand some of his business?"

Her eyes flickered as if she was choosing a response, but then she said, "All of it. With his health, and his hands often unsteady . . . He wouldn't allow me to put things in order here, but I kept his books and wrote most of his letters."

She soon revealed a depth of understanding that suggested she'd been doing most of the work. He caught himself wondering why she hadn't insisted on better business decisions but then knew he was ridiculous. She was eighteen years old. Was she to argue with and overrule a man nearly three times her age who had far more experience of the world?

They paused for refreshments at noon. Before Simon could return to work, a uniformed aide arrived commanding his presence at the lieutenant governor's residence.

"Damn," Simon said once the man was safely waiting in the hall. "I should have gone without being summoned. Hal, you'll stay here?"

"Of course."

"Will there be difficulties?" Jane asked, looking pale. "Over the duel?"

"No, don't worry. He'll be annoyed, but I've been

annoying him for months. This might work out well, in fact. He won't want the duel to resume."

The brief walk to the lieutenant governor's house was constantly interrupted by people wanting to express sorrow at Isaiah's death. Simon wondered if it was his imagination that saw blame in many eyes. He certainly blamed himself. His rash duel had led to Isaiah's death.

Gore, the man responsible for the whole of Upper Canada, was as annoyed as expected. "Messy business, sir. Very messy. I'll see if I can bring about a resolution, but it's dashed difficult when you questioned the man's integrity!"

"Better than dragging a lady's name in the dirt, sir. McArthur's comments about Miss Otterburn and her uncle were completely unwarranted."

Gore turned redder. "Yes, yes, but couldn't you have insulted his hat or something? I'll see what I can do to smooth his feathers."

Simon thought McArthur should be plucked not soothed, but he controlled himself. "I'd be grateful, sir. I have a wife entirely dependent on me now."

"Aye, and that's another thing. Would have been wiser to be more open about your understanding, St. Bride. And wiser of Miss Otterburn to attend more events. My wife was put out—put out, sir!—to have her kind invitations refused."

"My wife is somewhat shy, sir, and she has been in mourning for both a mother and a cousin."

"Aye, aye, but a concert wouldn't have hurt. Or a summer expedition to Castle Frank."

Simon grasped solid excuses. "Her pale skin easily burns, sir, and she seems to attract the mosquitoes."

He'd returned to York in July to find Jane covered with bites. He'd offered an Indian concoction that had given her some relief, but he hadn't thought the natives' preventative of grease would be appreciated. He didn't favor it himself, though at times he used it.

It was one of the impossible problems here that the settlers were often disgusted by greasy, smelly Indians while tortured by the insect bites the grease could prevent.

"The English climate will suit her better," he said. "I have passage booked on the *Eweretta*."

The *Eweretta* was the North West Company's fur ship. Her annual arrival in Montreal in April marked the true beginning of the Canadian spring. Her departure in late October signaled the approach of the long winter. She took few passengers, but for those few she provided all possible comforts.

Gore nodded. "Excellent. She won't wait for anyone this year, however, with that volcanic eruption playing merry hell with the weather. So the sooner you leave for Montreal, the better."

The message couldn't be clearer. *Take your troublesome wife and self elsewhere.*

Simon met his eyes. "I would not wish to appear to be shirking my obligations, sir."

"If McArthur isn't here, you can't be expected to wait on his pleasure and risk being trapped by winter."

So.

"Of course, I would always be available to him in England, sir."

"Quite." Gore escorted him to the door. "Happy to provide any assistance in settling Trewitt's affairs. Good, sound man."

Simon left feeling half a ton lighter. He wasn't a coward, but the aborted duel had served its purpose and he had Jane to consider. If Gore sent McArthur on an errand that would keep him away from York for the next few weeks, his honor might be satisfied without more shots.

"Thank heavens," Jane said when he reported back, her eyes bright. "So when do we leave?"

"The *Eweretta*'s set to sail on the twenty-eighth of October, and we should allow a fortnight to get to Montreal. All being well, it might take only half of that, but Gore's probably correct. This year, the ship won't wait for us."

"But that leaves under three weeks to deal with everything here. It can't be done. Inventory. Pack. Sell the house. Dispose of all it contains."

"You would prefer to stay until spring?"

He saw her readjust. "Very well. It *must* be done." She returned briskly to the desk and the papers.

Simon turned to Hal. "The *Ewqretta*'s prime passenger accommodation. You should send with haste to book. Galloway's a good agent in Montreal. If there's no space he may be able to find room for us all on another ship."

Hal sat to write a letter and then left to see it on its way.

In the hall, the clock chimed two. Six hours. Six hours since Isaiah's death. Simon turned to Jane, a black island of calm, seated at the desk, going methodically through documents. It was unreasonable to resent her composure, but he did.

Had she truly cared for her uncle at all? But he had only to think back to the morning to know just how deeply her feelings ran. This calm was simply more of the peculiarity of Jane Otterburn, his wife.

Since she had the paperwork in hand, he completed the job he'd foolishly given Hal and checked the books for loose papers. He added a great deal to the pile of scraps, letters, and currency notes. He kept an eye out for any book he or Jane might want, but they were things like gazetteers, bound journals, and trade directories, mostly out of date. He sighed.

"What's the matter?"

What the devil do you think is the matter?

He squashed down anger. "It feels damnable to throw away Isaiah's things, even books like the 1795 *Directory of Atlantic Ports*. He kept them and so I want to, in memory of him."

"He kept them because he couldn't be bothered to

throw them out. I don't think he treasured them, Simon."

Weren't women supposed to be the emotional ones?

He excused himself and went to sit vigil with Isaiah. A dark-clad mute stood in attendance, but the man slipped out of the room as soon as Simon entered.

Simon knew he'd come here as a reproach to Jane, which was flat-out wrong. Isaiah wasn't here, only his corpse. Jane had been correct to say that he would have no patience with them wasting time on his remains. All he'd required was that Simon take care of Jane, which he was failing to do.

He let the professional take his place, returned to do better.

Hal returned, bringing his two servants with him—a lanky young man called Treadwell, who'd been his batman once and was now his valet, and a short block of middle-aged muscle called Oglethorpe. His title was groom, but he looked able to deal with anything, including danger. Simon wasn't sure what to do with them, however, so suggested they could go through the stables and other outer buildings, sorting out rubbish, preparing for an auction.

"Why not sell all the contents with the house?" Hal suggested. "Clear out the absolute rubbish, yes, but leave the rest."

It was a blinding relief. "My God, yes." Simon turned to Jane. "Any furniture or other items you value we will ship home, of course."

She frowned. "That would be foolish. Carriage would be more than its value."

"I'm not a pauper. If you want a desk or chair, take it."

"Well, I don't." She stood up. "Excuse me. I must attend to dinner."

She swept out of the room and he knew some of her sharpness was in response to his. Damn. He still resented the fact that she was in control of herself. He wanted her to be a dissolved mess of tears. He felt a good woman, an honest woman, should be. Which was unfair.

He tried to pull his mind into focus and do some meaningful work, but by the time he and Hal were summoned to dine in the parlor, he wasn't sure he'd achieved much. When he discovered that Jane had efficiently arranged for a small table to be set up and a good dinner prepared, it stirred the same resentments.

He tried to act appropriately. "A miracle," he said lightly. "How clever you are."

She blushed—he hoped with pleasure.

As they started on Scotch broth, she said, "So, how do we ship our possessions to Montreal, and how much can we take on the *Eweretta*?"

Why on earth would he want a weeping, helpless wife when he could have a calm, capable one?

They made practical plans, but eventually talk dwindled as if the burden of the day crept in with the evening shadows. He saw that Jane hadn't eaten much of her meal, and nor had he. Work was a relief. Idleness might kill him. He noticed for the first time that Hal was cutting roast pork with a combination knife and fork.

His interest must have been too obvious, for Hal said, "It's called a Nelson fork. Knife-sharp along one thicker tine, and rocker-shaped. Clever thing, with the advantage that I could probably slit someone's throat with it if necessary."

Since the subject was in the open, Simon asked, "Would you not find a hook or some such useful?"

"At times." Hal didn't seem to mind. "It's the arm that's the problem. Very complex thing, an arm. I have a wooden one with elbow joint and all, but I can only move it with my other arm. I visited a man in Ireland who's working on something better. Complicated matter of moving the chest and shoulder muscles to operate joints. You never know what there'll be one day."

He spoke without distress, but it still sounded like an appalling problem. Simon didn't know what to say.

He was saved by Sal coming in, not for the dishes, but with a cloth sling full of wood for the fire. Simon remembered that most of the time Isaiah had brought in the wood. He rose and took the sling, saying he'd deal with it. In truth, he was escaping into work again.

He brought in two more loads, taking one up to his bedroom and then, after a hesitation, filling the woodbox in Jane's. Though he'd glimpsed into her room occasionally, he'd never crossed the threshold before and felt intrusive. He supposed a husband had the right, but he didn't feel that way.

He was certain he had no right to study the room, but he did it anyway, seeking answers to the conundrum she presented. It was sparsely furnished with a narrow bed, a chest of drawers, a desk, a clothespress, and a rocking chair by the fire. This all left quite a bit of space and he wondered why the bed wasn't larger. Some other nun-like choice?

Then he remembered that the narrow bed was because Isaiah had lovingly furnished this for two. When Jane had arrived alone, the extra bed, chest of drawers, and chair had been removed to spare her grief. It would seem that she'd not chosen to change anything.

She'd made it her own, but probably without spending much money. Why, when Isaiah would have delighted to buy her anything she desired?

The quilt on the bed was a patchwork of scraps—pretty enough, but not elegant—and the fine carpet was protected by the sort of country rug again made of scraps. A knitted blanket was folded over the chair. Perhaps she wrapped herself in it on the coldest days. A pleasant enough thought, but it reminded him of the dull, knitted shawl she often wore. Isaiah would have bought her the finest kashmir.

He realized the room felt like one in a simple house, or even in a cottage. If she was uneasy in Trewitt House, what would she make of Brideswell? And yet it was strangely comfortable. With bits and scraps and the work of her own hands, Jane had created a pleasant nest.

She'd surrounded herself with pictures from her past. That was hardly surprising. He had a picture of Brideswell on his own wall along with miniatures of his parents.

Hers were all crudely framed, however, apart from the not-very-good painting of Archibald Otterburn. No mistaking father and daughter even though Simon suspected that she had more energy and strength in one finger than her father had ever possessed. He'd died from getting caught out in the rain. That didn't surprise.

She got her strength from her mother, as was obvious in the pencil portrait of Martha Otterburn that he hadn't seen before. Here, caught in her kitchen, she looked more relaxed and kindly.

Beside that was a less successful work that must be a self-portrait by the cousin. The quality of the drawing equaled the others, but the pose had the awkwardness common in self-portraits. She looked so wooden it was impossible to imagine what she'd been like, but even so, the resemblance to Jane was remarkable between distant cousins. Nan Otterburn's face had been a little longer, perhaps her nose a little straighter, but assuming the coloring was the same, they must have seemed like twins.

Nan's talent had been remarkable for her age. A tragic loss of perhaps a genius. He saw no signature, but her drawings were finer work than the painting, which was boldly signed *B K McKee*.

Then he spotted one other small drawing sitting framed on the desk. He picked it up to see a two-story house that was clearly part of a terrace, even though the image faded to nothing on either side.

Their home in Carlisle, he assumed. Decent but modest. Very modest. Otterburn's school had apparently been well respected and had prepared many boys for grander ones, but he'd clearly not made a fortune at it. There was something in the front window. He held the drawing closer and made out a card saying: *Mrs. Otterburn. Haberdasher.*

He couldn't help it. His first thought was that Jane must never show the picture to his family or to anyone in her new circle.

He pushed the thought away, but it lingered like grit in a wound. He'd married a shopkeeper's daughter, one who'd worked in the shop, and though he could tell himself he didn't mind, he minded that others would.

He put the picture down, reminding himself that the Otterburns were respectable Scottish gentry headed, he gathered, by a Sir David Otterburn, a philanthropist of some note. Simon could make some comment about charity beginning at home, since Sir David had not taken in Nan, but still, it was a decent connection. Even her relationship with Isaiah was in her favor, for he'd done well for himself in the New World and mixed with the highest levels here in York.

He wasn't ashamed of his wife's origins, he assured himself.

It would simply be better if no one back home knew about the shop.

Chapter Six

*T*hey worked through the evening as if, thought
Simon, it all had to be done in the one day. Or
because work was escape from grief.

When the hall clock tinkled nine, however, Hal rose.
"I should return to the hotel."

Something made Simon think that Hal had realized
this was their wedding night. He was tempted to laugh.

"I thank you for your help. Will we be able to impose
on you tomorrow?"

"Certainly, and all the morrows."

When Simon returned from showing Hal out, Jane
was still working through papers. He drew her to her
feet. "Enough of that. You'll wear out your eyes."

"The writing is beginning to swim."

"Come on, then. It's been a long and difficult day."

Simon locked the room. He had no reason to think
anyone would pry or steal, but all these things were his
responsibility now. Then he was unsure what to do next.
As Jane had said, no one would expect them to treat
this as a normal wedding night, but without rituals, what
did one do?

Then Mrs. Gunn marched into the hall, strange to his
eyes in a good dress, black bonnet, and gloves. "If you
don't mind, sir, ma'am, I'll pay my respects to Mr. Trewitt for a while. I put a plain supper in your room, sir,

so you take your wife up there and have some peace and quiet."

An unlikely guiding light, but it didn't sound like a bad idea. There were matters to talk of. Simon thanked the cook, took Jane's hand, and drew her up the stairs. He felt her reluctance. "We need to talk, and then we can go to our separate beds."

"You must think me silly."

"Not to want to consummate such a marriage on such a day? Not at all. There's no hurry, after all. Come along."

His room lay at the far end of the corridor, so they had to pass Isaiah's door. Simon stopped. It seemed impossible that his friend wouldn't emerge with a genial smile and a cheery comment. "He'll never sleep there again."

"And everything in there has to be dealt with," she wearily pointed out.

All Isaiah's little treasures. He'd kept the horn buttons from the coat in which he'd arrived in Canada, and some rough whittled figures a friend had made up in the north. There were eagle feathers, a beaded belt, corn husk dolls, a scarred knife with a carved bone handle . . .

"I want to bury them with him," Simon abruptly said.

Jane's eyes met his, bright—with tears, he thought, but also with approval. "I'll get a candle."

She returned in a moment and they entered the room. The bed was still disordered from Isaiah's rising, and his nightshirt lay over a chair. The whole room spoke of a person leaving it who intended to return. Death could strike like a scythe into grass on a sunlit day.

Simon went to the chest of drawers and mantelpiece where the treasures sat. Jane picked up a porcupine quill basket and he put the items in. She added Isaiah's favorite ivory snuffbox, a new pipe, and some tobacco.

"The rest still has to be dealt with," Simon said, "but I'll be glad to send him on his way with these things for his journey."

They shared a smile and left the chilly room to go on

to his bright, warm one. The fire had been built up and the promised food set on a small table between the two comfortable chairs. The curtains were discreetly drawn across the alcove bed. Tactful Mrs. Gunn.

Simon seated Jane in one chair and served her with food and wine. She took it, but didn't eat or drink. When he sat in the other chair, he said, "Wine settles the nerves. Try some."

She shook her head. "I can't. I keep thinking that we should have found a decent way to avoid this marriage. Is there any way to escape it now?"

Simon was surprisingly hurt by the word "escape." "I'll look into it, but I don't think so. Am I really so intolerable to you?"

She looked up, those blue eyes huge. "No, but you can't want it. I'm not a suitable bride for you."

"I assure you, I could have had a *suitable* bride anytime I wished, here and in England, there being a remote chance I'll be an earl one day."

It was something he often joked about, but from her reaction, she hadn't believed it.

"That's not true, is it?"

"Well, yes."

She looked as if he'd announced he had the plague.

"It's not quite a fate worse than death." His light tone misfired, so he spoke plainly. "Jane, don't be a goose. My father is a distant connection of the Earl of Marlowe, and yes, he does stand in line. But for him to inherit, the earl's current heir, Viscount Austrey, would have to die without a son. Austrey's only fifteen years older than I, and last I heard his young wife had given him a couple of daughters. There's bound to be a boy or two soon."

"But if there isn't, you'll be an earl?"

"Yes, but far, far in the future. If Austrey doesn't sire a son, he'll still likely live another thirty or forty years. We St. Brides have staying power. His father's nearly ninety. So when doom descends on our heads, we'll be too old to care."

She didn't look much comforted, so he added, "If he dies sooner, my father's in the predicament, not me. And Father's a hale and hearty fifty-one without any interest in risky activities like hunting." He decided not to bother her with the detail that if his father did inherit the earldom, he would then have the heir's title, Viscount Austrey.

"If you don't care for the idea," he added, "you'll be a kindred spirit to my parents. The thought of having to leave Brideswell would keep them awake at nights, if they thought it was a remote possibility."

"You think me silly."

"No."

"You do, and with reason. But this is your world, Simon, not mine. It makes sense to you, but not to me. I won't know how to behave, how to fit in."

"Of course you will."

"I'll be an outcast."

"You'll be my wife," he said firmly.

"I'm a shopkeeper's daughter. I *helped* in the shop!"

"You certainly won't fit in if you keep throwing that like a handful of dung!"

A horrible silence gripped them, and then she looked down, biting her lip.

"Jane, I'm sorry, but truly, it doesn't matter."

That was a lie, and they both knew it. Simon felt mentally exhausted, without any capacity to deal with this now, but he must try. "Listen, Hal isn't treating you like a peasant, is he?"

"No, but he doesn't know."

"I'll tell him tomorrow. It won't matter."

"He'll hide it, but it will," she insisted. "I've avoided York society, but I know the finest here consider such as I a lower species of animal, no matter how graciously they condescend."

That startled him. Did the village women in Monkton St. Brides feel like a lower species when his mother and

sisters stopped to talk to them? Did they feel conde-
scension?

Did *he* make people feel that way? He didn't consider
himself a higher being—but yes, sometimes he felt he
was doing someone a kindness merely by taking an
interest.

Hell.

"Drink some wine." When she'd mutinously obeyed,
he said, "You've heard me mention the Company of
Rogues."

She nodded warily. "Your school-day friends."

"Hal's one. Some of them are married now, and not
to particularly highborn women. Your father was a
schoolmaster. The Marquess of Arden married a school-
teacher. That's no higher, and he's the heir to the Duke
of Belcraven. I very much doubt that anyone's making
Beth Arden feel like a lower species. Lucien would gut
them."

"But she's a marchioness."

"Eat some cake," he said, heartened by the story himself. "Lee, the Earl of Charrington, married the impover-
ished widow of a poet, and if I remember aright, she
had been a curate's daughter before her first marriage.
I don't think a curate rates higher than a schoolmaster,
does he?"

"You're making fun of me."

"I'm merely showing that your fears are overblown."

She fired a look at him. "Then why say I should keep
the shop a secret?"

"Oh, dammit, talk about it if you want. Open a shop
if you bloody well want." He inhaled. "I apologize."

She was scarlet, with mortification or anger.

He raised her from her chair, carrying her hands to
his lips. "Forgive me. We're insane to try to talk about
this now. It will all sort out, I promise. In a couple of
months we'll be back in England and you'll see that your
sordid origins will not matter."

He'd meant "sordid" as a joke, but she burst into tears. After a helpless moment, he pulled her into his arms and patted her back. "Come, come now. I didn't mean it. There's nothing sordid in your birth. Even Isaiah's family are respectable people."

She went on weeping in such a deeply anguished way, he was at a loss. He backed into his chair and took her on his knee, where he rocked her as he would a disconsolate child. He could understand the need to weep, but he didn't understand the trigger.

"Jane, Jane, even if the whole world discovers that your widowed mother made ends meet by selling ribbon and lace, and that you helped in her shop, only the most particular will mind, and who cares about them? Is it being a countess?" he asked desperately. "Truly, it can't happen for decades."

Oh, shut up, you idiot. This was exhaustion and grief over Isaiah. He could almost weep himself. He remembered then that Jane had found Isaiah and then been forced into a marriage. And dammit, perhaps the prospect of meeting marquesses and earls *was* terrifying for her.

He rubbed her back, silently begging her to calm.

What were the grounds for annulling a marriage? Insanity, he thought. Fraud. If a person pretended to be someone they weren't. One of the parties being under twenty-one. But Isaiah had been Jane's legal guardian and he'd clearly given his consent in front of a room full of witnesses.

There'd been no banns or license, but he knew that here, where ministers and churches were scarce, the laws were relaxed. A prayer book marriage freely entered into in front of so many and presided over by the parish clergyman was probably ironclad.

Her sobs subsided, so he eased her straighter and looked into her blotched and swollen-eyed face. The crying had marred her looks, but that only made him feel more protective. If there was a way out of this, and if she truly wanted it, he'd find it.

"Jane, for now, think of me as your brother. I have four sisters, so I'm highly experienced at the job. If my sisters were here I'm sure they'd give me excellent references. You shall have my protection, guidance, and care." He risked a joke again. "All I require in return is that you kneel three times a day and bow down before me as if I were the Grand Panjandrum himself."

This time his humor worked. The reference to the nonsensical potentate brought a weak smile. " 'With the little round button a-top,' " she quoted, sitting up straighter and pulling out a handkerchief to wipe her face. "I've made a terrible mess of your jacket."

"A sister's privilege. Though I'd say my jacket has made a terrible mess of your face." He touched her cheek. "I see a clear impression of a button."

She rubbed the spot and struggled off his knees to stand. "I'm so very sorry. For everything." She looked at him with intent seriousness. "There *could* be a way out of this marriage—"

"Hush." He rose and put a finger on her lips. "If there is, we can't do anything yet. Wisely or not, I let it be known that we intended to marry. We can't go back on that without reviving scandal. Let's cope with the immediate and consider the rest later."

Her fingers tangled in the damp handkerchief. "What if McArthur comes back before we leave? Oh, I wish women were allowed to issue challenges!"

"Can you handle a pistol?"

"I could learn."

"I'm sure you could."

Despite her conventional middle-class upbringing, he meant it. He saw her again, charging across a rough field and yelling scathing commands, hair flying loose.

Knowing it to be unwise, he untied the laces beneath her chin and pulled off her mourning cap. It took very little work to remove pins so that her hair fell heavily down her back.

She stared at him, wide-eyed, lips parted.

Kissable.

"Why do you keep it hidden?"

But his soul knew why. So her hair wouldn't drive men mad as it threatened to do to him. He wanted to gather it in his hands like an avaricious thief clutching guineas.

She grabbed it on one side—like a miser guarding guineas. As if she knew. "I've been in mourning."

Mourning didn't require a woman to hide her hair. Another puzzle, but this was no time to badger her with questions. He escorted her to her bedroom and then returned to his own room, wanting to tear things apart.

He couldn't sort out whether he wanted to be married to Jane or not, but he certainly *wanted* her. Perhaps he'd lusted after her for months, but her position here and, yes, her quiet manner and sober clothes, had put her out of bounds.

But now she was his wife. Taking off her cap and releasing her hair had been his *right*. He could strip her naked with the same holy blessing, kiss her, touch her, and handle her in any way he wished. . . .

His thoughts disgusted him even as his animal side growled with desire.

He poured and drank a glass of wine. Even if his honor didn't forbid him to behave like a brute, he absolutely must not take away Jane's chance to free herself. Surely consummating a marriage made it harder to break. It would certainly make it impossible for him to let her go. What if there was a child?

He'd talk to Baldwin tomorrow and to Stephen Ball when they reached England, but he strongly suspected that they were tied for life. And despite all the problems he saw now and in the future, he couldn't regret that.

*   *   *

Guilt and grief kept Jancy awake for most of the night, and she had to drag herself out of bed the next morning. In her mirror, she looked sallow and heavy-eyed, but she supposed no one would be surprised by that. Not even if they thought she and Simon had had a wedding night.

She dropped her hairbrush to cover her face with her hands. She had to free him from this marriage, and the fact that she didn't want to was more reason, not less. She was a wicked, deceitful sinner and she carried disaster with her like a contagion.

Martha had died.

Jane had died.

Isaiah had died.

She knew the strange code by which gentlemen lived meant that Simon would feel honor bound to meet McArthur if the man insisted on it. So he might die. She couldn't bear it. She couldn't bear it.

If telling him the truth would avoid the duel, she'd do it immediately. But it wouldn't. She'd gone around and around that in the night. No matter what the original trigger, the duel had ended up being over McArthur's misuse of funds. Her confession wouldn't change that, and here and now it would complicate things horribly.

Weighed down by misery, she completed her dressing and went to sit in final vigil by Isaiah's coffin.

Simon urged her to eat, but she shook her head, unable to imagine touching food. At least he didn't persist and he looked as drawn as she felt. Isaiah's friends and business associates began to arrive, each murmuring condolences. The only other woman present was Mrs. Gunn, who took a place by her side.

Jancy smiled slightly at the old woman in thanks and Mrs. Gunn patted her hand. In some ways she reminded Jancy of Martha, and the kitchen had become a favorite haven. She'd often wished she could confide the truth to her.

Reverend Strachan read the service and then Ross put

the lid on the coffin and nailed it shut. Even though Jancy did truly believe that a corpse was merely a shell, each blow hammered her heart. When Simon put his arm around her, she leaned.

"You shouldn't be here," he said softly.

"I need to be."

He had to leave her to be one of the coffin bearers, and Jane was grateful for Mrs. Gunn's support during the procession over to the churchyard.

Through tear-blurred eyes, the sunny day was a crazy quilt of blue, green, brown, and orange. The trees were turning, heralding winter, as did the touch of ice in the air. Jancy was glad of the fur-lined muff Isaiah had given her for Christmas, but also of the cold. It would be wrong for nature to be too pleasant today.

Reverend Strachan began the graveside service, but Jancy said prayers of her own.

Dear God, You know what a good man this is. Welcome him into heaven. Make him young and strong again, and give him seas to sail, lands to explore, and rivers to travel through the glories of Your creation.

But then her focus turned from God to Isaiah.

Dear Uncle Isaiah, by now you know the truth. Are you able to forgive me? I wish I'd found the courage to confess. I know now that you would have understood.

When Jane died, I was so frightened. I was on the seas and we'd both been terribly sick. I'd thought I'd die, but then Jane did. I was alone in the world, going to a wilderness. Aunt Martha always said that you lived where there were bears at the door and savages in the streets. And I'd be going into the power of a stranger who was no relative of mine.

I imagined you turning me from the door. Or even having me thrown in jail for using Jane's money to survive on, for I'd not enough of my own.

So I switched. No one on board knew us well, and we looked a lot alike.

I'm so very sorry I didn't trust you. Especially as then you'd not have made Simon marry me. Oh, I wish you hadn't. I wish I'd refused.

You have to help me make everything right. Guide me, Uncle. You don't mind me calling you that still, do you? Guide me as to how to behave, and how and when to tell him the truth. About the switch from Nan to Jane, that is. I'll never tell him or anyone that I'm a Haskett. . . .

"Jane?"

Jancy started and found Simon beside her. People were beginning to move away from the grave, back toward the house for the wake.

"Do you want to throw dirt on the coffin?"

She shuddered. "Why do people do that?"

"I don't know."

Instead she took out her black-edged handkerchief, damp with her tears, and let it flutter down into the porcupine quill basket that sat on the coffin. "Good-bye, Uncle Isaiah. Happy journey."

Simon linked arms and led her back to the house. "We only have to survive the wake and the worst will be over."

Jancy sighed. If only that were true.

The funeral rites did bring some good news. Jancy overheard Lieutenant Governor Gore mention to the room in general that McArthur had unfortunately been obliged to travel west to deal with unrest near Amherstburg. Jancy hoped it was violent unrest and McArthur was caught in the cross fire.

Mrs. Gunn had returned to the kitchen, so when Simon urged Jancy to lie down and rest, she took the escape offered. She'd done her duty by Isaiah, and if the men wanted to get drunk, talk business, or both, she was happy to leave them to it. Except that being alone and idle left too much space for thought.

To escape that she began to go through her room, sorting out what she would take back to England. Nearly

everything she'd brought, of course. Jane's drawings.
The locket holding a coil of Aunt Martha's graying hair,
to which she'd added a wisp of Jane's rich coppery gold.

Strangely, she'd never prayed to Martha and Jane as
she'd prayed to Isaiah today, so she knelt and did so,
begging their forgiveness for any sins and asking for
their guidance. A sweet feeling of peace crept over her.
It was Jane, she knew. Sweet, loving Jane, and she could
almost feel her stroking her hair.

*It's all right, Nan. Truly. You did what seemed best at
the time, and I will watch over you. I suppose you'd like
me to call you Jancy—*

"No," Jancy said aloud, startling herself out of a kind
of trance.

The powerful sense of Jane's presence fled, but the
effect lingered. "Oh, Jane, love, be with me. Help me.
But call me Nan. To you, I'm Nan. Always."

If anyone heard her they'd think her mad. She crawled
up on the bed and fell into a deep sleep.

When she woke, she was crusty eyed and misty
headed, but she felt better. For almost a year she'd been
confused and afraid, but now everything seemed clear.
She would be Simon's helpmeet as he sorted out Isaiah's
affairs and arranged their journey back to England. But
as soon as they landed, before he took her to his home,
she would tell him the truth.

The whole truth.

Even the Haskett part.

The fact that he'd thought he was marrying a different
person had to invalidate the marriage, so he'd be free
to return to his home unburdened.

She changed into one of her plain dresses and white
caps. When she arrived downstairs the house seemed
empty except for three of Mrs. Gunn's relatives cleaning
up. They were even chattering, though they fell silent
when she appeared.

The wake was over. Life must go on. But the transi-
tion seemed painfully abrupt. Death one day, burial the

next, and then onward. Perhaps mourners should be offered a formal period to become adjusted, as a married couple was allowed a honeymoon. A "bittermoon," she named the idea, but that described too well her situation—honeymooning amid grief.

She heard Simon's voice from the parlor and her heart moved. It really did feel like that. Not quite a dance. More like a devoted puppy quivering with excitement at its master's voice. She composed herself and entered to find Simon with Hal.

"We have an offer for the house, with all contents we wish to leave." He looked braced for objection. "Gilbraith."

It did feel rather like vultures gathering, but she smiled. "One less thing to do, then. Don't worry, Simon. I've lived here less than a year, and all I really cared about is dead." Hastily she added, "Apart from you, of course. And you don't come with the house. I mean," she said desperately, "I don't have the attachment to this house that I had to my home in Carlisle."

"I understand, Jane. Well, back to work."

Perhaps they all seized eagerly on that sanctuary.

Hal Beaumont tried to excuse himself from dinner, but both Simon and Jancy urged him to stay. She knew why. They didn't want to be alone. After the meal they played a game of dominoes in memory of Isaiah, who'd been fond of the simple game and treasured his ebony and ivory set.

"This must go home with us," she said and then wondered if she would be allowed to keep it after the parting. Isaiah hadn't left his possessions to her, but to Jane.

She probably looked distressed, for Simon said, "You must be very tired, Jane."

Hal again rose to take his leave, but she smiled and told him to stay and then left the men together. There was no question of going anywhere but to her own room, but once there, she stood, hands clasped in anxiety. Simon had said they'd wait to consummate the marriage, but he wouldn't wait forever. What was she going to do if—when—he came to her bed? If they were to break the marriage, they mustn't . . . *swive,* the Hasketts called it.

That was a battle for another day, however, and Simon had been correct. She was unbelievably tired. She undressed, washed, and went to bed.

Chapter Seven

*A*fter breakfast the next morning, Simon said, "I have to attend the inquest, but later, we should deal with Isaiah's room. There are bequeathed items that must be in there."

Hal hadn't arrived yet, and Jancy could see that Simon dreaded the task as much as she did. "I'll do it if you want."

"No, we'll do it together."

"The inquest won't cause any problems, will it? To do with the duel?"

"I don't expect so. Baldwin will speak to Isaiah's health. As for circumstances, Saul Prithy told him about the duel and then left to get Isaiah's horse. By the time he returned it was all over. I'm sorry you had to find him, Jane, but I don't think they'll require your testimony."

"I'd rather not relive it."

"Then you won't." He pressed her shoulder as he went out.

She busied herself with the repetitive task of writing death announcements for distant people, but when Simon returned, she looked at him anxiously.

"Brief and routine. Death by accident. Now we should deal with his room."

She rose and went to him. He took her hand as they

went upstairs, and the warm touch, skin to skin, was both comfort and torture.

"This is going to be worse than the funeral," she said outside the door. "A more absolute farewell."

"Yes." He opened the door and they went in.

But the cold room felt nothing like Isaiah any longer, not even with the rumpled bed and abandoned night-shirt. Perhaps the absence of his special treasures was the symbol that he had gone. All the same, the room was still full of his belongings.

"Where in heaven's name do we start?" Jancy asked.

"You don't have to do this, Jane. Treadwell and Ogle-thorpe can help me."

"No. I want to." She looked around. "We'll go through the room systematically, emptying all the draw-ers and cupboards."

"Very well. Anything bequeathed on one pile. Things you or I wish to keep on another. Anything of value that we don't want on a third to be sold. Other items . . ."

Thrown away hung in the air.

"Reverend Strachan," she said. "For the poor. It's sur-prising what can be of use to the desperate."

He smiled. "Thank you. Yes."

She straightened the bed and then started on the chest of drawers. The first drawer, full of breeches, had her at a loss. "None of these will fit you."

"And are not really my style."

She looked at him, startled into a laugh that she smothered with her hand. "I suppose not. But what do we do with them?"

"Reverend Strachan, I assume."

"Yes, of course. I'm sorry. It's just . . ."

"I know."

They worked steadily and in silence, though Jane fre-quently blew her nose. Sometimes they'd pause for a memory, so a memorial of Isaiah was woven between them as they worked. Perhaps something else was cre-ated, too. Jancy realized that they had never before been alone for so long, and here their shared love for Isaiah Trewitt was intimate and profound.

Often their eyes met, and she was sure he, like she, knew that no one else could understand these things as the other did. Once, coming across a lock of blond hair in a fold of yellowed paper, they wondered whose it was, what loss it marked. They held hands as they accepted that the only thing to do was put it aside to be burned.

Simon raised her hand to his lips before returning to work. She pretended to move on to the next drawer, but she stroked the place where he'd kissed and tried to calm a rapid heart.

Moment by moment she was rebelling against fate. Something powerful existed here. Something glorious. Why should she have to shatter it and live forever in the desert? Why couldn't she respond to the message in Simon's eyes and let him kiss her mouth, let him take her to his bed and seal their union once and for all?

She picked up a bundle of letters absentmindedly but then gasped.

"What's the matter?" he asked.

She wanted to hide the small bundle, but that was impossible now. "Letters. From . . . my mother."

She'd almost said "Aunt Martha"! What to do? "It's so cold in here. If you'll build a fire, I'll get a light."

She dashed out and into her room, guiltily aware that Simon would think her crying over sorrowful memories instead of shivering with panic and fear. Her hands shook as she unfolded the first letter to skim the contents. It was an early one, from before Martha's marriage. She put it aside and unfolded the next.

Though the letters covered nearly twenty years, there were only a dozen or so. More had been sent recently than in the distant past. Jancy hurried through them, looking for any sent around the time she'd gone to live with Martha.

What had she told her brother?

There. Written in September 1808.

As Jancy had feared, Martha had told Isaiah everything. A filthy Haskett had produced a little girl who was so like dear Jane that the woman's story had to be true.

Jancy read through a full half page about Martha's struggle to forgive her dead husband for his sin. She paused to appreciate that her foster mother had never let that struggle affect her kindness.

Martha went on to explain her stratagem. Perhaps her distant brother had been the only person to whom she felt she could be honest.

Even though I detest all lies, Brother, the girl will be known as Nan Otterburn, an orphan of the Otterburn family. Pray God forgive me the deceit and protect us from discovery.

For a moment Jancy thought that Isaiah had always known the truth about her, but then she realized not. He'd thought her to be Jane, and this Nan Haskett dead on the high seas.

She put that letter aside and continued. After that one revelation Martha never again referred to Hasketts, and Jancy was "dear Nan" or more often one of "my dear girls." Tears flowed then, and she had to struggle not to cry all over the precious sheets. What a good woman Martha had been.

The last letter was the one written in wandering handwriting when Martha was ill, asking her brother's kindness for "my dear girls." Jancy remembered Jane offering to write it for her mother, but Martha insisting on writing it herself. Now she saw why.

They are both good girls, Brother, and I most particularly ask that you forget what I once wrote about Nan's origins. If I had ever expected to come to this I would not have told you. Nan is a little bolder than Jane, a little more impulsive in her ways, but I promise you there is no Haskett contamination in her soul. She is a good girl and I beg that you will treat her as you do your true niece Jane.

Jancy clutched the letters, hating that she was going to have to destroy them, but she must. Only look how Martha on her deathbed had worried about her Haskett blood.

Contamination.

Then she realized that she didn't have to destroy them all. There was nothing anywhere to reveal that she was Nan, not Jane, and only a couple that spoke of the deeper shame. They would have to go.

She hated to do it. She sobbed as she did it. But she put the two letters on the fire and watched to be sure that they disappeared entirely into ashes.

There. The Haskett contamination was gone.

She slipped the remaining letters into her desk then used the tongs to take a burning piece of wood to Isaiah's room to light the fire that Simon had made. Soon it was burning brightly warming and cheering the room as they completed the task.

He didn't comment on her lengthy absence, but Jancy was wound tight with dread of finding something else that would betray her. She took an opportunity to look inside Isaiah's Bible to be sure he hadn't recorded family there. Nothing, and he wasn't the sort to keep a diary or copies of replies he had sent to his sister.

But when Simon said, "Ah, look," she started as if jabbed.

He was only handling a cumbersome ancient pistol. He put it on the pile to keep and they continued with their task.

Simon hated stripping Isaiah's room, but it was a healing ritual. A final farewell. He was sorry Jane had found letters that opened old wounds, but she seemed to have recovered. They'd both be better away from here, however, and on their way to a new life.

Together.

In England.

That prospect seemed more promising by the moment.

Her neat, graceful movements around the room and even her composure soothed him. Their shared memories were a treasure. With whom else would he be able to talk about Isaiah? With whom else could he hold hands in just that way?

When he'd kissed her knuckles, a wave had passed through him that he might have dismissed as lust but had known was a deeper longing. A dangerous longing, when he was resolved to return her to England a virgin, with some possibility of freedom.

When they'd finished with the room, he arranged for the items as they'd agreed, and she went to summon the servants to give it a thorough cleaning. This became the pattern for their busy days. He sorted out Isaiah's business and property. She helped, but also organized an attic to cellar cleaning of the house. It seemed important to her to leave it spotless for Gilbraith and his family.

He supposed it was important to him to leave Isaiah's business affairs in order.

Even though Gilbraith was willing to buy the furniture and fittings, and Gore had sent a clerk called John Vincent to oversee the inventory, there was still a mountain of work to hide in. Thank God Hal stayed to dine every night. But every night eventually Hal left them alone in the house and Simon's mind turned to lust.

Jane still wore her prim caps, but now that he knew the hair they confined, they were more tantalizing than protective. From a few brief embraces, he knew the shape of her body and its soft, warm allure. Her subtle perfume tormented him with wicked thoughts of meadow pleasures.

He wasted time looking at her, and sometimes she caught him at it. He probably blushed. She certainly did, looking even prettier, and flustered, and shy—and desirable.

Now and then he'd remember the lurking threat that McArthur would return to complete the duel, but he couldn't seem to give that the weight he should. Instead he lay awake at night wondering why he wasn't making love to his wife.

There was the issue of annulment, but that felt less important every day. Jane was gracious, intelligent, hardworking, efficient, and beautiful. Hal liked her. Hal's menservants seemed to adore her. What more could any man want?

He was not arrogant enough to assume she must want to remain married to him, but the look in her eye, the way she blushed, even the way she moved sometimes suggested that she did. There was certainly no hint of dislike or disgust.

The main reason he didn't court his wife into bed, the insurmountable reason, was that he still wasn't sure that he *loved* her. He wanted her, but was it more than lust?

He was sure it was idiotic, but he needed to love his wife—any wife. To desire her, yes, but also to like her, to enjoy her company, to feel lessened when she was away. And to trust her.

Which was the thorn on this rose.

Despite all Jane's glorious charms, there was something secretive and perplexing about her. He could never pin it down, but it was there. When he turned conversation to her past, to her family and home, she appeared to talk about it, but he realized later that he'd learned very little. She was like a jeweled box, lovely but locked so that he had no idea what lay inside.

He tried to talk to Hal about it. Jane was upstairs making an inventory of the household linens and deciding which to take with them for use on the journey. Treadwell and Oglethorpe were packing up Isaiah's business papers to stay with Baldwin.

Simon took his friend into the parlor and offered him wine. "Have you ever been in love, Hal?" The silence made him wince. "Sorry."

"I am in love."

Simon eyed him. "Tricky subject?"

"You could say that. You never asked why I'm here."

"Escort duty, didn't you say? We've been too busy to get into details. But I did think it odd that you'd undertaken a grueling two-month journey to the edge of the wilderness only to turn around and repeat it in the other direction."

Hal looked at his drink, swirling it. "I did it because the woman I love won't marry me." He looked up, smiling wryly. "I decided separation might bring her to her senses, but I knew I'd not be able to stay away. So I put an ocean and half a continent between us. And," he added, finally sipping, "I miss her more than my damned arm."

Simon drank, too, wondering if the missing arm was the reason Hal's beloved had rejected him. "Would I know the lady?"

"Probably not, except by reputation. She's an actress. Mrs. Blanche Hardcastle."

Simon almost choked.

Nicholas Delaney kept him informed on Roguish matters, so he knew that when Lucien de Vaux had married, Hal had inherited his famous mistress, the White Dove of Drury Lane. He'd thought it excellent news—proof that Hal's life had returned to normal.

But he wanted to *marry* her?

He managed, "Ah, yes, Nicholas wrote."

"Busy keeping everyone in the fold, whether they want to be or not."

Simon assessed the acid edge on Hal's comment. "Has Nicholas been irritating you?"

"Everyone is irritating me. Especially, at the moment, you. Why the devil are you asking about love?"

Hal was by nature as steady as they come. He'd dealt with the loss of his arm with wry stoicism. Things were clearly bad.

Simon leaped with relief to his own problems. "Because I can't decide whether I love Jane. That story of us intending to wed was a fabrication. Isaiah demanded that we marry as he lay dying and I couldn't see a way out, especially as her reputation had been smirched."

"You are married, however. Locked in wed."

"It's remotely possible it can be broken. If it can't . . ." He shrugged. "I had hoped to marry for love. The kind that strikes like a thunderbolt, driving one to adoring knees."

"They say love can grow."

"But not for you?" The question escaped before Simon could prevent it. "I mean, if you chose someone more suitable . . ."

"Not," Hal said, "when one is riven by a thunderbolt. The effect is somewhat permanent." He looked, clearly without seeing, toward the fire. "Blanche was born Maggie Duggins, daughter of a butcher. She bore a bastard when scarcely more than a child herself and then used her beauty and her body to make a better life." He looked at Simon, a hard glitter in his eyes. "I have a list of all the men. She forced it on me."

Simon had to say something. "Which makes it hard for you to love her?"

But then he remembered the thunderbolt.

"I only care because I wish I'd known her when she was thirteen and protected her from all suffering. Which is bloody stupid, as I was a child at the time. She's eight years older than I. And that life, the one I'd save her from, has made her the magnificent woman she is today. She's my mistress. She gives me anything and everything except the wedding. And I'm here, without her, fighting for that one thing."

Simon was speechless. Before inspiration struck, Hal added, "She's fighting to protect me from my own insanity because she loves me. I'm so miserable that I'd swim the bloody ocean if I could to get back to her side faster. And that, Simon, is love. Avoid it if you can."

"For God's sake, why are you lingering? Take the next ship."

Hal drained the glass and put it aside. "I told her I'd hear her decision on her birthday, December fifteenth. I have strength enough for that."

"And if she still says no?"

Hal smiled. "Then I'll take what crumbs I can. And she must know it."

That could be the end of the matter, but friendship pushed Simon to say, "Have you thought that she might be right? How can she fit into our world?"

Immediately he realized that he wasn't talking only about Hal and his actress. He was thinking of himself and his shopgirl. And Jane had an impeccable reputation and acceptable family.

Hal laughed. "I've not only thought, but had it beaten into my head by Blanche herself. The situation's not helped by the fact that she almost certainly can't bear another child. It doesn't bother me, but it weighs on her."

"Then will she not be more comfortable as your mistress?"

"Probably, but I'm a selfish bastard, and I want my ring on her finger to show that she's locked with me for eternity."

Simon thought of his ring on Jane's finger—and knew that he, too, wanted a woman locked to him for eternity, mysterious or not. Riven by a thunderbolt? It didn't feel like that. More like the unnoticed effect of water beneath a wall, eroding the foundation, causing it to tilt and one day fall.

He pulled back to Hal's inappropriate beloved. "Perhaps Mrs. Hardcastle doesn't want to give up her profession. I gather she's an excellent actress."

"She won't have to."

Simon would have laughed at anyone who described him as conventional, but that did shake him. Bad enough for Hal to take a wife with a scandalous past, but to have her continue to act on the stage? Even, he assumed, in breeches parts?

A wife, he realized, he would be expected to introduce to Jane?

Hal's expression suggested that he guessed what Simon was thinking. "Blanche and Beth Arden are best of friends."

"What?" Luce's wife and his ex-mistress?

"Staunch allies," Hal assured him, bitterly amused. "Especially in trying to apply the principles of rights for women to all levels of society. Add in that Nicholas dictates that all wives become Rogues, fully accepted, and you're returning to a madhouse."

Simon drained his forgotten wine. "Bloody hell. It'll take a bit of getting used to."

He'd been bracing himself to introduce a shopkeeper's daughter to his family and friends. Now he wondered how Jane, with her conventional upbringing, would react to an introduction to an immoral actress or to revolutionary notions about women's equality.

Hal asked, "If you discovered that Jane had a similar background, you think you would be unable to love her?"

"I know all about Jane's background."

"But?"

Simon gave the question thought. "I suppose Cupid's lightning bolt can strike anyone at any time, but no, I wouldn't marry someone like that. Sorry, Hal, but I would not. It wouldn't be fair to my family or my children."

A moment later Jane came in with tea. Simon hoped to hell she hadn't heard his last words and misinterpreted. She looked undisturbed.

Perhaps he should tell her that the conversation had eased his mind. So Jane's mother had kept a shop and Jane had assisted in it. Compared to the career of the White Dove of Drury Lane, that was nothing.

Chapter Eight

*J*ancy had heard Simon's words.

I wouldn't marry someone like that. Sorry, Hal, but I would not. It wouldn't be fair to my family or my children.

She didn't know whom they'd been talking about, but she was sure it could be no one lower than Jancy Haskett. Soon she received another blow.

Simon said, "I suppose we must attend church tomorrow."

"Must we?"

"Not to do so will cause talk. That's the last thing we need."

"True," she sighed. "But a bride's first appearance at church after the wedding is something of an event."

Especially the dramatically wed bride of Simon St. Bride.

"Don't worry," Simon said, making her think, *All very well for you to say!* "Hal and I will provide escort."

"Then I will be the envy of all," she said lightly. But that evening, she excused herself early to prepare for battle.

She'd attended St. James's with Isaiah and sat in his pew but never lingered afterward. Now she would be a center of attention for the York elite, and for Simon's sake, she had to do him credit.

Traditionally the bride attended church in the fine gown she'd worn for her wedding. That wouldn't do. She and Jane had brought their better gowns, but she could hardly wear colors.

It would have to be the black mourning gown. Though plain, it was stylish. Martha had been a seamstress by trade and had trained her girls well. Jancy's York gowns were *unstylish* by intent.

Next she considered headwear. Her two bonnets were dull and showing their age. She studied one, seeking a way to refurbish it, but it was hopeless. Then she remembered a lady newly come from England who'd worn a kind of beret trimmed with a feather. The "Scottish cap" was apparently all the latest thing.

She could make something like that. But there was only one source of material. She opened a trunk, lifted off the top layers to reach Jane's clothing.

It had been wasteful to keep these gowns when she herself could never wear them. Jane had been a little shorter and of slighter build even then. Now, any of the bodices would burst.

She'd clung to any connection to Jane, but there was no excuse to pay the costs of taking the clothes back to England. She resolutely piled them on the floor to go to charity, but then burst into tears over Jane's favorite forget-me-not sprigged muslin. Jancy had done most of the work on it, for she'd been the better seamstress, and Jane had always preferred drawing to needlework.

She remembered Jane sketching her as she'd worked. . . .

She pulled herself together and put it with the rest, but then snatched it back. Perhaps she could remake it in some way. Put inserts in the bodice. Or a whole new bodice and a flounce at the hem to lengthen it.

How stupid. Jane had loved it so much she'd almost worn it to death. But there was enough good cloth to make a pretty dress for a little girl.

For a daughter.

For a daughter of hers and Simon's named Jane St. Bride . . .

She put the dress aside to keep and then picked up Jane's mourning dress. It was almost identical to her own and had been cut from the same bolt of cloth. Though it hurt as if she slashed her own skin, she cut out a large part of the skirt and began to fashion a soft, brimless hat.

She did it by trial and error, but she'd always been good at this sort of thing. She lacked time to make the stitching fine, but she soon saw in the mirror the effect she wanted. The Scottish cap. It needed some sort of trimming. Jane had also had a mourning cap similar to her own. Jancy formed a rosette from the black lace and fixed it on one side.

It was gone midnight when she tried it on for the last time. Her hands and eyes were weary from the work, but she was satisfied. Tomorrow she would not shame Simon any more than necessary.

Even so, the next morning, when she heard the bell of St. James's church summoning worshippers, her knees wobbled and she had to brace herself to go down to where he and Hal waited.

Simon smiled, particularly at her hat. "Where did that charming miracle come from?"

"I made it. I'm sorry."

"Why?"

"I'm sure real ladies don't make their own hats."

"I'm sure they would if they were so clever at it. Don't be a goose. Wait a moment." He ran upstairs and returned with a silver filigree brooch set with amethysts. "This would look stylish in your rosette."

A gift. A gift from Simon.

Jancy took off her hat and fixed the brooch in the heart of the rosette. She went to the mirror and put the hat on again. "It's perfect. Thank you."

She turned to smile and his echoing smile caught her with its warmth and admiration. It gave her courage as she walked with her handsome, nobly born escorts to the clapboard church. They were part of a steady stream, but it would seem people didn't know what to do with a bride in deep mourning. Most acknowledged the three of them with an inclined head, but that was it.

After the service she would have liked to hurry away as she always had, but Simon took her to speak to the Strachans and the Gores. They were even approached by the inappropriately named Humbles, who had never deigned to notice her before. They sneered at anyone not of noble birth.

Within minutes Mrs. Humble managed to mention her cousin the duke three times and Simon's connection the Earl of Marlowe twice. And to convey with chilly looks that Jancy was an upstart interloper.

As Jancy and Simon moved away, she muttered, "I don't know why she doesn't have her escutcheon tattooed onto her forehead. Then she wouldn't have to make sure everyone knows about her fine connections."

He choked on laughter. "Don't."

Jancy pursed her lips to hide her own laughter as she faced Lady Chisholme, wife of a Scottish major who was also a baronet.

"Your father was Scottish, I believe, Mrs. St. Bride?"

Something in the jowly woman's sharp eyes warned Jancy of an inquisition.

Hiding sick dread, she said, "Yes, ma'am."

"From the Roxburgh Otterburns?"

Jancy agreed, thanking heaven that she knew about Archibald Otterburn's family. "But I'm afraid we never visited my father's family, and he died when I was nine."

That should deal with that.

But Mrs. Humble had followed. "Your mother, I believe, was of a lower station, Mrs. St. Bride."

Jancy and Simon became the center of a group of ladies. Ambushed at the church door? A wild desire surged to shock them into a collective faint by saying, "Very low. She was a vagrant called Tillie Haskett."

Simon saved her. "My wife's mother was Isaiah Trewitt's sister, Mrs. Humble. That is high enough for me."

Flags of angry color flew in the lady's cheeks, but she smiled, with her mouth at least. "How romantic."

That put an end to the inquisition, however, and the other ladies melted away. With the excuse of so much to do before leaving York, Simon eased them out of the throng.

"Thank you," Jancy said, "but I'm going to encounter the same thing back in England, aren't I?"

"Only from cold trouts like Humble."

She looked at him. "I'm not going to be constantly asked about my origins?"

"Yes, of course, but tell the truth. There's nothing shameful."

"Not even the shop? What do these people think we should have done when the money began to run out? Starve in genteel dignity?"

"Probably. Which shows how ridiculous they are. No, it won't be like that back home. The Humbles and Chisholmes are trout pretending to be salmon because the stream is small."

He said it so casually that Jancy found his words convincing, but then where did a small fish like herself fit? As salmon food, probably. She worried about it all the way back to the house, but as she changed into working clothes she remembered that it didn't matter, because once she told Simon the truth, she'd be in another stream entirely. A puddle, more like.

It was becoming so easy to slip into believing that their marriage could last, and oh, how she wanted it to.

Long days in each other's company had made him even more precious to her. They had constant need to confer and consult, and more and more, their practical conversations became lighthearted banter. They even seemed to think alike on most subjects.

She couldn't imagine being apart, never seeing him again. Despite the gulf between their stations, they suited very well. Why couldn't it work? Did she have to confess? She and Jane had been very alike. As long as she avoided Carlisle and the people there who'd known her well, perhaps the lie could hold.

She went downstairs, fighting temptation, and she found Simon in the office with a ledger open.

"I thought we'd settled all the accounts," she said.

"Almost."

She peered at the page. "Oh, yes, there are still some debts outstanding."

He tapped his finger on the page and she wondered what had him uneasy. She could read him now, read his every mood. "I wondered if you'd mind if we forgave them."

She glanced at the list, trying to remember details. "Why?"

"First, because Isaiah had let them ride for quite a while. He'd have his reasons."

"He was very softhearted."

"Yes, but the sums are so very small. Twenty pounds, twelve, even five. Nothings, but to these people, a burden. I don't know where Saul Prithy would find twenty pounds."

She wanted to say, *The rent for our house in Carlisle was less than twenty pounds a year.* A question escaped. "What's your income, Simon?"

He looked startled but said, "Six hundred a year."

Jancy's heart sank. She'd slipped into the illusion of them having so much in common, but it wasn't true.

Six hundred pounds a year was a fortune to her, but she remembered him once saying that his allowance as his father's heir should be larger. His father refused to pay it all unless he returned to live at Brideswell.

Isaiah's entire estate would amount to under two thousand pounds, and she could live on the interest of that for the rest of her life. It would be genteel poverty, but she could survive, especially with the skills of her needle.

It was true, however, that the debts he considered petty probably were keeping people awake at night.

"By all means. You're correct. Isaiah would want them forgiven."

"Good. Now let's talk about your income."

She stared at him. Was he planning to put her aside? "What do you mean?"

"The marriage settlement. Your security in case anything happens to me."

"Nothing's going to happen to you!"

But awareness of McArthur shivered suddenly through the stripped office.

"Fate is unpredictable, but in any case you will need pin money."

"Pin money?"

"Money for your use alone."

Alone. Her head was buzzing with panic. "I won't be alone."

"Jane . . ." He took her hand. "I'm sorry, I'm not explaining very well. In my circles it's usual for these things to be set up legally so that the wife has income regardless of her husband's whim and will be secure if he should die."

"I see. But I have Isaiah's money."

He grimaced. "No, you don't. By marriage, it's now mine. But normally you would have been protected by a settlement that guaranteed you income in compensation. I've had Baldwin draw up my will, which will put Isaiah's money back in your hands if I should die. Because of your age, I've named my father as your guardian. I know that would be difficult, but I can trust him to keep you safe."

"Simon, don't! I don't even want to think about you dying." She gripped his hands tighter. "Is McArthur back?"

"No. I didn't mean to frighten you. These things simply need to be done. To keep you safe."

She was upsetting him with her foolishness. "Very well. Thank you. Now can we talk of something else?"

"If you wish. But once we're in England I'll have a

proper marriage settlement drawn up. As I have little income, it will need my father's guarantees, but you'll have your pin money and a secured jointure. It will also provide for our younger children."

Children.

"I have," he said, watching her, "been wondering if you'd given any thought to the matter of children."

Fire and ice ran over her skin. She tried to pass it off with a joke. "Troublesome creatures."

"That's the sort of thing a man's supposed to say. I confess I like children. I look forward to filling Brideswell with another generation."

It was a question, one that threw her into whirling disorder.

They mustn't.

Her body, however—her skin, her nerves, her breasts, her very womb—had other ideas, particularly when he drew her against him and brushed his lips against her neck.

Why not? They were married, and she wanted to stay married. . . .

She pushed sharply away, stumbling in her urgency. "Not until England!" she gasped. They mustn't consummate the marriage until she'd told him the truth.

He stared. "Not until *England*? Jane . . . Do you still want an annulment? I thought things had changed."

"Yes. No!" She desperately sought some rational excuse. "I was so sick on board ship. J— . . . Nan died. If I were with child, I might die."

He ran a hand through his hair. "Then of course it will be as you wish."

Not as I wish, my love. As it must be.

"Thank you," she gasped and fled to the safety of the kitchens.

Mrs. Gunn looked up from a pot. "What's put you in a tizzy, then?"

"Nothing." Jancy took an apron from the hook.

"Aye, a husband's usually nothing."

"What vegetables should I prepare?"

"Chop some onions. It'll give you something to cry about."

"I don't need onions to cry over Isaiah."

"Maybe not, but everything'd be simpler if you took your husband to your bed."

Jancy grabbed three big onions. "That's none of your business."

"True enough, except that the pair of you are acting like mooncalves." Mrs. Gunn thumped her pan onto the central table. "Anyone can see he's burning up with wanting you."

"Truly?" Jancy didn't need assurance on that, but she wanted it anyway.

"And you're as keen as he is, so don't pretend you aren't. If you weren't married, I'd lock the two of you in separate rooms. So what is it? Frightened?"

"No." The truth came out before she thought, stealing Jancy's best excuse.

The cook began to attack a lump of bleeding venison with a sharp knife. "Then what's the problem?"

Lacking anything better, as she skinned the onions and began to slice, Jancy gave her the reason she'd given Simon.

Mrs. Gunn humphed. "I can see as how you'd be nervous, dearie, your cousin dying an' all, but if you're sick with the sea and sick with a child it'd probably be no worse in all. And think of all the fun you're missing."

"Mrs. Gunn!"

"What? Never tell me your mother made it out to be torture. Trust your feelings, dearie, and enjoy yourself."

"Maybe," Jancy mumbled, hoping Mrs. Gunn took the tears running down her face to be caused by the onions. Some of them were.

When the braised meat was in the oven, Jancy put together a tea tray and carried it back to the house, hoping Hal wasn't back yet. Her mind swam with forbidden longings, and perhaps it wouldn't be so wrong.

Martha had never spoken about the marriage bed at all, but there'd always been an implication that it was an unfortunate necessity for the blessing of children. A price to be paid. Jancy remembered something Tillie had said when explaining who her father was. "Once his wife knew she was with child, she refused him his pleasure, silly biddy, so he took to long walks. And there he met me."

Jancy didn't want Simon taking long walks, and she didn't need telling that the marriage bed wasn't torture. Hasketts took it for granted that swiving was jolly fun for women as well as men. Sometimes they'd called it "pleasuring," too.

She wanted to pleasure Simon and be pleasured in return, and whether it was nature or her Haskett blood, she understood what it meant.

She entered the hall, tussling with her conscience, and heard a man in the parlor say, "McArthur's back."

She froze to listen.

"Have you spoken with him?" Simon asked, as if talking about the weather.

"No, but Delahaye sought me out."

The bearer of bad news was Captain Norton, Simon's second. Jancy hurried into the parlor to protest this insanity.

Simon saw her. "Don't distress yourself, my dear. I have no intention of making you a widow for, oh, sixty years or so."

"All very well if intention had anything to do with it."

Hal was there as well, jaw tight, but the three men presented a silently solid front against women and reason. Jancy thumped the tray down on a table so that it rattled and turned to run up to her room.

Chapter Nine

Simon watched, wanting to run after her. And say what?

"Hardly surprising if she's fearful," Norton muttered, looking uncomfortable with domestic complications.

"Not at all," Simon said. "I'm sorry she overheard and that you'll be troubled by this again. I do have passage booked, so McArthur will have to agree to a hasty meeting."

"Delahaye suggests tomorrow."

Simon hoped no trace of his shiver showed. "Very well. Everything the same as before?"

"Yes."

Simon escorted Norton out and then paused in the hall. His unsteadiness wasn't exactly fear, though he had no wish to go through the damned business again. It was because of Jane. She mustn't be left alone in the world.

But also he didn't want to die without making love to her. Their conversation earlier had turned swirling hungers into solid form. He was riven by the thunderbolt and would only be whole when completely joined with her.

But it wouldn't be fair. Not when she might be a widow tomorrow.

He returned to Hal. "Whatever happens, Jane must be taken care of."

"Of course."

"I've drawn up a marriage settlement, but it needs my father's consent. I'm sure he'll honor it."

"If he has any doubts, I'll explain more fully. And I'll make sure your papers get into the right hands. If you die in this cause, this McArthur will feel the wrath of all the Rogues."

"I'll cheer you on from heaven." From out of nowhere, however, a new loss struck. "Dammit, when I haven't seen Dare for years and thought him dead, why does it matter so much that I might not see him again?"

Hal didn't try to answer an unanswerable question.

"This is like the night before a battle, isn't it?" Simon said. "Tendency to become mawkish."

"We could always sing sentimental songs about girls we've left behind."

It was the right tone and Simon laughed. "I'll get those papers now in case sentiment makes me forget. Help yourself to tea."

Upstairs, Simon paused outside Jane's door, wondering if he should try to comfort her, but what comfort did he have to offer? He continued on to his own room and retrieved his papers. So much pain and trouble because of them. If he had his time over, would he take the same road?

Yes. Some roads, no matter how rocky, couldn't be ignored.

Jane didn't come down to dinner, so Simon and Hal ate braised venison alone, deliberately talking of the past. The atmosphere failed to be natural, however, so Simon excused Hal early by claiming to need a good night's rest.

Hal took the satchel of papers but said, "If you don't mind, I'll attend the duel."

"I'd be glad of it."

Simon went up to his room, trying to be sure there was nothing left undone.

His will was properly drawn up this time. He couldn't bear to rewrite the letter to his parents so simply added a postscript: *Jane is very dear to me, as I hope she will be to you.*

He decided to write to Dare, though he wasn't sure what to say.

> *Few things have made me happier than hearing that you'd survived, and now I'm distressed that I won't see you again, for if you ever read this I will be dead. My work here in Canada has been worthwhile, I believe, and I am one of the few who could do it, but my absence now feels neglectful. Proof, I suppose, that none of us are God.*
>
> *Hal gives me hope that you are recovering, but he left England shortly after your return. I'm sure it's not an easy road, but if it encourages you at all, live well for me. And if you have the opportunity, ensure that my dear Jane lives well, too.*

My dear Jane.

Too late, Simon was realizing that any secrets Jane held on to were irrelevant. Everything he knew about her was crystal clear and pure. And he loved her with that mad fire described by poets. Should he write to her? Tell her how he felt?

No. That could only be a burden from the grave.

He sealed and addressed the letter and then wandered his room, reviewing the previous duel, seeking insights that would help him survive.

He needed to stay as calm as possible. McArthur had fired when Jane startled them. Had that indicated nerves or quickness? Had the fact that he himself hadn't pulled the trigger meant that he was slower? Perhaps he'd been slowed by intensity, his flaw in times of crisis.

He remembered in the war once having a key target in his rifle sights and being overtaken by tremors of such urgent excitement that they had cost him the moment. He'd felt something similar hover at the last duel. Tomorrow, it could be fatal.

And he'd not made love to his wife. He looked toward Jane's room at the same moment someone knocked on the door, stealing his breath.

It could only be her.

He opened the door and found her there, covered chin to toe in her green wool robe, her nightgown visible only as a white ruff at neck and wrists, as it had been the night before the previous duel. This time, however, her hair was uncovered, hanging in a plait down to her waist.

Simplicity itself.

Ravishing.

"I'm sorry. I couldn't . . . I don't know. Couldn't sleep. Couldn't leave things in anger."

He stepped back, inviting her in.

Intensity was transmuting into a fierce desire for sex. As his heart thudded, he was aware as if at a distance of directing her to a chair and offering her brandy. She took a glass, but he could tell by the way she sipped that she was unused to it and unsure she liked it.

He drank a whole glass before sitting to sip another.

She was staring at him, puzzled, and he realized he'd not spoken a word.

It took effort to find a calm voice. "What exactly troubles you, Jane?"

The same desires that trouble me? Please, God.

"That you could die."

"There's nothing to be done about that."

She rolled the glass between her fingers. "Couldn't we leave now? No, I know we can't. But it seems so stupid. I want to change fate."

"That's your nature, isn't it? To grasp fate and twist it."

Her eyes widened. "No."

"Then why are you here?"

She looked down, took another sip of brandy, grimacing as it went down. "I couldn't sleep. It's too early anyway."

His mind seemed poised on a balance point, ready to

tip either way under the slightest pressure. Alas, he was still too much himself to force her or even to pressure her if she'd come here in innocence. She was young, he reminded himself, innocent, and had suffered many losses. Of course she was horrified at the thought of another death. He should soothe her and send her back to her bed.

Beneath these civil thoughts a drum of animal desire pounded.

"Loosen your hair for me."

The words came without control and she stared at him, lips parted. To refuse?

But she put aside her glass and pulled her plait forward. She tugged free the ribbon on the end and undid the heavy strands, all the time looking down. Then she ran her fingers through it, loosening and spreading it, and looked up.

He'd never watched a woman do that before and it was powerfully erotic. The still-rational part of his mind laughed.

At the moment, a woman cleaning her toenails would jolly you on, my boy.

"Thank you. It's beautiful."

"I wish I could do more."

Simon breathed. "Do you?"

He saw her understand. And falter. The balanced tipped. Clearly she'd not come here with that in mind.

"Would you like to play cards?" he asked.

"Cards?" She looked as if he'd suggested standing on their heads.

"It would pass the time. Piquet? Isaiah taught you, didn't he?"

"Yes, but I don't think I can concentrate."

Was he reading her wrongly? All he needed was a sign. A shift of her body would do. A lick of the lips. She simply looked at him, apparently at a loss.

"The attempt will do you good." Simon rose and

found his pack of cards, a paper, and a pencil. Then he poured himself more brandy. *Not too much,* he reminded himself. *You don't want to lose control, and you certainly don't want a hangover tomorrow.*

He was amused to realize that spending time with Jane was a treasure on its own. He'd not have believed that. Love clearly was magical. That didn't quench the fire in his blood, but he could contain that, if her company was all he could have.

He moved his chair closer to hers and put a table between them, and then took out the lower cards, shuffled, and cut for deal. "The results don't matter anyway. What's mine is yours and what's yours is mine."

"I suppose so."

It did help to concentrate on the game, though Jane didn't present much of a challenge. It left his mind too much space to roam.

To the pure, white frill of her nightgown cuff framing each hand. Capable hands with smooth, oval nails. His wedding ring, making permissible what his blood sang for.

The soft shade of her robe's sleeve, reminding him of the darker depths of an English woodland. And of something else. Ah. The uniform of the Green Tigers, the irregular force of Canadians that had been so effective during the war, in part because they were almost invisible in the woods.

He'd fought with them for a while. Cheated death so often. Had it finally hunted him down? Waited for the time when life was supremely precious?

The soft green scent of her tormented him, all springtime leaves and herbs. It made him think her a creature of the fields and forest though she was a town girl, born and raised. Here in York she'd always been nervous of anything beyond the right-angled streets.

Absurd to imagine her wandering barefoot through wildflowers, her hair flowing loose, but he did. And with that wild, wanton creature he could strip off loose garments to lie with her amid wildflowers, to nuzzle between warm breasts, to lick between moist thighs . . .

"Are you tired now?"

He realized he'd not played on her latest card. He gathered his wits and put down his hand. "No, but you're right. I can't concentrate."

"Or I'm not giving you much of a game." Her lips curved in a rueful smile. Her full, pink lips that sank deeply at the corners when she smiled, in the most delightful way. "Isaiah only played with me when he couldn't find anyone better."

"You don't have a competitive nature."

"I don't know about that." She began to neatly gather the cards. She stilled, and he wondered why. Then she looked up, the cards still in her hands. "Would you like me to tell your fortune?"

"You can?"

Pink touched her cheeks as if she were caught in a sin. Hardly surprising. He couldn't imagine Martha Otterburn approving of fortune-telling.

"A Gypsy taught me once," she said, looking down as she shuffled.

A Gypsy? Another of those strange Jane mysteries. But now he would relish the chance to explore them, along with the mysteries of her doubtless lovely body.

It would be the color of milk from head to toe, but with gold between her thighs and dainty, pink nipples on full, soft breasts.

"Are you drunk?" she asked, peering at him. Then she said, "Do you want me to go?"

"No." That was the last thing he wanted. "Go ahead. Tell my fortune, though I don't believe in such things."

She was still shuffling. "I'm not sure I have the gift, but I've seen some remarkable results."

He leaned back, drinking more brandy. Probably more than was wise, but it helped. "If it predicts imminent death, don't tell me."

"Very well."

"Oh, hell. Tell me the truth."

She looked up at him, and he thought an older intelligence showed there, something he couldn't place in the Trewitt-Otterburn milieu. Families were strange things, however. Characteristics could lurk, like the dark infernal streak that ran through the placid St. Brides.

"I designate you the king of clubs," she said. "Clubs are outgoing, determined, and focused on their goals. They seek action and results."

"What are you, then?"

"A diamond. Fair in color, hasty in nature."

"I will shower you with diamonds."

"Don't be foolish. I'm a creature of earth and air. You are fire and water."

"Don't I extinguish myself?"

She glanced up. "Or turn to steam. The question is how these things balance. In you, I think fire rules and water moderates."

"And in you?"

She looked down. "I don't know."

"Perhaps your elements war with each other. You're full of contradictions, wife of mine."

Contradictions he wasn't going to be allowed to explore tonight, so he settled to being grateful for what he had. His lovely wife, here with him.

Chapter Ten

*J*ancy concentrated on the cards, trying to still her rapid heartbeat. She'd been impelled here against all her better judgment, unable to bear parting from Simon with angry words or losing the hours that might be his last on this earth. She'd known the risks, and a part of her had welcomed them. She couldn't bear the thought that Simon would die tomorrow without them at least kissing.

Kissing properly.

As lovers do.

Mostly, however, or so she'd told herself, she'd come to offer him company in what had to be a difficult time. She thought she'd done that, but she was aware with a purely Haskett instinct of the passion building in the room. She could almost smell it.

He'd never force her, but she knew she had only to signal with a look, with a gesture, to unleash the power that built in her as strongly as in him.

It was like a crescendo of craving. A need that could overwhelm every scrap of will and strength. Like the need for water when parched with thirst. Or for heat when the body ached with cold. The relief would be as shiveringly wonderful and all the reasons against it were evaporating like water drops on a hot griddle, sizzling away to nothing.

But she didn't want to do wrong here. She didn't want to make everything worse.

Perhaps the cards would be her guide.

She handed the pack to him. "Shuffle, please."

Their hands brushed, and sizzle was exactly the word. Their eyes held for a moment, and Jancy felt the heat rise in her body and surely flame in her face. She broke contact of eyes and hands. He shuffled and then put the cards down.

Avoiding such contact again.

She fanned them on the table. "Take eight."

When he did so, she dealt them in a half circle and then did the same with the next eight and the next, adding them to the piles until all the cards were in the eight piles. She turned up the first layer, stating each one in the detached way she'd learned as a child.

"Don't think, dearie," Sadie Haskett had said. " 'Tis not for thinking, the cards. Just let 'em speak through you."

"The ace of spades brings you business affairs and problems, and the king of diamonds says that a man with fair hair stands your friend. The seven of hearts says that you are unsure of your path."

She glanced up. She couldn't imagine Simon unsure. He'd slid down to lounge in his chair and was sipping his brandy, eyes mostly shielded by his lids.

She looked back at the cards, reminding herself not to think but only to let them speak. "The ten of clubs predicts a journey. The jack of diamonds warns of a young or fair-haired man who could betray you, and the queen of diamonds of a light-haired woman who can't keep secrets."

"Not you, then," he said.

She looked up sharply. "Why do you say that?"

"Are you claiming not to have secrets?"

"Everyone has secrets."

"True enough. Keep yours if you can, but I warn you, Jane, I intend to uncover them all in time."

She looked desperately back at the cards and turned the next. "The eight of clubs. Good friends." She turned the next and faltered. Almost she lied, but that wouldn't change anything. "The nine of diamonds. Be careful around sharp objects and firearms."

Steadily he said, "Does that predict a deadly wound?"

"No." But she wished that card hadn't turned up in the first rank.

"Does any card predict death?"

"They are never so specific. The nine of spades is a card of ill omen, and the ten and eight imply bad news."

"You've turned up none of those, so all is well. Rejoice!"

True, it was a good spread, which eased her mind. Simon wouldn't die tomorrow. But she didn't like that nine of diamonds.

Her recent upbringing said that fortune-telling was superstitious nonsense, even devil worship, but in her youth she'd seen too many predictions come true not to have some belief. Over the years she'd secretly consulted the cards, and given their lack of specifics, they'd been right.

"Do you want to see your longer predictions?" she asked, knowing it was weak to want to know herself.

"Why not? The next layer?"

"No, the bottom layer." She flipped over the piles one after the other. When she completed the set without the nine of spades, she breathed a sigh of relief. Everyone dies in the end, but a premature death would show in the bottom layer.

"The queen of hearts. A loving, fair-haired woman." She couldn't help but look up and smile at that, and see his echoing smile.

"I'm coming to believe in these cards more and more. Go on."

"Eight of clubs. You are and always will be rich with good friends."

"Another hit."

"The ace of diamonds predicts ample money in your future. Good news for me. The ten of clubs tells of a pleasant journey, and the seven of clubs of success and renown. The nine of hearts . . ." She paused, unsure how to phrase the nuance she sensed. "A treasure you do not want, I think. The king of hearts says again that a blond man will be your true friend, and we end with the king of clubs, which is you, reinforcing your many virtues."

She swept the cards together and smiled at him. "It's an excellent spread, Simon. All will be well."

"Good." He rose. "So, if I'm going to live . . ."

She thought he was going to send her away, but instead he raised her to her feet and began to unbutton her robe.

Chapter Eleven

*S*he stared into his eyes, knowing that the slightest flicker of fear or rejection would end this now. Desire burned in her, however, flaring higher and higher with each touch of his hands, breathed on by the dark hunger in his gaze.

She shrugged off her robe herself as he worked on the buttons that fastened her nightgown up to the high neck. Then some Haskett part of her nature made her step back and lift it off herself to toss it aside. She shook her head so her hair spread around her.

He looked stunned. She shouldn't have done that—

But then he crushed her to him for the kiss she'd longed for, dreamed of, starved for over weeks, months, a year. She surrendered to instinct and him, swept into the flames by every touch of his urgent hands. Then she was in the tent of his bed, a place well suited for the hot mysteries of his mouth at her breasts and then nibbling up her inner thighs, creating aching, burning hunger deep inside.

She gasped his name, clutched his hair, cried out, and arched, but knew what she wanted, wanted above all. She fought free and began to tear at his breeches' buttons. He took over, stripping quickly.

He lowered himself over her, settling between her thighs, the most perfect weight imaginable. His cock—a good Haskett word, that—pressed at her . . . *cunny,* she thought. Another good Haskett word, banned in Abbey Street. She'd felt wanting there before and known what it was, but not like this. Not with yearning, and needing, and a kind of demanding pain.

Then he sucked her nipple and she gasped at a sensation she'd never even imagined. He laughed and at last began to push into her, even as he licked and sucked and teased. She laughed, too, as she raised her hips to him.

Then it hurt, making her catch her breath.

They both stilled, but urgently she said, "Go on, go on!" She'd die if he didn't complete her now.

He broke through her maidenhead.

"Give me a moment," she gasped. "It feels wonderful, but I need a moment."

As he stroked her and murmured things she could hardly hear never mind understand, she shifted to fit. He was breathing like a runner, but still talking. "Lovely Jane. Darling bride. Celtic sun. My love, my love . . ."

His love? Hunger roared to cover pain and she rose to join with him, ignoring soreness, rolling her head back to breathe, to gasp in air.

She should probably be speaking love to him, but she was dumb. Blind, dumb, and numb to everything but the wild pleasure of their sliding together, slapping together, humping and bumping accompanied by little screams she couldn't help.

And then locked in an astonishing explosion. It rippled on through her gasping breaths until he and she were tangled together, limp and sweaty.

Ah, Tillie, no wonder you liked the men so much.

His mouth was at her breast again, tonguing lazily. "My wife," he murmured, sounding perfectly content. Then again, "My love."

She cherished his hair and his shoulder, unable to be anything but content as well. This was what she'd promised not to do, but she'd brought him pleasure and forgetfulness, and it had been spectacularly wonderful.

And he loved her.

How could she give him up if he loved her?

He moved to look at her, stroking hair from her face. "Did it hurt a great deal?"

"No. Well, a little, but I didn't mind. And now it's over." She smiled into his smiling hazel eyes. "Like getting a tooth drawn."

Delight danced there. "Horrid woman. You must be sore, though."

She supposed she was. Every sensation down there seemed overwhelmed, but yes, there was soreness. Then she realized what he was asking. "We can do it again?"

"Undoubtedly, but don't let me be a brute."

Hunger was already growling. "You'd be a brute to deny a poor lady her pleasure."

He laughed. "You are a splendid woman, Jane St. Bride."

He moved over her and off the bed to walk in gorgeous nakedness to their glasses and the brandy decanter. She shifted to her side, head supported on her hand to watch.

"And how come there's not a pasty white spot on you, sir?"

He turned back, already half ready for her. "I swim naked—most men do—and the sun here is hot in summer. I'm sorry I don't have anything but brandy."

He strolled back to the bed to put the decanter and one glass on the floor and then lay on his back and gave her the other glass. "Dribble it on me and lick it off. You might like it better that way."

She bit her lip but did as he suggested. "Mmmm. I see what you mean." Licking his torso was certainly the most delicious taste ever, brandy or not. When some pooled in his navel, she sucked it out and he bucked beneath her. She glanced at him and then repeated the treat.

"Why not dribble some lower and suck there?" he said, watching her with heavy eyes.

She looked at his jutting cock and then dipped her finger in the brandy and stroked it onto him. Slowly she licked it off, feeling him move, quiver. Then she did the same with the bag below.

Baubles, the Haskett women called it. *Pretty baubles,* she thought, inhaling a musky scent.

His thighs tensed and she knew he was fighting himself. Wickedly she sucked there. Heard him curse, but not in a bad way. Smiling, she licked over his pretty baubles and up his hot, hard cock, right to the tip.

His lips were parted, his eyes looked drowned, but he said, "Where did this wild, wanton witch come from?"

Panic flashed through her, but before she could think what to say, he rolled her onto her back and slid into her again.

He didn't seem able to hold back this time but raced to his pleasure. It was like riding out a wild storm at sea. It left her dazed but wanting, but she didn't mind. To give him pleasure was enough.

But then he stirred and kissed her, his hand sliding between her thighs to exquisitely sensitive flesh. She flinched and his touch gentled.

"I only want to pleasure you, my love, my precious. Relax and tell me if it hurts."

She felt the war in her body between pleasure and pain, but she did tell him and he found the right sliding touch, circling and circling as his mouth made magic on her breasts and lips so that the dizzying fever built again.

It was like but unlike the ecstasy she'd felt before, because she was so aware of it this time, free to concentrate on the coiling tension and deep ache and the wild fever of longing that eventually climaxed in spasms of absolute pleasure that left her heart-poundingly blank.

Eventually she opened her eyes and looked at him. "Marriage is a very wonderful thing, isn't it?"

"In all honesty, my Celtic jewel, I have to point out that marriage isn't essential."

"That's very sinful, sir."

"I consider my sinful past training for you, Jane."

The name jolted her. "Would you call me Jancy, Simon, here in our bed?"

"Jancy?"

"My childhood name." It wasn't really a lie. "A fond name, you might say."

"Jancy, then. It suits this wild, wanton wonder better than plain Jane. I could call you that all the time."

"No." No one in her Carlisle life knew the name Jancy, but still, it felt dangerous. "It's . . . it's a baby name. Not suited for a wife."

"That's foolish, but I like the idea of a private name. I'm sorry I don't have one to offer you."

"No one called you Sim?"

"That's my father. First sons are always called Simon in our family, and we alternate between Simon and Sim." As they cuddled close he said, "My oldest brother's Rupert, after my mother's father, and the youngster's Benjamin. Lord, he's fifteen now. Almost a man. I wonder if he still lets people call him Benji."

She understood that he needed to talk about his family now.

"Two brothers and three sisters, I think?"

"Four. Ella's married with a child of her own. Then there's Mara, Jenny, and Lucy. She was an infant when I left. I'll be a stranger to her."

"But she'll soon learn she has an excellent brother."

He rubbed his head against hers. "I hope so."

"Are they all at home, other than Ella?"

"I assume Benji's at school, but yes. Even Rupert and his wife. He's Father's estate steward, on the assumption, I think, that I will never take on that job."

"Do you mind?"

"Lord, no. It's most unnatural of me, but agriculture bores me."

"What about when you inherit?"

"Perhaps I'll mellow with age, but I hope Rupert's there to carry on."

"What do you plan to do, then? Travel again?"

Despite love, this distressed her. She'd sealed her fate here and joined with him for life, but she really didn't want to wander the world's wildernesses.

"I've burned that out of my system, but I need battles to fight. I'm thinking of standing for Parliament."

She rolled onto his chest, looking up at him by the light of the guttering candles. "Shaping the laws of the land. That's wonderful."

He drew her closer for a kiss. "With you by my side, Jancy St. Bride."

They made love again and talked more of his dreams until sleep claimed them. Claimed them too well. They were woken by Sal knocking at the door, saying, "Captain Norton's here to see you, sir, right urgent, and it barely seven!"

Simon cursed and rushed out of bed and into his clothes, apologizing to Jancy and the universe. She sat there, clutching the covers to her, cold as much with shock as because the fire had died long ago. She managed to say, "Are you late?" but it came out from a strangled throat.

"Not yet." He hastily brushed his hair and then turned an anguished look on her. He pulled her to him for a ferocious kiss. "I fully intend to be back here for breakfast, but if I'm not, you're to go to Brideswell—Hal will take you—and let my family take care of you. Promise me that."

"I promise. God go with you, Simon!"

"If I were God I'd have no part in this sort of thing, but yes. Pray."

Then he was gone. He couldn't die. He couldn't possibly die!

And yet he could.

Jancy couldn't bear to wait here for news. She scrambled out of bed, pulled on her robe, and rushed to her room to drag on clothing. She left the house to run toward Elmsley's Farm as she had once before.

As before, the morning was chilly and overcast but

this time with no threat of rain that might prevent the duel. As she reached the edge of town, the sun broke through to illuminate the distant group of men. It didn't look as if the duel had started yet.

She couldn't race there directly as she had before but had to circle to where some trees provided concealment. As she did so, two of the men took positions, facing each other.

Simon, Simon!

She came to rest behind a tree, panting. Simon looked so calm and steady. McArthur, may he rot, looked less so, but she could tell how he burned to kill. She read it on his face and had to clench her hands over her bitten lips to stop herself from screaming at them to stop.

The cards had promised Simon would be safe.

But there was that nine of diamonds.

She heard the count, saw the guns raised and aimed, the pale handkerchief fluttering in Captain Norton's hand.

McArthur's pistol flamed before it dropped.

Simon staggered.

Jancy began to race to him, but he steadied, even though hunched and with his left hand to his side.

She froze as he slowly straightened and raised his pistol.

McArthur backed, raising his hands as if to ward off a shot. "No, no. It was an accident. . . ."

Jancy expected someone to stop Simon, but all the men stood still. Norton finally let the handkerchief waver to the ground.

Simon fired.

Lancelot McArthur clutched his chest, letting out a cry that sounded as much shocked as agonized. Then he crumpled into an ungainly, twitching heap.

The pistol fell from Simon's hand, and he sank to his knees and then to the ground. Jancy ran to fling herself down beside him. He still breathed but in a way that spoke of agony. Blood oozed from his side.

She remembered the talk about Isaiah's wound. How no one survived a belly wound. This was surely higher. To the side.

Don't be dying, my love. Don't be dead.

Chapter Twelve

She realized she was saying it. "Simon, don't you dare die. Don't you *dare*!"

His lids fluttered open, his lips moved.

"You shouldn't be here," Hal snapped, and it was as if he spoke for his friend.

She replied to Simon. "I had to."

Then another man was there, pushing her aside and unbuttoning Simon's coat. "Someone make sure McArthur's dead, though he looks it."

The doctor probed. Simon choked back a cry.

Jancy put out a hand to stop the man. Hal grabbed it and wrenched her to her feet. She turned away from the horrible sight.

"McArthur fired first," she cried. "Before the sign. I saw it!"

"We all did," Hal said. "Don't worry. Simon was entitled to his shot."

It was what Jancy wanted to hear, but it still made her shiver to think of Simon shooting the man in cold blood.

The two seconds were hunched over McArthur, but Norton came over to them. "Heart. Gone in moments. Damn good aim, especially under the circumstances. I would never have believed he'd stoop to murder."

"Simon's not *dead*!" Jancy snapped and then whirled back to make sure.

The doctor had Simon's bloody shirt cut away, but

Jancy couldn't see the wound for his gory fingers. So much blood. Simon's teeth and hands were clenched and he was white. But not dead and surely the wound was too low for the heart. It seemed to be in his side near the bottom of his ribs.

She knelt again and asked, "Can he live?"

"Possibly." The doctor grabbed a pad of cloth out of his bag and pressed it on the long, bleeding wound. Though he seemed to do it gently, Simon choked back a cry.

"Ribs. Ball's broken at least one, but at least that means it didn't reach a vital organ."

Thank you, God.

"Better pray it hasn't splintered."

"Why?"

The doctor threw her a look that said, *Idiot.* "Because a splintered rib can't knit, and the bits will puncture a lung and kill him eventually."

Jancy grasped one of Simon's clenched fists. He relaxed his hand enough to take hers and even found a faint smile for her.

"This won't kill me, love. Remember the cards."

She leaned to press a kiss on his lips.

The doctor muttered something and she turned to see that he'd raised the pad and was grimacing at the wound. It looked shallow, and apparently the ribs had stopped the pistol ball. Her frantic panic began to subside.

He shoved a thick piece of leather between Simon's teeth and then probed.

Simon choked deep in his throat and Jancy did the same. His hand was crushing her fingers.

"Idiot woman," the doctor growled. "Beaumont, give him something useful to grip. I need to get the ball."

Simon understood. He let Jancy go and Hal knelt to put his one hand in his friend's. "You didn't do her any damage, and I doubt you can even bruise me."

Simon might have weakly laughed, but then he was in agony again as the doctor dug deeper. The wound must be painful enough, but beneath lay those broken ribs.

"Can't you give him opium?" Jancy demanded.

"For this?" Playter scoffed, taking out a long metal implement and probing with that. Simon fainted.

"Oh, thank you, God," Jancy said.

The doctor dug deeper, twisted, and with a smile of satisfaction produced a misshapen piece of lead. He inspected it carefully and then nodded. He wrapped it in a bit of cloth and then passed it to Jancy. "Knowing these young fools, he'll treasure it as a souvenir."

Jancy didn't want the thing, but she hoped he was right. That would mean that Simon would be alive to care. She disliked the brusque military surgeon, but his casual manner soothed her. He must have seen many wounds and he showed no concern.

He took out another pad of cloth and poured what smelled like brandy over it and then pressed it to the newly bleeding wound. Simon stirred and groaned, but seemed only half-conscious.

The doctor tied a rough bandage around Simon's chest and then rose. "Now to get him inside where I can sort him out properly. But I don't want those ribs shifting. Need a litter. Delahaye, can I bother you to ride to the garrison for one? The rigid sort. My orderly will know."

The shaken officer hurried away.

The doctor looked at Jancy. "Ma'am, go home and prepare a sickroom."

Jancy hesitated, knowing he only wanted to get rid of her, but Hal pulled her to her feet. "Come on. I'll escort you."

She would have stayed if she could be of any use, but the sooner Simon was in a warm bed the better. They walked briskly into the town, where people were beginning to emerge to a new day. Jancy saw strange looks, which wasn't surprising. Her hair was loose, and her clothes were probably muddy.

Hal would have come in the house with her, but she said, "Go back, please. I can deal with everything here." She grabbed his arm. "Keep him alive!"

He freed himself and patted her. "Don't worry. It's not so bad a wound."

Jancy watched him stride away, wishing she could wipe away all fear.

It wasn't a fatal wound, but even though the ball was out, even if the rib was cleanly broken and didn't puncture Simon's lung, the wound could become infected. That was doubtless why Hal's arm had been cut off. But one couldn't amputate ribs.

Stop panicking and do something useful, she told herself and hurried to prepare for Simon's arrival home. At least McArthur was dead. Dead and gone to hell, where he belonged.

He'd need warmth. She went to the log pile and filled a sling and then carried it upstairs. At the head of the stairs, she froze.

A figure was coming out of Simon's room.

For a dreadful moment she thought it was Simon, that it must be his ghost, that he was dead. But then she realized the man was no one she knew.

"Who are you?" she demanded. "What are you doing?"

The roughly dressed man in the wide-brimmed hat whirled to her in alarm. Even as she inhaled to scream, he hurtled toward her. By some instinct, she stepped aside instead of trying to stop him, and he stumbled down the stairs and out of the house.

For long seconds she leaned against the wall, clutching her sling of wood, staring after the intruder. Then everything fell into place. He'd been after Simon's papers!

She hurried to the room. It was in disorder, but only as they'd left it. The bed was rumpled, and some of Simon's clothes from last night's hasty undressing were still strewn around. The scent of their lovemaking wove in the air, making her face heat with embarrassment and yearning.

She pulled herself together and looked around again, but it was no good. She had no idea where Simon kept his papers and wouldn't know if they were missing. Had the intruder been carrying anything? No, and surely all Simon's work wouldn't fit in a pocket.

But it was sinking in that Lancelot McArthur had not only set out to murder Simon, he'd arranged to steal the papers, too. Presumably he'd expected her to be asleep in her own bed. She hoped the devil was toasting him, but now she had work to do. She put down her logs and dragged the coverings off the bed but then realized that the alcove it sat in was impossible for the care of an invalid.

Her room?

Too small.

Isaiah's. Plenty of space there, and access to the bed all around. She picked up the sling and then realized her wits were scrambled. She didn't have to do everything herself.

She dropped the wood and ran downstairs and out to the kitchen. Mrs. Gunn was tending the stove. Sal and Izzy looked up fearfully.

"Yes, Simon met McArthur again, and he's wounded. Simon is. McArthur fired ahead of time. The foul scum cheated! But he's dead. McArthur is, I mean."

She was gasping and babbling like an idiot, and all three were staring at her. She tried to do better. "They're bringing him back here. Soon. The fire must be made in Mr. Trewitt's room. I took up wood. What else do we need?"

She said that looking at Mrs. Gunn, for she felt suddenly empty-headed and lost.

"Warming pans. Cloth for bandages. Hot water." Mrs. Gunn was already turning to the big fireplace, but it was to take a teapot off a trivet and pour dark tea into a cup. She added milk and two lumps of sugar and put it in Jancy's hands.

"Sit down and drink that, dearie. Mr. Simon'll be fine, I'm sure. Off you go, Sal, and build the fire. Izzy, find sheets and help make the bed. Then come back here."

Jancy was thankful to sit and drink the tea, but she couldn't stop babbling—about McArthur cheating and Simon's pain. About ribs and infection. She ran out of words at last and realized Simon could already be in the house. She leaped up and fled back through the walkway.

But the house was silent.

Silent as death.

Then low voices broke the eeriness as the maids came downstairs.

Jancy gathered herself and went up to check everything was in readiness. Isaiah's room was already warming from the new fire, and the bed was freshly made. As she fussed with the pillows, Izzy returned with a big jug of hot water that she put on the hearth.

Fire and water. Simon's elements.

Turning to steam. Insubstantial steam.

Where *were* they? Had something gone wrong?

She wanted to run out to meet them, but that horrible doctor would only make some other scathing comment. She knew Simon had a high opinion of the army surgeon, but if things went badly, she'd call in Dr. Baldwin.

Went badly. Tears spilled and she pressed her hand over her mouth. So little time since she'd held Simon, whole and healthy, in her arms, and now he could die. People died of cuts and broken bones. Of bad teeth, even.

The cards. She seized on to the message of the cards. They'd predicted this wound, but they hadn't predicted death. They *hadn't*.

She repeated this to herself as she found one of the worn sheets set aside for charity. She took it to the window in her room and began to rip it up for bandages, imagining she was ripping the skin off Lancelot McArthur.

"You're in hell now, where you belong," she muttered. "I hope the devil is ripping you apart just like this. And this. And this."

The front door.

She dropped the sheet and ran out. By the time she reached the head of the stairs, the men were in the hall. Simon was flat on a board carried by four uniformed soldiers. Hal was there, and the doctor. And someone else in uniform. Oh, Simon's second. Captain Norton. Jancy took in all this as she skimmed downstairs to Simon's side. His eyes were shut and he was gray. . . .

"He's fine," Hal said. "But movement is painful."

She breathed again. "I've prepared Uncle Isaiah's room. Upstairs," she added to the men carrying him.

"Not yet," barked Playter. "No point dragging him about until I've cleaned the wound and strapped him up. Dining room?"

So again the dining table was put to service. Jancy followed, but Playter turned on her. "Out! Go and make tea or something. You'll be no use here."

Jancy looked to Hal for help, but grim-faced, he pushed her through the door and shut it in her face. She was standing there helplessly when Mrs. Gunn came into the hall carrying a tray.

"You come into the parlor with me, love. We'll have a nice cup of tea and a bit of som'at to eat as we wait."

Jancy wanted to stand vigil, but she obeyed like a sleepwalker. When Mrs. Gunn closed the door behind them, she realized that the parlor lay at the back of the house, as far as possible from the dining room. If Simon screamed, she might not hear.

As far as Jancy knew, Mrs. Gunn had never taken tea in the house, but she had no objection. She had no will or strength at all and, shivering, allowed herself to be put in a chair and even to have Isaiah's old lap rug tucked around her.

"There, there, dearie, it'll be all right."

More strong, sweet tea helped, but Jancy couldn't touch food.

"I wish I knew what was happening."

"Now, now, if anything had gone amiss, they'd not still be at it, would they?"

Jancy stared in the direction of the dining room. "But I wish I knew!"

"These things can't be hurried," Mrs. Gunn said, her thin, gnarled hands unusually idle in her aproned lap. "He's a healthy young man, and that's what matters. Not but what dueling ain't a nasty business. Gunn, now, he loved a fistfight, but it was me as had to patch him up, and him cursing me for hurting him as he hadn't cursed the ones whose knuckles had done the damage. I cursed him right back, I can tell you. . . ."

The old woman rambled on and it flowed over Jancy like balm so that when the door opened and Hal came in, she neither leaped at him nor fainted.

"It went well. They're ready to move him to the bed."

Jancy's heart was racing again, and she didn't know why. Everything was all right now. Or at least, good enough. "I'll show you."

She guided the men with the litter up the stairs and into the big room. Simon's eyes were closed but she didn't think he was unconscious or asleep. She suspected that he was simply enduring.

"Bolsters," the doctor demanded. "He'll be most comfortable sitting up, but the support must be firm."

Jancy hastened to get the hard bolsters from her bed and Simon's. Dr. Playter arranged them and then marshaled the transfer to the bed like a captain commanding the tricky docking of a ship. Simon's clothes had been removed other than his drawers—which were horribly bloodstained at one side. His chest was half covered with bandages. For a shallow wound around the lower ribs?

Perhaps her puzzlement was obvious, for Hal said, "To discourage movement while his rib knits."

"But won't the dressing have to be changed?"

"Do and undo," said the doctor. "Which is why they're knotted at the left side. The ribs didn't shatter, so they should knit. I believe I removed all the bits of cloth. That's what kills most men, ma'am—bits of cloth driven into the wound carrying contagion. And for what?" He shook his head like an angry bull. "A fine, healthy young man one moment and now look at him."

He glared at someone behind her, and Jancy turned to see Captain Norton was still present, looking almost as haggard as Simon.

"I'm sure there was nothing you could have done, sir," she said and then turned back to Playter. "So with proper care he'll live?"

"I'm a doctor, ma'am, not a fortune-teller! It's in God's hands. Do you have nursing experience?"

"Only with sickness, not with wounds."

"He'll *be* sick. He'll run a fever as his body burns contagion. His greatest peril right now is movement. Don't let him move!"

Perhaps she flinched at his bark, or the tears in her throat showed in her eyes, for he pulled a face and moderated his tone.

"I'll return this evening to change the dressing and inspect the wound. Don't fiddle with it. The body heals itself. He must have a lowering diet. Bland food. No meat or alcohol. Plenty of fluids. Barley water. Clear broth. Weak tea. Do you have an invalid cup?"

"Yes, I think so."

"Good. He won't want to even flex for a while."

He began to march out, but Jancy said, "Why is his arm bandaged? Did you bleed him?"

"Not yet. The ball creased it en route. He probably moved it to block when he saw McArthur fire. Might have saved his life, for it took some of the ball's power. It's a flesh wound. His ribs are the danger. Keep him still."

He left and Jancy turned to gently stroke damp, dark hair off Simon's forehead. How easily his flesh could be cold rather than warm—perhaps but for a twitch of the arm.

He opened his eyes, and despite a crease of pain in his brows, she saw something that might be a smile. He moved—and gasped.

She pressed back on his shoulder. "Don't do that!"

"Trust me, I won't. Gads, but it hurts." His eyes wandered the room. "Ever broken ribs, Norton?"

The captain came over to the bed. "No."

"Don't. The wound's nothing, but the ribs . . ."

"That's why you have to stay still," Jancy said. "Very still."

He frowned. "We're leaving in four days."

"We'll leave when you're fit to."

"We'll miss the *Eweretta*."

She stroked his shoulder. "There'll be other ships."

"Not once the river freezes. Jancy, this is serious. Half our belongings are already in Montreal."

Chapter Thirteen

*H*e'd called her Jancy. Part of her flinched, expecting some dire revelation, but most of her remembered their night. Which had made him unalterably hers. Hers to take care of.

"If our possessions reach England before we do," she said soothingly, "so be it. Put your mind to healing, love." She gently kissed him.

He looked at her with a lazy smile that was unlike him—except that she remembered it from the night.

"Stop smiling at me like that."

His smile deepened. "Why?"

"It makes me blush."

"You're delightful when you blush. Even your freckles blush."

She put a hand over her face. "Stop it!"

"Lie beside me?"

Jancy looked around, but they were alone. The other men had tactfully left.

"Still shy?" he teased.

"Still wicked?"

"When I have to be."

"Oh, but you're terrible." And the most wonderful man in the world.

She took off her shoes and climbed carefully up on his left side. He'd been put in the middle of the bed, so there wasn't much space, and his mound of bolsters made things difficult. She hooked one leg over his and tucked her head on his bare shoulder, one arm carefully across his bandaged chest, her hand feeling the steady strong beat of his heart.

"Thank heaven you're alive, Simon. I was so frightened."

"Playter's the best gunshot man in Upper Canada."

"I don't like him. But if he keeps you well, I'll kiss his feet."

"Not necessary. Now mine . . ."

His hand moved against her hip, sending tremors through her.

Her conscience still nibbled at her for keeping her secrets, but with ever weakening teeth. Simon was hers and she would not lose him, to death or to the law.

She'd never before realized the roaring power of love. To separate herself from him now would feel like cutting off her own arm.

His fingers still played lightly against her. "I think you're my guardian angel."

"I've brought you nothing but trouble."

"Silly. This is none of your doing. I was a fool not to realize that McArthur always planned to fire early. Your interrupting us that first time probably saved my life. Today, something drew my eye from the handkerchief to you. That could have been fatal, but I must have seen him begin to fire so I twitched and took some of the ball with my arm. Guardian angel."

She snuggled back against him. "May I ever be so, then. But I wish I were a fine lady, for your sake."

"Jane, if you don't stop this I shall rise from my bed to shake you, and thus, according to Playter, die. I admit, if I took home a coarse criminal type, my family would find that difficult. But a well-raised lady of courage, intelligence, and generosity? They will thank heaven."

A coarse, criminal type . . .

"In fact," he said, relaxing, "you're very like my mother. She's a sensible, practical woman who does what needs to be done and gives the men a piece of her mind if she thinks they need it. She helps in the kitchens sometimes and makes creams and polishes in her stillroom. She pins up her skirts and tackles the spring-cleaning with the servants."

She shifted to read his face. "Truly? I thought Brideswell was very grand."

"A chilly, pillared mansion? Devil a bit. It's a rambling country home run in a country manner, and my family are very down-to-earth people."

"But your father's in line to be an earl."

"Put that out of your mind as firmly as he does."

She obeyed but said, "You'll have to prepare me, Simon. I don't want to shame you."

"You won't."

"I don't think you realize how different my life has always been."

"Then tell me."

Jancy winced. She'd walked straight into that pit. But now they were irretrievably married she had to make it work. She had to fit into his world, which meant impressing on him how different it was from hers.

Remembering to speak as Jane, she said, "When my father ran his school, we lived in a large house, but most of it was used for the school. After his death, mother and I moved to Abbey Street. Our house there was a modest one. Smaller even than this. Two bedrooms and a boxroom upstairs. A parlor, dining room, and kitchen down. And of course the front parlor was eventually given over to the shop.

"I can't remember if my parents mixed with Carlisle society before my father died, but Martha certainly didn't afterward, though she put great store on our well-born Scottish connections. That meant we didn't mix with many people at all. She was reserved, with little interest in what she called 'gadding about.' Then, of course, she became a shopkeeper."

She waited for his judgment of this.

"Will I have to teach you how to dance?" he asked.

"Yes."

"How delightful."

He still wasn't taking it seriously. "And how to curtsy to lords and ladies. How to behave at a grand meal, and even how to treat servants. We had one maid of all work, and here hasn't been so different. Don't try to tell me your mother doesn't have a host of servants."

"I suppose she does, yes. Very well. No need to bludgeon me any more. We have a couple of months before we reach England. Time enough for lessons. And when we arrive we'll visit Dare before going on to Brideswell. That will be a useful trial."

She considered this. "Isn't he at his family home?"

"As far as we know."

"And isn't his father a duke?"

"Yes."

She rolled off the bed to glare at him. "Simon!"

He simply smiled. "Trust me, Jancy. You are my wife. Your happiness and comfort are my duty and my pleasure."

Even though she'd described her Carlisle life, he clearly still didn't grasp the gulf between them. And lurking beneath everything like a threatening bog lay her true origins.

A duke meeting a Haskett? There was probably a law against it.

"At least McArthur's dead and gone," she said but then remembered the intruder. Strange how dramatic events could push things from the mind. She told him what had happened.

"He not only went out to kill you, he sent a thief to get your papers. And he might have done! I'm sorry, Simon. The man wasn't carrying anything, but he might have found them. I should have stopped him—"

He moved. Then cursed. "Hush. No, Jancy. He didn't."

"How can you be sure?"

"Because Hal has them."

She frowned at him. "In the hotel? Are they safe there?"

"McArthur's dead," he reminded her.

"But he never acted alone, did he? And didn't you say others are mentioned in them?"

"My remarkable Jancy. Names are coded, but some people could be worried, yes. Treadwell and Oglethorpe aren't to let them out of their sight, but for safety's sake, perhaps they and Hal move in here. In any case, you'll need help in caring for me."

Jancy almost protested, but then she realized Simon would probably rather have a manservant deal with his intimate care.

"Where could they sleep? We have only three bedrooms."

"Hal can use my room. Isn't there a closet off this one with a cot for a servant? Hal's men will be able to make do there."

Jancy opened the door and considered the small room. It was lit by only a tiny window, but there was one narrow bed and room for a mattress on the floor.

"Very well. I'll see to it."

"And food?" he asked, like a child asking for a treat. "I'm recovered enough to be famished."

"You're supposed to eat a lowering diet."

"Do you want me lowered? A rare steak, now . . ."

"Definitely not."

"Tyrant."

"If I have to be."

But their eyes smiled.

"Not gruel, which rhymes with cruel," he pleaded. "I'm hollow, love."

She shook her head at him but was delighted at his rapid recovery. She went toward the door but then she turned back. "I think Captain Norton feels guilty. Or responsible in some way."

"Nothing he could have done, but if he's still here, send him in. He can share breakfast."

She found Norton pacing the corridor and then told Hal about the plan for him and his men to move in. He agreed and left. Jancy stood and breathed.

Simon would survive, and she would become the wife he needed. Though Martha had chosen to live quietly, she'd raised her girls to be worthy of her husband's family, determined that they would both be considered ladies.

It had probably always been a faint hope, for Archibald Otterburn's family had cut him off for marrying a seamstress. That was how the world worked.

Jancy knew she was quick-witted and a good mimic, however. She'd soon learned Abbey Street ways when she'd been taken there. She could learn Brideswell ways, too, and yes, even how to behave in a duke's house.

She turned her mind to the moment. Simon's room needed readying for Hal. The servants would need bedding and a spare mattress from somewhere. Simon was hungry.

He'd do best with food he could eat out of his hands. He'd need company, too. She and Hal would eat with him at a small table in Isaiah's room.

She went to the kitchen and realized the servants hadn't received a full report. "All's well. Mr. St. Bride only needs to rest and let his ribs knit." To Mrs. Gunn she said, "The doctor prescribes a lowering diet, but he'd do best with food he can eat with one hand and without flexing."

"Not porridge and stewed apples, then," the old woman said with a grin. "A sandwich won't hurt him, and I can bake pies."

"What about an invalid cup? I thought I'd seen one."

The cup with the long spout was soon found and breakfast under way. As the servants were all busy, Jancy went to strip the sheets off Simon's bed herself.

When she realized the state of the room, she was profoundly glad. What they'd done here hadn't been
wicked, but it felt like it.

Wickedly wonderful. She scooped up a fallen brandy
glass from the floor, inhaling the medley of scents that
told the story. The cards were still spread on the table.
She put them in their box and then noticed the letters
on the desk.

My will. To my parents. To Lord Darius Debenham.

She wanted to read them simply because they were
part of Simon, but she put them in a drawer with the
cards, tidied the scattered clothing, and dragged off the
stained, blood-streaked sheets.

Then she stood there, hugging them for comfort, inhaling the scent of Simon and lust. She longed to sleep
here, to wrap herself in everything that was him, but she
could hardly suggest Hal sleep in her room.

She pressed the sheet to her eyes to stem tears. For
not being able to sleep here. For fears of punctured
lungs and infected wounds. For not being able to tell
Simon the truth. For fear of the future, of having the
golden promise snatched away . . .

She pulled herself together, bundled up the sheets,
and took them down to the laundry bin by the kitchen
door.

She stole a moment in the garden, pinching off a sprig
of mint and smelling it as she studied the clapboard
houses of their neighbors, each hardly visible because of
the large lots and the trees. She was very glad Hal and
his men were moving in, for a sense of danger still prickled her neck.

York was so neatly laid out, so full of ladies, gentlemen, and officers, that it felt civilized, but in truth it was
as wild and dangerous as the forest around it. They
would leave as soon as Simon was able. Even if they
missed the last oceangoing vessel, they'd make it to
Montreal or even Quebec. They'd be away from here.

Then Sal and Izzy came out of the kitchen bearing

trays. Jancy hurried to open the back door for them and followed them in. When they'd delivered the food, she instructed Izzy to make up the bed in Simon's room. She turned to see Hal coming up the stairs with his men and explained the arrangements. The house was positively crowded and she loved it. Now Simon and his work were safe.

When she followed Hal into the bedroom, however, she heard him say, "The inquest is set for tomorrow."

Chapter Fourteen

"*I*nquest?" she gasped.

Simon was eating a sandwich left-handed. "There has to be one, my love, if someone dies like that. I doubt it'll go to trial, not least because Gore wants as little attention paid to this whole matter as possible."

"But you could be tried for *murder?*"

"Highly unlikely," Hal said. "All correct forms were followed. Right, Norton?"

"Absolutely." He sounded a little too hearty, but then he added to Jancy, "If they weren't, ma'am, the seconds would be liable for prosecution, too."

"Will Simon have to testify? He can't be moved."

"If so, they'll come here," Hal said. "But I doubt it will be necessary. His being wounded will work in his favor, but it's the fact that McArthur fired before the signal was given that will clinch it."

Norton left to take up his military duties. Jancy put on a cheerful face and busied herself with housekeeping, but the thought of the inquest beat in her head like a drum. She couldn't blank out the image of Simon struggling to stay on his feet and deliberately shooting to kill. He had apparently been entitled to do that, but what if a court saw it differently? He might *hang*.

The men didn't seem much concerned, so her terror must rise out of Haskett experiences. Hasketts had no faith in justice and the law.

When she returned to Simon, he suggested whist so she sat to play, with Treadwell making the fourth. Hal produced a frame in which he slotted his cards.

Later Hal and his servants left them alone and she read to Simon. Playter returned and reported that all was well, though he didn't unbandage the wound. "Don't meddle with nature" seemed to be his law.

As darkness fell she hoped Simon would fall asleep, for he looked exhausted, but when he did he moved and woke from pain. She read more to him, trying to soothe him, but in the end she had to leave him to Oglethorpe before she fell asleep where she was.

When she returned the next morning, Simon looked haggard, and she heard that he'd tried to get up to use a chamber pot instead of the invalid receptacle. She scolded him, but how was he to get well like this? When she heard the doctor downstairs, she intercepted. "Can't he be given something for the pain? He couldn't sleep."

Playter dumped his gloves, hat, and cloak on a chair. "Does it hurt him to move?"

"Terribly."

"Then he won't, will he?"

She followed him upstairs feeling a fool but still disliking the doctor intensely.

This time Playter unbandaged Simon's chest, raised the lint pad, and inspected the brown and yellow stains on it. Then he sniffed at it. All Jancy could smell was the brandy.

"Is it all right?" she asked. The swollen, crusting flesh looked horrible.

"Thus far."

"Why brandy?"

He scowled at her, so she scowled back. "I need to know how to care for him, Doctor."

He grunted but said, "A spiritous compress assists in the healing of gunshot wounds. You'll see that the bleeding has stopped, and there is excellent fungus."

"What?" Jancy was horrified.

"The swelling flesh, Mrs. St. Bride. It's part of the healing process. The crusting"—he indicated it with his finger—"we call eschar. This only occurs with heated wounds such as burns or gunshot. It is healthful in the beginning, but care must be taken that it does not seal up the wound, for the wound must drain. Trapped fluids poison the body."

"I am here, you know," Simon said.

"And will stay still and let others take care of you." Playter took a new pad of lint out of his bag. "Do you have brandy, ma'am? Don't see why I should use my own."

Jancy brought it. He soaked the pad in it and covered the wound.

"I'd rather that brandy was inside me," Simon said, tension showing that even these gentle ministrations were painful.

"And inflame your blood?" Playter tightened the chest bandages. Simon hissed.

"They must be tight to keep your ribs in place, sir," Playter said, not, in Jancy's opinion, without some relish.

"How soon before I can travel?"

"Perhaps two weeks, and that assumes you continue to heal appropriately."

"What happens if I travel in two days?"

"You'll probably kill yourself."

Simon's lips tightened.

"If it's movement that's the problem," Jancy said, "couldn't he travel on a stretcher, as he came here?"

Simon's objection to the very idea clashed with Playter's response. "Why take the risk?"

"Because we want to sail to England before the river freezes," she said. "Travel by boat down to Montreal wouldn't be too strenuous, would it?"

"Young lady, Lake Ontario can storm like the Atlantic, and the Saint Lawrence is broken by rapids. He stays here until I say it's safe, or I wash my hands of him."

She opened her mouth to argue, but Simon said, "Jancy."

She obeyed the silent request, but a new fear had occurred to her. How did they know Playter was telling the truth? If there were people who wanted to stop Simon taking his papers to London, the longer he was kept here, the better for them. She would send for Dr. Baldwin.

Playter took out new instruments.

"What are you doing?" She couldn't keep suspicion out of her voice.

"The wound has ceased to bleed, so it is necessary to release some blood to avoid mortification. If you're likely to faint, go away."

Though Jancy hated to see Simon hurt even in such a minor way, she certainly would not faint and she wanted to be sure Playter did nothing suspicious. She'd often attended the doctor bleeding and cupping Aunt Martha, so she knew how it was done. All seemed to go as usual, however.

When Simon's left arm was bandaged, he said, "I must look a sorry specimen."

"At least your arms match," she teased, but added to the doctor, "Shouldn't you look at his arm wound?"

"A mere crease, ma'am. A child could attend to it." But he unwrapped the bandage. "There, see. Good eschar, and when it sloughs, there'll be a healthy discharge. All's well."

"So I should dress it? With brandy?"

"Leave it be, woman! I tell you, the body heals itself."

When Hal took the doctor downstairs, Simon said, "Jancy, if I can't leave before the river freezes, you must."

"No."

"There might be danger. Remember that intruder."

"All the more reason for me to stay."

"Don't I have some authority as your husband?"

"If you do, you've no way to assert it."

"Oglethorpe."

"Yes, sir?"

"Would you beat my wife for me?"

"No, sir."

"Traitor."

Jancy laughed and kissed Simon's cheek. "Be good. The *Eweretta* won't be the last ship to leave. You said yourself that it always makes sure to sail from Montreal before there's any danger of being blocked. As soon as it's safe, we'll leave York, but your health is more important than anything."

Thought of the inquest hung silent in the room. Jancy wished she'd asked Playter what he would tell the jury. Surely he'd have to tell the truth, but now that suspicion had germinated, she couldn't get rid of it. What if he lied? What if they all lied? If there was a conspiracy to have Simon hang?

Hal. Hal was her only hope.

When he left to give his evidence, she flung herself into cleaning. She should probably sit with Simon, who could be as fearful beneath his calm, but instead she wore herself out scrubbing the parlor. She even hung the parlor carpet in the yard and beat the dust out of it.

"Is it dead yet?"

She whirled to see Hal. "What happened?"

"All's well." He took the wicker carpet beater from her and tossed it on the ground. "Come on."

She dusted off her hands. "You must think me silly."

"No. I had concerns." He put his hand on her back to steer her toward the house. "The judge frowned on Simon taking his shot, but Norton, Delahaye, and I all agreed that McArthur fired before the handkerchief dropped and fired to kill. A couple of others testified to hearing McArthur say he was going to get rid of Simon. It was enough, especially when Simon was right. Gore apparently made it clear that he wanted the matter closed, not dragged on. It's over."

In Simon's room, a celebratory party was taking place.

"I told you not to worry," he said.

If she'd had the carpet beater she might have

thwacked him with it, and she did confiscate his glass of wine. "So we're free to leave as soon as you're able?"

"Yes."

A tight knot inside her unraveled. "Isn't Gore worried about what you'll do in London? McArthur's crimes occurred during his administration."

"He probably hopes it'll suit the government to bury the whole matter. There, McArthur's death is to his advantage."

"But that would waste all your work."

He shook his head. "No. My main aim all along has been to stop McArthur and get reparation for those he hurt. I'm not on a witch hunt."

"Then I hope other people know that," Hal said.

Simon gave him an exasperated look. "This house is as safe as a fortress now."

"Remember Troy."

"So admit no horses."

Jancy decided to share her fears. "I'm wondering about Dr. Playter."

"Gads, ma'am," Norton said. "Very sound man. Remarkable reputation."

"But he's so brusque."

Hal said, "He's an army surgeon, Jane. They have to become calloused."

So they can deal with the aftermath of battle, she realized. *Cut off limbs until they pile up around them. Ignore the wounded who can't be saved.* Given that, Simon's wounds must seem nothing, and she a silly, fussy child. But she would send for Dr. Baldwin, just to be safe.

She took Simon's hand. "So all that remains is for you to behave yourself and let your ribs heal. What can we do to amuse you now, sir, who reclines on his divan like the Grand Panjandrum himself?"

Their eyes met in memory of that first, terrible night, when he'd been so kind.

"With the little round button a-top," he said. "Can you recite it?"

The nonsense poem had supposedly been created to test an actor's ability to memorize, and thus was used to torment children in the schoolroom.

Jancy took a thespian stance. " 'So she went into the garden to cut a cabbage leaf to make an apple pie, and at the same time a great she-bear, coming down the street, pops its head into the shop. What, no soap? So he died, and she very imprudently married the barber. . . .' "

Simon picked up, " 'And there were present, the Picninnies, Joblillies, the Garyulies, and the Grand Panjandrum himself, with the little round button a-top.' "

Together, grinning, they completed, " 'And they all fell to playing the game of catch-as-catch-can, till the gunpowder ran out at the heels of their boots.' "

Their audience applauded. Simon laughed—then swore under his breath, but tension had fled. Even so, Jancy sent to Dr. Baldwin and he came.

"Purely as a neighbor," he insisted. He refused to inspect the wounds, saying that would intrude on another doctor's domain, but he considered Simon's general state and confirmed Playter's advice.

"If there was necessity, I'd say you could leave sooner, St. Bride, if you were willing to endure considerable pain, but you'll be a great deal more comfortable in a week or two."

Jancy had to accept that. She put those fears out of the way and settled, with everyone, to waiting.

The next day Dr. Playter again announced himself satisfied with Simon's wound. He tweezed off a bit of his precious eschar, which clearly hurt, though Simon didn't complain. When he'd inspected the discharge that resulted, he said, "All's well," and redressed the wound.

"He is fevered," Jancy pointed out.

"Which is excellent." Playter bled Simon again and left.

The other men had left during the doctor's examination, so Jancy indulged in a kiss, a real kiss, closing her eyes to enjoy it. When she straightened, she caressed his hot face. "Be patient, love."

"I'll atrophy from lying here."

"You're probably grumpy from hunger. I'll go and get lunch."

When she returned with the tray, she found Simon trying to get out of bed.

"Stop that!" she cried.

He'd already stopped, swearing and white with agony.

Oglethorpe rushed out of the dressing room to help him back onto his bolsters. "Now, now, sir, none of that with your lady wife present."

"It's time she broadened her vocabulary."

Jancy almost told him she'd heard it all—she'd scandalized Martha when she'd first been in Abbey Street—but instead said, "I think I should start a penance pot. A penny for every infraction."

Hal had come in behind her. "Make it a guinea. Milk him for all he has."

"Which is damn little," Simon snapped. "How would you like being stuck here like a waxwork when you're perfectly fit?"

"Not at all, which is irrelevant," Hal retorted. "You're a fool to risk those ribs and you're not fit. You're running a fever."

"If this was wartime I'd not be lying around. I'd probably be thrown back into battle."

"No, you'd doubtless be dead."

Jancy intervened before a fight broke out. "Eat." She thrust a sandwich into Simon's hand.

"Damned sandwiches." But then met her eyes. "I apologize, but this is enough to try a saint."

"Even a St. Bride, it would seem." She poured tea into the invalid cup, seeking a safe subject. "Was there ever a Saint Bride?"

He swallowed his mouthful. "Doubtless many. It comes either from the Irish Bridget or the Swedish Birgitta. In Lincolnshire, the Swedish connection seems most likely. She was a highborn wife and mother, given to speaking her mind to kings and popes."

"I'd have thought that would earn her hell, not heaven."

"Astonishing, isn't it? Perhaps things were different in the past." He ate more sandwich as she poured for Hal and herself.

"There was a monastery in her honor near Brideswell, which is why the village is Monkton St. Brides. There's no trace left except the village church, which was part of it. There's a natural spring in the village street with an interesting legend attached."

"What?"

"Brides are supposed to drink from it before entering the church. If they're impure, they'll drop dead."

She half laughed, half frowned. "That's terrible. Does it happen?"

His eyes danced. "We're a very pure lot in Lincolnshire. It's also supposed to guarantee fertility and godly children. That seems to work."

Tales of his village and home charmed her, so she encouraged more, hoping and praying that this truly would be her world.

Chapter Fifteen

After lunch the tactful men again left them alone. Simon held out his left hand to her and she put her right one in it.

"I never courted you, did I, my love?" He raised her palm to his mouth and kissed it. "Shall I court you now?"

"How can you—atrophying here?"

"The Grand Panjandrum has minions. Have you never been courted?"

"No. Have you courted?"

His brows flicked up and down. "Not, I confess, with marriage in mind."

She laughed and gently tweaked his nose. "Wicked, as I said. And what should I do as the courted lady?"

"Blush, which you do so prettily. Say, 'Oh, la, sir!' Perhaps," he added, eyes lazy, "make me a modest gift in return."

She deliberately chose the most boring thing she could think of. "A handkerchief?"

"Perfect."

Jancy had begun to make some handkerchiefs for Isaiah for his birthday, so later she considered one of the squares of fine lawn. Instead of a monogram she would copy the design of Simon's signet—an S arising from flames. It would be slow work, however, if she was to do it out of his sight.

She wondered what Simon intended. Nosegays? Trinkets? Gloves? When she returned, he gave her a perfect scarlet leaf.

"I had to send Treadwell to find it for me."

Jancy was surprised, but then she smiled. "Nature creates such beauty, doesn't it?"

He was smiling at her when he said, "Yes."

She blushed. "Oh, la, sir!" As an immediate reward, she poured a little brandy into a glass, dipped her finger, and stroked his lips. He licked and said, "More."

She did it again, and he captured her finger to suck it, his eyes on hers. The play of his tongue made her knees wobble.

"Soon," she whispered, sliding her finger free.

"I could have a brandy kiss right now."

Perhaps his temperature made him heavy-eyed, but she didn't think so. She felt as fevered. She took brandy into her mouth and then bent to kiss him, letting the liquid slip slowly into his mouth. When he swallowed, she closed her eyes and explored his mouth, gripping his head with one hand, aching inside for what they couldn't have.

Yet.

When complaining muscles compelled her to straighten, she said, "I believe I have come to like brandy."

That evening he gave her a book—a slim volume bound in blue cloth with gold lettering on the spine. "I bought it just before McArthur returned, intending it for you."

"Angel Bride," she read on the spine, "by Sebastian Rossiter. I'm flattered, sir." She dropped a kiss on his lips, noticing more heat. "How do you feel?"

"Hot and irritable. Read a poem to soothe me, my angel bride. I bought that, by the way, because one of my friends is married to his widow."

"A Rogue?"

"I do have other friends, but yes. I mentioned him.
Leander, Earl of Charrington. Why do you always frown
if I mention a titled friend?"

"I don't."

"You do."

She pulled a face at him. "All right, I do. What will
they think of me?"

"That you are a treasure and I'm a lucky man. Read
me a poem."

She opened the book at random.

How sweet the home that is by angels blest,
At hearth, in schoolroom, at the mother's breast.
A man alone is but a withered thing,
No matter how the raucous rakes do sing
The joys of single state.

Chaste angel! How you raise the lowly mind,
Directing heavenward more base mankind.
With smiling lips and orbs of innocent hue
You gently chide all those who carol to
The joys of single state.

My little cherubs sitting at my feet,
Or running with glad cries papa to greet,
Are treasures greater than a pasha's hoard.
What man would choose instead some common bawd
And the joys of single state?

Jancy looked up at Simon. "Isn't there a quote about
someone protesting too much?"

His lips quirked. "I gather he wasn't quite the ideal
husband he portrays. But he's very popular. I remember
my sisters mooning over his work."

"I'm sorry, I'm not being politely grateful for the gift,
am I?"

"A lesson for me to check the gift horse's mouth before I offer it. I'll do better."

She put the book aside and took his hand. "There's no need."

"What else do I have to do?"

She saw him wince and realized she'd taken his right hand. "Did I hurt you?"

"The arm hurts. Playter's beloved eschar, I suppose."

She put a hand over the bandage. It felt hot there. She almost unwrapped it but remembered the instructions to leave it alone. Heat healed. "We'll ask him to look at it tomorrow. Perhaps it's not draining."

Later, she was amused to find Oglethorpe absorbed in *Angel Bride*. She caught Simon's eye and bit the inside of her cheeks to fight laughter. The stocky ex-marine was the last person she'd imagine enjoying sentimental verse.

She mustn't have succeeded in hiding her thought, for with an amiable smile, Oglethorpe said, "War's a grim business, ma'am. I've come to enjoy anything with a bit of sweetness and light, and I've been privileged to meet Mr. Rossiter's Angel Bride as was."

"Is she ethereal?"

His eyes twinkled. "A bit of what they call poetic license, I think, ma'am, but a very pleasant lady with two charming children, Miss Rosie and Master Bastian. His little cherubs."

"Little imps, more like it," Hal said.

"Sir," Jancy protested, "you destroy all our illusions."

"It's Blanche's opinion that anyone who describes children as angels has only viewed them from afar."

"Blanche?" she queried, intrigued at a hint of a lady fair.

He blushed.

Jancy raised her brows at Simon, who shot a look that said, *Don't pursue it.*

Oh.

"Were you an angel?" Simon asked.

Jancy was assailed by contrasting visions—of she and Jane, who had not exactly been angels but had certainly been little ladies. And of the Haskett children, where all, boys and girls equally, could be described as imps.

"I don't think so." She offered Hal more cake. "What news of travel?"

"No one's willing to predict, but we have at least a week."

"Then we leave in a week," Simon said. When Jancy tried to protest, he said, "My ribs feel much better, but I'll travel on a damned stretcher if I must."

But that night, the enemy struck. Simon's fever soared.

Oglethorpe woke Hal, and at three in the morning, Hal woke Jancy.

"It's supposed to be normal," she said, hurrying to the sickroom. "Part of healing."

But the degree of heat shocked her. Simon shook her hand away. "Don't fuss. I'll be fine."

She retreated and murmured to Hal, "Should we send for Playter?"

"What could he do?"

Jancy remembered her earlier thought. He couldn't amputate ribs.

She undid the chest bandages, knowing Playter would berate her, and peeled back the top dressings on the wound. She couldn't see the actual wound, but didn't smell putrefaction, or see swelling or any spreading redness.

"Perhaps it's some other cause," she murmured, relieved as much as anything. She looked at the others. "What do you think?"

"Bound to be," Hal said, "so he'll get over it."

"Cool water, then. To bring down the fever." She began the treatment herself, patiently wiping a damp cloth over Simon's head and shoulders, soothing him when he tried to brush her away.

But then pain no longer seemed to keep him still. His skin burned and his pulse was rapid. Dawn was brightening the sky, so she sent Oglethorpe for the doctor.

Playter arrived complaining but then muttered a curse. He, too, undid the bandages and then stripped all the dressings off the wound. The final dressing brought the crusty scab with it. A copious, smelly discharge spilled out.

Jancy gasped, but the doctor said, "No contagion there."

"No?" she queried.

"No. Water! Light!" He cleaned the wound and then peered into it with a magnifying glass. "Even a little granulation. Healing tissue," he said, looking up at her. "The fever must be something else. Does he suffer from malaria?"

"He's never had it. And surely . . ." She stopped herself pointing out that the symptoms weren't right.

He checked Simon's bloodshot eyes and then his dry mouth and tongue, muttering to himself. He pushed and poked at his abdomen.

"His arm's particularly hot."

The doctor unwrapped the wound and Jancy saw him turn gray. "God forgive me."

The beneficial crust had shed on its own to reveal more stinking pus but also swollen, scarlet flesh.

"Brandy!" he snapped and poured it over the long wound.

Jancy choked back a cry. Where once it had been shallow, it now cut deep.

"The arm'll have to come off."

Jancy stared at him. "No!"

"No," Simon whispered, as absolutely.

"You'd rather die?" the doctor asked.

Jancy was intensely aware of Hal Beaumont standing behind her. She didn't know what to do. Her heart was pounding and she felt dizzy. As she understood it, Hal's arm had been shattered. This had to be different.

"It doesn't have to be now, does it?" she asked.

"The earlier, the better his chances of survival. And there's no point in putting it off."

"No," Simon said again, begging her with his eyes.

God help her, but she knew they must at least wait. From a dry throat she said, "Not yet. So, what do we do to help him overcome the putrefaction?"

The doctor snapped shut his case. "If we knew that, woman, don't you think we'd do it? You can try compresses to draw out the poison, but it'll do no good." He turned to Simon. "My deepest apologies, sir. I neglected to clean that wound as thoroughly as the other. I was in error."

"Then can't you clean it now?" Jancy demanded.

Dr. Playter said, "It's too late," and left.

Jancy collapsed into the bedside chair, her eyes locked with Simon's. She didn't want to show how much this appalled her because if it happened, it if had to be, she didn't want him to ever think it made him less in her eyes.

She saw in the set of his lips that he was never going to agree. So if the doctor was right and he grew worse and worse, she might have to make the decision. As his wife, it was her right. Would he hate her for it later?

She should probably say something cheerful and bracing, but all she could think was, how could life be so *cruel*?

Hal said, "Brandy does seem to help. Why don't we apply brandy compresses?"

It was something to do, but Simon's fever stayed high and the redness around the wound spread. Simon soon turned delirious. When Playter didn't return, it was clear he wouldn't come back except to amputate. Jancy knew she should send for him, but she delayed.

As she bathed Simon's hot forehead, feeling steam should rise, she said, "You will not die. You know the cards didn't foretell it, so it will not be."

His eyes moved beneath his lids. "Superstitious . . ." he whispered. "Anyone . . . think . . . Gypsy."

She was glad he wasn't looking at her. "Don't be silly, and save your strength."

After a while, he said, "If cards say . . . no need to cut off arm."

"Precisely."

She knew, however, that the nine of diamonds didn't rule out an amputation. And that she wouldn't let Simon die. If he wasn't better by morning, she'd send for Playter.

She caressed a cheek that was rough with bristles and gently kissed his cracked lips. "Don't worry. I'll take care of you."

Remembering how soothing Mrs. Gunn's ramble had been, she tried to talk about practical matters. She refused to leave his side, clinging to an irrational faith that while she was present, Simon, at the very least, could not die. But in the deep hours of the night she remembered feeling the same way about Jane and waking up on board ship next to her corpse.

They kept cleaning the wound with brandy, but she knew rot was eating into him.

He came to himself once. "Glad you're back," he said, faintly but clearly.

She'd not left his side for hours, but she said, "I'm glad you missed me."

"Missed your smell. Let me smell your hand. Something here stinks."

She had put on hand cream after last washing her hands. She stroked around his face. "Soon you'll smell a real English garden."

"Take you to Brideswell. But it'll be winter, not spring. . . ."

She put her fingers over his lips. "Don't talk anymore, love. You need your strength."

"Come up on the bed with me and I'll be good."

Despite Hal and Treadwell in the room, Jancy climbed up and snuggled close—he was so dreadfully hot!

He smiled. "Best medicine."

"I'm glad then. Try to sleep."

Perhaps he did, and perhaps she did, too, for she dreamed, of fire. She woke and saw Hal rising from a chair. Treadwell was already leaving.

"Smoke?" she asked, slipping off the bed.

The smell was stronger. It *was* smoke.

"Wake Oglethorpe," Hal said and ran out.

She dashed into the adjoining room and shook the man awake. She didn't ask the pointless question, but inside she was screaming it. *What do we do about Simon? He can't be moved yet.*

In this wooden town, every house had a fire bell and buckets of water ready. She heard the bell ring and sent shirtsleeved Oglethorpe to find out what was happening.

She looked into the corridor and saw only wisps of smoke downstairs but she was frantic with indecision. "Come back quickly!" she screamed after the man. "With Treadwell."

If necessary, they'd carry Simon out.

She heard a sound and whirled back to the bed. He was trying to sit up. She ran over to hold him down. "Don't. It's all right. Lie back."

"So hot. Fire."

She quickly bathed him again. "Don't worry. You're not on fire. We're not on fire. Just a little problem." She kept babbling nonsense, wanting to scream for someone to come and tell her what was going on.

She could hear other fire bells and clamoring voices outside. Then it grew quieter. She couldn't bear it and ran out into the corridor. Her nose wrinkled at the stink, but was it the acrid smell of an extinguished fire?

Was it out?

"Is anyone there?" she yelled. "What's happening?"

Hal appeared at the bottom of the stairs, soot-streaked, his hair on end. "It's out. It's all right."

She clung to the newel post in relief. "Thank heavens. Where was it? What damage?"

"In the parlor. I'll talk to you in a moment."

He turned away and she realized there were people in the house, probably concerned neighbors, but it could be anyone. She fled back to Simon's side.

All was well.

In a laughably terrible way.

Simon still raged with the fever that might kill him. In hours she was going to have to allow Playter to cut off his arm. But at least no one had burned them in their beds.

She was sure that had been the intent.

It seemed an age before Hal came. He'd taken the time to wash and change his clothes and she resented that.

"Someone started the fire. Broke the parlor window and threw in papers and oily rags and then set fire to them. A clumsy attempt, but I suppose if we'd all been asleep it might have gained a better hold."

"Simon's bedridden. We'd have carried him out, but then his rib could have killed him." She couldn't bring herself to say that he was dying anyway. Then Jancy realized something else. "Hal, only consider what lies above the office."

He inhaled. "Simon's room."

"A fire that consumed at least the back of the house would destroy any papers there. Thus, once Simon died of this infection, everyone would be in the clear." She put a hand to her throat. "We have to get away from here! Even with risk, we have to get away. Tomorrow."

"Jane, he might not be alive tomorrow."

She looked at Simon and asked very quietly, "How soon after an amputation could he travel?"

"If he survives the operation, immediately."

Chapter Sixteen

W hen dawn's light crept into the room, Jancy was gritty-eyed and exhausted, but Simon still lived. He was burning up with fever, but he lived. Praying she hadn't left it too late, she sent for Playter.

She went to her room with some notion of tidying herself, but when she looked in her mirror, she shrank from the image of the wild, disheveled creature there. She saw Jancy Haskett, as might have been, and after today she might as well tell Simon. He'd hate her anyway.

She washed and pinned up her hair, but as she did so, her mind insisted on swirling around her Haskett life. Wild Haskett hellions. Fire. A baby had fallen into a fire and been badly burned. The wounds had crusted. Eschar, though no one had called it that. Granny Haskett had said to leave it and it had healed well.

Granny Haskett. Treating a nasty knife wound in Uncle Malachy's arm, a wound that had gone bad . . .

A rap at the door heralded Playter. Mouth dry, Jancy ran down to meet him in the hall. "Maggots."

"What?" He was obviously primed to do his grisly duty.

"People use maggots to treat infection."

The doctor turned red. "I'll have you know, madam, that I am an Edinburgh-trained physician, not an old woman casting spells. Maggots," he growled. "Beaumont. Take Mrs. St. Bride away. She's becoming deranged."

"No!" She dodged away from Hal's hand. "I want to try maggots first."

She was almost crazed with fear of her decision, of having to defy these men, but she had to. She'd remembered it all—watching Granny Haskett, fascinated by the squirmy treatment, seeing it work.

"Maggots work. I've *seen* them work. They eat the infection."

Playter glared at her. "Are you or are you not going to let me amputate that arm?"

She stared at him, sickness churning, but then said, "Not."

He turned and marched out. She sobbed and looked to Hal for reassurance.

"Maggots?" he said, pale.

She'd been only nine when she'd seen it done, and if it worked, wouldn't a doctor know that? Perhaps it had worked from sheer luck. Perhaps there were dangers she knew nothing of. She was committed now, however. "I need to try. We can amputate later."

"Later might be too late."

"Hal, I have to try! Maggots," she said to herself. "Where?" Then she knew. "Saul Prithy. Send one of the men for him. Quickly!"

He jerked with astonishment at her command but then bellowed, "Oglethorpe!"

Jancy told Oglethorpe what she needed. He looked as worried as Hal, but he didn't question her.

She went back to Simon's side, wishing she could talk to him, explain, ask his wishes. Instead she unbandaged the festering wound and cleaned it again.

Red marks were spreading from it. The red spiders, Granny Haskett had called them. Hal was right. If this didn't work, she might have left it too late. She teetered in indecision again, but the red spiders had started around Uncle Malachy's wound, too.

It seemed an age, but was only half an hour by the clock before Oglethorpe returned with a wooden box. He was handling it squeamishly, but Jancy grabbed it, opened it, and saw white maggots crawling upon a bed of bran.

"Thank you, Saul," she breathed.

Saul still mostly lived by hunting, so she'd known he'd have hanging game, which was a good source of healthy maggots. He'd use them for fishing bait, too, keeping them in a bran box as the Hasketts had.

"Now what?" Hal asked.

She wanted to say, "I was a child. I don't remember," but if she did, Hal might stop her.

Trying to appear confident, she picked maggots from the top of the bran and put them on the swollen skin around the wound. She feared they'd wriggle away from the heat, but they didn't. Instead the first one crawled in. She heard someone mutter in disgust and she felt the same way, as she hadn't at nine. Then she'd simply been fascinated.

Moment by moment her memory was clearing, however, so her confidence grew. Granny Haskett was an unlikely guardian angel, but Jancy did feel as if someone was guiding her. She even remembered why people kept maggots in bran. Crawling up through it and eating it cleaned them inside and out. She put more and more in the wound.

They're doing good, she told herself. *They're eating the rot that's killing Simon.*

When the wound was as full as could be, she put a loose bandage on top. "Now we wait."

"Are you sure?" Hal asked, sounding appalled.

Of course I'm not sure! "I have to try."

"We wait, then."

Treadwell took up the job of bathing Simon's hot body while Jancy picked out more maggots as they wriggled to the top of the bran, collecting them in a covered dish.

She drank some sweet tea when it was brought to her, but she could stomach nothing more.

Treadwell tried to get water into Simon, but not much made it past his cracked lips. At every moment, Jancy fought the terror that she was killing him. That the maggots wouldn't work. That it really was an old wives' tale, and that Edinburgh-educated Dr. Playter was right.

That when she admitted it, it would be too late and Simon would die.

She even began to worry that the maggots were eating Simon's good flesh—burrowing deeper and deeper into his arm, down to the bones. She kept looking beneath the bandage, but she couldn't tell anything from the squirming mass.

Then maggots began crawling away from the wound, fatter, darker, gorged, disgusting—marvelous.

"They're full!" she exclaimed, scooping them back into the bran box and adding new ones.

She heard Hal say, "Dear God," more in disgust than wonder, but she ignored him. This was exactly as it had been when Granny Haskett had done it. She sent Ogle- thorpe for more maggots and prayed.

Was Simon a little cooler? There was no way to tell.

Were the spiders shrinking? She wasn't sure, so she marked the end of the red lines and then cleared away more gorged maggots and added fresh. How long did she do this for? How long should it take?

She lost all sense of time.

Then Simon swallowed a few mouthfuls of water and muttered something about his arm crawling.

"It's all right, love," she said, daring to hope. "It's all right."

She kept watching her marks, wanting to believe, but not wanting to fool herself that the lines were shrinking when they weren't.

A gentle hand and voice stirred her. "The lines have shrunk."

She blinked, finding herself fallen forward so her head was on the mattress. She pushed painfully up and focused bleary eyes.

She laughed for joy and murmured prayers of thanks as she inspected the wound. It was still red and swollen and it crawled with maggots, but the red spiders had shrunk away. She placed a hand on his forehead. Cooler. Not cool, but not an inferno.

Surely now his body could, as Playter said, heal itself.

"Praise be to God, and to you, you lovely little creatures!" She scooped off some that had fallen on the sheet. "Hal, try to get Playter to return."

"It's the middle of the night."

She looked around, surprised. "Oh, very well. We'll let him sleep. We've done it, though, haven't we?"

"Perhaps" was all he would say.

Hal probably wrote a long explanation to Playter, for he did come the next day, albeit suspiciously. But as soon as he saw Simon, he said, "By the holy hounds of Hades!"

He quickly examined the wound, scowling ferociously. Jancy waited for some blessing, but he said nothing until he straightened. "Coincidence, of course, but perhaps you were right to wait. A healthy constitution can work miracles, despite those who meddle. And it was only a minor wound."

Jancy stared at him but could see there was no point in arguing. "So, now he will live?"

"He has a chance, especially if you remove those disgusting creatures. Anyone would think you were a Gypsy, ma'am!"

Jancy realized that her knowledge of maggots could betray her, but even so, she'd not have done anything different. Simon would live, and he would be whole.

"We intend to leave immediately," she told the doctor. "How do we manage it?"

To her surprise, he didn't argue. "Those ribs are still

a danger. A stumble could harm him. But if you get him to a boat on a stretcher and then are lucky enough to avoid storms, perhaps no great harm will be done."

His agreement surprised her, but he might simply want to be rid of someone who challenged his medical beliefs. Or did he, too, think Simon in danger here?

When he'd left, Hal said, "When do you want to leave?"

"Do you think it foolish?"

"No. In fact, if we can, we should leave tomorrow. We'll hire a boat for ourselves alone, so if the water turns rough we can put in to shore."

"Won't that be terribly expensive?"

His blank look reminded her of the different world these men inhabited.

"I wasn't sure," she confessed. "About the maggots."

"You're a remarkable woman, Jane."

"But what if I'd been wrong?"

"What-ifs are pointless."

A grim set to his mouth made her realize he was thinking about his own arm. Might maggots have saved it? Why would doctors reject a treatment that might help simply because it didn't fit with their beliefs?

"Simon is whole and recovering," he said. "We'll get him safely to Montreal, and if the journey goes well, we might even get there before the *Ewheretta* sails and be home for Christmas."

Jancy left to organize a flurry of packing.

She'd left out Jane's self-portrait until now, but as she put it away in the portfolio with the others, she felt guilty. If Jane had lived, none of the recent events would have happened. But if a similar disaster had struck, Isaiah would have forced Simon to marry Jane, not herself. The idea was intolerable. Simon St. Bride, husband, hero, and lover, was *hers*, and if Jane were alive, she'd fight her for him. She slid the drawing inside the stiff portfolio, ashamed but unrepentant.

* * *

Simon awoke from terrifying dreams and immediately looked to where his arm should be. Was!

He raised it to be sure. Oh, thank God. In his dream it had been hacked off and he'd been searching through piles of discarded limbs, many crawling with maggots, sure that if he found the right one it could be stuck back on.

He wriggled his fingers. Though he felt a fierce burning beneath the bandage, everything seemed to work.

"Awake, sir? How do you feel?"

Simon looked at the lanky man by the bed, for a moment unable to recognize him. But then his tangled brain sorted itself out.

"Treadwell." He cleared his throat, but his voice still rasped when he said, "Chewed up and spit out. What happened to me?"

"Bit of bother, sir. All sorted out now. Here, try some water."

Simon drank from the spouted invalid cup and never had water tasted so good. "What sort of bother?"

Treadwell adjusted his bolsters. "Well, sir, you ran a bit of a temperature."

Simon frowned. "Don't I remember smoke?"

"And there was a bit of a fire."

"I want my wife." Simon heard himself sound like a child wanting its mother, but he wanted Jane. Like a storm-tossed ship seeking a harbor, he wanted Jane.

"Good idea, sir. I'll fetch her for you. And some light food, I'm sure."

Simon lay there, trying to sort out dreams from fevered memories. Had his dream been a premonition? Did the throbbing of his arm mean it was infected and Playter was coming to cut it off?

Then Jane entered in one of her sober gowns, her hair pinned up, but smiling, eyes bright. She wouldn't look like that if anything was wrong.

He spoke his thought. "Beautiful angel. Perhaps Sebastian Rossiter isn't so far out in his poems."

She laughed and, still radiant, came to kiss his cheek, to cradle his face.

"I prefer your hair loose."

"That's hardly practical." But, blushing, she pulled out pins and shook her hair free. Then she ran her fingers through it, raising it, letting it fall.

"I see you're recovering," she teased.

He looked down, but he wasn't tenting the bed. Of course not. She was too innocent for a comment like that, despite one remarkable night.

"Recovering from what? What happened, Jancy? Treadwell said a bit of a temperature and a bit of a fire." He hadn't meant to tell her, tell anyone, but he added, "I dreamed that Playter amputated my arm."

She took his right hand in both of hers. "He almost did. That minor wound became infected."

"It's all right now?" He looked at his arm again, to check that he hadn't imagined its presence. "I remember . . . I forbade it, but how?"

"I thought of something I'd seen once. Maggots."

"Maggots!"

"Now you sound like Playter. They saved your arm, Simon."

He stared at his arm again. Was he imagining a crawling sensation? "Then thank you, and thank the maggots. But how?"

"They eat the corrupt flesh, the way they eat rotting meat. Don't look like that."

"I can't help it. I'm profoundly grateful, but I can't help it. *Maggots?*"

She leaned forward with a mock grimace. "Crawling into and out of you, yes."

He laughed, but then hissed at the catch in his ribs. But he assessed the pain. "Not as bad as it was. How long has it been?"

"Since when?"

"Since the duel, I suppose."

"Five days."

"How strange. So we've missed our boat."

"We can hire another. If you're up to the journey."

"How? And, why?" When her eyes shifted, he said, "Don't, Jane. You're not a good liar. Tell me the truth. Why this urgency to leave?"

"Someone set a fire. It could have burned the house down and us in it, but as we were awake tending to you, it only scorched the office. We think it was an attempt to burn your room above. To burn your papers."

"Those damn papers. I wonder if they're worth all this."

"Of course they are, but even Playter agrees that we can go tomorrow if you'll be sensible."

He was worried about all aspects of this, and bitterly frustrated about being weak and stuck in this bed, but even so, he smiled at her stern care of him.

"Who are you, Jane St. Bride?"

Her eyes flew to his, alarmed.

"Don't worry. I'm not delirious. But I thought I knew you once. Plain, sober Jane who preferred a quiet life and wouldn't say boo to a goose. Now you're a golden tempest, a warrior goddess, a shining angel. I adore you. I'm profoundly grateful. But if this is the real Jane, why the other one?"

She blinked at him. "Perhaps events have changed me."

"You've never been like this before?"

"No. But I wasn't angelically quiet back in Carlisle. Before Martha died—

"Why do you call her Martha, not Mother?"

Her cheeks flushed. "She preferred it."

It seemed unlikely, but why would Jane lie about something like that? Yet he felt strongly that she was lying and concerns rushed back. The jeweled box was even more magnificent, but he still didn't know what it contained.

"Before *Mother* died," she said stiffly, "I was something of a tomboy. I suppose it was two deaths and coming to a strange place that quenched me."

"Until now."

She kissed his hand again. "Until *you*. If I'm a warrior goddess, Simon, it's because you've made me one. I'll fight to keep you safe, but you must rest, eat, and get stronger. Hal's hiring a boat for us alone so we can stop if there's rough weather. We're leaving, and with God's blessing, we'll reach home."

Weak and in pain, he wanted home, but he wanted Jancy just as much. It must be fever and weakness that made him feel that she was watchful and wary. How could he love and adore a woman he didn't trust? But Simon couldn't push away all questions. He lay staring at the ceiling, wishing he knew what was inside the box he was taking to his beloved home.

Chapter Seventeen

*J*ancy made an excuse to escape. She was ecstatic that Simon seemed to be recovering his strength so quickly, but she wished his mind weren't so sharp. How had she not noticed she'd started calling Martha by name? It was a wonder she hadn't called her Aunt Martha under all this stress.

She longed for truth between them as a parched throat longs for sweet water. True lovers should never lie to each other, but in addition it would seem true love loosened the tongue—or weakened the brain.

She took refuge in her room to think.

Perhaps she should tell Simon about the switch from Nan to Jane. He might understand and forgive, and once he knew, he might be able to sort out any legal complications. That information, however, felt like the locked door that kept the Hasketts out of sight.

That, he must never know.

But why would he doubt that Nan Otterburn was who Martha had said she was—an orphan from the Scottish Otterburns? But then she realized that he might think it appropriate to inform the head of the Otterburn family of their marriage. That would explode everything.

No. The door must stay locked.

She could carry off the deception. The few people who knew Jane and Nan well enough to tell them apart were all in Carlisle and unlikely to travel or invade noble spheres. What's more, every passing day made exposure less likely. People changed. All she had to do was keep her head and not make silly mistakes.

A knock on the door made her aware that her hands were clenched, her nails digging into her palms. She relaxed them and opened the door to find Oglethorpe.

"Captain Norton's here, ma'am, asking to speak to Mr. St. Bride."

Jancy wanted to shield Simon from everyone, but she went to ask his wishes.

"Bring him up. Norton's not going to slit my throat."

Of course he wasn't, but as Jancy escorted Captain Norton to Simon, she had the feeling he came bearing news. She doubted it could be good.

As soon as he left, she returned. "What did he want?"

"To slit my throat," Simon teased. "In fact, to ask to travel with us. Gore's given him charge of some extra documents to go on the *Eweretta,* and he's to leave for Montreal tomorrow and take the place of the courier already there."

"Isn't that strange?" she asked uneasily. "Too coincidental?"

"Jancy, you're letting your imagination run away with you. The explanation is simple. Gore's getting rid of everyone connected to the duel."

"What of the other second, then?"

"Delahaye? Posted west to the Red River Valley debacle, poor man."

"And Playter?"

"Nothing yet, but Gore would start a riot at the garrison if he tried."

She still felt a creeping sense of threat. "What of the people who conspired with McArthur? Might they still pose a threat?

"They're insignificant people who've probably made themselves scarce since his death. It seems to me that the words 'coin' and 'land' are often used awkwardly and might indicate a person of some importance, but I can't work out who. I hope someone in the Foreign Office can match the references with time and place and work it out."

She'd rather know now. "Initials? But that would be a long string of names."

"More likely a similarity. There's a Captain Penny in the garrison, but also a Lieutenant Moneysworth. Then we have Sir Peter Field and Frobisher Glebe. I'll leave it for others. Will you mind Norton traveling with us?"

"Not at all. He'll be extra protection." She went to put more wood on the fire. "He must regret standing as your second, however."

"Devil a bit. He's ambitious. He's been thinking of making a future here, but this opens up much better opportunities. I gather he twisted Gore's arm for some excellent recommendations. And of course I, too, owe him some assistance."

For a moment she wondered what he meant. Then she realized. A St. Bride of Brideswell could apparently advance a man's career.

"What's the matter?" he asked. "I do owe him something."

"It's that you take on everyone's causes."

He laughed. "It's in the blood, my love. Lost causes a specialty. An ancestor on my mother's side was Lady Godiva, who rode naked through Coventry so that her husband would reduce taxes."

"You mean that if riding around naked would get the Indians their homeland, you'd do it?"

"Without hesitation, but I doubt my naked body would carry much weight with the government."

She grinned at him. "You'd have all the ladies on your side."

"If you'll remember, out of respect the observers were supposed to close their eyes. Are you saying you wouldn't?"

"No. I'd be peeping Thomasina. She must have been a remarkable woman."

"And beloved by her people and her husband. She passed her spirit of fighting injustice on to her son, Hereward."

She stared at him. "Not Hereward the Wake."

"Valiant leader of the hopeless resistance to the Norman invasion, yes."

"*He's* an ancestor of yours, too?"

He looked at her quizzically. "Over time, one acquires rather a lot of ancestors."

"But most people don't have ones from the history books."

"He's not a direct ancestor, if that's any consolation. His sister carried Lady Godiva's blood down through the Baddersley family to my mother, and thus to me."

"Hereward's rebellion led to his death," she pointed out.

"Not according to my family's version. He accepted reality and settled for peace and a handsome property not far from where Brideswell now sits. And there he and King William would sit by the fireside to talk about the good old days."

"Really?" She didn't try to hide her disbelief.

He grinned. "You're a cynic, love. There's no proof either way, so why not believe the pleasant story? I, too, am driven to fight for justice, but see"—he held out his hand to her—"I already have my happy ending."

Jancy took his hand and asked questions about Lady Godiva and Hereward, but underneath she was quivering with the effect of idle words.

It's in the blood.

Carried the blood down through the family . . .

Simon didn't doubt that the blood of a woman dead eight centuries ago could shape him. What would he think if he ever found out that she brought the blood of vagrants and thieves to his line? A need to tell him and get it over with rose in her like vomit. She was saved by Hal returning with the news that he'd found a vessel leaving tomorrow carrying cargo to Kingston.

"It can take us, and for an extra fee, the captain agrees to put in to shore if a storm rises."

Jancy's "Excellent" clashed with Simon's "I'll be able to walk there."

She turned on him. "No, you will not! What if you were to fall? Do you want to be brought back here? Playter said you could try standing when you're on the boat and no sooner."

"He's an old woman, and so are you."

She put her hands on her hips. "I'm a *young* woman, and I've known old ones who could eat you for breakfast."

His stormy expression eased. "Your mother?"

Jancy hadn't meant Martha. Martha had been strong in her way, but not in the knife-wearing, hard-swearing ways of some of the Hasketts.

"Among others," she said and escaped to attack the last of the packing.

As soon as Jancy had left, Simon said, "Help me up."

Both Hal and Oglethorpe looked dubious, but at least they didn't argue.

Flexing upright to sit on the side of the bed was the worst. Simon froze as pain spasmed around his ribs.

"Lie back," Hal said, but Simon pushed on upward and found a bearable position.

"That was," he said, "extraordinarily painful, but I'm all right now. Move the steps beneath my feet."

The bed was high enough to need steps. Once his feet were on the lower one, Simon cautiously stood, aware that he was hunched and unable to do anything about it.

"I feel like a wizened ancient, but this isn't too bad. . . ."

As soon as he was upright, however, his head swam and his legs threatened to buckle. He clutched the two men. "Hell, Jancy's right. *She* could eat me for breakfast."

"Any day," Hal said. "Lie down again, you fool."

"No, not yet. If I'm to get my strength back, I need to move." With help, he stepped carefully onto carpet and managed to hobble to the fireplace and back—even if a careless turn froze him with pain again. He didn't say how grateful he was to be back in bed, supported by his damn bolsters, but he was sure they knew.

"I hoped to walk to the ship."

"It's too risky, Simon. But we can rig up a chair. You can go in state like the Grand Panjandrum himself."

"Better than on a stretcher. Thank you. I feel so damned useless. Jancy looks exhausted."

"She's worked like a Trojan, but once we're on board she'll have nothing more to do."

"Except worry. She hides it, but she seems tense with worry all the time."

"Her uncle died. You were shot—almost murdered. Then you almost lost your arm and would have done if she hadn't saved it. Then someone tried to burn you in your bed. You're surprised that she's a little tense?"

Simon laughed, resting his head back. "You're right. It's me who's disordered simply from lying here. Do something for me."

Hal agreed.

After dinner Simon asked that the female servants come up so he and Jancy could take farewell of them. The maids and Tom would stay on with Gilbraith, but Isaiah had left Mrs. Gunn a generous annuity, so she was moving to Scarborough to live with her daughter.

"Lucky daughter," he said to her, smiling.

Perhaps she blushed a bit. "Go on with you. You take care of yourself, sir, and take care of your wife. She's had a lot to put up with from you."

"I will."

He gave them all an extra gift and sent money to Saul Prithy, too—enough to live on as especial thanks for the maggots. Then everyone left him alone with Jancy.

"The house feels so strange," she said. "Furnished, but lacking all the small things that make a place a home. Waiting."

"Gilbraith has a wife and three children. It'll soon be more lively than it's been since Isaiah had it built. He would have liked that, I think. Come here."

She stared at him, almost as if afraid. "Why?"

"I have something for you." Held out his closed hand.

"What?"

"How suspicious you are. Trust me."

She relaxed. "Of course I do." She came and pried up his fingers. Then said, "Oh." With a grin she corrected it to, "La, sir. You shouldn't have!"

"Put them on."

She took out her plain hoops and put in the pearl earrings he'd bought so long ago. She went to the mirror and said, "They're beautiful!," her reflected, shining eyes as bright as if he'd given her the moon.

"I'll add a string of pearls once we're home."

In the mirror he saw the flicker of a real *You shouldn't* before she smiled. It wasn't really to her discredit that she was frugal, and she would learn to enjoy pleasure and beautiful things. He would teach her.

"You can wear your pearls, and nothing else, in our bed."

She turned, trying to be severe. "You're wicked."

"Guilty as charged." Then he said, "Tantalize me."

"What?"

"You know the story of Tantalus, who was chained in a lake, dying of thirst, and the water rose every day, but only to his chin?"

"You feel like that?"

"No, but I want to."

Her brow wrinkled. "You want me to torture you?"

"Yes, please. Take off your stockings."

She laughed slightly, blushing, glancing at the door, clearly worrying about Hal or the servants returning.

"They'll knock," he said, "and fear of discovery can even add a little spark."

He thought fear would win, but then she put her shoed foot on the chair and slowly raised her dark gray skirt and plain white petticoat. She pulled them up just to the knee, so she could untie her garter. Her very plain garter.

Silk, he thought. He'd buy her silk garters trimmed with ribbons, perhaps even with pearls, and they would hold up gossamer embroidered stockings. . . .

Glancing at him sideways, her smile deepened as it did when she was thinking wicked thoughts. Slowly she rolled down her thick cotton stocking, letting her skirts fall as she did so, so that he never saw her naked leg.

"Oh, cruel lady."

Her eyes sparkled. She raised her other foot and began to slowly lift her skirts again.

Someone knocked.

She froze.

"Go away," Simon called.

Footsteps receded. Her cheeks flamed. "They'll know. I mean, they'll assume . . ."

He grinned. "Yes. I'm beginning to think it would be worth the pain."

She put her foot down, twitching her skirts into place. "We have the rest of our lives as long as you're careful now."

"Spoilsport. Aren't you going to do the other stocking?"

"No. It gives you ideas."

"My dearest love, the air as you pass gives me ideas."

If eyes could kiss, hers kissed his, but she looked uncertain.

He held out a hand to her. When she took it, he said, "I forget how young you are. You should be just leaving the schoolroom, thinking only of dancing and flirtatious delights."

"Silly."

"No, it's not. I promise you dancing and flirtatious delights. And I'm sadly behind in my courtship."

She touched one earring—"No, you're not"—and leaned to kiss him slowly, deeply. It was the stuff of heaven and the torments of hell.

As they rested cheek to cheek, he said, "Better let people in, my love. And you should go to your own bed. We need to be up early tomorrow to be on our way."

Chapter Eighteen

Jancy hadn't anticipated how hard and nerve-racking leaving Trewitt House would be. It was scarcely dawn and the wind blew sharp, which might have explained her shivers, but didn't.

She felt sorrow at breaking the final tie with Isaiah, but the shivers came from fear. The house had become a sort of fortress, and now they must leave and be exposed. When she'd seen Simon in the wooden armchair mounted with poles, her only thought had been that he made an excellent target.

The town was barely stirring, but the empty street felt threatening to her. They took a last farewell of the servants and then set off, Hal in the lead, Treadwell and Oglethorpe carrying Simon, and two of Mrs. Gunn's grandsons bringing their luggage in a handcart. It should be escort enough.

"Behold, the Grand Panjandrum passes!" Simon declared, waving to a passerby as he swayed down toward the wharf. "Bow down and worship."

"Stop it!" Jancy hissed at him.

She'd persuaded him that all the men should carry loaded pistols, but he'd clearly thought her demented. "Who could possibly feel strongly enough to try to assassinate me as I leave, especially as they probably all want to see me gone?"

He was proved right. The few people they passed either stared at the display or saluted in farewell, but they reached the ship without incident.

She hadn't thought to worry about the ship. It was very small and it bobbed against the wharf, already making her feel sick.

"Behold the good ship *Ferret,*" Simon declared. "Take me aboard, slaves."

Jancy looked at Hal. "You've hired a boat called the *Ferret*?"

"I sailed on one called the *Weasel,* which seemed preferable to the *Haddock*. Ferrets are clever little beasts and skillful predators."

Jancy wanted to roll her eyes at anyone teaching a Haskett about ferrets, one of the prime tools of a poacher, but mostly she was frightened. After the journey here, she hated ships.

The men were carrying Simon up the narrow, wobbly plank. Once he was safely aboard, she exhaled, but now it was her turn. Reminding herself that this was the only route to safety, she focused on Simon and rushed across the rickety plank.

A black-toothed sailor had to almost catch her, and he seemed typical of the small crew.

"How safe are *they*?" she muttered to Simon once she reached his side.

"I doubt they have mischief in mind, but if they do, we have five armed escorts."

She hugged herself. "I don't like boats. They're just bits of wood and they go down all the time, even on the lake."

Captain Norton was already aboard, positively gleaming in his scarlet-and-white uniform. "Hearts of oak and all that, ma'am," he said.

"If the *Ferret*'s made of hearts of oak, I'll eat my hat."

"It probably is, you know," Simon remarked. "One thing Canada does not lack is excellent timber. Try to relax, love."

"I hate the way boats move. What if I'm sick?"

He took her gloved hand and squeezed it. "You're thinking of your cousin. That won't happen to you. I swear it."

"Is Canute one of your ancestors, too? Are you able to control the waves? If God had meant people to go on the water, He'd have given us feathers and webbed feet!"

"Don't make me laugh."

She made herself calm down. "I'm sorry." She looked around. "So this is our domain."

The men might be right that it was sturdy and safe, but the *Ferret* had little else to recommend it. The deck was dirty and crowded with boxes, sacks, and even crates of poultry and squealing piglets, so that there was little space for passengers at all. Perhaps the livestock explained the stink, but she suspected much of it was more established than that.

The one hatch in the middle of the deck was open, and the ruffian crew were lowering their luggage down there. She almost wanted to protest, but there was nowhere better. She hoped the *Ferret* didn't leak.

A wooden structure at one end probably contained the captain's quarters. There had to be a captain. She sought the man giving orders and found someone no smarter in appearance than the rest except for a battered old braided bicorn hat.

When the loading was done, he lit a long clay pipe, puffed on it, and came over with a rolling gait. "Angus Lawrie," he declared in a thick Scottish accent, revealing only a half complement of teeth. "Welcome to the *Ferret*, sir, ma'am. She's a sturdy ship, and we'll have you safe to Kingston within the week."

"What news of the weather?" Simon asked.

"Aye, well," the captain said, chewing on his pipe. "The river's a wee bit ahead of itself this year. But don't you worry. It'll stay open for some weeks yet."

Captain Lawrie turned away to bark unintelligible commands, and his men set about casting off. The plank,

their last link to land, was dragged in, leaving them at
the mercy of the water.

Mrs. Gunn's grandsons waved and Jancy waved back,
even though bile was rising in her throat. The ship was
hardly tossing at all, so if she really was about to be sick
it would be from fear of being sick. She focused on
Simon. "How are you?"

"In perfect trim." He was not, however, immediately
attempting to stand, so she knew the journey must have
been painful.

"Can you breathe properly?"

He inhaled in and out. "If I'd rebroken the rib and
punctured my lung, I'd know it. Help me up."

She wanted to protest but summoned Oglethorpe to
help, for if Simon started to fall, she couldn't catch him.

Halfway upright he hissed, but he made it, and after
a moment, he said, "That's better." He made it to the
rail, which gave him some support.

Jancy glanced at Hal and rolled her eyes, but she
didn't blame Simon for wanting to be on his feet. She
joined him just as the sails caught the wind, and the
Ferret shuddered, as if excited to be off. The water between ship and shore lengthened. They were now truly
at the mercy of untrustworthy water.

"I'll miss the colors," Simon said.

She looked at him, astonished that he could be so
calm—but then everyone was, from the pipe-puffing captain to the crew member who was coiling rope. She was
the only one panicking. She clutched the rail and fixed
her gaze on a scarlet tree.

She even began to appreciate the beauty. The rising
sun broke through clouds, highlighting the town and garrison set against a glorious patchwork of greens, golds,
yellows, and flaming reds. As they moved farther from
shore, the scenery was reflected in the lake, creating a
rippling tapestry.

"Better now?" he asked.

She smiled for him. "Yes." She asked Hal, "Where are our accommodations? Simon can't go below."

"If I have to . . ."

"Don't worry," Hal said. "The captain has surrendered his cabin. It's not much, but it'll do."

"Happy to oblige, ma'am," the captain called in so cheerful a voice that Jancy was sure he'd been paid a ridiculous amount.

Hal opened a warped door that led to the hut, and Jancy went in, ducking slightly. She didn't need to, but the beams were low enough to make her feel her head was threatened. On shore, this space would count more as a hovel. It had two windows, both dirty. She tried them, and one actually opened. Thank heavens. The room had a sour, stale stink.

"It's not much, I know," Hal said, "but the *Ferret* was the only possibility, and despite appearances it's said to be a sound ship and Lawrie to be a good seaman."

"This room can be reached without a ladder and has fresh air. It's perfect."

"You're very gracious. The *Eweretta* will be a grand improvement. She's famous for her comforts."

He went back on deck and Jancy took stock of the room.

Much of the limited space was stacked with cargo, but at least there was no livestock in here. Some of the smell could be coming from the barrels and boxes, but she thought most was simply long-term lack of cleanliness. Regretfully, she closed the window. A black metal stove was providing heat and they'd need that.

She was tempted to roll up her sleeves and scrub, but it would be a labor of Hercules, and anyway, she was sure Mrs. Simon St. Bride wasn't supposed to scrub her own floors.

Remember your Haskett days, she told herself. *Then this will seem like luxury.*

At least they'd brought their own bedding. And the

bed would fit two—just. She pulled back the greasy gray coverlet, thinking things were looking up.

Someone tapped on the open door.

She turned to see Treadwell ducking in. "I'll do that, ma'am."

Jancy stepped back, aware of a faux pas. She must learn to use servants, to assume they would do things rather than doing them herself. When he'd stripped the bed, however, she stared at the stained mattress. "I wish I'd brought our own bed."

"Indeed, ma'am. Excuse me."

He left and soon returned with a roll of canvas. He spread it over the mattress and tucked it in on either side. "A little trick I learned, ma'am. Ships always have extra sailcloth."

Perhaps using servants would be wise. They were, after all, professionals. Jancy left Treadwell to his expert work and went back on deck to join Simon. "Shouldn't you sit again?"

She had expected a fight, but he agreed. Yes, he was in pain. The cabin, for all its shortcomings, would be theirs alone and quite far from others, but clearly there'd be no lovemaking yet.

"I feel like a decrepit ancient," he complained as he sank carefully back into his chair.

"Consider yourself to be a Turkish pasha."

He grinned. "What an intriguing idea. A pasha would have a hundred wives."

"Which I'm sure would be a great relief to them, pashas being pashas."

"And what do you know about pashas?"

"Nothing, but I assume they are all Grand Panjandrums."

"With horses' tails instead of little round buttons," Hal said.

"What?" Jancy and Simon said it in unison, turning to him.

Hal was leaning against the rail nearby. "I served for

a while in the eastern Mediterranean. The importance of a pasha is shown by the number of horse tails hanging from his pennant. If I'd known you were going to take this fancy, Simon, I'd have raided the stables."

Suddenly everything felt brighter. They were away. The threat of York was shrinking with the town, and if the crew were ruffians, they wouldn't take on Hal, Norton, Treadwell, and Oglethorpe, not to mention Simon, who was probably up to a fight now if necessary.

Even nature smiled on them. There was just enough wind for steady travel without choppy waves and the sun came and went. And after days of terror and urgency, suddenly there was nothing to do. Soon, she suspected, she'd be bored, but for now, idleness felt like luxury.

The *Ferret* had an eating area belowdecks, next to a crude galley, but as Simon couldn't get down there, they ate picnic style on the deck and enjoyed it. They were all warmly dressed, and the simple food was surprisingly good.

Breakfast was strong tea, bread and butter, sliced ham, and hard-boiled eggs. For the midafternoon dinner they were served bread and stew, but good bread and stew, with apple pies and cheese for dessert. As the sun set, they were offered bread, cheese, and ale.

They'd brought their own supplies, so they had fresh fruit, wine, and coffee as well. Simon offered coffee to the crew, but they declared themselves happy with tea, ale, and grog—watered rum.

That evening, Jancy sat on the hatch by Simon's chair, sipping coffee and watching the sky pale as the sun disappeared. "It's like mother-of-pearl."

"Nature's magnificence."

When she turned to him, he was looking at her. "Don't."

"You are magnificent, Jane. What remarkable courage and strength you've shown."

She looked back at the sky. "I'm nothing out of the ordinary."

"There's nothing out of the ordinary about the setting of the sun. It happens every day, yet people are regularly brought to awe by it. Like love."

She turned back to him. "Nothing out of the ordinary?"

"It's common enough coin, there for the beggar and the king, the sinner and the saint. Yet wondrous." He took her hand and carried it to his lips. She wasn't wearing her gloves.

"You're cold," he said. "Do you want to go inside?"

To their private room with their private bed? Longings vibrated between them, but they couldn't. Not yet. "Of course. Do you want to walk there?"

"I believe I can manage that."

Jancy gave him her arm and they made the short, unsteady journey. She knew Hal and Norton were standing by in case. They made it, however. Simon was getting stronger all the time. Was it possible?

Treadwell was waiting to prepare Simon for bed. Of course, servants.

Jancy backed away. "I'll return in a few minutes."

Norton went down the ladder, but Hal came to join her at the rail. The last trace of light had faded, making a mystery of the universe. A sailor lit a lantern hanging on the mast, and the *Ferret* rattled down an anchor for the night.

"I'm not used to servants," she confessed, tucking her hands in her muff.

"You will be. It's like a clean, warm bed—easy to take to."

Remembering her transformation from vagrancy to middle-class comfort, she was soothed.

"You came here for such a little while," she said. "Was it worth it, all this traveling?"

"To assist Simon, yes."

"Did you come to find him, then?"

He was leaning his left hip against the ship, facing her.

"In a way. I had reasons for making the journey, but Simon's parents asked me to seek him out and bring him home."

"What if he hadn't wanted to?"

"Guilt is a powerful weapon."

"Why guilt?"

"They want their wandering prince home."

"Prince?"

"You know that St. Brides tend to stay close to the hive, as Simon puts it?"

"No." Next to being with Simon, talking about Simon was her most precious delight.

"They're famous for it," Hal said. "They don't wander. Don't go to sea or into the army, and if the sons choose the church, there's always a parish somewhere within fifty miles or so. The daughters marry into local families."

"They say that isn't healthy."

"Not that local, but they don't go to London, meet a gentleman from Sussex, and make their home there. The boys don't go far to school. Simon shouldn't have been at Harrow, but he had wanderlust even then, and his passion for just causes. It really is as well he didn't join the army. Even at school, he was often in hot water."

He told some school stories that illustrated Simon's tendency to seek out adventure and fight injustice. Stories, like Simon's, full of titles.

Treadwell emerged and went below. It was time to go, but Jancy had to ask, "Simon really is in line for an earldom?"

"Yes. Marlowe. It bothers you?"

"Is that like a clean, warm bed?"

In the weak candlelight she saw him smile. "With rich, heraldic hangings."

She said good night and went into the captain's cabin. It was lit by a single, glass-guarded candle, which softened the squalor. Treadwell had hung a sheet around a box that held a basin and washing water. Simon was in bed, lying down normally, with room beside him for her. "Welcome," he said softly.

This was their first night for going to bed together in a normal way. She smiled at him as she discarded her muff and cloak.

"We should have hired a maid for you."

"I don't need one."

"True. I'll be your maid on the voyage, and you my valet."

It was a delightful prospect. She went toward the shielding curtain, but he said, "Will you undress for me?"

Heat rising, she almost refused. It felt so much more deliberate than their mad stripping the night before the duel. But when Simon looked at her like that, she could deny him nothing.

Exposed in candlelight, she unfastened the front of her gown, her unsteady fingers clumsy. Then she untied the lace that tightened the gown beneath her breasts and took it off, aware of how plain her undergarments were. He didn't seem disappointed.

"You men are easy to please, aren't you?" she teased.

"Of course, but I'm hoping for more."

Remembering her play with her garter, she took her time about removing her stockings, but then let her shift drop again. She slowly unhooked the front of her bodice, wondering if an ordinary woman, a decent woman, would enjoy this as she was. Would dally, eyes on his, drawing out the moment.

She thrilled to the change in his face as her breasts were freed, even though they were still covered by the shift. When she shrugged off the bodice and dropped it on the floor, his eyes darkened. She covered her suddenly swollen, tingling breasts, not to hide them, but to comfort them.

They couldn't, could they?

He closed his eyes. "Alas, you'd better blow out the light."

Swallowing disappointment, she washed behind the screen and hurried into her nightgown. She blew out the candle and then slipped into the bed beside him. He took her hand.

"On the *Eweretta*," he said. "But no more games until then. I don't think I can bear it."

Commanding her body to calm, she snuggled against him. "This is good, too, though, isn't it?"

"A small compensation. No, more than small." He kissed her hair. "To be together, in peace, and on our way to a happy lifetime, is almost enough."

Chapter Nineteen

*N*ancy woke the next morning to cold air. The stove had gone out, but she didn't care. She was warm beneath the covers, and Simon was by her side. He was right. It was almost enough.

They'd talked in the dark, going over events in York, both recent and distant. He'd told her something of his experiences during the war that made her grateful she hadn't been in love with him then. She gave silent thanks that Britain was now at peace.

She'd told him more of her time in Carlisle, blending her own experiences and Jane's. If this was to work, she had to overcome her squeamishness about lying. It was all true, just not all about her. Now, in the morning light, she felt more rested and at peace than since before Isaiah's death. Even the motion of the ship, now clearly under way again, seemed pleasant.

"Sleeping with you is a cure for all ills," she told him, rolling to kiss his cheek.

Lazily smiling, he asked, "Should I advertise?"

"I'd have to shoot all customers." She sat up. "It must be late."

"Late for what?" His fingers played on her back. "We have nothing to do but be carried by the wind."

She turned to look down at him. "But we should get up."

"Why?"

She laughed and kissed him. "Just because." She escaped the bed. Despite last night, she couldn't feel comfortable about dressing in front of him and went behind the sheet. When she took off her nightgown, she saw a bloodstain. Only then did she feel a heaviness inside. She blushed with embarrassment. Was there a stain on the bed?

And her cloths were in her chest, which was out in the room.

At least her valise was here, so she had a fresh shift. But how was she to wash the other? She couldn't, absolutely couldn't, let Treadwell do it, even if a gentleman's valet was supposed to do such things.

Dressed but without her drawers, she emerged and unlocked her chest. She dug around until she found her cloths and the sling that kept them in place, and then stood to retreat behind the sheet again.

Simon was looking at her. He knew.

"There's a blood spot on the sheet," he said. "I'm sorry if you'd rather not talk about it, but I think in this situation it would be rather difficult. No child, then."

A touch of sadness in his voice made her ask, "Do you mind?"

"No, of course not. As you said, you don't want to be with child during an ocean voyage. But our children will be welcome when they come. Will you have a hard time of it?"

"No, but . . . Never mind."

"What is it?" he asked, so prosaically that she told him.

"I can't imagine how to discreetly wash my nightgown and cloths. And Treadwell will see the sheet."

"I can't do anything about that, but as for your nightgown and cloths, throw them away."

"That would be a sinful waste!"

"Slave, your pasha commands. Throw them away. The cloths, at least. If necessary, buy more in Kingston or Montreal."

"But . . ."

"I can, I believe, afford rags for my wife. I'm not rich, but I'm not a pauper."

"You don't know the meaning of rich and poor. You have no idea!"

"Oh, don't I? Hal's laying out most of the money for this journey."

She opened her mouth to score a point, but he quickly added, "But I'm not so poor that my wife needs to launder her monthly rags."

"And your wife's not so foolish that she'll throw money away!"

They glared at each other, but then Simon asked, "What are we arguing about?"

She straightened. "I'm sorry. I get short-tempered at this time."

"And I'm impatient with pain and frustration."

"Didn't you sleep well?"

"I don't think I've had a decent night's sleep since the duel. I'm not complaining, given the perils I've avoided, but it's wearing."

"I have some laudanum. Playter forbade it because pain would keep you still, but surely your ribs are mostly knitted by now."

"It's tempting," he said. "Perhaps too much so. My friend Lord Darius is apparently addicted to opium because of being given too much for too long when injured."

"A dose of opium to help you sleep is scarcely the same thing."

"No, but the pain is easing."

She couldn't insist, so she went behind the sheet and fixed her pad in place. "I'm sorry for being a fishwife."

"Simply a wife. I rather like it. Marital bickering and apologizing. We've had no chance to be a normal married couple, have we? Imagine if we'd married in England in the usual way—we might never have had a time like this. I'd have my valet, you your maid. We'd have separate bedrooms and dressing rooms and only see each other at our best."

Jancy tied the waistband of her drawers.

The usual way. Would they really have to live separated by servants? She didn't want to be slave to some haughty maid who knew far more about fashion than she did.

When she was dressed, she emerged from behind the sheet. "I'll get Treadwell for you."

She put on her cloak and gloves and went on deck. She'd once traveled toward a wilderness that had proved to be not at all as wild as she'd thought. She could only pray that the luxury at the end of this journey would be not so grand. Simon's descriptions of cheerful, crowded Brideswell didn't fit with the cold, servant-ruled life he'd outlined. He must have been teasing her.

She found Treadwell and then sat in Simon's chair to watch the forested shore flow by. Trees, trees, trees. Habitations were few, though an Indian in a canoe glided by at one point, ignoring their existence. What had this land been like when lightly populated by people and without the complexities that Europeans took for granted?

Then an eagle circled, plummeted, and rose with a flapping silver fish in its talons. It had been wild, and still was.

She shivered in the nippy air, out of sorts. She should have expected her monthly, but now she was realizing that there'd be another visit halfway across the ocean. She prayed that she wouldn't be seasick at the same time. And how was she to manage it all discreetly now she had a husband and servants?

Throw away her cloths? It went against every frugal instinct drilled into her by Martha, but she was Jane St. Bride now, who would soon have a terrifying lady's maid. Heavens above, that terrifying maid would have to know about her monthly visitor and perhaps deal with her cloths.

If being a good wife to Simon meant she had to get used to having personal servants, however, then she would do it. She would become as haughty as Mrs. Humble if she had to. As Hal had implied, it was hardly a hellish fate. Most people would love to have servants at their beck and call.

Treadwell emerged from the cabin. "Mr. St. Bride suggests you and the gentlemen eat in the cabin, it being cold today, ma'am."

She went in, finding he'd lit the stove, as well as arranged boxes by the small table as extra seats. Soon the other men joined them for a cheerful breakfast. Then Norton let out a curse, blushed, and apologized, and she was aware of being a solitary woman in the company of three handsome men.

Were there female pashas with male harems?

It was such a wicked thought that she blushed, which made Norton think she was deeply embarrassed, so she assured him she wasn't but then worried that gave the wrong impression.

Laughing, Simon extricated her with a new topic of conversation. Jancy drank her tea, sure that a true lady would not think the idea of a harem of men even slightly exciting.

Of course she actually wanted no one but Simon, but even so, the idea of surveying a group of men like this, all with different charms, and saying, "That one. Bring him to my bed tonight," made her want Simon even more.

In thinking that, she'd looked at him. Their eyes met and it was as if he knew. She looked away, blushing even more hotly, and then stole a glance to find his eyes dancing at her. Perhaps that was why the other men excused themselves, leaving them alone.

"We can at least kiss," Simon said, so she sat beside him, and they did.

"Care to share with me what put that sparkle in your eye?" he murmured against the corner of her mouth.

"No."

"Ah-ah. Something wicked. Tell me. Perhaps I can make it come true."

She chuckled. "I don't think so."

"Now you really have to tell me. I promise not to be shocked."

"How can you promise that?"

His brows rose. "That outrageous? My imagination is running riot. You'd better tell me before I assume worse than the truth."

She pushed him playfully. "Oh, you. Very well then. I was wondering . . . I was there with three fine gentlemen. . . ." His brows rose again, and some bold part of her *wanted* to shock him. "I was imagining a woman with a harem of men."

"Jancy, you treasure! Of course I'd never permit it any more than you'd permit me a harem of blushing damsels, but you are full of surprises beneath your sober plumage."

"I'm sorry."

"No. I like it. You're like a set of puzzle boxes. Each day a new delight, and one day I'll reach the secret heart of you."

Jancy smiled, praying that never come true.

She soon realized that it wasn't going to be easy to keep her secrets. Simon grew stronger every day, but many movements still hurt and he preferred to sit most of the time, either in the cabin or on deck. Hal and Norton joined them for cards but also frequently left them together. Sometimes he read to her as she sewed, but often he wanted to talk—about her.

"Was it strange to move from a large house to a small one?" he asked one day.

The sun was shining so they were on the deck, warmly dressed, watching nature's colorful display pass by.

She had to think how it might be. "We had our own rooms, and Mother and I rarely entered the school proper."

"Didn't she have care of the boarders?"

Help. She'd never thought about these things. "I suppose so. But she didn't take me. I was only just ten when my father died and we left for that smaller house."

"I saw a picture."

She looked a question at him.

"In your room, when I took in wood. Your cousin was very skilled."

Jancy suddenly wanted to talk about Jane, even if in deceitful terms. She missed her so much. "Yes, but houses and landscapes weren't her forte. She loved portraiture. She created quite a stir last year. Our chapel— we attended the Evangelical chapel, not the Anglican church—decided to raise money for soldiers wounded by the war. We held a summer fete, and the minister persuaded . . . Nan"—*Be careful!* She'd almost said Jane—"to do portrait sketches at two shillings a time.

"She took some persuading, for she was shy, but she also had a most generous heart." She smiled at him. "She raised over five pounds, because those who could afford it gave her much more. It was for a good cause, of course, but people were truly delighted. I do believe she could have made it her profession, but as I said, she was shy and then Aunt Martha fell ill."

"Aunt Martha?"

Ice ran down Jancy's spine. "Her Aunt Martha."

He seemed to accept that. "When did she come to live with you?"

Still shocked by her mistake, Jancy hunted through her answer for traps before saying, "When I was ten. She was nine, but our birthdays were only four months apart."

"And she was an orphan from Scotland? No Otterburns up there to take her in?"

This was becoming an inquisition. Did he suspect?

"I assume not. Why do you ask?"

"I merely wondered."

Jancy grabbed on to the well-practiced lie that Martha had drilled into her. She'd lived this story so much that in a way it seemed true. "I gather Nan's father was a black sheep. He gamed and drank himself into disaster, so his family cast him off, and her mother had died when she was young."

"So they sent the 'bad blood' to England."

The words "bad blood" sank into her stomach like a stone.

Simon was enjoying this drifting time apart from life. He grew stronger by the day, and his ribs pained him less. Now that they had leisure, he was learning more about Jane and his old feelings of mystery seemed foolish. He might have seduced her if she hadn't been in her courses, but as it was, he was content to wait, talk to her, and simply look at her.

Not that there weren't problems ahead.

Though she hid it, she was clearly unhappy with the distant prospect of becoming a countess, and not even comfortable with Brideswell. She'd probably prefer a small home like the one she'd had in Carlisle, which made no sense to him.

She was as frugal as a miser. At this moment she was setting neat stitches that made a hole in her coarse stocking almost invisible. Admirable in a cottager's wife, perhaps, but he was used to women wanting to marry into wealth and position, not fearing it.

He looked away and saw a vee in the sky. He pointed it out and smiled at Jane's excited pleasure as the honking geese flapped overhead, heading south. Driven on their appointed course—as were they all. His course was to property, duty, responsibility, and a place in the heart of his world. Her course was now to be by his side.

He didn't want to compel her to anything, but he hoped she'd agree to a new wardrobe soon after arrival in England. She'd be more comfortable if properly dressed. If she wished, she could wear the muted shades of half-mourning, but he longed to see her in sky blue, clear green, and buttery cream.

Or out of them . . .

She turned to him then, and something in her parted lips showed that she'd picked up a message from his eyes. Her lovely blush rose like dawn.

"I hope you never stop blushing," he said.

"I only blush because you're a very wicked man."

"I hope I never stop being a very wicked man. Blame it on the hair."

"The hair?" she asked.

"I must have told you of Black Ademar's hair."

She nipped off her thread with her teeth and re-threaded her needle. "No, I don't think so."

"Another ancestor. Ademar de Braque was a Gascon adventurer who found favor with the young Edward I by his brilliance at jousting. The king was inordinately fond of jousting, and thus Ademar became rich and a great lord and married a fair lady. But he was famous for his 'devil's hair'—black shot through with red, like mine."

She cocked her head at him. "Was he wicked, then?"

"Trust me, my love, any nameless adventurer who rises to fame and glory is wicked. But it's the adventurousness that comes with the hair. Whenever the devil's hair appears in our family, it means the child will be a wild wanderer."

"Like you?" She slid her stocking off the smooth wooden lump she used to sew against and glanced up to tease. "What happens if your fiery hair falls out?"

"Cruel woman."

"Or goes gray?"

"Perhaps that's why we devil-heads tend to cool with time. So, would you want children with the hair?"

She colored again at the mention of children. Their children.

"I hope they all have sunrise hair," he said softly. "A different, gentler fire."

"Or they could be little Trewitts," she pointed. "Solid and brown."

She meant it to disconcert him, so he smiled. "That would be perfect, too."

That night in bed, Jancy lay spooned against Simon's back, pretending to sleep.

Trewitt blood. Ademar's devilish hair. Hereward's urge to fight for justice.

Blood will out.

Blood will out.

Children did take after their parents, or their parents' parents, or their ancestors. She ought to tell him the truth.

But she never would.

Chapter Twenty

*J*ancy rose the next day to find they were approaching Kingston, where they changed to a shallow-bottomed boat that could pass through the tricky water upstream. The talk on the Kingston wharf was all about the harsh weather, and people who had come upriver from Quebec or the Atlantic carried rumors of an early freeze.

A captain reported that the *Eweretta* had been in Montreal five days ago, but ready to sail. Jancy had hoped to visit the shops here for supplies not available in York, but they decided to leave immediately.

The boat could navigate the rapids, but she persuaded Simon to walk around them with her. He appeared recovered, but she knew he still felt some pain and still had trouble sleeping in the night because of it.

"You don't want to risk an accident that could set you back."

As they watched their boat hurtle and swirl through the rapids, she was grateful for their decision but a little wistful, too.

"Jancy," Simon said with surprise, "you wish you were on that."

She glanced at him. "A folly, but yes."

He grinned. "So do I. I've shot rapids for the sheer excitement." When she frowned at him, he shrugged. "It's the hair."

"I think I'll pluck out every red strand."

"Confess, you wouldn't really want me tame."

She pretended to glare and they walked on, picking their way over rough ground. She didn't want him tame, but she didn't want him plunging into any more dangerous adventures, either.

As they passed between more densely populated shores, getting close to Montreal, a flurry of rain turned to hail. Jancy felt everyone's tension. Even though they had passage booked, the *Eweretta* would not risk being trapped by ice.

The tin-roofed city came in sight, startling Jancy with its size. As they approached the harbor, Simon called out to a passing vessel. "Has the *Eweretta* sailed yet?"

And the blessed reply was *"Non, monsieur."*

Jancy hugged Simon—carefully—for joy.

"Not many ships left, though," Simon said, scanning ahead.

The harbor looked busy to Jancy, but she supposed there weren't many grand oceangoing vessels. "I hope we have time to buy some supplies."

"No matter if you can't. The *Eweretta* is famous for providing well for its passengers."

As they worked their way closer, weaving between other boats, she pointed to a tall monument. "What's that?"

"In honor of Lord Nelson. Strange, don't you think, that they've positioned him looking inland? But then, he apparently was plagued by seasickness."

She squinted at him, wondering if he was joking. "Nelson was? Then why become a sailor?"

"It would seem his love of the sea outweighed the pain. Love frequently drives men mad."

He clearly meant nothing by it, but it felt like an ill omen to her. She'd pinned the rightness of her actions on love, hers and his, but was it enough?

They pulled into the riverbank and a rough plank slammed down onto the muddy earth. They climbed carefully down it.

"I wouldn't mind an hour or two on solid ground," she said.

But Simon took her hand. "Come on. Once we've announced ourselves, perhaps we can explore the city."

They'd already decided that she and Simon would walk to the *Eweretta,* while Hal, Norton, and the servants took care of their possessions.

Though it was unlikely the ship would up-anchor and sail before their eyes, they hurried toward the wharf and along it. The *Eweretta* was huge and very grand with its fresh paint and gilding. Even the plank for them to go aboard was solid and had a handrail, with a smartly turned out sailor at top and bottom as guide and guard.

Once on board, however, Jancy saw the main deck had little more free space than the *Ferret* and was as crowded with crates and barrels. Some might be going below, but most seemed to be lashed in place. She saw pens containing animals.

"Pigs?" she asked Simon.

"Roast pork on the trotter."

"Oh, dear."

"Didn't you have fresh meat on the ship you came over on?"

"I fell sick so soon. Perhaps some of the hellish screams I imagined were real."

"Squeamish? But then you're a town girl, aren't you? Used to your meat already dressed."

"I suppose so," she said, remembering helping skin rabbits and gut chickens. Stolen chickens.

A blond, fresh-faced man hurried over and introduced himself as Lieutenant Jolley. Once Simon identified himself, he said, "Very glad you've arrived, sir. We can be off. Kirkby!" he bellowed.

This summoned the cabin steward, whom Jancy knew would be chiefly responsible for their comfort. The steward on the *Wallace* had been a dour young man who seemed to resent anything demanded of him. Kirkby appeared a little old and thin for the job, but he was sprightly and cheerful as he led them directly off the main deck into a large room. Jancy saw what people meant about the *Ewceretta*.

She and Jane had been cabin passengers on the *Wallace*—the ones traveling in style. The *Wallace,* however, had been primitive compared to this.

Kirkby proudly showed off the central common room, or cuddy, and it could have graced a fine home. Three large, curtained windows lit its white-painted walls, and a carpet lay upon the floor. No, she realized, the carpet was painted on, but skillfully done. A carpet would certainly be difficult, for in an ocean storm, water could slosh in here, even over the raised barrier at the doorway.

The thought of ocean storms stirred her stomach, but she commanded it to behave. She'd been fine on the *Ferret*.

A gleaming mahogany table and chairs ran down the center of the room but left space for some easy chairs, a couple of small tables, and a desk. There was also a glass-fronted bookcase and other cupboards with solid doors. The room was warmed by a large stove covered with blue and white tiles. In her cloak and gloves, she was already hot.

Six doors opened off this room, three on either side, and Kirkby opened one. "Neat as you like," he declared, gesturing them into their stateroom.

A way of saying "small," Jancy decided, but their bedroom was still astonishingly elegant, and passengers were expected to spend most of their time in the cuddy or on deck.

Unless ill.

Don't think of that.

This room had only a small porthole for light, but the walls were glossily painted, and a mahogany washstand was built into one corner with a mirror above it. Only hooks were provided for clothes, but there was also a polished wooden chest for their possessions. When closed, as Kirkby demonstrated, it made a convenient seat.

The beds were provided with clean mattresses and bedding, he assured them, but in other respects they were like the ones she and Jane had used on the way out—narrow and one above the other. Suddenly the dirty bed on the *Ferret* seemed like paradise.

"You just let me know, sir, if there's anything you want," Kirkby was saying. "We prides ourselves on our passengers' comfort, we do, on the *Eweretta*."

"I can see that," Simon said. "Are there any cabins with larger beds?"

His eyes met Jancy's with a smile.

"Bless me, sir, but no. We're full, and the two family cabins have been taken by Colonel and Mrs. Ransome-Brown. They have their children with them, you see. Mrs. Ransome-Brown has one room, with her older daughter, her infant, and the governess. The colonel has the other with his two sons and his batman."

"Clearly their need is greater than ours. Whom else do we travel with?"

"Well, sir, apart from your party, we have Mr. Shore, a clergyman, and we're to pick up a Mr. and Mrs. Dacre in Quebec. An excellent company, as I'm sure you'll find."

When he left, Jancy smiled. "Does he protest too much?"

"Perhaps the colonel is a tartar, or his children monsters. Or the Reverend Shore a prosy bore. The hazards of sea travel. I'm more concerned about the beds." He eyed them. "I do believe two people could sleep in one if they had no objection to being very, very close."

Their eyes kissed again, but she said, "Your ribs?"

"Are fine. And besides, you'd stop me rolling about."

"There's a high board on this side for precisely that purpose, sir."

"All the better to tuck us together, my dear. We could test it out. . . ."

Jancy laughed as she drew him out of tempting privacy. "You are to behave. I'm quite in awe of all this and determined to create the right impression."

She said it lightly, but she meant it. The *Wallace* had been a much simpler vessel, and her fellow passengers simpler people. She'd not expected this grandeur and knew she had neither the wardrobe nor the training for it. It couldn't be helped, but she'd insist on best behavior to compensate.

"Perhaps we have time to go to the shops," she said as she led the way out onto the deck. A new bonnet. A fancy shawl. Some pretty caps. Some items to smarten up her plain clothes.

The ship was now a merry dance of sailors doing mysterious things under barked commands. A rotund, rather hard-faced man with short, brindled hair marched up to them. "Captain Stoddard, sir, ma'am. Welcome aboard. If you have no objection, sir, I intend to get under way as soon as your luggage arrives."

Jancy wondered whether to beg for a little time, but Simon said, "No objection. The weather?"

"Reports of freezing in the gulf, sir. No problem if we leave promptly, though I've not seen a year like this. That infernal volcano."

Simon nodded. "Astonishing how widespread an effect an eruption in Asia can have. I gather parts of Europe are in a bad way."

"Aye, sir. I hope it doesn't affect the price of furs. I've summoned the rest of the passengers from shore and I had them on orders to be ready, so we should be under way shortly." As if he could read Jancy's dismay, he added, "You'll find everything of the finest on board the *Eweretta,* ma'am. Fresh bread, meat, eggs."

Jancy realized that clucking and squawking was coming from the longboat that hung the length of the deck. It was packed with crates of poultry.

Somewhere a cow lowed.

"Milch cow and nanny goat," the captain boasted.

"Goat at the request of Colonel Ransome-Brown's lady. She prefers goat milk for her youngsters. If you have any special requests, ma'am, do not hesitate to make them known. We can delay long enough for a last-minute purchase or two if you will allow me to send a man. Can't afford to lose you."

"Do you have a doctor aboard, Captain?" she asked.

"No, ma'am, but the bosun is quite skilled and we keep good medical supplies. And I assure you, you will not find us lacking for such things as fresh fruit and good wines."

She suppressed a sigh. "Then no, thank you, Captain. I think we have all we need."

He nodded and marched away to bark orders at someone.

"He seems eager to please," she said.

"That's because we're his perquisite." When she looked a question, he said, "Didn't you know? The carrying of passengers on a merchant vessel is at the captain's discretion and to his profit. He fits up the accommodation, provides the amenities, and pockets the passage money."

She wanted to ask how much passage on the *Eweretta* cost but didn't even dare.

They worked their way around the busy deck to look out for Hal and Norton and saw them coming along with a small army of barrows. They paused to let another party come aboard, led by a stately lady in a green fur-lined cloak, an enormous fur muff, and a large tartan Scottish cap tilted modishly to one side.

Jancy wanted to slide down out of sight. Mrs. Ransome-Brown, for sure.

Simon leaned to murmur, "A Grand Panjandrum herself."

Jancy saw that the beret had a button on top and bowed her head to hide an explosion of laughter.

When she'd recovered, the lady was aboard, accepting the captain's bow as her due and revealing a sinewy man

behind her, presumably the colonel. He was escorting a
young man and woman who looked to be perhaps twelve
and fifteen but were dressed in the latest adult fashion.
The lad's starched shirt collar covered his ears, and the
girl's flower-trimmed bonnet added a foot to her height.
The procession was completed by a soberly dressed
woman carrying a toddler, a maid with a child by the
hand, and a soldier who was presumably the batman.
They all disappeared into the cabin area.

"Oh, dear," Jancy said.

"What's the matter?"

"She looks as grand as the queen."

"I'm sure she'll be a source of great amusement, she
and her Picninnies, Joblillies, and Garyulies."

Deliberately or not, he was deflating her panic. She
laughed, greeted their friends, and set to arranging what
boxes should go below and what to their stateroom, but
she couldn't ignore the fact that she was plunged into
high society before she was ready.

She hadn't planned to wear her best black on the voyage, but she pulled it out of the chest that was going
down to the hold. She was tempted to keep out some
of her Carlisle dresses, but she knew they'd be too tight,
and even at their best they'd not been up to Ransome-
Brown standards.

She sent the chests away. "Will we keep your papers
here?"

"No, Hal has them. He's sharing his cabin with
Treadwell and Oglethorpe, so they'll keep an eye on
them. It's hardly necessary in any case, unless you think
the Grand Panjandrum was playing Guinevere to
Lancelot McArthur."

It made her laugh, but she wouldn't feel entirely safe
until she was sure that none of their fellow passengers
had links to York.

She was finding a place in their cabin for an extra box
when the ship's whistle blew. She took Simon's hand
and they hurried on deck to witness the end of her time

in Canada. With a noisy rattle, the gangplank came up and was neatly stowed below the rail. Then the *Eweretta* was towed out into the river to begin her great journey home.

Chapter Twenty-One

*T*hey didn't meet their fellow cabin passengers in any formal sense until dinner, which on the *Ewaretta* was to be served at the fashionable hour of five. There would be breakfast at eight, nunch at, of course, noon, dinner at five, and a supper at eleven for those who cared for it. Apart from supper, they were all expected to be at the table on time if they wished to eat because the cuddy had to alternate between dining room and drawing room.

After a struggle, Jancy had decided not to wear her black for the first evening. She wanted to make a good impression, but as she could hardly wear the black every night, there seemed no point. Gentlemen had an easier time of it, she thought. Simon's simple brown coat, fawn pantaloons, and plain waistcoat would suffice, especially when Treadwell arranged a neckcloth for him.

"I can do a tolerable job," he told Jancy, chin raised, "but it still hurts to flex my right arm that much. For a slight wound, it's proving to be more trouble than the ribs."

With dismay, she watched him transform before her eyes. In York, his neckcloths had been soft and casual. Now Treadwell deftly arranged folds and tucks in a stiffer one, and fixed the arrangement with a jewel-headed pin she'd never seen before. What was that golden stone? A topaz?

She glanced at herself in the mirror, in a dress no better than the Ransome-Browns' servant's, her hair simply pinned up and without cap or ornament. She had no ornament, and she knew her style of cap would consign her to the servant class. She pinned the amethyst brooch to the front of her gown and added the pearl earrings. They gave her some dignity.

She turned and found Simon watching her.

"I'm sorry," he said. "I should have thought. I traveled across on a naval vessel."

She liked the fact that he wasn't ignoring reality. He raised her chin with his finger. "You are Jane St. Bride of Brideswell. That is enough."

She smiled. "Very well. Let's face the Grand Panjandrum herself."

The captain presided at dinner, explaining that a pilot had charge of the ship for the first little while. He began the meal with a toast to the *Eweretta* and the company and to a smooth, fast journey to England. They all said, "Hear, hear!" with sincerity.

Then the formal introductions were made.

The colonel, in his scarlet, braided uniform, introduced his wife, in low-necked, dark blue satin and a matching turban set with a feather spray of jewels. *Pasha,* Jancy thought and became terrified of losing her composure. She dared not even glance at Simon. At least her fears about McArthur conspirators were laid to rest. The Ransome-Browns had been in Canada for only three years, all spent in Montreal.

Miss Ransome-Brown was present, in pale pink, with curls clustering around her sulky face, as was Master Ransome-Brown, in an even higher collar and a brightly striped waistcoat. Apparently the younger children and governess would eat in one of the cabins.

A shame, Jancy thought. She felt she might have more in common with that lady.

The Ransome-Browns, the colonel explained, were returning to England to take up a position in London. A smirk on his wife's face indicated that it was an excellent one.

"Reverend Shore," said a tall, thin man with wispy white hair. He looked over seventy and frail. "I have spent my adult life ministering to the Anglican settlers of Quebec, but now age carries me homeward for my final years. I intend to spend the voyage writing my reminiscences from my diaries and notes."

In other words, leave me alone. A less likely McArthur associate was impossible to imagine.

Hal and Captain Norton introduced themselves, and then Simon said, "Simon St. Bride, and my wife, Jane. We are returning home to Brideswell, Lincolnshire."

Jancy had gathered that "Brideswell" was a magic word, and that was confirmed by the way Mrs. Ransome-Brown's bosom expanded. He'd done it deliberately. A kind of raised, warning sword.

Do not discount me or my wife.

If she didn't already adore him, she would have done so then, even if the Grand Panjandrum was staring at her with disbelief.

He added, "We're both in mourning for my wife's uncle, but as he didn't approve of lengthy gloom, we won't cast a damper on the company here."

"Excellent, excellent," said Captain Stoddard. "My passengers generally enjoy card parties, music, and have been known to stage theatricals. All as you wish, of course. Some of my guests prefer a quieter time of it. In clement weather we have even had dancing on the deck, but I fear that will not be on this voyage. Excellent soup, what?"

It was excellent soup, but Jancy's throat was tight.

Card parties, theatricals, and dancing? Before arriving in York the only skill she'd had with cards was in fortune telling. She'd never acted—Martha would have fainted on the spot—and though Martha hadn't actually objected to country dances, they hadn't had occasion to dance any. She suddenly felt much as she had when she'd arrived in Castle Row in rags.

At least conversation became a masculine affair with much talk of Canadian and British politics, economics, and the weather. On the state of Europe, Hal was the best informed and he had bleak things to say about the effect of the cold spring and harsh summer in many parts, adding to the depression caused by the end of the war.

The meal drew to a rather somber close. Reverend Shore retired early, but the rest seemed inclined to linger, talking of these problems, and income tax, and the new currency. Colonel Ransome-Brown was concerned about the fate of ex-soldiers but had no sympathy for what he called the "idle poor."

Simon said, "With respect, Colonel, the newly unemployed can't be thought idle by choice."

"True, true, but there's always some who don't want steady work."

"Very few, I suspect."

Oh, Simon, you should meet my family. Jancy suppressed that thought and then noticed Mrs. Ransome-Brown's attention.

"You are from a York family, Mrs. St. Bride?"

Jancy's heart jolted in alarm, but she said, "No, ma'am. I've been there only a year."

"Ah, so in England, you come from . . . ?"

There seemed no way to avoid it. "Carlisle, ma'am." To get it over with, she added, "My father was a schoolmaster there, but he died some years ago. When my mother also died, I went to live with my uncle in York."

"I see. And now your uncle, too, is dead. How very unfortunate." Jancy heard a suggestion that she was in some way to blame for fate, but no increase in disdain. Perhaps a schoolmaster was respectable.

"And you, ma'am?" Jancy asked. "Where is your family home?"

Not in the north, she prayed.

"Rutland, but we will be purchasing an estate near London, as my husband's position will require him to be there most of the time."

And Reverend Shore was from Devon. She was safe but newly aware of dangers. She'd foolishly imagined that her life with Simon would be similar to her life in Carlisle, within a limited circle, even if it was limited to an important family in Lincolnshire.

But in Simon's world she would meet people from all over. She could, would, meet people from Cumberland, even from Carlisle. The chance of meeting anyone who had known her in Carlisle was remote, but it still set up a nervous twang of alarm.

She was safe on the *Eweretta,* at least, unless one of the officers was a danger, but she would have to prepare for future encounters. To develop some sort of defense. As soon as it was excusable, she claimed tiredness and retreated to the stateroom, where she sat on the chest to think.

She probably was worrying over nothing. The grand society of Cumberland and Carlisle didn't know Jane and Nan Otterburn existed. If one of the ladies had come into Martha's shop—and she couldn't remember such an event—they'd not know who had assisted them. Such people did not attend the chapel.

A knock on the door made her jump, but when she opened it she found only Kirkby offering a steaming jug of washing water. She took it, thanking him. Every luxury on the *Eweretta.*

She poured hot water into the china bowl, telling herself it would be all right. There was no danger, and if she'd read the signals right, Simon would soon be joining her, with lovemaking on his mind. She quickly stripped down to her shift and washed, cradling her own breasts as she soaped them beneath the cotton, her mind sliding toward pleasures to come.

When she was clean, she quickly swapped damp shift

for nightgown and pulled her warm robe on top. She unpinned her hair and teased out the plait, and then sat on the chest to give it its hundred strokes. When Simon knocked and slipped in, she truly felt her heart tremble. In love, in desire, and in fear of ever losing him.

"My wife."

Such simple words to bring everything to the one important point. *Simon.*

"Keep on brushing," he said. "Please. I love to watch you do that."

So she tilted her head and continued with the long strokes as he began to undress. Shoes first. Then jacket, waistcoat, cravat.

"What next?" he asked.

Jancy remembered to continue brushing, even though the strength was leaving her hand. Abbey Street propriety suddenly overwhelmed her. "Your . . . unmentionables."

His eyes danced, but he took off his pantaloons. "And the even more unmentionables?" he asked, meaning his drawers.

"You're a wicked man to tease a lady so. But yes."

In short order, he stripped naked. "Is this less teasing?"

The brush fell from Jancy's hand with a clatter as she rose to take him in her arms. But the light of the one candle shone on his long, jagged wound. She bent to kiss it.

"You nearly died, Simon."

"And would have except for you." He raised and discarded her nightgown and they kissed.

Beyond the door, a burst of laughter made her hide her face against his chest. "People will hear us," she whispered.

"We're married," he whispered back. "We're allowed to do this."

"Even *naked*? I'm sure we're not supposed to do it naked."

She felt his chest shake. "Why ever not?"

She looked up. "You're laughing at me."

"You're being silly. But if you're worrying about the others, you'll have to be very, very quiet, won't you?"

He sat on the chest and drew her to straddle him, and then began to play his mouth over her breasts, then her belly. When she muttered something, clutching, he said, "Hush."

"Wretch."

"Rogue," he corrected.

His left arm supported her, but his right hand slid down her belly and into her slit to find the sensitive spot and circle there. She gasped, and right outside the door, someone—the colonel, she thought—said, "Good night."

She went very still, and again, Simon laughed.

She muttered furiously at him.

"Then don't make a sound."

"Or?"

"Alas, I've forgotten my horses' tails. So scream if you wish, love." He grasped her hips and slid deeply into her.

She managed to keep most of the cry in her throat and cradled his face to kiss him as she clenched around him. Her hips flexed on their own and he leaned back. "Go on."

"Or?" she asked again.

He smiled. "I'll make you scream and embarrass yourself."

She hummed, teasing him, but then rose and rocked, watching his beloved features show the pleasure and torment she was causing him. He gripped her hips and control fled. They could be shaking the whole ship *Ewcretta* like the mightiest storm, but she didn't care and neither did he. But she managed to keep her cries of "Simon! Simon! Simon!" to mostly gasps.

They clung together afterward, she kissing his hair, he nuzzling her breasts, but then cold had them scrambling into the bottom bed. It was a tight fit, but they lay face to face, kissing, stroking, whispering.

She had to make it clear. "I love you more than words can say, Simon. Always remember that."

"How could I forget? Especially as we'll be doing this every night." He raised her leg and adjusted, pressing against her, sliding in again. "It's been so long, my love," he said as he rocked against her. "I'm ravenous for you. Feed me."

His lips sealed hers.

Simon was woken by the steward's little bell announcing breakfast.

He turned in the tight space to look at his wife, all ivory and gold beauty in the thin sunlight coming through the porthole. She'd not plaited her hair before bed, so it tangled around her, and she had crease marks on her cheeks.

He soothed those marks and stroked hair off her face, adoring the smell of her, the feel of her. Her eyes flittered open, confused for a moment and then smiling— as if he were her sunrise. He prayed he would always be worthy of her love.

"We're summoned to eat. Sleep well?"

"Astonishingly well."

"Nothing astonishing about it after all that exercise."

"Stop it."

He grinned. "Yes, my love."

"Don't!"

"Call you my love?"

"Look at me like that. We can't."

The little bell rang again and she hurried out of bed, grabbed her shift, and began to dress. He indulged in watching her, savoring complete happiness, and then followed more carefully.

She stopped, dress half on. "Are you all right? Did you hurt yourself?"

"I am wonderfully all right. I even slept well. But you can help me dress if you're worried."

She shook her head at him but brought his clothes

and dressed him, and then he helped her, and they kissed. The bell rang again, insistently. Laughing, he grabbed her hairbrush and untangled her hair, and then brushed the long length of it. She stilled and he could almost hear her purr.

"So many delightful ways to please you," he said, kissing her nape. He plaited her hair and tied it with a ribbon. "Leave it like that. It's pretty."

She turned to him. "It's childish. I want to look like your wife."

"Oh, you do. I assure you."

She whirled to the small mirror. "Everyone will know!"

"Everyone," he said, turning her toward the door, "will be very jealous."

Chapter Twenty-Two

As the *Eweretta* sailed down the Saint Lawrence, Simon's support and natural confidence shrank Jancy's nervousness. It almost felt as if they were setting a tone for casual dressing, for after that first night, Mrs. Ransome-Brown did not again appear in glossy splendor. Was that the power of Brideswell?

The lady had quizzed Jancy a few more times about her origins. She'd looked down her nose at the Trewitts but accepted the Otterburns as some compensation. She herself was one who needed her escutcheon tattooed on her forehead. Jancy soon knew that the Ransomes were a *very* important family in Rutland, and that she was also connected to the Manners family and the Wallops.

That night Jancy asked Simon who they were.

"Manners, Duke of Rutland. Wallop, Earl of Portsmouth."

"I had a hard time keeping a straight face at thought of the Wallops. Am I supposed to know these things?"

"By rote." But he grinned. "As you can see, people will tell you, directly or indirectly, if they think they're important."

Jancy considered this, which wasn't easy when he was undressing her. She slapped his hand away. "Listen."

"Why?" He began on the pins in her hair.

She twitched away, laughing. "I want to be serious a moment."

"Nonsense."

He kissed her and she kissed him back, but then she put her fingers between their lips. "I do think I need to know some of these things. It's all natural to you, like . . . like types of lace and embroidery stitches are to me. But I know as little about dukes and earls as you do about sewing. You'll have to teach me. It will give us something to do."

His eyes laughed at that, but he freed himself and said, "Very well. The king is our head. . . ."

He worked on her pins and then ran his fingers through her loose hair.

"The royal dukes are your eyes." He kissed the lids of each.

She bit her lip and laughed.

"Your lovely lips are the ordinary dukes. Very important, dukes are, even ordinary ones."

Perhaps that was why he lingered there, teasing her until she grasped his head and kissed as she wanted to.

He trailed his lips down her throat, murmuring, "The mighty marquesses," working on her gown until it fell open and then unfastening her bodice beneath.

A tug on the drawstring of the neck of her shift and her breasts were at his mercy. "The earls, our most ancient nobles, rulers of counties before the conquest."

When his lips settled on one nipple, she held his head there. "Why not counts, then?"

He switched to the other side. "Nasty French things, counts are."

"Why are Earl's wives countesses, then?"

"God alone knows." He pushed her clothes off her shoulders so they slid down, sinking to his knees to explore her navel. "The viscounts. The minor counts, mere newcomers." His tongue swirled.

Her knees wobbled. "I think I have it now. King, dukes, marquesses, earls, viscounts . . ."

"And barons . . ." His tongue traced a line but stopped. "No, that is too wondrous a place for barons, ancient form though that be. They shall be your pretty knees." He kissed each as he untied her garters. "Remind me," he murmured, "to teach you all about orders. The Garter. The Bath."

She clutched his shoulders. "Simon . . ."

He rose to his feet, took her hands, and kissed each palm. "Not lords at all, but not to be discounted. The baronets—knights and their fair ladies."

He brought her hands together and then stepped back. She was naked; he was still mostly dressed.

"Now," he said, "repeat the lesson on me."

So she did, proving she was a very clever student indeed.

The next day she watched the approach of the city Quebec, Canada's capital, without any premonition of trouble.

It looked to be a handsome city, high on the cliff that great Wolfe had climbed with his army to defeat the French sixty years or so ago. Captain Stoddard was still anxious to escape the river, however, so they could not disembark to explore. Supplies were taken on, especially fresh water, and the final passengers arrived.

The Dacres seemed a pleasant couple of about the same age as Jancy and Simon. They were both brown haired and well dressed, but in a quiet way. He had a rather chunky, high-colored face, whereas she was long faced, doe eyed, and pale.

Mrs. Dacre was either quiet or shy, and her husband was exactly her opposite. Everyone soon learned that they were newly wed—the lady blushed—and traveling to his home so that she could meet his family. He had been in Quebec for five years, had an excellent government position, and had hopes of rising higher. She was from a prosperous Royalist family—those who had come north when the Americans had rebelled against the Crown.

He could, Jancy thought, have been unbearable, but

he was so cheerful and good-hearted, and so blissfully in love with his wife, that she liked him. It wasn't until dinner that they all introduced themselves fully to the Dacres.

Simon said, ". . . and my wife is from Carlisle," and Dacre perked up like a terrier.

"Carlisle! A fellow Cumbrian. How splendid!"

Jancy stared at him, so shocked that she feared she'd faint.

He cocked his head, studying her. "In fact, I feel we might have met."

Before Jancy could even attempt to respond to that terrifying statement, he carried on, "But no. Can't pin it down, and I'm good at faces. I'm from the Penrith area myself, but I know Carlisle pretty well. Do you travel there, ma'am?"

Jancy wasn't sure she could force words out of her tight throat, but she managed, "No. I no longer have family in the north, sir."

"Shame, but we'll have to share memories, what?" Then he was off talking about his plans, which apparently required some time in London on government business before he could visit his home.

Simon said softly, "Are you all right? You look a little pale."

"Oh, yes." But she needed to escape, so she said, "No, not really. I think it's the motion of the ship."

In fact it was no different from any other day and she seemed to be tolerating the roll well, but Simon made her excuses and supported her to their cabin. He sat her on the chest. "Do you need anything?"

Feeling like a deceitful worm, she shook her head. "I think I'll just go early to bed. I'm sure I'll be recovered by tomorrow."

He kissed her. "I hope so."

When he'd left she sat there feeling her stomach churn, but it was with fear.

Dacre thought he knew her, but he couldn't! She certainly didn't know him. She hadn't moved in his circles, and a young gentleman like that wouldn't have patronized Martha's shop. He wasn't even from Carlisle.

Her hands gripped each other and she forced terror down.

Hadn't he said he'd been in Canada for five years? If he had met her, or Jane, or both, they would have been children. Surely he couldn't tell one from the other now, and that was the important point.

She sucked in a deep breath. He was no danger, and she couldn't have a fit every time she met someone from Cumberland. She'd already accepted that it must happen. It was him saying he thought he knew her that had thrown her into a panic, but that was impossible.

She was still shaken, however, and went to bed, falling asleep before Simon joined her. She woke in the morning alone. After a frantic moment she realized that Simon was sleeping in the upper bed.

She knew it was only out of consideration for her, but it felt like an ill omen—that her secrets and fears would drive them apart. To overcome that, she climbed up to join him and woke him with intimate attentions. Which seemed to delight him, even if they did almost fall off the high bed.

Despite her every effort, when she went out to face the Dacres again her heart pounded with nervousness, but soon she relaxed. He hadn't recollected overnight that he knew her to be Nan Otterburn. In fact, he didn't mention Cumberland at all.

The days settled again into pleasant patterns.

The Dacres were wrapped up in each other. Jancy hoped she and Simon were less obvious about their feelings but doubted it. People tended to leave them alone.

Reverend Shore spent all his time at the desk in the cuddy, writing. The colonel was usually with his sons, which made Jancy think well of him. The Grand Panjandrum mostly sat in the cuddy reading or sewing, her sulky daughter under her eye. The governess came and went silently with the toddler.

In the evening, some social interaction was expected. Whist was popular, especially with the colonel and his lady. Norton and Simon were the ones most likely to make up the four. Jancy was happy to sit and sew and Hal to observe.

She wondered if he didn't like to use his card frame in front of strangers. When she remembered how Simon could be struggling to manage without his right arm, she shuddered.

Sometimes they had music. Eliza Ransome-Brown had a dulcimer, thank heavens, a pretty voice. Otherwise, it would have been torture. Hal had an excellent voice, too, and was willing to sing duets with the girl. Lionel Dacre played the flute, and Simon—somewhat irreverently, Jancy thought—proved to be expert on, of all things, the spoons. He could take two spoons and play such excellent rhythms with them it was almost music on its own.

One evening, in their warmest clothes, they even danced on deck. Some of the sailors obliged with music and they made a set of eight. Norton partnered Eliza. Jancy supposed dancing, with the gentlemen passing ladies arm to arm, was something else Hal found awkward to do.

She was nervous, but it was a simple dance and Simon guided her. Soon she was loving it. As she spun with him, arm in arm, she said, "This is wonderful! Look at the moon and stars."

He looked up, too, and they almost collided with others. But then everyone was looking at the moon and stars as they danced, and laughing.

But after Quebec the river had turned north, and every day grew colder. When they paused again to take on more fresh water, they saw ice glinting at the river's edge, and that night it snowed. Only a trace was left when they rose, but the dire predictions were correct. The river would freeze early this year, and ships that had dallied in Montreal might not make it to the Atlantic.

It wouldn't trap the *Eweretta,* however. Sails full, she sped into the gulf and toward the ocean, hitting rougher seas. Jancy put on extra clothing and stayed in the fresh, frigid air, despite the fiercer rolling of the ship, praying, praying, praying. . . .

But when the colonel threw up over the rail, her stomach took charge, and she fled to the stateroom and the waiting bucket.

"Jancy, love . . ." Simon tried desperately to think what to do.

"Go away!"

"How can I?"

Jane looked up from the bucket, a disheveled misery. "Go. Go! Leave me alone."

"You wouldn't leave me in York. I won't leave you here. Let me at least wipe your face."

Eyes closed, she said, "If you don't go away, I shall shoot you."

"You don't know how."

"I'll learn. Go!"

Then she retched again.

Simon stood and reluctantly did as she commanded, having to cling to handholds to avoid being thrown about by the turbulent sea. He winced as a particularly vicious roll dragged at his healing wounds.

It was after dinner—which few had eaten—and everyone had retired to sleep. Or to be sick. He heard sounds of vomiting from various cabins. His own stomach wasn't rock steady.

The steward came out of his little room, carrying a bucket of charcoal for the stove. "All right, sir?"

"I am. My wife isn't. How many others are ill?"

"Mr. Dacre, Captain Norton, the colonel, and his

older son." The man lowered his voice. "Testy about it, if you see what I mean."

"My wife's testy, too, but she won't let me tend her."

"That's the way they often are, sir. Seasickness puts even angels in a mood."

"I have to do something. Are there any steerage passengers?"

"Just one family, sir. We don't normally take steerage other than servants, but as there's a light complement of servants this time, Major Beaumont wanting his men with him, the captain took on one family of eight. Respectable enough people who took against Canada when one of them died."

"Any woman I could hire?"

"There's the young widow, sir. Any extra money might be welcome."

"See what you can do. Tomorrow, I suppose."

"Aye-aye, sir." The steward refueled the stove and disappeared.

Simon found himself alone in the cuddy, surrounded by moans and sounds of vomiting. He'd go on deck but for the bitter cold. Jancy was right. People would be better off flying. Perhaps balloons would someday carry people across the oceans. But then, people would probably be air sick.

And where the hell was he to sleep?

He heard a door open behind him and turned just as the ship lurched. He caromed into an easy chair, cracking his ribs against the wooden edge.

"Hell almighty!"

"Sit down, damn you." Hal thrust him into the chair.

Simon was clutching his side. "God, I'm so fed up with this." But then he looked at Hal's empty sleeve. "How petty of me to complain."

Hal shrugged. "Brandy?"

"Yes, please."

Hal went to a cupboard and took out two heavy-bottomed tumblers and put them on the table, managing remarkably well in the tossing ship. Then he took out a silver flask and undid the cap one-handed.

When the brandy was poured, Simon sipped it. "Good stuff." But then something about Hal's movements made him ask, "Are you drunk?" He'd been wrapped up in Jancy, but he thought Hal might have been drinking a lot since the voyage began.

Hal took another mouthful of brandy. "My arm was badly broken, but it might just have been some use to me."

"Ah. Maggots."

"A troubling thought. Brandy helps."

"It could become another kind of infection."

Hal's mouth moved into a bitter twist. "What would they cut off then? Dammit, a leg would have been better. Or an eye. I'm sorry. Not good form."

"What are friends for if not to share grief?"

Hal looked at his glass. "Yes, grief. That's what it is. Do you think I'll be reunited in heaven?"

There was nothing to say to that, so Simon changed the subject. "Jane's turning inside out and I don't know what to do for her. She was badly affected on the way out. Her cousin died of it."

He hadn't admitted that deepest fear until he spoke it.

Hal carefully sat down opposite him. "But Jane didn't die on the way out, did she?"

"No. No, she didn't. But she screams at me every time I go in there."

"That's a good sign of life. Oh, you don't have a bed. Why not cram into my cabin? We've already got one hammock slung for Oglethorpe. Your papers are under the bottom mattress, by the way, if you ever want them."

They seemed irrelevant now. "Abandon her?"

"You'll be more use to her after some rest."

Simon went to ask Jane if she approved this arrangement. Though her response couldn't be described as sweet and loving, it did sound fervently sincere.

*   *   *

The next morning, when Jancy heard the door open, she groaned. She knew Simon meant well, but she couldn't bear him seeing her like this. She'd managed to sleep now and then through the night, and if she lay very still her stomach only churned and ached. She knew she had to be a mess and she knew she'd scream at him again.

Like a fishwife.

Like two Haskett women fighting over a stolen skirt.

"Jane?"

There he was again.

"This is Grace Pitt. She's going to assist you."

Jancy opened her eyes a slit and saw a looming figure, but the door had closed and she thought Simon had gone.

"Grace?" she managed from a dry mouth. She was dying for a drink but she knew she'd throw it up.

"That's right, mum," the woman said in a thick accent that sounded like the Midlands. "I'll take away yer slops, shall I, mum?"

"Yes, please."

Perhaps without that stink in the room she'd feel better. But she knew she wouldn't. She knew the whole course of this misery. Including death.

There was a thumping and a clanking and the door closed again. Jancy simply lay still. She didn't want to die, not now, not when she had Simon. Yet at the same time, she'd welcome death as an escape.

Grace Pitt. Where had she come from? An ungracious-sounding woman, but that was hardly surprising. No matter what Simon was paying her, this was a horrible job. Even tending for Jane, Jancy had found it vile. But she was grateful to have someone other than the overworked steward to help her. Someone who was not Simon.

Perhaps she dozed, for she seemed to wake up to Grace saying, "I've some gruel here they say as you should try, mum."

Jancy wanted to put nothing in her mouth ever again, but she knew that was impossible. "Help me sit up, please."

The woman did so, proving to be big, strong—and pungent. Jancy was sure she stank herself, but her attendant had another sort of smell. The sour odor of a long-unwashed body.

Jancy took a mouthful of gruel, commanding her stomach to stay calm. Grace was short and stocky with an enormous bosom and arms like a strong man's. She was probably about thirty, but the rough square face was impossible to assess. She wore a skirt and laced bodice over a grubby shift in a style of fifty years ago.

Jancy took another mouthful. Perhaps it would stay down.

"Water, please."

"Yer wants to wash?" Grace asked.

"I wants to drink." She hadn't meant to mimic, and the woman didn't seem to notice.

"Beer, then, mum?"

"No, water."

"I wouldn't drink water misself, mum, especially not on board ship. Nasty stuff, water is, especially out of barrels."

The woman had a point, though the water should still be good. But what if drinking stale water caused the sickness?

"I'll try the beer, then."

Grace was back in a moment with a pewter tankard, and she helped Jancy drink. It was small beer, thin and weak, but that was exactly right for thirst and it felt wonderful in her mouth and throat. Jancy sat there, praying, but clutching the bowl in case. Just as she'd begun to hope, her stomach cramped and she threw up again.

Over the next days, every time her stomach calmed, she hoped. Every time she felt the vomit rise, she truly wished she were dead. Even the bells that marked the sailors' days felt like knives through her throbbing head. A shrill screaming one day made her sure some poor soul had given up hope.

"Don't you worry none, mum," Grace said. "They're just killing a pig. Roast pork for dinner t'night."

Jancy threw up again at the thought, wishing the hell-hole called the *Eweretta* would crash on some rocks and bring her happy release.

Memory of poor Jane's fate began to seem a blessing. Death would solve everything. Her wickedness would never be discovered, Simon would be free to marry a lady of his own station, and she'd escape this never-ending torture.

Simon came to check on her every morning and evening, knocking and asking Grace for news. Jancy huddled under the covers praying he wouldn't insist on seeing her, for she knew she was a haggard crone. He never did, and then she wept for being abandoned.

He'd realized he didn't really love her. That she was a lowborn wanton, not suited to be his bride. He was probably wooing Eliza Ransome-Brown, who was connected to the Manners and the Wallops. He wanted her to die. She lost count of the days and waited for death, and even wept wet tears and dry in Grace Pitt's burly arms, praying for the end.

That was, as they said, the darkness before dawn. Jancy woke to a real dawn feeling steadier. Weak as a blind kitten, but in some way settled inside. It helped that the weather seemed calmer and the ship only rolled.

When Simon knocked to check on her, however, she again pretended to be asleep. Her hair was a tangled, sticky mess, and she smelled worse than Grace.

She heard Grace at the door whispering that there was no change, but Jancy knew she'd be able to eat a bit today and keep it down. Tomorrow she might have the strength to get up and move around the cabin. This time she wouldn't have grief to crush her, so perhaps in a few days she'd be almost normal again.

Then she heard Grace say, "She might be a bit touched in the head, sir. She were weeping in the night, and told me she wun't a lady, but a basket!"

Jane was puzzling over that when Simon touched her brow. She knew his touch and her eyes flew open. "Don't. I'm filthy!"

"The question is, are you mad?"

"Don't bend like that."

He smiled his beloved smile, and tears spilled from her eyes.

He wiped them away. "You've been in here ten days, love. I can dance a jig by now. I suppose if you can nag me, you still have your wits. Did you really say you were a basket? What kind? Straw? Willow? Best Leghorn cane?"

Unwillingly amused, she muttered, "I don't know—" But then she stopped, horrified.

Not basket. *Haskett!*

Chapter Twenty-Three

$\mathcal{A}$ child's rhyme came into her mind.

> *A tisket, a tasket,*
> *A green and yellow basket . . .*

Her mind changed it to:

> *A tisket, a tasket,*
> *Your mother was a Haskett . . .*

What else had she said in her raving?

"What's the matter, love? What do you need?"

"Just a cramp," she lied. "I feel so foolish to be ill."

"Remember Nelson. It's nothing to be ashamed of."

His hazel eyes were full of love, but her heart was sour with fear. What else had she said to Grace Pitt? "I feel so weak. Literally, I mean."

"You've hardly eaten for ten days. What about some broth with bread in it? Do you think you could eat that?"

"I'll try."

He kissed her forehead and left.

Even sitting up to eat was a strain, but the broth stayed down, then some gruel, then some tea and toast. By afternoon, she could move around the cabin, though shakily, and that could just have been due to the motion of the ship.

She was intent on getting well so she could get rid of Grace, though she couldn't decide whether to try to find out what else she'd babbled, or ignore it. Clearly the woman didn't think "basket" had any particular meaning.

She looked out of the porthole but quickly turned away from the tilted, swaying view. She clutched one of the bedposts, eyes tight shut, trying not to think of the way the ship heaved beneath her feet. The clamminess started again, but she fought it, fought it, and things settled.

More or less.

She opened her eyes again and almost shrieked at the filthy, matted-haired hag with cracked lips in the mirror.

> *A tisket, a tasket,*
> *Your mother was a Haskett.*

She sat on the chest, panting with effort and panic.

Grace came in, swore, and hoisted her back onto the bed. "Don't you be trying to do too much, mum!"

Jancy obeyed, letting the woman think that it had been moving around that had caused her distress. In a way it had been, but in her frail state she felt as if her deepest shame could be revealed at any moment.

When Simon knocked that evening, Grace whispered to him, "She's eating well, sir. She'll soon be into roast pork."

Jancy's stomach roiled.

"Excellent."

He began to come in. Jancy pulled the sheet over her head, "Please don't. I'm in a horrible state."

"Jane, love . . . Grace, leave us for a while."

Jancy heard the door shut. "Sweetheart, you've seen me as badly off."

"No, I haven't. We bathed you every day."

He leaned closer and whispered, "Would you like me to bathe you?"

Part of her stirred, but she didn't want him touching her when she was like this. "Go away."

"Very well, if I can't tempt you that far, would you like to bathe yourself?"

"Bring me hot water, then."

"I can do better."

She lowered the sheet enough to look at him. "How?"

"Dacre complained of the lack of a shower bath. The *Eweretta* cannot lack anything, so now we have one."

"What is it?"

"A half barrel to stand in and another above with a pierced metal opening to let down warm water upon pulling a string. Very clever design. It uses seawater, but it has rained in plenty, so there's fresh for rinsing."

It sounded like paradise. "When?"

"Don't try to do too much too soon, love. Wait until tomorrow."

"I long to be clean."

"Tomorrow. First thing. I'll arrange it." He went to the door but turned to smile. "Welcome back, my love."

Over the top of the dirty sheet, she smiled back at him.

He left but didn't close the door because Grace was outside. Jancy heard the woman whisper, "Pardon me, sir, but did you call your wife Jane?"

"Yes. Why?"

"Well, sir, when she were at her worst, she called out for a Jane. 'Jane, oh, Jane!' she cried. 'Don't die.'"

A clammy sweat broke out over Jancy's body.

"She must have known some other Jane," Simon said. "At such times our minds can reach back."

The door clicked closed and Grace took up her watching post, sitting on the chest. Jancy lay there surprised her heartbeat wasn't shaking the ship. Twice, she'd as good as declared her deception to the world.

That night she tried to stay awake in case she talked

in her sleep. But then Grace was snoring in the upper bunk and nature had its way. The next she knew was daylight through the porthole with even a bit of sunny brightness to it.

It was a new day and she must face her future. She knew now, however, that it would be as treacherous as the sands of Morecambe Bay—so smooth and unthreatening on the surface, but turning to quicksand when the tide rushed in.

And in her case, the tides would be unpredictable. First there'd been her slips in the way she referred to Martha. Then the arrival of Dacre. Now the babblings of sickness. What would it be next time?

And when would it suck her down?

She was almost too weary to fight, but like a thing apart, her brain began to come up with ways to explain away the inconvenient Jane.

They said stealing became easier each time a person did it. So, it would seem, did lying. Perhaps she could blame everything on Tillie and Martha, who'd made her a liar at a young age. Sick at herself, she wove a new thread into her tapestry of deceit. A childhood friend called Jane—who had drowned. When they were both . . . six. An age a person could remember, but long, long ago.

Carefully she sat up. Grace wasn't in the room, so she climbed out of bed. Her legs felt weak, but that would correct with movement. She staggered over to the chest to find clean clothing. If she had such a thing after what—two weeks at sea? She'd not changed during the past ten days, however, so there was still plenty.

When Grace came in, she sent her to ask that the bath be prepared and then sat to attempt to comb her hair. It was in such a state she wondered if the woman had combed it properly once during her sickness.

Combing out Jane's hair so it lay like silk even as she faded and died . . .

She pulled back from that and worked at the knots,

feeling the filth. Seawater was terrible for washing hair, but it would have to be an improvement.

Simon came himself to say the bath was ready. She would have hidden from him if there'd been any way.

"Where is it?" she asked.

"In the corner of the cuddy, behind the stove. There's a curtain."

"Is anyone out there?"

"Just Shore. Everyone else is on deck enjoying the sunshine. I'll persuade him to do the same for a while."

Jancy gathered her clean clothes, dragged a blanket from the bed to hide in, and scurried to the curtained area.

Half an hour later, she felt like a different person.

The bathing arrangement was surprisingly pleasant and the stove kept the chill off this corner. Every time she pulled a string, a bit of warm seawater poured down on her. Even though her soap wouldn't lather, the smell of it refreshed her, and there was something about scrubbing with warm saltiness that made her feel especially clean. The shower arrangement definitely made it easier to wash her hair.

When she'd finished, she poured fresh water over herself from a jug. It had been heated but had cooled by then and she shivered. She toweled herself dry and pulled on her shift, bodice, and gown, and then combed her wet hair. A small mirror hung on the wall and she checked herself before emerging. Ah, that was better.

No trace of Haskett.

She came out from behind the curtain to see only Simon in the cuddy.

He smiled. "My love, you're alive again."

She went to him with her hands outstretched. "Yes, I think I am. I do apologize."

"Don't be foolish. Grace and Kirkby are cleaning our room, so sit and have some tea."

"I'm afraid that will be quite a job," she said, doing as suggested but braced for questions about the Jane

who had died, or even Hasketts/baskets. She suddenly
wondered if Lionel Dacre knew about Hasketts.

But Simon talked about what had been happening
while she was ill. "We're making excellent time. Stoddard says we might make the crossing in under a
month."

"It might be half over?"

"Yes."

"Was I the only one sick?"

"Not at all. I think we all were, especially in one major
storm, but only you, Dacre, and the colonel suffered
badly."

"I don't think I noticed a storm. Or I imagined it part
of my hell."

He covered her hand with him. "Poor love. Do you
want to keep Grace as a maid for the rest of the voyage?
She'd have to sleep below, but she could come up by
day."

"No." Grace had probably told Simon all she'd heard,
but if there was a way to get her off the ship without
cruelty, Jancy would have paid every penny she owned
to do it. "I don't need a maid. I'm not used to one, and
she is somewhat rough."

He looked more relieved than disappointed, thank
heavens.

"So is all harmony," she asked, "or have factions and
fractures developed?"

"Harmony. Despite mal de mer, everyone's in good
spirits. We have a fishing competition going."

"Who has?" she asked, suddenly blissful to be back,
to be talking with Simon again.

"The gentlemen, though some of the sailors fish in
their off time. We've run into a school of tunny fish.
Enormous creatures, but the young can be about twenty
pounds. We're competing to see who can catch one and
bring it in."

The door opened and Reverend Shore staggered in,
muffled up in a greatcoat, enormous scarf, and a well-

pulled-down hat. He gave Jancy a sour look and disappeared into his cabin.

"How is Norton coping with sharing with him?" she
murmured.

"Easily, I think. He's no trouble to anyone."

The clergyman appeared with one of his journals and
paper and sat again to his work. Simon asked, "Do you
want to take the air?"

Jancy did, but she was already feeling exhausted.
Kirkby came out of the cabin then and announced it was
ready, so she said she wanted to lie down for a little.

As soon as she entered her room, however, a foul
smell hit her. The room was clean and the beds freshly
made. The smell came from Grace Pitt.

What to do?

Grace had probably enjoyed being up here. Despite
the dangers the woman presented, perhaps she should
keep her on out of charity.

She put on a cheerful manner and asked, "Would you
like a bath, Grace?"

The woman reared back. "What? I'd catch me death!"

"I just bathed, and I feel much better for it."

"Time'll tell, won't it? Rotten bad for the skin, bathing is, and in winter, it'll kill yer!"

Jancy could have pointed out that it wasn't winter yet,
but it would do no good. If Grace wouldn't bathe, she
had to go.

She knew Simon would get rid of her if she wished,
but she was a married woman. Dealing with servants
was her job, especially the female ones. Shaking inside,
she said, "You've been a great help to me, Grace. I'm
sure my husband has paid you, but I'd like to give you
a little extra."

The woman's eyes narrowed. "Like that, is it?"

"Like what?"

"Now you've no use for me, you want rid of me."

Though her mouth was dry, Jancy said, "I no longer
have *need* of you, Grace."

"You need someone to help you dress, do your hair and such. Ladies do."

Jancy gestured to her hair and gown. "I'm quite used to taking care of myself, as you see."

She turned away from more confrontation and opened the chest. As she took out her knitted purse, she realized how easy it would have been for Grace to steal from it. Her money seemed all there, however, and she was ashamed of her suspicions.

She rose, took a guinea out of her purse, and offered it. "Thank you."

Grace's eye sparkled at sight of the gold, but as the coin disappeared into her dirty bodice, she gave Jancy a sneering look. "You're no true lady. Anyone can tell that." With that salvo, she marched out of the cabin.

Jancy stared at the door, telling herself that parting shot had meant nothing. Grace couldn't possibly suspect the truth. Nor would she make anything of the things she'd heard. Despite the cold, she opened the porthole to air out the room and then lay under the covers for warmth, but also like a small creature burrowing for safety.

She couldn't lose Simon. She couldn't bear it.

She fell into a doze, to be woken by his kiss. "It's nunch time. You should try to eat a little more."

"I do feel empty."

She climbed out and moved into his arms. "I've missed you so," she said, resting against his chest.

"And I you. No more sea travel for you, Jancy St. Bride."

She looked up at him. "I don't want to trap you on an island."

He smiled. "A smaller one than Britain would be ample, love, when I'm with you."

"For me, too." The bell rang for the meal and she moved apart from him. "All steady."

She went to the mirror to check that her hair was still

in order. It was, but in such a simple style. Grace's words stuck in her mind. "Will I ever be a true lady?"

"You are a true lady."

She turned to him. "You're bound to say that."

"My love, I'll try always to be honest with you. You are a lady and my wife, but yes, your appearance must change. I hope you'll spend a great deal on pretty clothes and accept a skilled lady's maid to assist you with them."

"I'm good with my needle." It was only half a tease.

"But you won't be able to make everything. A true lady has many demands on her time."

He'd said exactly the right thing and she didn't think it was calculated. Unlike her own words, which were always weighed to the ounce.

"I dismissed Grace Pitt."

"I'm not surprised. I'm sorry. There wasn't much choice."

"She did all that was necessary, and heaven knows I was noisome enough company. I paid her off. A guinea. Probably too much."

"She had been paid."

"I guessed as much, but it seemed mine to do."

"Because you're my wife." He touched her cheek. "It's been an unsettled marriage thus far, hasn't it? I promise smooth sailing from here."

"Really?" she challenged.

He laughed. "No, I can't drive away storms, but you won't be sick again, will you?"

"I pray not."

"No miraculous maggots? No folk remedy for mal de mer?"

"As Dr. Playter said, if I knew of anything, don't you think I'd have used it?"

He dropped his teasing. "I'm sorry. I forgot about your cousin. Nan, wasn't it?"

It struck like a blow that he not be sure.

"Now I've said entirely the wrong thing. Jane, I'm sorry. I forgot how much she meant to you."

She found a smile. "It's all right. You can't help it. You never knew her."

"Then why not tell me about her?"

Jancy wanted to talk about Jane, so much it blossomed as agony in her heart, but she couldn't. She couldn't speak the truth, and she couldn't bear to spew lies to Simon. She was going to burst into tears.

"My love, my love, I'm sorry." He drew her into his arms. "I'm a clumsy oaf. We'll visit Carlisle. You can show me where you both played. Your favorite spots. Your old friends. Your mother's grave . . ."

Jancy screwed her eyes shut but wanted to moan. How had she ever thought she could carry this off? "I'm sorry. I'm weak still. I think I'd better go back to bed."

"Of course." He helped her to lie down. "I'll have some food sent to you. Do try to eat."

Jancy lay there with her hands over her face. How could she live like this, having to lie to Simon again and again and again? Never able to talk honestly about Jane. Never able to relax. Could love survive that? She wasn't sure she could.

The steward knocked and brought a tray. She asked him to put it on the chest, unable to imagine eating.

She kept to her room that day, and whenever Simon came in to check on her, she pretended to be asleep. When he came to bed, he "woke" her.

"I'm sorry, Jane, but I'm not sure you should be sleeping so much. Are you sure you're all right?"

Looking into his concerned eyes, guilt and love brought tears to her eyes again. He gathered her into his arms and rocked her. "Hush, my love, hush. I can't bear to see you cry."

"I'm sorry. I'm just so tired. I think I'll be better tomorrow."

He stroked her cheek and kissed her. "I pray so. I want my strong, spirited Jancy back."

For him, she would fly to the moon. "She will be."

"Tomorrow?" he asked, his eyes telling her what he really wanted.

She found the strength to play the game. "Perhaps. If you're very, very good."

"Oh, I will be. I promise."

He undressed, deliberately leaving the candle lit, and desire overwhelmed even fear. She held out her hands to him and he came to her. "Are you sure?"

"Oh, yes. Love me, Simon."

As he slipped into bed beside her and took her into his arms, her need for him, need in every way, was as palpable as the urgent beating of her heart. She turned the lock firmly upon truth. Nothing would ever come between them.

After breakfast the next day Simon insisted that Jancy take some air on deck. Mrs. Ransome-Brown protested that it was too cold, but Jancy declared herself desperate for fresh air. She dressed warmly in both a long pelisse and a waist-length cloak. With a firmly tied-on bonnet, warm gloves, and her muff, she was ready for the elements.

The wind hit brisk and icy, but she laughed with delight. "Oh, that feels wonderful!" She tilted her head back farther and saw a sailor high in the rigging. "I don't know how they can bring themselves to do that."

"A head for heights," he said. "Should I confess that I climbed up to the crow's nest on the voyage out?"

She turned a frown on him. "You're not to do it this time."

"Or you'll whip me with horses' tails?"

She fought a smile. "No, with ribbons and silken thread. And I, sir, do have some of those in my luggage."

He wriggled his brows. "I can't wait."

Laughter escaped and she turned away to look out at the silver sea, trying not to think of how deep it was, and how frail even a ship like the *Eweretta* was by comparison. Simon came up behind her and put his arms around her, resting his head against hers. She felt warm, safe, and perfectly content.

"I missed you so much, love. Despite all the strife, we've hardly been apart since our wedding. If I have my way, we will never be apart again."

She covered his hands with her own. "That sounds perfect."

He rubbed his head against hers. "Who was the other Jane? The one you fretted about. Tell me, love. I want to share all your sorrows."

Quicksands sucked at her feet.

Chapter Twenty-Four

Jancy fought tears. Why now, at this idyllic moment? Eyes closed, she produced her lie. "A childhood friend. She drowned."

"I'm sorry."

Some force led her to turn and elaborate, as if a complex lie was less wicked than a simple one. "She drowned in the river. In Carlisle. We'd slipped away from home and were playing at the edge, trying to catch sticklebacks. She fell in. I screamed for help. Some men dragged her out."

Then some truly demented force took control. "They were Hasketts. Nobody likes Hasketts. Decent people, I mean. I suppose Hasketts like Hasketts." She was babbling and couldn't stop. "They're dirty and thieving, but they were kind to me. They tried to save her. But she died."

She stood there, appalled, but deep inside a part of her was bubbling to be able to speak a truth about her childhood family.

They were kind to me.

They would try to save a child from drowning.

In their own Haskett way, they were good people.

She'd fallen into the Abbey Street way of seeing things—if people were footloose and dirty, they had to be wicked. But she knew now that it wasn't true. Not in the real sense of wicked. Not as clean, home-owning McArthur had been wicked.

How could she not have known how strangling her long denial had been?

"I'm sorry," Simon said. "That's obviously still a very distressing memory." He took her gloved hand. "A friend of mine, a cousin, died. We were eight, not six, but playing. Simply playing in a hayloft. He fell. A rotten ladder shattered and—he was impaled. I've seen many other deaths, but I will never forget that one."

Jancy gripped his hand. "Oh, Simon, I'm so very sorry." She meant it in more ways than one. His painful memory was true and hers was an entire fabrication.

He smiled. "It was long ago. Then he looked beyond her and turned her. "The tunny are back!"

A huge silvery blue shape arched out of the water, then another, and another. Simon took her hand. "Come on. Hal and Norton are fishing on the other side."

They ran around the longboat to where Hal and Norton were fishing. Or rather, to where they were leaning against the rail in conversation while holding the wooden frames around which fishing line was wrapped, the rest of it trailing in the water.

"Wake up, you two," Simon said. "They're back."

The two men took a firmer grip on their frames. A memory popped into Jancy's head. Playing with similar frames—a hand line it was called. Children whiling away summer afternoons dangling their lines into streams. The best she ever remembered catching was a useless little gudgeon. They hadn't been allowed to play where they might catch trout, salmon, or pike. That was poaching territory. Hasketts might use their children for begging, but they guarded them from serious trouble with the law.

Hal shouted as his hand line jerked and he began to turn it with his wrist, reeling in the taut line. Simon rushed to help. Jancy wondered if Hal might object, but he was grinning as they worked together. Then it snapped, staggering them both backward.

"Too big," Simon said, grabbing a new hook and a piece of meat. He fixed it to the line and Hal let it down into the water again.

Jancy hung over the rail, watching the great fish flicker beneath the water and sometimes leap out. "They're all too big."

"There are small ones," Simon said. "The colonel caught one yesterday." His attention was on the water and the line, but she didn't mind. Not at all.

Abbey Street might not have taught her much about men, but her Haskett days plus her time with Isaiah had. This was Simon's ordinary life, enjoying sport with friends, and she wanted it for him. Ordinary life for both of them. Surely that wasn't too much to ask?

Colonel Ransome-Brown rushed out with his son to try to catch another fish. Dacre was close behind. Even Reverend Shore emerged to observe. Bait was snatched, but lines snapped. Then Norton began to reel one in.

"I think I can handle this one!" he cried, gritting his teeth as he fought the fish and the fish fought back.

It flashed out of the water, big and strong, but tiny by tunny standards. Perhaps only a couple of feet long. That was big enough for a fierce fight, however, and the men gathered to help as Norton slowly hauled it in. The colonel reached over with a big hook to help bring it over the side. Norton slammed the fish on the head with a mallet to kill it.

Everyone, including the sailors and even the captain, let out a mighty cheer.

That evening, the whole ship enjoyed the results. The cook baked the tunny over a fire on the deck, and it was quite meaty, not like the fish Jancy was used to, but delicious. She made sure Grace Pitt and her family weren't forgotten in the treat. The captain proposed a toast to the fish and the hero who'd caught it. They all raised their glasses and Captain Norton colored, but with pride.

Talk turned to ports of arrival. The *Eweretta*'s destination port was London, but it had already been arranged that she would put in to Plymouth to let off Mr. Shore, whose sister lived nearby, and Simon and his party, in order to visit Lord Darius.

Jancy asked the captain, "Why do so many ships sail around to London? Why not use western ports such as Plymouth or Bristol?"

"Transportation, ma'am. There's the old saying 'All roads lead to Rome,' but today, all roads lead to London. Now, it's different if goods are going to or from the west or north; then Bristol, Liverpool, or even Glasgow are more appropriate."

"Sailed from Glasgow outbound," Dacre said. "We'd be sailing back there if not for commissions in London."

"We sailed from Glasgow, too," Jancy said.

"We?" asked Mrs. Ransome-Brown. Why did the woman always seem so suspicious? Was dull clothing a sign of sin in her eyes?

"My wife traveled with a cousin," Simon intervened, "who sadly died. I mentioned her when Jane was sick."

"Ah, yes, you were both Miss Otterburn at the time."

Lionel Dacre exclaimed, "Otterburn! Never say you're old Otter Otterburn's daughter, Mrs. St. Bride? Little Janey? But of course you must be. *That's* why you look familiar."

Jancy stared at him, straining to keep a smile on her face.

Was this it, then?

Here, in public, where she was trapped by the endless ocean?

Say something.

But he chattered on. "You won't remember me, of course." He laughed. "You were a young thing when I went on to Sedbergh."

Of course she had been. Or Jane had been. Jane had been only ten when her father died and the school was sold. At that time, Jancy was still with the Hasketts.

Breathe.

"You and your mother attended prayers each morning," he reminisced. "I remember your pretty hair. I did hear about Dr. Otterburn's death. My condolences. I say, I hope you didn't mind my using that old nickname. Schoolboy nonsense."

"Not at all, sir."

Jancy was still braced for the ax to fall, but he started to tell stories about her father that needed no input from her at all. A reprieve, but she bleakly knew that execution was still likely. Inevitable, even.

She'd persuaded herself that there was little danger of meeting people whom she'd known well in Carlisle—but she'd overlooked the school. Many young gentlemen of Cumberland, Westmorland, and northern Lancashire had spent a year or two at Otterburn's before going on to grander schools. Simon's world could be full of them.

Desperately playing her part in the conversation, Jancy tried to imagine what an ex-schoolboy might know or say that would trip her up. There were so many details of Jane's early life that she didn't know. Her toys, her pets, Martha's baby name for her. Dacre had referred to her as Janey, and she'd told Simon Jancy was her baby name. Had he noticed?

Simon took her hand beneath the table. She knew he thought she was distressed by sad memories, not fear.

Conversation had moved to principles of education, so she concentrated on appearing carefree. *See,* she tried to tell herself, *you have met one of those young men and all is well. What notice would a schoolboy take of a child?*

She made herself believe it and was almost calm by the time the meal ended. Everyone rose so Kirkby could clear the table, and she was thinking she could make an excuse to retreat into privacy, but Dacre came over.

"I don't wish to impose, Mrs. St. Bride, but I wondered if you still executed portraits."

It was as if a great stillness settled around her. For

far too long her mind was empty, but then she managed, "I'm sorry . . .? Oh, no. It was not I, sir, but my cousin who was the artist. However did you know about that?"

He seemed taken aback. "My apologies. I could have sworn . . . I have a picture of my sister, you see, sent to me last year, and I thought you might do one of my wife. Here, let me get it. I'm sure everyone will be interested, for it is so excellently done."

He was gone before she could protest, and how could she? But she was icy and unsteady. Thank heavens Simon was setting up the card table and unaware of any crisis. She sat in one of the side chairs, fighting faintness.

If she insisted Nan had been the artist, surely Dacre couldn't contradict her. He couldn't be *sure* of such a detail, especially when he hadn't been there. She was trying to remember if Jane had signed those charity drawings. Surely not. She hardly ever signed her work.

This wasn't the end, then. Only yet one more battle to fight.

But if the limited world of the *Eweretta* held such traps, what would the whole of Britain hold? Many of Jane's pictures, for a start.

Dacre came back with a framed picture and announced, "I have a treat for everyone. A drawing executed by Mrs. St. Bride's cousin!"

He related the story of the young artist doing pencil sketches to raise money for the soldiers and displayed the picture on the desk. Everyone gathered to look, and Jancy felt she must go, too. It was small, as were all the ones done at the fair, but even without knowing the sitter, Jancy could tell that as always Jane had caught the likeness. A shy, nervous smile and a kind heart.

All present voiced their admiration.

Then Simon said, "We have more. Would you mind sharing them, my dear?"

Numbly Jancy said, "No, of course not." If doom was to strike, she wanted Jane to get her due.

He brought back the portfolio and everyone sat at the now cleared table to pass them round.

"A remarkable talent," the colonel said.

"A sad loss," murmured Norton.

"You were something of a hoyden," stated Mrs. Ransome-Brown, looking at the picture of Jancy in the tree. "Ah," she added, picking up the self-portrait. "The artist." She looked from the picture to Jancy and back again. "A remarkable resemblance between cousins."

As usual, it carried a hint of suspicion, but no one, not even the Grand Panjandrum herself, could suspect the truth.

Jancy said, "Yes, we were often mistaken for each other by those who didn't know us well. Our coloring was exactly the same."

The lady produced a lorgnette and peered at Dacre's picture. "What tiny initials. JAO. What was your cousin's name?"

Jancy's head went hot, her hands and feet cold. There was only one thing to say. "Jane Anne Otterburn, ma'am. We were both called Jane Anne Otterburn."

The lorgnette was turned on her. "A remarkable coincidence."

"They are Otterburn names, I understand."

"How very confusing it must have been."

"That's why one of us was Jane, ma'am, one Nan."

She braced for the next blow, but when it came, it was from an entirely unexpected direction. The pictures went the rounds, were admired, and then arrived at her to be put away.

That was when Jancy realized that before Simon brought the pictures out, he'd removed the one that showed their simple Abbey Street house. The picture with the sign in the window saying *Mrs. Otterburn. Haberdashers.*

For all his grand words, he was ashamed of even that minor failing.

She tied the portfolio and then excused herself.

She stood in the small room, still and hopeless. How had she ever thought her lies could hold? In York, especially living quietly, there'd seemed no danger. Perhaps that had lulled her.

For a while, the ship had seemed equally safe, even when Lionel Dacre turned out to be from Penrith. In fact that had reassured her, proving that even people who knew Carlisle posed no threat.

But the *Eweretta* was Simon's world in miniature. They would not live quietly but in the midst of a world full of Grand Panjandrums with nothing better to do than scrutinize every detail of her life, men like Dacre who'd attended her father's school, and all the people who treasured Jane's charity sketches.

Dear God, Simon wanted to become a Member of Parliament.

She remembered the captain saying, *"All roads lead to London."*

She couldn't stop her mind from reeling out a scene. Some elegant London party, attended by Simon's eminent friends and all sorts of important people. Someone bringing over the Member from Carlisle and the Member's wife.

"Ah, yes. I remember you from Mrs. Otterburn's haberdashery, Mrs. St. Bride. You were the Scottish cousin, were you not? So good of Mrs. Otterburn to take you in."

It was so clear to Jancy that she sat on the chest, as faint as if it were happening now. She could argue that it was unlikely that the wife of a Member of Parliament would patronize grander shops, and that even if such a lady had once visited Martha's haberdashery, she wouldn't remember who had served her.

But she'd reached a breaking point.

She could not live like this, and more important, she and Simon could never build a good life on such shifting sands. She must confess to him. About the switch, at least. If he could understand, could forgive, then perhaps they could fight this together, but she couldn't do it alone any longer.

But—she didn't know if it was cowardice or true concern—not yet. How could she hurl such a thing at him when they were trapped here by the ocean, pinned under scrutinizing eyes? He would have no escape.

As soon as they reached land, however.

As soon as.

Agonizing though it was, her decision eased her, but there were ramifications. They must not make love again. It would feel in some way dishonest, but above all, they must not risk a child. Simon must be free to decide what was best, and a child would bind him to disaster.

It was possible that she was already with child, but she doubted it. Could a baby take root in a body during such protracted illness? And they'd made love only once since her recovery. Her courses should start again at any day, and then she'd know for sure.

If they didn't . . .? She'd have to reassess, but until then she must be resolute.

She couldn't imagine how to reject him, so she hurried out of her clothes and into bed. When Simon came in she pretended to be asleep, face burrowed into a pillow damp with tears. He climbed into the upper bed.

Her trickster mind did not give up easily. She lay awake for hours, but no amount of frantic thought brought her a miraculous solution. When she did sleep she dreamed of a storm, of the ship springing leaks and taking on water. She ran frantically from place to place, trying to patch the holes, but new ones kept spurting and no one came to help.

"Jancy, Jancy, hush . . . ."

She woke to Simon holding her, comforting her, tucked behind her in the narrow bed.

"I dreamed of a storm," she gasped, holding his strong arms to her heart, shattered by what was to come.

He stroked her. "It has turned a bit rough. But nothing serious."

"How can you tell?"

"No sounds of urgency on deck. Go back to sleep, love. You're safe. I'll never let anything hurt you."

Oh, my love, my dearest treasure. If only I could say the same to you.

She couldn't sleep again, so as soon as daylight shone in, she slipped out of bed. If she stayed, she knew, he'd want to make love.

She dressed with some difficulty, for the ship was tossing in the strong wind. Even so, she put on her cloak and gloves. She needed fresh air, as if it might scour her clean.

When she went into the cuddy, Kirkby was setting out pewter plates for breakfast, balancing like an acrobat. "Nice brisk morning, ma'am," he said cheerily.

Jancy clutched at a chair for balance, thinking that the steward had an optimistic term for everything. She expected that one day he'd say, "Lovely bit of hurricane today."

What would he say about her affairs?

Interesting bit of a pickle you're in, ma'am.

She went out on deck but had to stay within the shield of the overhanging poop deck, for the wind was wild and occasional waves slapped over the deck. The sailors staggered about their work, drenched, and the poor cow and goat were mooing and bleating their complaints. Clearly nature was in sympathy with her situation. Or howled in horror at her wickedness.

The door opened. She looked over her shoulder to see Simon in his greatcoat. "What on earth are you doing out here?" he demanded.

"I wanted some fresh air."

He looked as if he was worried about her sanity, which wasn't surprising. He took her arm and dragged her back inside. It was the first time he'd truly compelled her to do anything. He steered her roughly back into their cabin but then took off her cloak and wiped her face and hair with a towel. She'd forgotten a bonnet and not pulled up her hood.

"What is it, love? Are you feeling sick again?"

Grieving, she took the escape offered. "Perhaps a little. I don't want breakfast."

"Then go back to bed." He unfastened her gown with skill grown from experience, stripped her down to her shift, and tucked her under the covers. "I'll bring you some sweet tea. And some bread and jam. Try to eat, love, please.

Chapter Twenty-Five

*S*imon took Jancy the food but had no appetite himself, so he returned to the howling winds and the whip of cold, wet air, frantic with fear. Jancy had become like breath itself to him. Essential.

The long days of her illness had felt like an eternity in limbo. He'd hated to know she was suffering and be unable to do anything. Though he'd told himself that she couldn't die of seasickness, that her cousin had to have been particularly frail, he'd been deeply afraid. Once she recovered, he'd thought all would be well.

Hal joined him, taking a firm grip on one handhold. "Trouble?"

Neither of them had bothered with hats, which would have been pointless in the wind that slapped their greatcoats about them.

"Jane," Simon said. "Perhaps it's just seasickness, but I don't know."

"Sea travel is hard for the ladies. Even on the *Ewer-etta* it's a rough life with little privacy, and this weather . . ."

"I don't think that's it." Simon was sure it wasn't, which was part of the problem. "Do you trust Blanche?"

"Of course."

"I don't mean to be faithful. I mean with everything."

"Of course," Hal repeated. "You don't trust Jane? Why not?"

"I don't know." Simon rocked with the ship's sudden lurch. "That's what's driving me demented. She's done nothing wrong, nothing. Yet I feel . . . I don't know, full of doubts. How can I love someone and feel like that? And I do love her. The lightning has struck. I feel"—he looked up the tall masts to the rigging and mighty sails— "like canvas without wind when away from her."

"Yes." After a moment, Hal added, "I saw the way she tended to you when you were ill, Simon. It was not the behavior of a dishonest woman."

"Does that make sense?"

"I think so."

"But what about maggots?"

"What *about* maggots?"

"How did she know about them?"

Hal stared at him. "You're accusing your wife of heaven knows what because she saved your arm with maggots?"

"No. Yes. No! I simply don't understand how she knew."

"Ask her."

"She says she knew someone interested in folk cures. Is that enough to cause her to stand firm against a doctor and risk my life?"

Hal rocked with the heaving ship for a while. "When you put it like that . . . But it's hardly a black sin."

"It's part of so many things. You didn't know Jane before Isaiah's death. She acted like a middle-aged nun. Again, not a sin, but I know now that was an act. It isn't who she is. I much prefer the real Jancy, but I can't stop wondering *why*. And now she's becoming peculiar again."

" 'Jancy'?"

Simon thought of all that the name Jancy meant to him. "A baby name. She likes it, for private moments."

"Didn't Dacre say that at the school they knew her as Janey?"

Simon considered that but shrugged. "An easy error.

What do you remember about the masters' families from your school days?"

"One had a very pretty daughter," Hal said with a smile.

"Not, I assume, a child."

"No."

The wind was dropping. It still dragged at hair and clothes but in a tamer way. Shouted commands caused new activity up in the rigging. The *Eweretta* settled beneath his feet and then surged forward. A marvelous machine, a ship, and how nice to be a captain, able to control it with ropes like a puppet master.

"Did Jane's uncle perhaps prefer her to be quiet and subdued?" Hal asked.

"The very opposite. When she arrived in York she was sick from the voyage and in mourning for her mother and cousin, so he understood her quiet ways. But by spring he was hoping to buy her pretty clothes and take her to dances. He'd have loved to see her the belle of York, but instead she became his housekeeper and sometime clerk."

"Shy?"

"What do you think?"

After a moment, Hal said, "No."

"Then what's the matter with her?"

Hal shifted to lean more comfortably. "Last night, I thought she might be frightened of something."

Simon frowned. "Of what? Of McArthur I could believe, but he's dead."

"I sit opposite her while you sit beside. She looked alarmed."

"When?"

"I'm not sure. When she was talking to Dacre, perhaps. About the north."

A suppressed worry uncoiled in Simon. "I have wondered if she did something there. Something she's ashamed of. I can't imagine it can be too terrible, but I need to know. . . ."

"Then get her to tell you."

"With thumbscrews? She's like a locked box."

How long was it since he'd thought of that image? He'd believed the box open and revealing only wonders.

"She could simply be afraid of what's to come," Hal said. "Blanche is a very different case, but she's shown me how exclusive our world can be. Perhaps all worlds. We each live in a kind of sphere composed of family, friends, and those we naturally meet in our activities. But each sphere is as limited as a glass ball. Most people never go beyond to meet those whose ways are strange.

"The army stirs things to some extent. It's hard there not to learn about men whose lives and interests are completely different. Travel can be a shock, which is probably why so many people try to travel firmly within their secure sphere. But perhaps we all fear the strange. Look at this ship. How much have we mixed with the officers, never mind the crew?

"Blanche's world isn't mine, and mine isn't hers, even though she's moved in high circles for years. We each still take things for granted only to realize that the other doesn't. Sometimes it seems that we speak different languages. I, of course, want her to learn to speak mine, but why should she, any more than the Iroquois or the French *habitant* should learn English?"

"Because people have to be able to talk to each other?" Simon asked, trying to understand what Hal was saying.

"Shared words don't always have shared meaning." Hal grimaced. "I don't know. I think my point is that until a short while ago Jane's sphere was entirely different to yours. I don't suppose she minds moving into yours, but it won't be easy for her. What's normal and natural for you is not so for her, and many will be like Mrs. Ransome-Brown, regarding the invader with suspicion. I'm sure Isaiah Trewitt was a noble soul, but the Trewitts aren't what our world considers admirable."

"They're solid, honest stock."

"Confess it, Simon. You're worried about what your family will say."

Simon sighed. "No. But I worry about what they'll *think*. It will all work out, however, as long as she stops her peculiar behavior. If she carries on as she is, they'll think I've married a madwoman."

After a moment, Hal asked, "Are you worried that you have?"

It was the point Simon had been both circling and avoiding. He knew his silence was revealing.

"Wait until we land," Hal said. "It's not surprising if ships distress her, and it's an uncomfortably tight sphere. Stoddard seems to think we'll sight land within the week."

It was as if a clenched fist inside Simon relaxed. "Thank you. That's exactly what I should do. For some insane reason I've been feeling I have to sort out everything before we arrive." He smiled as he added, "She's a wonderful woman."

"Yes."

Simon grinned at his friend. "Of course, I'd have to knock you down if you disagreed."

"Remember," Hal said, "that the same applies to Blanche."

Jancy had eaten the tea and bread, and perhaps something in her stomach did help to bring her back to earth—quicksand earth, though it be. She wanted to hide, but clearly that was impossible. Therefore she would face everyone and for Simon's sake try not to appear insane.

She dressed, took up her sewing, and went out into the cuddy. A number of people were there—not Simon, she instantly noticed. She headed for a chair by Mrs. Ransome-Brown, but Lionel Dacre dashed over. "Feeling a bit queasy again, Mrs. St. Bride? Come and sit with Rebecca and me."

She couldn't think how to refuse, and avoiding him completely was impossible, so she went with him to one end of the table, where Rebecca Dacre was also sewing.

Rebecca looked up with a smile. "Very rough, isn't it? I can't imagine venturing out on the deck."

Jancy sat and took her needlework out of its bag. She was keeping her flaming handkerchief for private moments, which meant she wasn't making much progress with it. For now, she would embroider a plain S on another. "I did go out for a moment, but it was too much for me."

"We're making excellent time, however," Dacre said. "Soon be home. Fancy you being from Carlisle, Mrs. St. Bride. I've been telling Rebecca about the school. Not a bad place . . ."

Jancy fiddled with her sewing, not wanting to set stitches that her unsteady hands would make a mess off, but gradually she relaxed. He wasn't at all interested in quizzing her but only in telling yet more stories to his adored wife. All he seemed to require from Jancy was an occasional, "Yes, I believe so," or "That's true." She even became comfortable with, "I don't remember."

It was a soothing interlude. His chatter confirmed that the schoolboys had seen Jane only at morning prayer. Jancy worked on the plain monogram as she tried to store away details that might be useful one day. In that impossible one day when she and Simon faced the world together, confident that the deception would hold.

Simon came in from the deck with Hal, his devil's hair wet and windblown, his cheeks damp with sea spray, his hazel eyes moving immediately to hers. She smiled, partly to reassure him that she was well, but also because she couldn't help it. Love truly did blossom like a rose, even in a storm, even in a desert.

His answering smile came more slowly but then deepened. When he went into their cabin, she watched until the door closed.

"You love him very much," Rebecca said softly.

"As you love your husband." Dacre had risen to speak to Hal.

"It is a special blessing God sends to us, isn't it?" She glanced at Jancy's sewing. "You do beautiful work."

"Thank you." Jancy looked at Rebecca's work and smiled. "For a baby?"

Rebecca blushed. "Yes."

"Unfortunate on a voyage. Are you well?"

"Very. I wasn't even sick in the early days, whereas Lionel was. I joked that he was suffering in my place."

"How long will you stay in England?"

"We intended to return on the *Eweretta* in the spring, but that is about when the baby should arrive, so we'll wait. Probably in London, for Lionel will be employed there for a while." Rebecca smiled at Jancy. "Perhaps you and your husband will be there in the spring. I understand many people go there for the Season. Of course, I will be in no state to enjoy it, but if you are there, I hope you'll visit us."

"Of course," Jancy said. By spring everything would be settled, one way or the other.

"I'm very happy we have peace at last," Rebecca said, setting neat stitches. "I want my child to be born into a world of peace."

Jancy smiled. "Amen."

"Amen, indeed," Dacre said, having caught the last of the conversation. "A world of peace and prosperity. I make no secret, Mrs. St. Bride, of wanting to found a dynasty in the New World. There's land and opportunity for everyone. Canada and America will reach the Pacific within decades, mark my words, and we will be part of it." He rested a hand on Rebecca's shoulder. "We and our children."

Jancy made a fastening stitch and cut her thread, sighing for Simon's cause. No mention of land for the Indians in Lionel Dacre's all-too-plausible plans.

It hurt that she probably wouldn't be by Simon's side to console him.

And that tonight, she would have to again find a way to deny him simpler comforts.

But that night, Simon took her hands. "Jancy, dear heart, I don't think we should make love again until we reach land. You're clearly not well," he said quickly as if fearing an argument. "It's not that I don't desire you— I'm sure you know that. I just don't like to see you distressed."

"I'm not distressed by the thought of making love, Simon. Truly."

"Then can you tell me what is upsetting you?"

Why had she protested? She grasped the excuse he'd offered.

"Perhaps it is that I'm still not recovered." She stroked his cheek. "It might be worth the wait. Imagine how it will be. Steady ground. A big bed. Freshly laundered sheets. A bath using copious amounts of water."

But I'll have to tell you first, so this is only a dream.

"A wedding night. I never did complete my courtship of you, did I? So let it be as if we're stepping lightly toward our appointed wedding night, each day building anticipation. I will shower you with gifts."

"How?" she asked, amused despite everything. "You're somewhat far from a shop."

"I am famous for my ingenuity."

Jancy blinked but couldn't clear tears. "You are the most wonderful man."

"Far from it, but I love you, Jancy St. Bride, and I hope you love me."

What could she say but the truth? "With all my heart and soul."

He rested his head against hers. "Then how can we come to grief, no matter what the storms?"

Chapter Twenty-Six

As there was no escape and no point in showing a sad face, Jancy threw herself into acting the unworried lady. She sewed with Rebecca, listened to Mrs. Ransome-Brown's accounts of grand occasions, and cheered the men during a shooting match. She also wondered what Simon would do about courtship gifts. Remembering the leaf, she half expected a fish.

Instead he took her to a quiet corner of the deck and gave her a pale rose. It was wood—pine, probably—neither painted nor varnished but delicately carved. Her vision blurred. "Where did you find it?"

"One of the sailors makes them. Next summer, my love, I'll shower you with real roses. There's a white one with a sweet smell that rambles near the stables at home."

There would be no Brideswell roses for her, but she would have this to treasure.

She wanted to reciprocate, so the next morning she woke early and slipped out into the cuddy to finish her flaming handkerchief.

She was enjoying the peace and quiet, but then Miss Ransome-Brown came out of her cabin, yawning, in a frilly robe over her nightgown. Jancy thought that inappropriate, but the sulky girl wasn't hers to instruct, thank heavens.

"What's that?" Eliza asked. "A colored handkerchief

for a gentleman? How peculiar. And"—she leaned closer—"flames?"

"It's a joke between my husband and me."

"Oh." The girl sat beside her. "Do gentlemen like jokes?"

"Of the right sort," Jancy said.

"We're going to London, but Mama says I may not take part in any formal entertainments for *years*." With disgust, she added, "I'm to be sent to *school*."

"You might enjoy it. Girls of your own age."

Eliza cast her a disbelieving look. "Captain Norton is handsome, isn't he? Of course, Major Beaumont is more tragic."

Jancy hoped Hal didn't hear that. She'd never spoken alone with the girl before and clearly hadn't missed anything.

"But both nearly twice your age," she pointed out.

"Fie for that. I like older men. I must admit that I prefer a *whole* man, but Captain Norton lacks prospects even though he's well connected."

Jancy stared at the shallow-minded twit.

"You're very lucky to have caught Mr. St. Bride," Eliza went on, oblivious. "Mama says he will be an earl one day."

Jancy was sure the conversation had continued on the lines of, *Such a shame he didn't meet you first, dear*.

"A very distant day, we hope, as it would require a number of deaths, including that of Simon's father."

"Mama says the earl and his heir are at death's door now."

Before Jancy could respond, Colonel Ransome-Brown and his son came out of their cabin. He sharply commanded his daughter to go and make herself decent and then took his son on deck for their morning walk. Kirkby appeared and began to prepare for breakfast. Jancy vacated her chair, incredulous that her situation could become even more complicated.

Was it true? Might Simon arrive in England to find

his father an earl and tranquil Brideswell in an uproar? Perhaps his whole family would be moving elsewhere. And this was to happen just as she shattered him with the truth?

She felt the sweet bite of temptation.

Don't tell him, then.

Take the risk that no one will ever find out. . . .

But she wouldn't do that. If he was about to be thrown into the highest levels of society, it was particularly important that he know that an ax hung over his head. Exposure would be so much more terrible.

The new burden on her was, should she tell him what Eliza had said? Warn him? Perhaps the girl had been wrong, but Jancy suspected that the Grand Panjandrum had excellent intelligence on such things.

Simon emerged from their room, looking immediately for her, his eyes lighting as they met hers. She quickly stuffed the flaming handkerchief into her bag and held out a hand. As their hands touched, dizzying warmth sealed them and their fingers locked.

How was she ever to bear life apart?

How could she bear to send him into pain without her?

After breakfast she found a moment to talk privately with Hal on deck. He was the person who had most recently been in England and might know the truth. She told him what Eliza Ransome-Brown had said and saw confirmation in his expression before he spoke.

"Marlowe's been at death's door for years, but Austrey . . ." He shrugged. "When I left he was dwindling away. He was a robust man last year and now he's a frail invalid, and no one knows why. He has the best doctors, of course, but it looks bad. That was part of the reason I was asked to bring Simon home. He'll be needed. I was prepared to tell him, but as he was returning anyway, why torment him ahead of time?"

Like an amputation, she thought, or any other operation. Far better to have it happen without warning than to have to anticipate the pain.

"So you'll tell him when we land?"

Must he bear multiple blows?

"I must. I know how much he wants to see Dare, but his parents will want him home."

"Will Long Chart be much out of our way?"

"No. Not far at all." He nodded. "Very well. I'll tell him there."

At least he'd have the visit that meant so much to him, and he would receive the blow with friends around him. She must confess her sins sooner, however. As soon as they were ashore and private.

Simon came over to them. "What are you two conspiring about?"

Jancy smiled, making it mischievous. "Never you mind."

"Saucy wench."

Hal excused himself. She wanted to take Simon in her arms and keep him from all pain, and the fact that she could only make his pain worse crushed her heart.

She did what little she could. After dinner, she persuaded him out on deck, despite a cold that whitened their breath. There, she gave him the handkerchief.

"It's wonderful," he said, his eyes shining as if the brilliant stars in the dark sky reflected there. "And a work of art."

"It's only sewing."

He raised the flames to his lips and kissed them. "Do you know there's a lady who's famous for her embroidered copies of great works of art?"

"No. But what's the point of that?"

He grinned. "Hush. But I suspect you're right. What was it Dr. Johnson said about a cat walking on its hind legs? That it wasn't remarkable for walking well, but for simply doing it at all. But this," he said, looking back at his handkerchief, "is done well and is original. A true work of art. Another way you and your cousin were alike."

He tucked it through a buttonhole of his jacket, where it would be in full display. "We men are very competitive, have you noticed? How fortunate that I have another gift for you, too."

He gave her a small box of a pale, smooth material, carved in some design.

"Ivory?" she asked.

"Just bone." He opened it and showed her a heart of polished bone inside. "You are keeper of my heart, my Jancy."

She swallowed tears. "It's lovely, and you're a miracle worker to find this."

"Shall I keep my secret? No? There's a thriving workshop belowdecks. The sailors while away their quiet times making things to sell on shore."

"Do they?" Jancy stored that information, and the next morning she found a quiet moment with Kirkby. "How do I find out if any sailors have made something my husband might like?"

His grin suggested that those belowdecks were aware of what was going on and that he might be earning a commission. "What do you have in mind, ma'am?"

That put her at a loss but then inspiration struck. "Does anyone do jewelry?"

"Of very simple sorts, ma'am."

"Would someone be able to work a bit of silver into something else?"

"Aye, likely."

She hurried to their room and returned with the misshapen pistol ball Dr. Playter had dug out of Simon and some silver threepenny bits. Simon had never asked for the ball, so she hadn't offered it, but now she said, "See if someone can mount this in the silver in some way so it could be hung as a fob."

He looked at the lump. "Caused him a bit of trouble, did it?"

After dinner, he popped his head out of his quarters and winked at her. Simon had gone on deck so she slipped over. He opened his hand to reveal the ball wrapped in a band of silver with a ring formed on top and a bit of braid attached. "Five shillings to you, ma'am."

It was probably robbery, but Jancy paid the price. She put on her cloak and went to give it to Simon.

It took him a moment to realize what it was, but then he laughed. "A very valuable reminder. Thank you." He promptly tied it to his watch chain. Then he handed her a rolled-up paper bound with ribbon. Ribbon she thought was from her own supply.

"A promissory note?" she queried. "Your ingenuity has expired?"

"Look and see."

She untied and unrolled it. "A poem?"

"I'm no Rossiter, but it seemed a suitable thing to attempt."

> Sunset hair, skin like snow,
> Gold on cheeks and nose.
> My love, my Jancy, all aglow,
> Like a wild Canadian rose.
>
> I was alone, I thought content,
> How foolish man can be.
> But then to me a rose was sent,
> My love, my bride. Jancy.

She swallowed tears. "That's beautiful."

"No, it's atrocious, but it comes from my heart."

"Which makes it beautiful," she said, meaning it. "How do I respond to poetry?"

"With a kiss?"

So she did, and it became long and slow. They were in a quiet corner of the deck, shielded to some extent by the stall, but they didn't even care. There was a special magic, she discovered, in a long, deep kiss that would not lead to sexual delight. A restrained, desirous brilliance.

"Courtship," he breathed against her neck, "is a wonderful thing."

Oh, my love, it can't be right that we must part. Perhaps I don't have to tell you. Perhaps I'm with child. I'm overdue a little, I think. No point in telling you if there's a child . . .

But the next day she felt a dull ache and found the first trace of blood on her drawers. She had probably made love to Simon for the last time.

She continued as she'd resolved to do, however, pretending all was well.

She attempted poetry, making it deliberately worse than his. He gave her a necklace of blue beads. She paid a sailor a shilling for a virulently gaudy neckcloth, washed it, hung it to dry, and presented it to him, daring him to wear it.

He did so to dinner, leading to questions, and general teasing and high spirits. This began a raid on the sailors' store of crafts and little treasures, which doubtless spread the joy belowdecks as well. Spirits were high anyway. Gulls had been sighted. Land must be close. Everyone spent time on deck searching the horizon, but of course it was the lookout high in the crow's nest who first called it.

Captain Stoddard used his telescope. He slapped it shut and turned to boom down at them from the poop deck. "Land, my friends!"

"Ireland, sir?" Simon called.

"No, sir. England, and in under thirty days!"

The passengers cheered the achievement, but Jancy burst out laughing. When Simon asked why, she couldn't tell him. She wasn't entirely sure why she was laughing instead of crying, but good winds, a sound ship, and a skillful captain had raced her to her doom.

Everyone lingered on deck that day, passing round a

telescope to peer at the shadow on the horizon that was, apparently, home, but as the sun set they had to go in to dinner. Jancy went with Simon into their cabin to tidy herself. As always now, he took her into his arms and kissed her, long and slow.

"Home soon," he whispered in her ear. "Terra firma. A big bed. Clean sheets. Unlimited fresh bathing water . . ."

She buried her head against his shoulder so he wouldn't see her expression.

When she pushed free, she looked behind and frowned.

"What's the matter?" he asked.

She was so used to guarding secrets that she almost lied.

"I don't think I left the chest like that, with that bit of cloth sticking out." She knew she hadn't. She was tidy by nature.

He turned to look. "You think someone has been in here? Stolen something?"

She raised the lid. The cloth was part of a pair of Simon's drawers. She grabbed for the small box in which she kept her bits of jewelry and Simon's precious gifts, but everything was there. She checked her purse, but if any of the coins were missing, it could be only few. Simon kept his money in his valise.

"I'm sure someone has interfered with this chest," she said.

She could tell he didn't believe her, but he said, "Let's see, then."

Together they took out everything—clothes, her box of medical supplies, the portfolio of Jane's drawings, some books and other small items—but when they'd finished, nothing was found missing.

"There, see," he said.

"Yes." But she added, "You didn't disturb things earlier?"

"I haven't opened it all day."

The thought was so horrible Jancy didn't want to put it into words. "Simon, what if someone was searching for your documents? What if one of the passengers is a colleague of McArthur's?"

He laughed, and she was ready to have her fears dismissed, but she had to add, "It would have been easy for someone to find out we were booked on the *Ewaretta*."

"True. But, my love, only consider. The Dacres and the Ransome-Browns booked months ago."

"As did you."

"As did I," he agreed more soberly. "But still, who among us could it be?"

"I don't know, but"—she lowered her voice—"whoever searched this cabin could also be looking for a way to kill you."

He put comforting hands on her shoulders. "Jancy, why now? We've been at sea for weeks, and I'm sure there have been times when I could have easily been pushed overboard."

"Don't! Oh, Lord, I thought you were *safe*."

"I *am*. Stop this. What has actually happened? One of us didn't tuck everything away tidily."

She pulled free of his hands. "I was in the chest only an hour ago to get my muff, and I wouldn't have left it like that. I wouldn't. Perhaps no one intends murder, but if someone wants to be rid of incriminating documents, this could be their last chance. The thief could hope we'd leave the ship none the wiser."

He inhaled. "Especially if he took only some. Very well, to be safe, I'd better alert Hal. I'll be back in a moment."

When he'd gone, Jancy shivered. She was certain the chest had been disturbed. The rest might be a flight of fancy, but it didn't feel like it. It was probably her disordered mind, but now she felt the presence on board of someone who wished Simon ill.

She could bear, just, to set Simon free and never see him again. She could not bear to lose him to death.

In turning out their chest, Jancy had come across the silk bag that held her cards—the crudely printed ones Sadie Haskett had given her. She'd slipped the bag past Simon's attention, but now she took out the pack. It was wrong to keep asking the cards the same question, but this was a new one. She needed to know about any immediate danger to Simon.

Praying he wouldn't come back soon, she shuffled, asking about his safety, and then dealt a simple spread. She exhaled with relief. The cards were very similar to last time with even less hint of disaster. And yet there was something in them. Something dark that she couldn't quite grasp. A twisted strand of good and evil. A two-sided person? Or two closely joined people?

The Dacres? She didn't want to think that. She didn't want to think that any of their fellow passengers was not what he or she seemed. She gathered the deck, wanting to ask again, but the cards could easily say something worse. There'd been no card of truly bad omen there.

She shuffled, wanting to ask about her own future, but put the cards back in their pouch and tucked them away in the chest. As Hal had said, what point in knowing about torture ahead of time?

Chapter Twenty-Seven

S imon had found Kirkby setting the table and all the passengers elsewhere, probably tidying themselves before dinner. He knocked on the door of Hal's room, and Oglethorpe opened it. "The major's still on deck, sir."

Aware of Kirkby, Simon asked, "Where's Treadwell?"

"On deck, too, sir."

Simon nodded. "Take care."

Oglethorpe raised a brow and nodded in return.

Simon turned away, trying to remember if everyone had been on deck in the past few hours.

"Everything all right, sir?" Kirkby asked.

"Oh, quite. Looking forward to reaching land."

"Aye, sir, but remember, the winds in the Channel are chancy as a lady. There's many a ship sighted the Lizard and took weeks to reach port."

"No reflection on the comforts of the *Eweretta*, but I pray we do better." He supposed Kirkby was a suspect. He certainly had access to the cabins. Did he have Canadian connections?

"What will you do when the ship docks in London? Is your home there?"

"Heavens, sir, my home's the *Eweretta*!"

"No thought of settling in the New World?"

The man's expression implied Simon had lost his

senses. "I've been at sea for nigh on forty years, sir. Started as a lad, and when I wasn't up to hauling lines anymore, I found this fine job."

Simon decided that the steward would have to be an actor brilliant enough for Drury Lane to be lying. He might have kept an eye on comings and goings, however.

"It's a marvel how you manage with so little space," Simon said. "Must make it a bit easier when everyone goes on deck, as recently."

"It does, sir, especially when I'm trying to set up a meal."

"Even Reverend Shore was out, I believe."

The steward gave him a grin. "He's run out of paper, sir."

"Ah." Had the clergyman become so desperate that he'd rummaged through everyone's possessions in search of more? *Don't be an idiot, Simon.*

"The good gentleman's been on the deck all afternoon," Kirkby said. "On the bench, swathed in a fur rug. It'll do him good, if you ask me. Excuse me, sir."

Kirkby slipped away, presumably for more mealtime necessities.

But that settled that. Unless Kirkby and Shore were conspirators, the clergyman was in the clear.

The whole thing was probably nonsense. Anyone could leave a bit of cloth sticking out of a chest, but he trusted Jancy's certainty about that detail, and she was right—she was neat by nature. With land, home, and a bed in Plymouth's finest inn waiting, he wasn't going to tolerate mischief now.

A hot bath, perhaps even shared. A big bed, fresh sheets, a lively fire, and endless time to explore and delight his bride. A blast of cold air was definitely needed, so he went on deck. Hal was chatting to Treadwell. Simon went over and told them what was going on.

"You take this seriously?" Hal asked.

"I'm not sure, but it won't hurt to be especially careful

over the next few days. If someone did search our cabin, they didn't find the papers. Yours is the next obvious spot."

"And possibly Norton's."

Simon nodded. "But they can search there with my blessing."

Treadwell said, "I'll return, sirs, and alert Oglethorpe. Don't worry. We never leave the place unguarded."

Simon watched the valet cross the deck. He's a good man and a dab hand with clothing. I'm tempted to bribe him away from you."

"Don't make me shoot you."

Simon laughed, tension easing. Any danger had to be product of Jancy's fretting mind, but she'd be fine once they reached land.

"If someone was in your chest," Hal said, "it could be a petty thief. Kirkby, for example."

"He wouldn't keep his job for long if the passengers began to notice things missing, and he loves the *Eweretta*. Besides, nothing was missing and there were coins there." Simon shook his head. "It has to be nothing."

"But your gut doesn't agree. How reliable is it?"

"My gut?" Simon met his eyes. "Very."

"Well, then. Scratch the colonel and his lady. It's impossible to imagine. They've only been in Canada for three years. They're delighted to be returning to England and show no interest in Upper Canada land or politics."

"And Shore is retiring," Simon said.

"He might still own property in Canada."

"But he's old, frail, and wrapped up in his memoirs. Which leaves the Dacres and the crew."

"Not the general crew," Hal pointed out. "Someone would have noticed a common sailor sneaking into the cuddy."

"One of the officers?"

"Slightly more possible, but I've become acquainted

with them. None of them appears to have any interest in Canada beyond some favorite haunts in Montreal."

"Dacre, then? I can't believe it." But then he remembered his suspicion of a code and thought, *Acre, land.* . . .

"He's very ambitious," Hal said, "and spent some time in Upper Canada a few years back."

Simon looked out to sea. "Damn and blast."

He returned to the cuddy wondering whether to tell Jancy that there might be something to her suspicions and that the villain was probably Dacre. He didn't want to distress her and she seemed to like the couple. He found the man a bit boisterous, but he wouldn't have thought there any vice in him. Ambition, however, was a harsh spur.

Kirkby rang the bell, which seemed a summons to honesty. It would be wrong to keep things from her, so he went into the cabin and told her all.

"Are you sure?" she asked. "About the code?"

"No, but there's definitely something odd about the phrasing of some of McArthur's papers."

She grimaced. "I can't believe it. Especially not of Rebecca."

"He'd never involve her, love."

"I suppose not, but I hate this."

"We're leaving at Plymouth and they're carrying on to London. That'll be the end of it."

Her eyes locked with his. "It could make him desperate."

"I'll be careful."

"What will you do when we land? Alert someone to his likely guilt?"

Simon shook his head. "No, I'll leave it in the hands of fate. As long as he doesn't trouble me or mine again."

"Yet you shot McArthur."

Simon touched the pistol ball. He'd wondered what she'd made of that. "Yes, and I don't know if it was right. I was angry, furious. But also, I thought I might die. I didn't want to leave him in the same world as you."

She came to him and kissed him. "Thank you."

"It was very Machiavellian. Never leave a defeated enemy alive."

"I think I approve of that." She turned to the mirror to tidy her hair and Simon settled to enjoy watching her. Her body shifted as she pulled out and then pushed in some hairpins. Her raised arms tightened her gown over her breasts—breasts that moved in ways that sternly corseted ones didn't.

He supposed she'd soon be wearing a corset, and he did look forward to seeing her in fashionable finery. But perhaps she'd keep her bodices for country wear. Decorated, though. She was clever with her needle. If he asked nicely, he was sure she'd ornament her plain undergarments in delightful ways.

He couldn't wait. For their first night ashore, but also for their life. Introducing her to his family at Brideswell. To his friends. Seeing her relax and lose her fears among the Rogues. Setting up their home. A London house, probably, where they could host small, informal parties. Nothing too daunting for her, and he certainly didn't want a grand establishment.

Despite another ring of the bell, he stepped forward to cradle her breasts and kiss the nape of her neck, where wisps of golden hair coiled against her creamy skin. He trailed his lips down the fine bones of her upper spine, feeling her shudder and her nipples peak.

She leaned back against him. He thought he heard her sigh. "We must go."

The bell jangled again.

"We could always eat each other."

She chuckled as if it were entirely a joke and eased away to tidy things into their chest. Yes, she was neat by nature. Before closing the lid, she carefully arranged the drawstring of a petticoat into an S.

"There. If anyone pokes around again, we'll know."

"Clever, but whomever it is won't return here. They have to know the papers are elsewhere."

"They're truly safe in Hal's cabin?"

"Our thief would have to kill Oglethorpe and Treadwell to get to them. I certainly wouldn't want to try. So yes. They're safe."

He saw in her eyes that she still worried about his safety.

"And I'll be careful, too," he said. "I promise."

They went to bed that night with the hope of landing the next day but woke before dawn to the howling of a storm. Jancy fought her way out of bed and, clinging to one of the posts, looked out of the porthole.

Water hurled at it, making her flinch back with a cry. Then she was tossed farther back, saw raging sky, and was sure the ship was turning upside down. It flung her forward again and Simon grabbed her, holding her and the post close. "You'd be safer in bed!" he cried over the shrieking, cracking pandemonium. "I could tie you there."

"Mind your ribs!" she yelled back at him. "We have to dress."

"Why?"

"If we have to abandon ship, I'm not doing it in my nightgown!"

Jancy grabbed her clothes and lay on the bed to put them on, where the raised side helped keep her safe. But her hands were almost paralyzed with terror. In the ocean a sound ship could ride out a storm, but here, with England to one side and France on the other and the Channel Islands scattered like traps, a storm had wrecked many a ship.

When they were both dressed, they lurched into the cubby, going from handhold to handhold. They found the colonel, Dacre, and Hal already there, in a room as cold and dark as their cabin, for stove and candles were too dangerous in such a storm. The painted floor already sloshed with an inch of water.

"I'm going to pin up my skirts," Jancy called to Simon and fought her way back to the cabin. She took a moment, clutching a post, to gather herself. They couldn't founder. Not so close to the end. But if their enemy wanted Simon dead, this could give him a chance. She found her pins and managed to kirtle up her skirts. She added her spencer, her plain shawl, and gloves, and then struggled with the door to get back into the cuddy.

Simon pulled her down into a seat at the table. As the table was fixed to the floor, it was probably the safest spot. He passed his tankard to her.

"Grog."

Jancy managed a mouthful of the rum and water mix without getting it all over herself and choked. It was mostly rum.

"Nice fresh water, at least," Kirkby said, bringing her some of her own. "That's the good thing about rain."

"Do you know where we are?" the colonel demanded. "With relation to shore, I mean."

"Can't say, sir. We'll see come light."

"Might be too damned late," the colonel growled.

Jancy wondered what he thought anyone could do. Abandon ship, she supposed. But to take to the boats in such a storm felt as good as suicide.

She was shaking with fear and ashamed of it. When Simon put an arm around her and pulled her against him, she looked into his eyes and said, "I do love you, Simon." If they died, she wanted that clear.

He rested his forehead against hers. "Don't sound as if you think this is doom."

Oglethorpe joined Hal for a quiet word and then left the cubby for the deck, managing to do it without letting in much water.

"He was a marine," Hal said to the room in general. "Used to ships. He'll see what's happening."

Colonel Ransome-Brown nodded. "Stout fellow."

Mrs. Ransome-Brown appeared in the doorway of her stateroom, her robe open over her nightgown, her hair hidden by a nightcap. She looked like any woman, and distraught. "Henry. The children?"

He went instantly to her. "My love, if necessary, I'm sure every man aboard will make their safety a prime concern."

There was a murmur of agreement, and Jancy was touched by the tender moment. She'd thought theirs an arid marriage. What a one she was for making harsh judgments from appearances—she who should know better.

Kirkby staggered out of his quarters again, this time with a high-sided tray loaded with slices of bread well covered with jam.

"All I can manage, ladies and gentlemen, but you'll need food to deal with the cold, so eat up."

They did. The bread was stale and they'd run out of butter days ago. The jam was still good, however, and it was nourishment.

Oglethorpe returned, drenched. "Close in to England, but not too close, the sailors think. Stoddard knows his business. We'll ride this out."

Jancy studied him, trying to decide how much was true, how much false reassurance. There was no way to tell.

Simon rose. "I'm going to see."

Jancy grabbed him. "You'll get half-drowned for no reason!"

"I have dry clothing."

She could see from his brilliant eyes that he longed to be out in the storm, not cowering in here.

He raised his brows at her. "You're not going to be the sort of wife who wants to keep her husband in leading strings, are you?"

She had to say, "No," and watch him go. Only then did she remember that his life might be in danger from more than a storm.

She looked around frantically. The colonel had gone with his wife. Dacre was here. Shore wasn't, but he'd surely be in his bed. No danger, then—unless the threat came from one of the crew. Someone needed to be out there to protect Simon!

Hal. But in the storm, his one arm was a serious handicap. Oglethorpe had gone into Hal's cabin, presumably to change into dry clothes. Treadwell?

But in truth, she wanted to go out and drag Simon back in as he had her.

She finished the last of her bread and rose. She inched her way to the door, knowing someone would try to stop her if they suspected her plan. Rebecca came out then, distressed, which drew every eye. Jancy seized the moment to open the door and dash out.

The wind almost swept her away. She grabbed a handhold for dear life. Was she mad? Was Simon? But then the wind slackened here, at least, beneath the poop deck. She fought the door closed and clung to her grip.

Rain and sea spray lashed the deck, and when they hit her they were whips of ice. A surly band of light told of dawn struggling to push up leaden clouds, but she saw only dark chaos around except where three turbulent lanterns cast hellish glimpses on forms and faces.

Where was Simon?

She wanted to scream his name, but the wind would carry it away. The captain's bellows and the piercing whistles used to send commands could hardly be heard above wind, waves, and shrieking ship. She realized the sails were rolled up, stealing the gale's power to hurtle them onto rocks, at least. But there were men up in the rigging. How did they do it?

Ropes were strung around the deck like low washing lines. The sailors held on to them as they moved about, so they wouldn't be swept overboard. No matter how much she wanted to search for Simon, she couldn't do the same. Her strength wasn't up to holding on against a mighty wave. She was useless out here. She could only watch, trying to make sense of chaos, trying to prepare to act if she saw the chance.

*   *   *

Simon clung to one of the ropes lashed around the mainmast, being careful to keep out of the way of the sailors, laughing at himself but loving every moment of the storm. The air flared with wild energy and even the icy waves that slammed across the deck were glorious.

This was like riding the wildest horse.

Like the wicked elation of battle.

Like sex.

Perhaps that was what was wrong with him. Pure frustration.

Dawn was breaking but not clarifying the mayhem around him. Instead it turned black to confusing gray. But then he saw Jane. He was sure he had to be mistaken, but he focused again. It was. Her eyes met his with wild relief and she let go with one hand to wave at him.

Damned idiot!

He grabbed one of the lines and staggered toward her, working from rope to rope.

Until one snapped.

It broke under his weight just as a wave hit him, so he was helpless, swept like a ball on a chain to slam into something. Pain blinded him for a moment, but he was intensely grateful that it was his back, not his side.

He heard Jancy scream his name. Then the ship leaned in the other direction and he began to slide. Let go of the rope to try for another? He was whipping toward the mast when a hand grabbed his wrist.

He looked up into Dacre's grimacing face. The man had his other arm hooked over the bolted-down bench, so Simon surrendered to him and was hauled to safety.

Clutching the bench for himself, he laughed. "Another madman, I see!"

"Not at all," Dacre yelled at him. "Your wife came out after you, and mine asked me to follow. But you, sir, *are* a damned madman!"

Simon tried to sober. "I apologize for endangering you."

"Aye, well, you're a bit of a pair, aren't you, you and Jane?"

Simon laughed again. "Yes. Yes, we are. Let's return together to safety."

They worked their way down a rope to the cuddy door.

"What the devil are *you* doing out here?" he shouted at Jane, but he was grinning.

"What the devil are *you* doing out here?" she yelled back, furious.

"Enjoying myself."

She suddenly smiled. "Me, too."

Dacre gave their laughter a disgusted look and fought the door to get inside.

They laughed even harder. It had to be the brush with death, but clinging to the ship for dear life, they kissed with hungry, burning lips that didn't part even when a wave drenched them. They only gasped into each other as it drove them together and kissed and kissed and kissed.

Then they stood together, stuck by wet clothing and the pressure of the wind, freezing and burning at the same time.

"We should go in," she said into his ear.

"I know. We could freeze to death here."

"Pneumonia."

"Yes."

They still didn't move, but then Jane pushed at him a bit. "When you hit, did you hurt yourself again?"

"I'll have a hell of a bruise, but no."

The separation, slight though it was, let in sanity. "Come on." As he put his hand on the door latch, he said, "There's one thing. We can cross Dacre off the villain list."

Chapter Twenty-Eight

*W*ith dawn the storm eased, so that by daylight the Channel was merely its choppy self. The *Eweretta* and her captain had proved their worth. The sails were loosed again and they were soon making good speed up the Channel.

Kirkby lit the cabin stove and while it heated, two sailors mopped up the water. The galley must have been working again, too, for soon tea and bowls of porridge appeared for anyone who wanted them. The *Eweretta* was back in order.

Hal and Simon both lectured Jancy on going out in the storm, but she knew Simon didn't truly regret it. Who could ever regret such a moment, such a kiss? If only he didn't have his family and his responsibilities perhaps they could head off to adventures where her identity didn't matter, seasickness be damned.

After breakfast everyone went on deck to inspect the damage and feast their eyes on the clearly visible shore of England. The captain strolled about the deck like a conquering hero, accepting the congratulations of his passengers and graciously passing off some of the glory to his crew.

But he paused by Simon. "Mr. St. Bride, as you may realize, we have overshot Plymouth and I cannot put back. I can offer you a landing at Poole, however, for I will stop there for Reverend Shore."

"Poole will suit us just as well, Captain. When will we arrive?"

"This evening, all being well. See," he said, pointing, "there is Portland Bill behind us, and Swanage Bay not far ahead."

Simon looked at Jancy. "Home, at last." His eyes sent a special message about baths and bed. "We'd best look to our preparations."

In their cabin, Jancy opened the chest to find the string in place. "I must have imagined the problem. I'm sorry."

"Why think that? The storm provided no opportunity for a villain."

"I suppose not, but the only possibility was Dacre, and see, he's a hero instead."

"I'm happier to have it so."

She smiled. "As am I."

Sailors brought their baggage and they began to pack. Jancy felt she should separate her possessions from Simon's in preparation for their parting, but didn't see how.

"I said we'd contact the Dacres when we pause in London," he said. "Assuming the *Eweretta* arrives by then."

Jancy handed him a pile of underwear. "Why should we? Pause in London, I mean."

"I have friends who will probably be there. Stephen Ball, for one. He'll know what I should do with the papers. I'm keen to pass that whole business on to others."

Friends, she thought. Support for him. She, however, would be alone in the world.

Once they were ready, they went on deck, where most of their fellow passengers were scanning green headlands atop brown cliffs, announcing glimpses of village spires. Each bay had its cluster of fishermen's cottages, and the Channel bobbed with their boats, which often hailed the *Eweretta*, home safe from the storm. Farther away other great ships drove along under the power of bellied sails, but a few limped brokenly toward safety and repair.

"I suppose some were wrecked," Jancy said to Simon as they watched the shore draw close. It looked so unthreatening now.

"Alas, yes, but more likely behind us on the coast of Cornwall or Devon. That's the ships' graveyard."

"A boat's coming," she said.

"A pilot. It must be a tricky harbor." He turned to smile at her. "It is so very good to be home."

He saw no shadows ahead and she wanted more than anything in the world to shield him from them. Instead he faced not only her confession, but also the news about the earldom of Marlowe. There was hope there, at least. It might only be rumor, or the heir might have made a miraculous recovery.

"We'll be only forty miles or so from Long Chart," he continued. "We could reach there tomorrow, but if you want to rest in Poole for a day or two, we will. Then on to Brideswell."

She had to act as if all this would involve her.

"What of London, then?" she asked.

"All roads lead to London, remember? It's the only sensible route."

"And we'll pause to deal with your papers." This might be the last opportunity to learn Simon's mind on that, so she took it. "What do you think will happen? About the Indians. Do you think they'll ever have a territory of their own?"

"I'm an optimist by nature, but no. We let that chance slip in the peace negotiations. The Americans will never agree to it now. And anyway, one nation wouldn't suffice. The Indians are as diverse as the whole of Europe, perhaps as the world. Some tribes are primitive, but some are highly cultured. Some need forests, some seas, some fertile valleys or plains of buffalo. There are even some who inhabit by choice the icy wastes of the north."

"Then what do you hope for?"

"Apart from miracles, simple justice. When we buy their lands, we should pay a fair price. When we make promises, we should keep them. And those who murder them should receive the same treatment as those who murder us."

"But you'll leave this to others now?"

"My place is here, in England, and I confess I'm too much of a St. Bride to throw my life away on a lost cause."

"You almost did," she pointed out.

"I had a purpose there, but if it was foolish, blame it on the hair."

"On the blood of Black Ademar and Hereward the Wake."

He obviously thought her comment strange but said, "Precisely."

Jancy considered the tranquil shore. "I suppose we're not far from where the invading Normans landed and swept away the Anglo-Saxon culture. Was that such a terrible thing? You say Hereward made his peace with the Normans, and we have peace and prosperity now."

"Time buries the bones."

She turned to look at him. "So what will you fight for now?"

"For justice for my own people. Fair wages. Education. Wresting voting power out of the hands of the few and into the hands of the many."

"A noble battle, but can it be won?"

"I believe so, yes. The changes are already happening." He smiled into her eyes. "And with you by my side, I can never fail."

She turned away, afraid of showing her agony, and they watched the careful negotiation of the *Eweretta* through the narrow opening that allowed the only access to the almost-landlocked Poole Harbor. Jancy sighed. If only . . .

She pulled away from dreams to reality. "How strange

to be surrounded by land after so many weeks in limitless ocean."

Simon put his arms around her from behind. "Embraced."

She covered his gloved hands with hers, savoring every last moment.

The pilot left, but port officials came aboard to deal with formalities to do with passengers and cargo. Jancy felt a tremor as Simon produced his passport, but no one could dispute that she was Jane St. Bride, his wife. Sailors were hauling up their chests and crates from the hold. Simon and Hal went to observe, checking off lists.

Jancy returned to their cabin to make sure nothing had been forgotten. For all the problems, she thought, touching the bottom bed, there had been some precious moments here. She returned to the cuddy to find Norton there. He was carrying on to London with Gore's papers.

"This will be farewell, Captain," she said, holding out a hand.

He took it and, to her surprise, kissed it. "It's been a pleasure to travel with you, Jane St. Bride. Perhaps in parting, you could call me Noll? For Oliver?"

Jancy pulled her hand free and smiled vaguely. The last thing she needed now was some man flirting with her, but he was Simon's friend.

"Perhaps we'll meet again in London, Captain."

"I hope for it. But winds being as they are in the Channel, you could be at Brideswell before we reach Greenwich. You do not plan to go north to your home?"

"No. As I said, I no longer have family there."

"But friends and neighbors, surely?"

"Very few. I must go, Captain."

On deck, she found their possessions were already being lowered into boats to be taken ashore. Time for farewells. The Grand Panjandrum herself was gracious in a haughty manner.

"When your husband brings you to London, we must

take tea, Mrs. St. Bride." Jancy was sure it was only her own mind that supplied, *And I hope you are more suitably dressed by then, you lowborn creature.*

The colonel made a similar comment, but more warmly. He complained, however, that Captain Stoddard would not permit them to spend the night on shore.

"Says he needs to catch an early tide tomorrow and he won't have his passengers wandering. But at least he's bringing fresh supplies aboard, and the sooner we reach London the better."

Rebecca Dacre cried as she said good-bye, and her husband seemed sincerely sorry to see them leave. "Perhaps we will see you again in London," he said. "And I know my family and friends in Cumberland will be interested to know that I traveled with the cousin of the artistic Miss Otterburn."

Once that would have terrified Jancy, but now it was toothless.

She was let down into the boat in the swaying bosun's chair, as was Reverend Shore. Hal was, too, which he must have hated. Simon and the two servants used the ladder. They all waved as they were rowed to shore.

As the sun began to set, everyone and everything arrived on terra firma in the small town of Poole—even if terra firma was heaving like the sea.

Jancy clutched Simon. "I don't remember this from last time."

"You were weak and ill. Peculiar, isn't it? Come on, I gather the Antelope has rooms."

She thought they must look like drunks as they staggered their way to the Antelope, a solid old inn fronting the harbor, but they were received cheerfully. Soon she was approving a pleasant room, thinking sadly that it fit their shipboard dream.

It wasn't large, and the diamond-paned window was only a few feet in either dimension, but that looked out on a garden and let in warm evening light. The walls were bright and clean, and the high tester bed had curtains and coverlet the color of bluebells. The sheets were freshly laundered, but above all, the room was still, quiet, and free of the stink of the ship.

She held her hands out to the fire, amazed at how wondrous such a simple thing seemed after so long without it.

A maidservant had guided her here and asked, "Do you require anything, ma'am?"

A bath. A real bath.

Jancy was ready to rush around boiling kettles herself, but she'd promised herself that she'd tell Simon at the first opportunity. That meant now, so she thanked the maid and sent her away.

Where was he? She wanted to get this over with, but he'd stayed downstairs to discuss something with Hal. Transportation to Long Chart, she supposed.

She roamed the room, wanting it over. But also wanting to never tell him—to carry on to Long Chart, London, and Brideswell and defy fate one more time.

She began to pray.

It wasn't my fault, Lord, that I was forced to live a lie as a child. It wasn't my fault that my father sinned with my mother. It's not my fault that I'm a contaminated Haskett!

She moved on to bargaining.

Please help me have a second chance. I promise never to lie again. I'll be the best wife in the world, the best daughter to his parents, sister to his sisters and brothers, aunt to his nephews and nieces. I will shape my life to make him happy. To make them all happy. I ask nothing for myself except the chance. That he understand and forgive—

Simon came in. "Dinner's ready."

She turned to him. She had to *eat*?

"You can't be *land*-sick, can you?" he asked. The impatient tone had her hastily going with him. Her prayers certainly hadn't helped. Why should they? They were purely selfish.

Dear God, turn everything to the best for Simon.

They dined in a private parlor with Hal, and Jancy even ate a little for Simon's sake. The food was delicious after the ship's rations, especially the limited ones of the past weeks. Baked perch. Plump roast turkey breast. A Florentine of kidneys. Fresh vegetables—cabbage, cauliflower, and spinach.

When the innkeeper presented a platter of pears, plums, and plump grapes, Simon said, "Fresh fruit. I see you know the ways of arriving passengers."

The man bowed and smiled. "Indeed I do, sir. Indeed I do."

When the meal ended, Simon rose.

Now.

But he smiled at her. "Why don't we take a walk and shake off the sea? After such a confined world, we now have miles."

An evening stroll. She could not deny herself that everyday pleasure. Just once.

But darkness was falling and the wind was cold. When they were hit with spots with rain, they hurried back to the inn. As they climbed the stairs to their room, Jancy's heart started to pound and her throat stuck with dryness. This was like facing an amputation. As they entered the cozy room, she wondered if she'd be able to force out words.

"What's the matter?" Simon asked, coming to help take off her cloak. "You're shaking. My love, you should have said. Come, sit by the fire and I'll order hot punch."

She was in a chair and he was gone before she could protest. She put a hand over her face, expecting tears, but this agony lay too deep for that. A rock of pain was lodged in her heart.

She held out unsteady hands to the fire, aware as if from a distance of her mind scrabbling for an excuse to keep her secrets. To enjoy the bed, where the handles of two warming pans stuck out invitingly from under the covers.

Simon returned, smiling. "It'll be here in a moment. And I've ordered baths."

Heaven alone knew what he saw in her face, but his smile faded.

"What is it? You look terrified."

He turned as the maid brought in a bowl of punch and glasses and put them on the table near the fire. When she'd left, he poured a glass and cradled her hands around it. "Drown your sorrows and trust me, darling. Everything will be all right."

Jancy sipped to lubricate her throat, distantly appreciating that the drink was delicious, tasting of lemon, sugar, spices, and rum. "Thank you."

"Better now?"

Though she heard the deeper question, she said, "Yes," then quickly blurted out, "Simon, I have something to tell you."

Chapter Twenty-Nine

*H*e sat, considering her. "You're with child? No, it can't be."

"No, not that."

"If you're about to tell me *you're* McArthur's ally . . . ?"

He was joking and she managed a smile. "No. Please just listen. This is going to be very hard."

She watched his features still.

"I'm not sure where to start or how to put this, but I want to say that if you don't want to be married to me that will be all right. No, not all right. Not at all. But *right*. I won't . . . Oh, I don't know."

"Jancy, for heaven's sake. We *are* married, to hell and back."

She was going to have to just spit it out. "I'm not Jane Otterburn. Or wasn't. I mean, I am not Isaiah Trewitt's niece."

He frowned. "What do you mean?"

It seemed easier now, as if a stone blocking a stream had been forced out of the way. "I'm the person known as Nan Otterburn, Jane Otterburn's cousin. Jane died on board ship and I took her identity."

His skin seemed to tighten on his bones. "Why?"

She looked away, looked down. Saw that her hands were tight around the punch glass. Saw his wedding ring. Should she take it off?

"It's hard to know why now." She'd mumbled it, so she swallowed and spoke more clearly. "I wasn't well. I'd been very sick, and then I'd nursed Jane, but she died. I felt so alone in the world. I *was* alone. And frightened. I was traveling to a strange, wild land and a strange man."

She looked up. "Isaiah was a wonderful man, but I didn't know that then. He was a stranger and no relative of mine. He loomed like a monster. I imagined him turning me from his door to survive in a wilderness full of wild animals. Or," she whispered, "doing worse."

"A surprising awareness for a girl raised quietly in a small town."

The cold suspicion in his voice struck her like a dagger, but she tried to respond calmly. "Small towns are not free of sin."

"I suppose not."

He stood and turned away from her. Tears rose, stinging her eyes and clogging her throat.

"I don't know what to say. I'm tempted to ask if you're sure, but you'd hardly make this up. And it does explain some things." He turned back. "Once you knew Isaiah, why not tell him the truth?"

He was blurred by her tears. "I kept putting it off. I feared to lose the refuge I'd found. Without him, I had no one. No one in the world. Perhaps . . . I think in a way I slid into believing it was true, and that if I lived quietly and virtuously and worked hard, it would *be* true. That I could carry on that way forever."

She looked straight into his guarded eyes. "But of course my behavior caused all the disasters."

He didn't deny it.

"And we're not really married. We—"

He raised a hand to silence her. "I need to think, Jane. Nan . . . What the hell do I call you?"

The swearing startled them both.

"Jancy?" she offered. "It truly was my childhood name."

In a childhood I still haven't confessed. With despair she recognized that she'd reached the limit of her endurance. She simply couldn't throw the Hasketts at him now.

"I'm sorry," he said, appearing almost a stranger with his stark features. "I have to go. Just for a while. To think." He fixed her with a look. "You will stay here?"

"Where could I go?"

"I was falling into theatrical imaginings of you running away into the night, or even into the sea."

"If I'd wanted to drown myself, I've had many better opportunities."

He looked as if he'd respond to the dry humor of that, but left.

After a still moment, Jancy pulled out her handkerchief and blew her nose. Running away into the night or even into the sea had a certain grim appeal, but she was too practical for such gestures. Hasketts no more abandoned life than did a cornered rat. She poured herself another glass of punch and sipped at it.

He hadn't immediately cast her off.

Did that allow hope?

Should she hope? He'd be better off free of her, but she loved him so much, as he did her. Didn't that count for something?

She sighed. She couldn't let him carry on with the marriage without telling him that she was a Haskett, and if she did, he'd certainly want to be rid of her then. She bounced from thought to thought like a fly trying frantically to escape a bottle.

She refilled her cup, wondering why it was so hard to know the right thing to do. Books of moral advice and preachers in their pulpits made it all seem so easy, but it never turned out that way for her.

She rose, needing to move as she struggled for answers, but the room whirled. She still didn't have her land legs. But as she clutched the back of the chair, she realized the horrible truth. She was drunk!

Her mind rocked at memories of her mother and other Hasketts staggering around, laughing at their own garbled wit, falling all over one another, often ending up sprawled snoring, clothes askew.

> *A tisket, a tasket,*
> *Your mother was a Haskett.*

She eyed the bed and lurched her way over to it. As she lowered herself carefully onto it, she fumbled her skirts decently over her legs and then sank her spiraling head on the pillow.

Better. And in a little while she'd be recovered.

In a little while . . .

Simon returned to the bedroom because there was nowhere else to go. The public rooms of the inn were busy and he knew of no private ones he could use. He could only lurk in the corridors for so long without becoming an object of curiosity. Outside, it was raining. Catching his death would hardly help matters.

He was tempted to go to Hal, but until he worked out what to do, the fewer people to know, the better.

He was trying to persuade himself that Jane . . . Jancy . . . his wife—maybe—was suffering some form of dementia. Some malady caused by being on dry land after weeks at sea. Strange to *want* her to be mad, but it wouldn't wash. Bizarre though her story was, it held the ring of truth. It explained so much of her strange behavior, including the fear Hal had noticed when Dacre said he'd attended the Otterburn school.

Dacre had recalled the name Janey, not Jancy. The initials on the drawings, JAO, had indeed stood for Jane Anne Otterburn, not Nan. His Jancy wasn't the artist. In a year, he hadn't seen her draw anything. Moreover, if she had such a talent, his Jancy wouldn't mark her work with a tiny, self-abasing monogram.

His Jancy.

The woman he loved. Who was breath and blood to him.

It was as if a telescope twisted into focus. Whoever she was, he loved Jancy St. Bride and would not let her go. So what the devil did he do?

The only way to sort this out was to return and talk to her. The rising tempo of his heart told him that was what he wanted more than anything in the world.

He entered the room, unsure what to expect. She wasn't in the chair. For a frightening moment he thought she had run away, but instead she was on the bed. On top of the covers, laid out as neat as a corpse.

He dashed over, his heart missing beats, but saw that she was simply asleep. She'd tossed that missile at him then gone to sleep, damn her?

He headed for the punch bowl—and saw how little was left. Despite everything, his lips twitched. His wicked, lying wife was passed out drunk. He scooped out what was left and went back to lean against one of the oaken bedposts and studied her as he sipped.

The voyage, and perhaps other stresses and strains, had thinned her face, making her look older than her years, but the sea air hadn't darkened that wondrous alabaster skin. Freckles still dotted it with gold, the same burnished gold as her long lashes and the hair that straggled in wisps around her face.

In her plain, stained gown she looked like a pauper, but that gown outlined her shape, the shape he'd explored and delighted in. Not nearly as often as he wished. He wanted to run his hand over breast and hip now.

Not until he'd decided what to do.

She was his wife. His brave, resourceful wife. If he could swap her for shy, artistic Jane Anne Otterburn, he wouldn't. He wanted this one—Nan, Jancy, whoever she was. He wanted the woman who'd charged in to stop a duel. Who'd fought the doctor to save his arm. Who'd laughed with him in the madness of a storm, and kissed him as if lightning ran through her blood.

The woman he was lightning-struck in love with.

He could even appreciate the courage it had taken to tell him the truth.

But if what she'd said was true, then she was right—by the strictest letter of the law they were not married. She had been impersonating someone else.

They were married by intent, however; by body, by heart, and by a minister of the church according to the prayer book. If he didn't make any difficulties, and she didn't, who would ever know? A leap within told him that was what he wanted.

He wished she'd trusted him sooner. He needed her to trust him.

But then he remembered how young she was. She was still eighteen. She'd been just seventeen when she'd faced tragedy on the seas when still shattered by the recent death of the woman who'd raised her and the loss of her home and country. No wonder she'd been terrified into a mistake.

Everything became clear.

She was his beloved Jancy, and he would take care of her. She would never again be alone or afraid. He would take her home to Brideswell and wrap her in the loving warmth of his family. Somehow, he'd find a way to make her identity secure.

Tenderly he eased off her shoes and maneuvered her so he could pull down the covers, extract the warming pans, and tuck her in. He put the pans outside the door, stripped to his shirt and drawers, and got into bed to take his wife into his arms.

It was the devil of a mess, but Jancy St. Bride was his precious wife, and the world would spin out of its orbit before he would let anyone tear them apart.

Chapter Thirty

*J*ancy woke, strangely light-headed, snuggled up against Simon in a big soft bed. Wonderful . . .

Then she remembered. She jerked away. It was pitch-dark, but she *felt* when he awoke.

"Headache?" he asked calmly.

She thought about it. "No."

"Good. Do you want to talk?"

She wished she could see his expression. "If you wish."

His warm hand linked with hers. "Let's deal with the important point first. Do you want to remain my wife?"

Jancy breathed, exploring every nuance of the question. "Not if it will harm you."

"Do you love me?"

"You'd believe me if I said yes?"

"Yes."

She turned toward him, even though she still couldn't see anything more than shadows. "Then yes, I love you, Simon St. Bride."

"And I love you." He drew them together in the sagging middle of the bed. "I think that settles it."

He kissed her, but she turned her head away and tried to hold him off. "No, it doesn't. What happens if someone finds out? You must think about that, Simon. It could be a horrible scandal."

"How likely is it?" His lips returned to brush where

they could. Her temple, her cheek and, when she turned back, her lips.

"Stop it. Pay attention!"

"Oh, I am," he murmured, amusement in his voice. "From the drawings, it's obvious you and your cousin were very alike, and my impression is that you lived very quietly in Carlisle. So who is going to shout the accusation?"

"We had friends. We went to church. And there was the shop. The customers."

He ceased his teasing kisses. "A very small shop, I gather. Weren't the customers local women?"

"Yes."

"Simple people?"

"People like us," she pointed out.

"And you aren't simple. I apologize. But are your customers likely to turn up at Brideswell, or in London?"

"No, but occasionally grander ladies would come in to see the wares."

How hard it was to be firm and rational when he was stroking her shoulder and back.

"Consider, love. If a passing lady entered the shop to look at ribbons, and you assisted her, would she now know if she had encountered Jane or Nan?"

"No, I suppose not."

"So we can dismiss that fear."

"But our friends and many of the congregation would," she pointed out.

It felt insane to be fighting so hard against what she wanted so much.

"What church did you attend?" he asked, steady as a rock.

"The Episcopalian chapel."

"Not a hub of Carlisle society, I assume."

"No, and the minister died last year. He used to come to dinner every week. . . . But *many* people knew Jane and me. Knew which was which."

A silence marked his thought and she feared she'd

won, even though his hand moved on her still, declaring a connection he seemed determined not to break.

"It's over a year since you left Carlisle. If we avoid the north, you may never meet any of those people again, especially as you'll be moving in very different circles. Thus if you do encounter any of them, it could be years from now."

"But—"

"Hush. Listen. You've changed since arriving in York. Your figure has filled out, but your face has changed, too, blurring any differences. Then consider fashion. You are beautiful as you are, but you will be changing in other ways."

His fingers moved up into her still-plaited hair. "I hate to lose a single strand, but the current style seems to require curls around the face. That will make you look very different. It will hide, for example, your lovely high forehead." He kissed it. "Your brows," he added, tracing them with his lips, "could be thinned and arched a little more. And simply, time will blur any differences."

He could be right. Jancy wondered why this didn't seem heavenly. And then she knew. "I had hoped to be able to stop lying, Simon, to stop living in fear."

His cherishing fingers stilled. "More than you want to remain with me?"

She turned closer, pressed closer. "No."

"Then surrender." He rolled over her. "I will not lose you, Jancy. I will *not*. We'll fight the hounds of hell if we have to, but we will never be torn apart."

His kiss seared her, as did his words, and she was helpless to resist. Even as voices clamored that she shouldn't, she kissed him back, tore at his clothes as he was tearing at hers. Then they simply pushed them up, aside, down until he was between her thighs, until they were slickly, wonderfully joined.

Her bodice was apart, so he could kiss a breast. She'd dragged his shirt loose so she could knead his back.

Stockinged legs tangled as they soared into passion, gasping love and desire until they ended, sated, in a tangle of skirts and sheets that threatened to knot them together for eternity.

What could be more perfect than that?

"You are mine," he said in a voice that was almost a growl. "Nothing will part us. Nothing. Trust me. Trust me always, my wife, my jewel, my heart."

Jancy closed her eyes and breathed.

You are mine.

What could be more perfect, and if Simon said it would be so, surely it would be. He knew his world better than she. She would believe.

A knock at the door woke Jancy, and she found it was bright daylight. Simon muttered but got out of bed. Or tried to. They were still knotted. "Wait a moment!" he called as they pushed and pulled.

Jancy smothered laughter, but it bubbled up anyway from a heart full of joy. It was a new day, and they need not part.

"It's Hal. I'm about to leave."

Simon gave up the struggle. "Safe journey, then. We'll see you in London." As footsteps receded he lay back, smiling at Jancy. "He's going to find Stephen Ball. If he's at Ancross, he'll let us know. If not, he'll go on to London." He traced her forehead, cheek, and lips. "You look like sunrise."

She didn't resist as he kissed her or hold back as he swept her into bliss.

Much later he said, "We should rise and breakfast if we're to travel today."

"True, but we still haven't had our precious baths."

He laughed. "Are you suggesting, wife of mine, that we're not fit for good company? Strange how a person can become accustomed to squalor. Very well, I'll order them." He traced her lips. "Much though I'd love to teach you all about the Order of the Bath, I suspect the Antelope has only tiny tubs and we have a lot of scrubbing to do."

He climbed out of bed stark naked, and she unashamedly ogled him. He took some fresh clothes from a valise but grimaced as he pulled them on. "Hal was to leave his men here with the papers. I'll send Treadwell to buy something fresh for us both."

He left in only shirt and breeches, careless of decorum. Jancy lay back to go over their situation again, seeking traps by light of day. Her mind wouldn't cooperate. It danced around like the dust motes in the sunbeam.

They were to stay together.

Simon said they would triumph.

If he said they could dance on the moon, she'd fly off with him.

But then she sat upright.

He didn't know about the Hasketts!

Her cowardice sickened her, but she *couldn't* tell him now. After last night, she couldn't bear to lose him, but more than that, she'd seen how much he cared. He'd fought to keep her, pledged to defend her. He truly did love her.

She worked her way out of the madly disordered bed and found the small wooden box in her valise—the one Simon had given her on the ship, the one containing a heart. She touched the satiny bone. How could she batter him with more pain?

After all, the Hasketts presented no danger. If the world believed that she was and always had been Jane St. Bride née Otterburn, the Hasketts were irrelevant. Silence would mean her living with lies around her like a hair shirt, but that was her penance to endure, for Simon's sake.

She tucked the box away safely and stripped off what bits of clothing remained on her. What a ragbag. A button on one side of her gown's bodice had been ripped out, taking cloth with it, and the waist seam was torn open at the front. The dress was no great loss, but she'd better prepare for bed properly in future. She couldn't afford to lose many more gowns just yet.

When she found clean underwear, she saw what Simon meant. Her grubby, coarse linen could be restored by a good laundry, but she hoped Treadwell could find them fresh for now. One night in clean sheets made her old garments intolerable.

She put on her green robe and set to untangling and brushing out her hair.

Simon arrived ahead of servants carrying a tub and buckets of water. "Mine's being set up in another room," he said. He kissed her and left.

When the tub was ready, one maid remained. Jancy wasn't used to a bathing attendant, but she didn't quibble. Then, to her surprise, the woman took out a paper. "The gentleman as left asked me to give you this, ma'am. Privately."

Jancy broke the seal. Hal explained that Simon wanted him to find Sir Stephen Ball, but that meant she must tell Simon about the earldom. She should allow him no more than a day of peace at Long Chart because his family needed him.

Poor Simon. She folded the note and tossed it on the fire. When she looked at the maid, however, she caught a disapproving sneer.

"Major Beaumont and I have planned a surprise for my husband."

"Really, ma'am?"

Jancy was sure a real lady would give the woman an icy set-down, but she protested, "Nothing like that."

For some reason, the maid seemed to believe her and flushed in turn. "I'm sorry, ma'am, but you wouldn't believe what we see in a place like this. Come on now. Into the bath."

Jancy slipped out of her clothes and into the lovely warm water, sighing with bliss. The maid helped to scrub

her back and then to wash and rinse her hair. Jancy
scrubbed the rest of herself until her skin tingled. When
she stepped out, she apologized for the state of the
water.

"Never you fret, ma'am. We're used to people off
ships here. I'd never go across the oceans, having seen
the state some arrive in. Sit in front of the fire, ma'am,
and I'll comb your hair out as it dries."

Jancy put on her robe and did so, carried back to
bittersweet memories of Jane doing this for her. They'd
often brushed out each other's hair before the fire to
dry it, especially in winter when wet hair, they said,
could kill a person.

"Lovely hair, it is," the woman said, combing. "Not
quite red, not quite gold. Like a sunset. There, then.
That'll do. Do you want me to do it up, ma'am?"

Jancy stood, running her fingers through her almost
dry hair that finally was as silky as it ought to be. "No,
thank you."

The maid left and Jancy considered herself in the mirror, hoping Simon would bring the clean undergarments himself.

He did.

She smiled at him, deliberately running her fingers
into her hair and spreading it around herself. She saw
him inhale. He tossed the package aside and loosed her
robe to adore her with his eyes. There was no other way
of thinking about it, and it made her certain of her
course. She'd do anything to secure his happiness.

"I'm glad I please you, Simon."

"I never knew such pleasure existed. I want you now."

She spread her hands. "I am yours."

He led her to the bed and pushed her down on her
back, her legs over the side. Then he unfastened his
riding breeches and drawers so his cock sprang free, bold
and full.

He leaned over her, sliding into her, and even like that
it was the most perfect sensation, perhaps even more so

for daylight and sanity. Eyes closed, arms spread, Jancy did nothing but feel every slow, deep stroke, feel how her body responded with building, feverish need. She raised her legs around him in a different kind of embrace and gasped, "Love, love, love . . ." until the cataclysm stole her voice entirely.

Heart still pounding, she opened her eyes. "That was lovely."

His eyes were brilliant with laughter and more than laughter as he grasped her legs and stepped back, sliding out of her. He looked down at her, making heat rush through her, and then knelt to kiss her there.

"Simon!"

He stood. "Due homage." Then he grasped her hand and pulled her up. "I have a fresh shift and drawers for you. Do you need assistance?"

Still warm from embarrassment and loving, she said, "Are you offering, sir?"

So he played maid to her, though her simple clothes didn't require it, and even plaited and pinned up her hair. Then, before she could rise from the chair in front of the dressing table, he produced a cap—a lacy, frilly thing—and arranged it on her hair.

"Oh, that's pretty. Thank you!"

She would have turned to him but he held her shoulder with one hand and took something out of his breeches pocket. She could see by the smile in his eyes in the mirror that it would be another gift.

He put his hands around her and pinned a brooch at the neckline of her dark blue gown—a colorful spray of flowers made of semiprecious stones.

She touched it, smiling. "It's lovely. Thank you."

He leaned to kiss her hair. "I have your flaming handkerchief tucked in a pocket, and the fob on my watch chain."

He let her turn, and she rose to kiss him. "Thank you," she said again.

He took her right hand and slid on a cameo ring. "Just

simple things, love, but enough, perhaps, until I can do better."

"Simon, they're all lovely, but you don't have to."

"Yes, I do. For my pleasure."

She sighed. "I said the wrong thing again, didn't I?"

"Jancy, there is no wrong thing. But try not to deprive me of the pleasure of giving you things. I don't want anyone to doubt that I hold you in the highest possible esteem."

She bit her lips against tears. "Simon, I'm not worthy of that."

"Are you calling me an idiot?" he teased.

"No, but . . ."

"Or disputing the fact that a husband is always right?"

"Well . . ."

They both laughed.

"Impudent wench. Come along. Breakfast is waiting and a carriage is ordered."

Chapter Thirty-One

After breakfast Simon escorted Jancy out to the waiting carriage, feeling as if the sun shone especially for them. He'd finally arrived at the heart of the puzzle boxes and found a mystery, but also a profound treasure. His beloved wife was stronger and braver than he'd already imagined, and he'd already thought her strong and brave.

At the moment, he realized, she was nervous.

"A post chaise," she said, as one might say, "A winged dragon."

"Of course." He guided her into the light vehicle, bemused that it could be a shock to her but reminded that she wasn't used to his world. It would be his delight to lay all its pleasures and comforts at her feet.

As she settled into the seat, she said, "This can't carry our possessions. Where are they?"

He sat beside her and gave the postilions the order to be off. "Most are on their way to Brideswell by wagon. If we need anything en route, we can buy it."

"You, sir, are too careless with money."

But he could tell she was protesting to cover nervousness, and when the chaise picked up speed, she clutched his arm. He certainly had no objection to putting his arm around her. "I promise, you're completely safe."

"But we're going so fast!"

"Think of it as like rapids on a river."

"But that *is* dangerous."

He chuckled. "In the most enjoyable way. Come on, Jancy, enjoy the adventure, for this and riding are my preferred ways of traveling."

"Are we safe in other ways?" she asked, looking to one side and the other, where Treadwell and Oglethorpe rode escort. Simon had his papers in the carriage at his feet.

"Of course. Simple precautions. If there was a villain on board the *Eweretta,* he is far away by now. Unless you're willing to suspect Reverend Shore, and even he is back at the Antelope, recovering from the journey."

She smiled at him, her eyes brightening. "I think I could grow to like this sort of travel. Would I be able to learn to drive some sort of vehicle?"

"Why not? And ride, too. I'll teach you."

"For now, teach me more about Lord Darius and his family. Thought of a duke's estate terrifies me."

She worried about these things too much, but he told her about Dare and his family and what to expect at Long Chart. She was shocked all over again at the first change, where their four horses were changed for new ones, ridden by new postilions.

"So soon!" she exclaimed.

His mood grew more grim, however, when he saw evidence of the poor harvest.

"Few haystacks, and they are small," he said, half to himself.

"And more vagrants," she added, as they passed a weary-looking family dragging possessions in a cart. Simon would have given them money, but the fast carriage had already left them far behind.

"Work to be done," he said. "And in more basic ways than reforming laws."

"Laws are important, as with the Corn Laws. And surely this is mostly to do with the weather. The harvest will be better next year."

He turned to look at her. "But the deeper cause is the end of the war and shifts in trade and industry. Even from chatter in Poole it's clear misery is stirring unrest, but riots won't help. Men have been hanged or transported for violence. It's not the answer, but with wages being lowered and the price of bread doubling . . ." He pulled a face. "I'm sorry. Don't let me bore you."

"Simon!" Lord, but he loved her frowns. "Such things couldn't possibly bore me. I'm looking forward to being the helpmeet of a newborn Hereward, fighting against the invasion of injustice. I don't understand many of the things you talk about, but I am much more familiar than you are with the lives of ordinary people. People for whom twenty pounds is the difference between decency and disaster. Who work all hours and make do and mend because they have no choice. Those who suffer from unjust laws . . ."

She broke off as if she, too, was worried she was ranting on.

He raised her hand and kissed it. "We are a perfect team, aren't we? Isaiah knew what he was doing when he forced our wedding."

They spent the next hours in plans, talking of where he would stand for Parliament and where they would live. He suggested that they treat Brideswell as their country home but in fairness added, "You should wait until you've been there before deciding. I call it a hive for a reason. It's always full of people, family, servants and guests, who all think they're entitled to meddle. We could have a place of our own, but not too far away, I hope."

She smiled at him. "Don't try to hide that you love it there. No idea of living there all the time?"

He laughed acceptance of her observation but shook his head. "If I'm going into politics, I'll give it most of my time. I'd like a seat fairly close to Brideswell so that we can spend time there or nearby, but our principal home will be in London unless you dislike that."

"I'm a town girl, don't forget."

"London isn't like Carlisle. It's big, crowded, noisy, and dirty. I'm not fond of the place myself."

She squeezed his hand. "We'll find the right home."

They continued to make plans, weaving a golden future and Simon thought their path smooth until they arrived at Long Chart. He hardly noticed turning between the stone pillars carved with heraldic devices to go up the long, treelined drive, but Jancy stopped speaking to stare.

"Lovely, isn't it?"

"I've never seen anything like it in my life."

She didn't sound entirely thrilled.

He tried to look with her eyes and saw parkland more perfect than God had ever intended and the great house sprawled over a gentle rise like a vast crown of golden stone.

"That's one house?" she asked. "It's bigger than York!"

Before he could think what to say, she turned a pale face to him. "I don't belong here. I'm sorry, but I can't. I won't know what to do!"

"Of course you belong here—as my wife."

"But I won't know what to do," she repeated. "Tell me."

"Simply be yourself."

"This *is* myself!"

Her snappish tone irritated. "Treat the duchess as you did Mrs. Gore. Treat Dare as you did Hal. And follow the old adage—when in Rome, do as the Romans do. Jancy, most people would be overwhelmed by Long Chart. If you get lost, ask the way. If you want anything, ask a servant to provide it, just as you did to Sal and Izzy."

They were nearing the house, and he wanted her to snap out of this before she threw a scene in front of the waiting footmen.

"Those aren't Izzy and Sal," she muttered, staring at them.

"But they are employed to help you. When you worked in the shop, did you mind assisting a customer?"

"No."

"This is no different."

She glared at him. "It *feels* different. Oh, I wish I was in a finer dress!"

Suddenly he did understand. "I'm sorry, love. It won't matter—these people are friends—but I should have thought of that."

The chaise stopped beneath the porte cochere.

"See," he added, "there's the duchess waiting to greet us, and she's not dressed much finer than you are."

Jancy snorted at that, but she appeared to be pulling herself together. What he'd said was true. The Duchess of Yeovil wore a plain brown dress and a simple shawl. Her brown hair was piled under a cap no more elaborate than the one Jancy wore under her bonnet. And beside her stood Dare, shockingly thinner and paler, even sallow, but alive and smiling.

As soon as they climbed down, the duchess beamed at Jancy. "My dear, how lovely to meet you. Though I warn you, Amy St. Bride is going to be frantic to have missed her oldest son's wedding. Simon, what a rascal you are to have stayed away so long." She turned back to Jancy. "I'm sure the wretch hasn't paid any heed to your comfort—"

"Oh, no, your grace. I mean, yes, your grace."

Devil take it, Simon thought. She was going to be bobbing like a kitchen maid in a moment. Why hadn't he anticipated this?

Sarah Yeovil linked arms with Jancy and swept her toward the door. "Come along out of the cold. You will want to refresh yourself, and Simon and Dare have years to catch up on."

Jancy glanced back, firing a silent plea for help. Simon

ignored it. There was nothing useful he could do and he trusted the duchess to smooth the way.

And Dare was here.

Simon gripped the thin hand of his dearest friend. Then he pulled Dare into his arms. Almost immediately, he let Dare go. "Sorry. I'm just so damned glad to see you."

"Teach you to stay away so long," Dare said, but smiling. "Shall we pursue before Mama terrifies your bride to death?"

"She's one of the kindest women in the world."

"Yes, isn't she. And I caused her so much grief." Before Simon could think how to respond, Dare said, "Does that satchel contain some secret treasure or can you surrender it to one of the footmen?"

Simon felt foolish to be clutching his papers, but it would be even more foolish to lose them now through carelessness. "I need to keep it with me."

Dare's brows rose. "A mystery?"

"Not exactly, but something of an adventure."

"Ah. The Rogue returns. And here we were, thinking we might have some quiet time. You heard that Luce had a son?"

"Hal told me."

"And Francis. A daughter—Emma. Both Lee's wife and Con's are in that interesting condition, and with the plethora of weddings I fear that next year England will suffer a plague of roguelettes."

It was just the sort of thing the old Dare might have said, but given a harsh edge. It was also as if the flow of words was being used as defense. Simon couldn't believe that he was unwelcome, but it almost felt that way.

They were walking down a corridor familiar to Simon from his youth. He even remembered the smell. Did all houses have their own smell, perhaps simply a matter of the choice of polish? Youthful memories made the changes in Dare even more marked.

It had been four years since they'd last met, so Simon

supposed he was changed, too. Dare was worn thin by wounds and opium, however, not time. That wasn't the whole of it, either. He looked years older than he should, but he *felt* older, too. Had that bright spirit been crushed forever?

Simon took the bull by the horns. "How are you?"

"Much improved. If you're shocked by me now, only imagine the reaction of my rescuers."

"I'm sorry."

"Don't be. Please. I'm the one who should be sorry." After a moment, Dare added, "I sometimes don't know quite how to behave with people anymore."

"Dare, you don't have to 'behave' with me."

"But sometimes I can't help it. Do please put up with me, Simon. I'm working my way from the drug, you see. I'm told stopping it abruptly can be deadly and it would certainly be unpleasant. Having been without it now and then, I know that. But this is a great deal more drawn out." After a moment he added, "I don't like what it does to me, but I don't like to be without it."

Simon tried a joke. "I've known women like that."

And Dare laughed, showing a flicker of his old self. "I'm very glad you're home, Simon."

Simon smiled. "So am I."

Jancy went with the duchess along what seemed like miles of paneled corridors and through grand chambers where paintings hung on the walls and even the ceilings were works of art. All the way, she tried to do her part in a stream of light conversation, but by the time they climbed an immense staircase, she was feeling desperate. Though there was nothing inquisitorial about the Duchess of Yeovil, Jancy felt squeezed for facts.

She'd admitted to being from Carlisle and that her father had been a schoolmaster there. This didn't seem to shock. She told the duchess about going to Canada when her mother died and meeting Simon there because he lived in the same house. She'd managed to avoid details about the wedding because she wasn't sure what Simon wanted her to say about that.

"How excellent that you met," the duchess said. "Simon has always been a wild flame, so I'm sure a tame domestic bloom would not have suited. Here we are."

Jancy was ushered into a room that took her breath away.

Walls painted with flowers and birds. A flowery carpet on the floor that felt silky beneath her scruffy shoes. Damask hangings in pale blue. Delicate furniture touched with gilding and upholstered in flowered silk.

A maidservant awaited, smiling, curtsying—and dressed far better than Jancy was, even in a striped dress, pinafore, and mobcap. Jancy realized she had her hands clasped nervously and made them relax.

"I'll leave you here, dear, to refresh yourself. When you're ready, the maid will bring you down to the small drawing room for tea. Don't feel you must hurry."

Jancy was left with a maid more terrifying than the duchess, even though she looked to be about the same age as herself. Apart from a twist of fate, what difference was there between them?

"Your dressing room's over here, ma'am," the round-faced girl said, opening an adjoining door. This room was plainer but still three times the size of Jancy's bedroom in Trewitt House. It had its own fireplace and various pieces of ornate polished furniture that would swallow up her meager collection of clothes.

And probably spit them out in disgust!

"There's hot water, ma'am, and the necessary behind the screen there. Beyond that door is Mr. St. Bride's room."

The bedroom was for her alone?

Jancy wanted to dismiss the maid and fend for herself, but she mustn't shame Simon. She let the maid assist her out of her bonnet and spencer, but then asked her to leave the dressing room so she could use the necessary. She was sure she shouldn't do that, either, but enough was enough. She wasn't yet ready to have a stranger listen to her piss.

Afterward, she washed her own hands and face, trying to sort through a bewildering swarm of feelings. She was definitely grateful for the cap, the brooch, and the ring. Small things, but they gave her a little dignity here.

As she dried her hands, she found some comfort in the splendor around her. She saw what Simon meant about her new rank making her safe. Mrs. Entwistle and Mrs. Cubhouse, Martha's closest friends in Carlisle, would never be encountered here. And if by some freak of fate it was to happen, they would be too awed to announce that a lady of the house was an impostor.

He was probably correct that they wouldn't even believe it. Whatever their sight told them, they simply wouldn't believe it could be true.

On the other hand, this was Simon's world, where everything was larger and grander—including disaster. What happened at these heights was observed and spread around the country and even the world. If the world discovered that Simon St. Bride had married the bastard daughter of Tillie Haskett . . .

She pushed that away. If no one ever questioned her being Jane, that would never happen.

She returned to the bedroom, where the maid said, "Your luggage has arrived, ma'am. I'll tell the men to take it into the dressing room and I'll unpack it for you, shall I?"

Already there was a bit of something. Not quite a sneer, but a recognition that this guest wasn't all she should be. The clothes would seal it.

Jancy assumed the air of the Grand Panjandrum. "It hardly seems worth it, but needs must. My husband and I are newly arrived from Canada, where only the simplest clothing is required."

A lie, but in a good cause, and she doubted this girl would know any different.

"We lived virtually in the wilderness," Jancy went on.

"And then, of course, we arrived on dry land only yesterday after a month at sea." She shuddered. "Only seawater in which to do laundry. As soon as we reach London, I will need an *entire* new wardrobe. Everything is ruined."

The maid's eyes were huge. "My goodness, ma'am, what an adventure! Would you like me to see what the laundry here can do?"

Jancy gave her an honest smile. "How very kind."

"And I can freshen up your other things, ma'am. A good stiff brush can work wonders."

"Thank you. I think now I shall go down."

Jancy felt she'd pulled that off rather well, but she approached the drawing room door braced for new quicksands. However, she found a quite modest room, cozily warmed by a fire, where the duchess, Simon, and Lord Darius were already taking tea with no servants in the room. Jancy soon relaxed. Perhaps the secret was not to think of the whole, enormous house but simply of the room and the people in it.

She had no premonition of trouble, therefore, before the duchess said to Simon, "It is most excellent that you have arrived at last. Your parents must need you badly."

He frowned. "Why?"

Jancy felt as if she was watching someone fall. Why hadn't she and Hal realized that the duchess would know?

"Why, poor Austrey," the duchess said. "I assumed that was why you'd returned."

Chapter Thirty-Two

Simon paled. "He's dead?"

"No, but any day, they say."

Dare said, "I'm sorry, Simon. I know you and your father never wanted this."

After a moment, Simon said, "No chance Austrey's wife's carrying a boy?"

The duchess shook her head. "I doubt it. The poor man's been dwindling for months and it would be known if Dorothy Austrey was advanced. He is receiving the best care, but . . . I'm sorry, dear. I assumed you knew."

"What ails him?" Simon asked.

"No one knows, but he's wasting away, poor man. Down to skin and bones."

Simon sat in silence, obviously prey to bleak thoughts. *Oh, my love,* Jancy thought, *I wish you could have had the one day we wanted for you.*

"My apologies," he said at last. "I'm afraid we must leave tomorrow, Duchess."

"Yes, of course. But do let's enjoy this evening." She smiled. "I hear the children. Dare, did you tell Simon about the children?"

"Not yet." Lord Darius smiled at Simon. "I've acquired a pair of French waifs. We're seeking their parents, but I fear I'll be left with them."

Jancy didn't think fear came into it. As Lord Darius had spoken, he'd turned toward the approaching voices.

The door opened and a maidservant came in and curtsied, a child at either side. One was a brown-haired boy of perhaps six in nankeen trousers and jacket; the other a pretty, younger girl in white, with bubbling dark hair and enormous blue eyes.

Those eyes, both pairs of eyes, fixed brightly on Lord Darius but then flickered around, as if checking for danger. Jancy wondered why she thought that. Then both children ran to Lord Darius, laughing. A black cat came sauntering after as if completely uninterested in these events, but it ended up at their feet.

"Good afternoon, Papa!" they both said with a slight French accent and began chattering about lessons and games.

"Hush," he said, and they were instantly obedient.

Too instantly, Jancy thought. What story lay behind this?

"I enjoy hearing about your day," he said kindly, "but you must make your bow and curtsy to some new friends, Uncle Simon and Aunt Jane. This is Delphie and Pierre," he said to them.

The girl curtsied and the boy bowed, but almost suspiciously.

"My papa has many friends," the boy said to Jancy as if warning her.

"That is a blessing," she responded.

"My papa's friends, the Rogues, will *kill* anyone who tries to hurt us. They have promised."

"Pierre." Lord Darius's reprimand was gentle. "Aunt Jane is a friend, too. She is married to Uncle Simon, who is a Rogue."

Both pairs of eyes turned on Simon. "Truly?" the little girl asked.

"Absolutely," Simon said.

This seemed to solve all problems and they went to the duchess, whom they called *Grand-mère*, to repeat the account of their adventures.

Lord Darius said, "They are still afraid of strangers

and especially of women in sober clothing. Even the housekeeper here now wears colors."

It all seemed extraordinary for a pair of waifs, and they did call Lord Darius papa. If they were his bastards, however, why not simply say so?

When Jancy caught the little girl looking at her, she said, "I don't much like dark colors, either. I can't wait to wear a dress as pretty as yours, Delphie."

It seemed to work. Delphie beamed and spread her sprigged muslin skirts. "It's is *très jolie,* is it not, *Tante* Jane? And I have many such."

They returned to Dare, almost competing for his attention, even though it was clear they were also devoted to each other. They were begging him to go with them to the schoolroom to see the picture they'd drawn. He excused himself and rose to be towed away, obviously wanting nothing else.

The cat sauntered after them.

When the door closed, the duchess sighed. "I don't know what will happen if their parents are found."

"Is it likely?" Simon asked.

"We think not. We hope not, but then, imagine if they have loving parents who are searching for them . . ." She gestured helplessly. "It is in the hands of God, and we are truly doing all we can. They're not brother and sister. Delphie can tell us nothing about her origins. Either she was too young or events were too shocking. Pierre remembers a village and poverty and grandparents, and that his surname was Martin. Pierre Martin. It's like John Smith. And I can't help but pray that we can keep them. We all love them. But now," she added briskly, "I will make arrangements for your travel tomorrow. You can take our traveling chariot to London."

"Thank you," Simon said. "And there is one other thing. We had planned to pause in London to find Jancy some better clothes, but now we must reach Brideswell without delay."

The duchess's eyebrows rose. "And where, you foolish

boy, did you think to find decent garments in under a week? Were you going to take her to a rag shop?" She eyed Jancy. "You are much of a size with my daughter, dear, who has so many garments that her drawers overflow, and I'm sure she's buying more even now in Bath. Will you allow me to make some space for her?"

Jancy glanced at Simon but saw that he wanted this. "Your grace, I would be very grateful."

"Come along then."

Jancy was taken on a raid of armoires of lovely clothes; more clothes than she'd ever imagined one person owning; clothes more beautiful than any she'd ever touched. And the duchess was right. Everything seemed to fit—once, that is, Jancy had been laced into a proper corset.

She'd forgotten how a corset raised the breasts into the fashionable high profile. She considered herself in the mirror in a dress of brown wool striped in bronze, high in the neck with a ruff for a collar, and long in the sleeves. The casual eye might think it simple, but it was beautifully designed and made.

She finally felt like a grand lady.

"Excellent!" the duchess approved. "Marie," she said to one of the attendant maids, "where is that sage green? I always thought it made Lady Thea sallow, and I'm sure she would agree, for I don't think she wore it above once. But I do believe it will suit Mrs. St. Bride."

The maids pulled out garment after garment, and the duchess assured Jancy that each didn't suit her daughter or was last year's fashion. "Thea will never wear it again, I assure you." But then she said, "Mourning clothes! I fear you may need black before you have time to order it."

Because of the impending deaths of the Earl of Marlowe and his heir, Jancy understood.

"The dowager duchess died during Thea's season," the duchess went on. "Such unfortunate timing. I assure you, she'll be pleased to find these garments gone."

More garments were produced, these in somber

shades but lovely all the same. Spoiled for choice, Jancy settled on the brown; two warm walking dresses, one in dark gray, the other the sage; a pretty silk dress in ivory; and another in gray and black that clearly was for mourning but beautifully embroidered and flounced.

"Isn't there's a silver and black turban?" the duchess demanded, and in moments that was produced and fitted on Jancy's head. She had to fight laughter. She was becoming a Grand Panjandrum herself.

"You must have curls around the face, dear."

Anything for Simon. "Do you have someone who can cut my hair?"

The duchess frowned. "Not well enough, but there's a way of dressing the hair forward." She sent a maid for someone called Villiers. "Now, spencers, shoes, gloves . . ."

Soon Jancy had all the accessories to go with her outfits and new luggage to hold it all. The shoes were a little large, but she could stuff something in the toes.

She wore the brown for dinner, with her hair dressed by Villiers, the duchess's maid, or dresser, as she was called. The woman had brushed Jancy's hair up at the back and swept it forward. There it had been curled with the irons to cluster around her face.

Jancy thought it looked silly, but the duchess assured her it was all the rage among those who did not wish to cut their hair short at front. "It's that or false curls, dear, and matching your hair won't be easy."

That sounded even worse.

Jancy added the pearl earrings and went down to see Simon's reaction.

For a moment, he hardly seemed to recognize her. Then he came smiling to take her hands and kiss them. "You are exquisite. Thank heavens I found you before other men. And you do see?"

He was referring to the fact that when she was dressed like this, no one would know if she was Jane or Nan. "Yes, I do. It's going to work, isn't it?"

*   *   *

That night in her grand bedroom, wearing one of Lady Theodosia's silk nightgowns with her own prosaic robe on top, Jancy wondering whether Simon would come to her or she should go to him. She wasn't even sure if he was in his room. When she'd retired, he'd still been talking to Lord Darius.

Dinner had gone well. They'd dined in a small room, just the four of them, so it hadn't been terrifying at all. The duchess and Lord Darius were so kind that she truly felt she could live in this world without strain.

As long as her deception was never questioned, she had paradise. Suddenly she needed to check her appearance now against the drawings of her and Jane.

She took out Jane's self-portrait and compared it and herself in the mirror. She didn't know. She was clearly different from the Jane in the picture, but if Jane was here, she would be different, too. The curls around her face had definitely changed her appearance.

She looked at the self-portrait, wishing she could share this splendid house with Jane. She would have loved all the art. One wall she had paned this evening held breathtaking drawings, apparently by Raphael.

She put the drawing away but then something puzzled her. She went through the drawings again. And again. With a gasp she raced to the door of Simon's room and flung it open.

He was there, but so was Treadwell, assisting him out of his waistcoat. She began to retreat, but he said, "Stay." Then to the valet: "Thank you."

When Treadwell left she said, "The drawing's missing. The one of Martha and me!"

"Are you sure? You must be, but let me look." A moment later he said, "You're correct. It must have been left on the ship. Don't worry, we'll send word—"

"No. If it had been left out in the cuddy that night, it would have been found. We didn't have the drawings out after that." She took a breath, not wanting to make a fool of herself. "Simon, I think someone stole it. When they searched our chest."

He took her hands. "But why? It's very good, but not of great value."

"You'll think I'm mad." He really would, but she had to share her fear. "Dacre seemed doubtful when I insisted that Nan had been the artist, not Jane. What if he stole the picture so he could take it north and show people to discover the truth?"

She hoped he'd blow that away, but he rubbed her hands thoughtfully. "To have a hold over me?"

"He must have been connected to McArthur after all."

"Not necessarily. He never tried to disguise his ambition and he'd know I could advance his career."

She clutched his hands. "So what do we *do*?"

"It's not disaster, love. I'm disappointed in him, but the last thing he'll want is to spill the truth. When he plays his hand, I'll know how to deal with it. All the same, we'll spoil it for him if we can. When we pass through London, I'll leave a message for Hal to see if the *Ewueretta*'s docked. If not, he'll organize a way to stop Dacre and relieve him of his weapon. If it has, he'll discover his whereabouts and do the same."

He drew her into his arms and she held him close, trying to take comfort from the warmth of his body, his strength, his casual *certainties*. What a wonder it must be to feel so sure of victory.

"I hate living on this razor edge of deception."

"Anything is worth it, as long as we're together."

She let him reassure her and welcomed his love, but later she lay sleepless beside him, sick with fear.

Chapter Thirty-Three

*I*t took a long day to reach London even on smooth toll roads and in the luxurious traveling chariot. They took rooms at the Swan Inn and Simon sent the servants off to find Hal, carrying a message about Dacre and the picture. Because of his family's urgent business, he'd left the Canadian papers in Lord Darius's safekeeping and had no need to deal with those now.

Jancy tried to be calm, but she was keyed up with fear of Dacre being in London and appearing to denounce her. If he planned to take the picture north, her fears were idiotic, but she couldn't help flinching at every knock on the door. Thank heavens she'd told Simon, though it could still be disaster.

And the Hasketts lurked in the shadows.

As they were finishing their dinner, another knock alarmed her, but Hal entered to say everything was in hand. "The ship's docked, but we have Dacre under watch. He and his wife are at a hotel. Do you want to confront him?"

"No time," Simon said. "I gather you knew about Marlowe and Austrey."

"You knowing would have altered nothing."

Simon's lips were tight, but Jancy thought he understood the connection with an amputation, and he nodded. "We would prefer to retrieve that picture."

"Stephen's in town. He'll know how."

"Our epitome of law and order?"

"Who better to circumvent it? There are Nicholas's old associates, too."

"Who?"

Hal laughed. "I keep forgetting that you've missed all the action. Don't worry. Rifling a hotel room is nothing."

Thievery? Jancy felt she should protest, which was very peculiar. She'd thought they were the upright and she the one on a tilt.

"Who else is here?" Simon asked. "Perhaps we should have a conference."

But at that moment a sharp rap barely preceded the entrance of a stunning woman swathed in a hooded sapphire blue cloak. It covered all but her face, but only framed her beauty. When she pushed back the hood, she revealed a complex arrangement of white hair. For a moment Jancy felt sure it was a wig, but it clearly wasn't.

"There you are!" the woman gasped, speaking to Hal as if he were the only person in the room. "Thank God. I was afraid you'd run off again before I found you."

"Run off?" He spoke as stiffly as he stood.

This must be Blanche, which of course meant white. Hal's woman, whom Jancy assumed to be disreputable.

The woman's perfect skin had blushed pink, making her even more breathtaking. "I'm sorry. Don't be angry with me, Hal. I can't bear it. Any of it. You've won." She'd moved forward as she spoke and was right before him now, but she didn't reach to touch. All the same, they could as well be fused together. "These months apart have been the most painful of my life."

Abruptly, roughly, he pulled her to him with his one arm. "Oh, God, for me, too," he said, so quietly Jancy could hardly hear, but she could feel it, in her bones and in her heart.

Breathless, she quickly looked away, toward Simon,

whom she loved as desperately. Whom she feared to lose. They began to retreat toward the adjoining bedroom.

"No, don't. We're sorry."

They turned to find Hal and Blanche facing them, smiling, blushing. Joyous.

"Our apologies for embarrassing you," Hal said. "But you may congratulate us."

Jancy heard a slightly challenging edge.

"You have to tell them first, love," the woman said. She smiled at Jancy, but her eyes were anxious. "I'm an actress. Some call me the White Dove of Drury Lane. My past . . . I'm not a suitable wife for Hal. The man's mad."

Simon went to her, took her white-gloved hand and kissed it. "I'm delighted to meet you at last, but I thought the White Dove never wore colors."

"What? Oh, the cloak. Disguise." Her eyes laughed at herself. "Besides, white is so impractical, especially in colder days when the coal soot is thick in the air. I don't know if Hal told you—"

"He did," Simon said gently, then added, "Jancy, my love, come and meet Hal's future wife."

Jancy went, a little puzzled by the formality, but then she understood. By introducing her to Blanche, he was accepting the actress. She felt engaged in a complex dance whose steps she did not know, but as always, she trusted Simon.

"I'm very pleased to meet you, ma'am."

The White Dove laughed. "Oh, enough of this ma'am-ing, then. I'm Blanche. Blanche Hardcastle." She looked to Hal. "Soon to be Blanche Beaumont, I suppose, you idiotic man."

He, too, raised her hand to his lips. "If you hadn't surrendered, I'd soon have been insane."

Love shone between them like a lamp. "It's to be a quiet wedding, though," Blanche stated. "No fuss."

"As long as we are married, I care not one jot."

"There'll be difficulties. Don't ever say I didn't warn you." Blanche turned back to Jancy. "I haven't led the purest life, and that's to put it mildly. You need to know that."

Jancy wished then that she could tell Blanche about the Hasketts, but she simply said, "It makes no difference to me. I wish you both every happiness."

Blanche smiled. "Simon St. Bride is a lucky man." But then she added to Hal, "What are we to do about your family? Your mother, your sister and her family?"

"If they refuse to accept you, we avoid them, but I have an ace." Wryly, he touched his empty sleeve. "They'll approve almost anything to ease my tragic plight."

Clearly his family hadn't reacted well to his injury, but Jancy thought there was a philosophy lesson in this somewhere—that everything had two sides, and suffering could bring blessings to compensate. It was too tangled for her tired mind.

"We must want to get to bed," Hal said, then colored slightly. He'd been speaking his own thoughts and his arm around Blanche was eloquent, as was the angle of her body to his.

"Yes," Simon said, laughter beneath his words. "I wish we could stay to celebrate but I need to get home."

"Don't worry about Dacre. . . ."

Another knock interrupted, and whoever it was waited to be admitted. Simon opened the door to reveal a distinguished, silver-haired gentleman.

"Mr. Simon," he said. "It's good to see you safe home." All the same, he did not smile.

"Grilling. Come in."

Introductions were made. Mr. Grilling was the St. Bride family's London solicitor. His well-schooled features almost betrayed him when he was introduced to Blanche, especially as Major Beaumont's betrothed, but he had other matters on his mind.

"I regret to inform you, sir, that I received news this afternoon that Lord Austrey's state has worsened. To be blunt, he could already be dead."

"No hope?" Simon asked.

"God's power is inifite, sir, but . . . no."

Simon sighed and quizzed the solicitor for news. When the man left, he turned to Jancy. "Can you bear to push on a little farther tonight? If we do, we can probably reach Brideswell tomorrow."

Jancy longed for a bed, but she agreed. They left all their other concerns in Hal's hands, and soon they were hurtling north by the light of the moon. They arrived at Ware exhausted and fell straight to sleep, and were off again at first light racing north, then east to Louth, and farther east toward the sea.

Darkness had fallen by the time they passed through the winding streets of Monkton St. Brides, so Jancy saw little more than shadows and candlelit windows. She could tell when they reached Brideswell only by the chaise slowing to turn under an arch.

In her light-headed, exhausted state, Simon's home seemed only an irregular spread of lights, but the chaise had barely stopped before he was out of the carriage. He turned to hand her down, and by the carriage lights, she saw his smile. No matter what news awaited, he was home.

By the time they reached the door it was open, spilling light and people.

"Simon!" a young woman shouted and threw herself into his arms. The dark hair flashing red told Jancy this was Mara.

Then he was in a woman's arms—his mother. Jancy was soon in the same vigorous embrace. "So pretty!" his mother declared, beaming at her. "Welcome, welcome, though it's a terrible time." She turned to Simon as she steered them inside. "You know?"

"Yes."

There was no time for more as a large old hall filled

with people pouring out of rooms, down stairs, from corridors. A hive indeed. The throng was of all ages, including a wide-eyed youngster in a nightshirt and a babe in
arms. Servants, too. All, it appeared, to be hugged or at
least shaken hands with, all bewilderingly introduced.

Simon's father had been organizing luggage, but now
he was there, shaking his oldest son's hand and then
taking him into his arms. He was a tall, fit man who
looked so much like Simon apart from the hair that
Jancy knew she saw him in thirty years or so. No wonder
Simon didn't expect to inherit anything soon.

Simon's mother was youthful, too, in her trimness and
energy, with excellent skin and a head of thick brown
hair. Even the older people—Simon's paternal grandmother and a great-uncle, if she had it right—looked
good for another decade or two.

Perhaps all that energy sapped hers. She felt the air
thin and darkness gather. She tried to stagger to a chair,
but the next thing she knew, she was being carried upstairs by Simon. "Oh, I'm sorry. I can walk."

"Don't be a goose. I'm the one who's sorry. Dragging
you on such a journey. Hush now, here we are."

Someone with a candle opened a door, and then she
was on a soft bed. The candle bearer was his mother,
looking cross—at him. "Foolish boy. No consideration.
Go away and let me take care of my new daughter."

Jancy wanted to cry to him to stay, but with a rueful
look, he obeyed.

"I know, I know," said Mrs. St. Bride, touching Jancy's hair. "We're a terrifying lot, particularly to those
not used to us. But there's no vice in us. We don't bite.
What do you say to getting right into bed? I'll have a
little supper prepared for you, and after a good night's
sleep, we'll get to know each other."

With a knock, two beaming maids carried in warming
pans. Another followed with her valise.

Jancy climbed off the bed so it could be warmed and
took off her outer clothing. Once the maids left, she

allowed her mother-in-law to help her undress, too exhausted to even think about privacy or washing. Once in bed, she fell fast asleep.

Simon endured his mother's scold with delight and teased her out of it with a kiss, sharing a smile with his father. It was so wonderful to be home that he couldn't imagine how he'd endured to be far away for so long. Though he knew it was illogical, he felt that nothing terrible could happen as long as he was at Brideswell.

"And I suppose you haven't eaten yet," his mother concluded, as if that was his fault, too, and left for the kitchen.

The throng had been dismissed, even the reluctant children, who were so grown he hardly recognized them. Simon willingly let his father draw him away to his cluttered study and gave a brief version of recent events, leaving out Jancy's confusing identity and the missing picture.

His father was engaged in the complex business of lighting a clay pipe. "Perhaps you needn't tell her about the duel just now."

"Mother? Never, if you wish."

"Lord, no. If you kept it entirely from her, she'd skin us both when she found out." He fixed Simon with a searching look. "You are fully recovered, my boy?"

"Completely. Thanks to Jancy."

"Pretty name, that. Perhaps she's with child. Fainting, I mean."

"Possible, of course, but only recently if so."

For some reason, the subject embarrassed, as if his parents shouldn't know that he'd bedded a woman. It was wonderful to be home.

He was nearly as exhausted as Jancy, however, and soon excused himself. It was strange to join a wife in his old bed, but perfect, especially with her special woodland smell mixing with all that was home. He lay close to her warmth and fell instantly asleep.

He woke early, with only gray dawn hinted through the curtains. The air in the bedroom was nippy, but that, too, was a familiarity of his youth. Perhaps he should build a fire to warm the room for Jancy, but she was no hothouse bloom.

She was lying with her back to him, the covers pulled up high. He eased closer and brushed a kiss against her hair, but lightly, so as not to wake her.

She turned, however, blinking but smiling. "Good morning."

He smiled back. "It's hardly that yet. Go back to sleep."

She yawned and stretched. "No, I'm awake." Looking into his eyes, she asked, "How is everything?"

He sighed and settled on his back. "All in good cheer, but it's an illusion. Marlowe smolders beneath Brideswell like a lit fuse, but they don't talk about it. In the end I asked for the latest news. Father said Austrey was poorly and changed the subject."

She moved closer and put an arm over him, stroking, comforting.

"My father is a wonderful man," he said, covering her tender hand with his own, "and strong in many ways. He doesn't avoid problems."

"So this shows how difficult it is for him," she said.

"Yes. Leaving Brideswell has to be close to unthinkable."

"So why do it? I gather he has no choice about becoming earl, but he can still choose where to live, can't he?"

"Strictly speaking, but the earldom brings many obligations. A seat in Parliament, an honorary position at court, and such. But above all, it brings Marlowe. The house. That's its complete name. Just Marlowe. He'll feel duty bound to live there at least half the year."

"But why?"

He dropped a kiss on her temple. "As I said, duty. It's a great house with extensive property attached. It's lifeblood to hundreds, even thousands, from the lowest servants to powerful stewards, from local farmers to a host of businessmen. There are farms, villages, vicarages, mills. Even the paupers suffer without personal interest from a local magnate. An empty house is a blight on a whole area."

"Then lease it."

"Good God, no."

He felt her flinch as she said, "I'm sorry."

He held her close. "No, love, it would be the sensible thing, but it can't be done. Not a place like Marlowe. As well suggest the Duke of Devonshire lease Chatsworth. And besides, tenants never take the same care as a conscientious owner."

"So the family will have to move backward and forward?"

"I suppose so. Or perhaps just my parents. The youngsters should have the life I had here, with half a county as a playground and every soul for miles around a friend or relative."

"It sounds wonderful, but better than being with their parents? Surely the area around Marlowe is pleasant, too."

The area around Marlowe was as indescribable as Brideswell, so Simon didn't try. "Possibly. I suppose it will sort itself out, but it's going to be a painful mess, whatever is arranged."

He pulled Jancy closer into his arms, resting his head against hers. "Thank heavens for you, my love. You are my rock and my strength."

Her arms tightened around him. "I don't know how that can be when you are my blood and bones, but I thank God. What's the matter?"

He'd tensed to listen. "A galloping horse."

"It could be anything."

"At this hour?" He climbed out of bed and pulled on essential clothing.

She followed. "Go on. I'll be down as soon as possible."

He left in just shirt and breeches and knew as soon

as he started downstairs that he was right. The bad news hung in the very air.

His parents were in the family parlor, sitting on a sofa in their nightwear, holding hands. Almost like children, he thought. A liveried groom was standing there, looking at a loss.

"The news?" he asked the man, who looked relieved to turn his attention to him.

"Viscount Austrey died at ten last night, sir. The earl's in a very bad way. Lady Austrey sends to ask that Mr. St. Bride come to Marlowe to take charge of matters."

Simon wanted to say that if Austrey had been failing for months, there was no urgency now, but of course Cousin Dorothy needed support. Who better than the man who would soon own Marlowe and all it entailed? Putting it off wouldn't change anything.

But he said to his father, "Would you like me to go? You can follow."

His father seemed to twitch to life, or perhaps shudder. "No, my boy. Or rather yes, if you feel able to accompany me, I would appreciate that, but I must go. Poor Dorothy must be very low." He patted his wife's hand. "You stay here, my love. I know you can take care of everything."

Simon heard footsteps but knew before he turned that it was Jancy. She was in one of her plain York gowns, her hair loose down her back, her eyes clear and alert.

He held out his hand and she took it. "I'm going with Father to Marlowe to help Austrey's widow. It seems likely that the earl will follow his son soon."

"Can I come with you?"

Breath caught with longing, but he said, "I've dragged you around enough. Stay here and rest awhile."

"I'm perfectly rested and I want to come with you." But then she added, "Unless there's some reason that I shouldn't . . ."

"No, of course not. But we must leave after a hasty breakfast."

She nodded. "Then I must pack." She left with a briskness that reminded him wonderfully of his mother.

A cleared throat reminded him of the rest of the world. He turned to see his mother smiling. "You chose well, Simon. There's a girl with her feet on the ground and strength enough to be a good wife and mother. It's a delight, too, to see you starry-eyed over her."

He laughed, knowing he was blushing. Parents could be the very devil.

Jancy had been in Brideswell for less than a day, yet she felt the wrench of leaving as she took her farewells. The throng had appeared again, but she still hadn't sorted out most of them.

The young woman with the baby was Mary, wife to Simon's brother Rupert. He was the Brideswell estate steward, and he and his family lived in the home. A plump excitable girl and a plump quiet one were Simon's young sisters Lucy and Jennifer, but she wasn't sure which was which. The ancients were a maternal grandfather, a paternal grandmother, and a great-aunt and -uncle connected who knew where.

There were some other old people who might be family connections or retired servants, and two young boys she hadn't placed. She hesitated to ask questions, though she'd be comforted to learn they were accepted by-blows. It would make her own birth a little less shocking.

She wouldn't want them to be bastards of Simon's father, however. She wanted to believe his parents were as devoted as they seemed. When packing, she'd realized that this was her first experience of a happy family. She wanted it true as a model for her future.

Simon's mother hugged Jancy in a warmer way than undemonstrative Martha ever had but with tears in her eyes. "Take care of them for me, my dear."

She seemed to regard the departure of her husband and son as if they were heading off to Canada, rather than traveling fifty miles into Nottinghamshire. But perhaps that was the effect of Brideswell. Jancy found herself sniffing back tears as the post chaise rolled away, a dozen people waving, the lads running alongside until they were through the arch and into the big, wide world.

Jancy settled back, thinking that her life had certainly been one of continuous motion for a very long time. She would have liked to talk to Simon about his family, but they were sharing one chaise with his father so instead she asked about their destination.

"You said Marlowe is a grand house. Is it like Long Chart?"

"Grand in a completely different way," Simon said. "Do you know your architecture? It's Palladian."

She didn't mind admitting, "That means nothing to me."

His father spoke up. "Built after the fashion of Andrea Palladio. Italian fellow. Sixteenth century. Wrote books about classical architecture—Roman villas and such. Last century a lot of people took up his ideas and unfortunately Great-uncle Marlowe was one of them."

"It means," said Simon, "facades that look like the Acropolis and a central hall that goes up to a skylight in imitation of a Roman atrium. As England lacks Italy's climate, the effect is chilly. Perhaps to compensate, the style has smaller villas attached by corridors to house ordinary living. Marlowe is widely admired, however. People travel from around the world to see it."

It was impossible to tell what Simon thought about that, but his father let out something that could be a growl or even a moan.

"The park matches Long Chart in beauty," Simon continued. "There's a lake close enough to the house to reflect it on calm days. A remarkable effect, especially with a rise, darkly treed, behind it."

She smiled at his tone. "You make it sound fit for a gothic novel."

"Not at all. No dusty corridors, ancient chapels, or priests' holes. The entire place was built only sixty years ago and an army of servants keep it pristine. Any skeletal monk would be run out in a moment."

Talk turned to other matters, mostly father and son reviewing the state of affairs, locally, nationally, and internationally. Jancy listened and learned, impressed by the way they took it for granted that all these matters were their business and, to an extent, their responsibility. If problems were discussed, such as unrest and poverty, it was hand in hand with proposed action.

Hereward the Wake's bloodline.

Her bloodline was nothing but irresponsible trouble. She put the Hasketts out of mind. Simon had taken action to deal with Dacre and he believed her deception would never be revealed. Let it be so.

She began to look forward to playing a small part in steering the fate of a nation and was amused to see Simon persuade his father that a seat in the House of Lords was not a total burden—that he would be able to use it to promote rural causes dear to his heart. Mr. St. Bride even promised to lend his weight to Simon's fight for justice in Canada but added with a mock scowl: "I suppose I'll end up tangled with those Rogues of yours. London. Plaguey nuisance."

Traveling in luxurious efficiency, they arrived at Marlowe in the afternoon and Jancy peered for her first look. She needn't have strained. Some great houses sought privacy behind walls and trees or flickered coyly from behind carefully arranged hills and coppices. Marlowe stood on display.

The park was almost flat in this direction and lightly wooded. Now, with most trees bare, the white house glowed from miles away, framed, as Simon had said, by a rise of dark evergreens behind.

It did resemble a Greek temple, the central part presenting a triangular pediment supported by tall pillars. On either side, two pillared arms curved to the villas—miniature copies of the central house, even to pediment and pillars. Like offshoot plants, she thought, her wanton imagination seeing gardeners having to scurry around trimming buildings before they overran the park.

The curving arms could have looked like a welcoming embrace, but to Jancy Marlowe stood aloof. It did not say, "Enter and be warmed." It said, "Look on my beauty and bow low in awe." She was grateful to be dressed in Lady Thea Debenham's elegant black.

They came to a halt at the foot of massive double stairs, where somber servants awaited to open the chaise door and usher them up to large white doors hung with an escutcheon draped in crape.

As they entered the house, Jancy supposed that an army of servants constituted a welcome, but that was the only one she felt. She reminded herself that this was a house of long-term sickness and recent death. The powdered footmen and uniformed maids all wore signs of mourning—black armbands and gloves for the men, black caps and aprons for the women.

Perhaps sickness and death explained the overall chill, but this hall, lit palely by a domed skylight, could never be cozy. The floor and walls were gray marble, the wall broken at regular intervals by black half pillars separating black alcoves holding white classical statues.

There was not a touch of color.

Could the St. Brides ever warm this place or would it freeze them to death? She felt only relief when a gentleman in elegant black bowed and said, "Lady Austrey awaits, sirs, ma'am," and led them down a corridor.

Once away from the hall, the house did have some color. As the corridor curved—it had to be one of the arms—the walls were painted blue to better show off landscape paintings. They passed through a door and into another hall, but this time a small one, paneled in rich golden wood. Their usher tapped on a door and they entered a room made gloomy only by drawn curtains. It was a drawing room of modest size, well warmed by a fire and with a flowered carpet on the floor.

The slender woman rising from a sofa, dressed in

deepest black, must be the widow, Cousin Dorothy, Lady Austrey. She dismissed a hovering maid and smiled with obvious effort.

"Uncle Sim, thank you for coming. And Simon. I didn't know you had returned. How good that is for everyone. I'm sorry to send for you, but there are so many things." She gestured vaguely. "Legal matters, the funeral. Everyone seems to need direction. And I simply can't . . ."

Jancy had thought Lady Austrey calm, for the death couldn't have been a shock, but perhaps she had hoped until the end. She certainly looked exhausted, and the prominent bones of her face were probably not her natural state.

Simon's father took her hand and sat her down, taking a seat beside her. "Of course not, after all that nursing. Simon and I will see to everything, never you fear, my dear. How is Marlowe?"

She sighed and simply shook her head.

Mr. St. Bride sighed, too. "Ah, well. Now, here's Simon's wife, Jancy. Will it be all right if she sits with you while we have a look at how things are? And what about Lady Taverley or one of your sisters?"

"I've sent for Mama, but she's in Harrogate. I hope she'll arrive tomorrow." She looked at Jancy and tried a smile. "I'm sorry. What a way to meet."

"I'm sorry for your loss, my lady, but let me take care of you."

"Oh, not 'my lady,' please! Cousin Dorothy."

Jancy winced at the mistake but didn't let it distract her. She turned to the men. "I'll look after things here."

Simon smiled his thanks, and the men left.

"I'm so happy for you," Lady Austrey said.

Jancy realized she was still smiling after Simon and gathered her wits and sat near the widow. Remembering how much she'd wanted to talk about Jane, and how horrible it had been not to be able to, she said, "How long have you been married, Cousin?"

Lady Austrey was clutching a black-edged handkerchief, but her eyes were dry. "Eight years. Austrey is ten years older than I, but we never expected this. He was only forty and always so healthy until last year."

Jancy prompted her to continue to talk, hoping this was the right thing to do. It was slow to begin with, but then words spilled in a torrent, about courtship, plans, her husband's love of horses, two darling daughters, and the tragedy of a dead baby son.

A tragedy for so many, Jancy thought.

She better understood Simon's concern. The Brideswell community could never move to this chilly, formal house and thrive, but they would hate to be divided. Even a few months here could erode the health and welfare of Simon's parents. Even so, they would feel they must.

This was like a deathwatch of a different, but no less terrible, kind.

Chapter Thirty-Four

*C*ousin Dorothy talked on, detailing treatments, many of them horrible as the doctors became more and more desperate. Improvements had all proved fleeting, leading to a painful, drawn-out end. Jancy would rather not have heard about it but hoped spilling all this would bring the poor woman ease.

But then Lady Austrey started. "Oh, what am I doing? And you just arrived from a long journey! Refreshments! Would you like tea? Dinner? What time is it?"

Jancy took her agitated hand. "Don't concern yourself about such things, Cousin Dorothy. I don't want to take over your home, and Marlowe is certainly much grander than anything I've had to do with, but please let me handle housekeeping matters for now."

The sunken eyes studied her. "It seems an imposition. You are so young. But then, I suppose . . ."

. . . *this will one day be yours,* Jancy heard.

Far, far in the future, thank heavens.

For now, firmness would be merciful. "It will be no imposition," she said. "Would *you* like tea, Cousin? When did you last eat?"

Lady Austrey stared into space. "I'm not sure."

Perhaps the question should be, when did she last sleep?

Jancy posed the question, adding, "I have lost people very dear to me, and I know how it can be. Let me take you to your bed. You'll be more comfortable there, and can have a tray."

She put an arm around the widow and raised her to her feet—heavens, she was down to her bones—and guided her toward the door. "Where is your bedroom?"

"Next door. But . . . Aeneas is there."

For a moment, Jancy didn't understand. Oh, her dead husband.

"Where have you been sleeping recently?"

"On a pallet. There."

What now? She could make the widow comfortable on a chaise, but she needed a bed. A new thought occurred. "Cousin Dorothy, where are your daughters?" Were the poor mites abandoned somewhere?

"I sent them to my sister weeks ago."

Thank heavens for that. "Do you want them summoned to return?"

"Oh, no. Funerals are so dismal. I will join them after their father is laid to rest." She stated it fiercely as if someone, Jancy even, might insist she stay.

"Of course," Jancy soothed. But what to do? Then she realized that there must be a bedroom somewhere prepared for herself and Simon. Trusting Dorothy to stand on her own feet for a moment or two, she went to the bellpull. A footman appeared in seconds.

"Where are my husband and I to sleep?" she asked.

"In the guest wing, ma'am."

There was a wing especially for guests? Hoping the widow wouldn't object to being far from her husband's corpse, she said, "Take us there."

She supported a good deal of Dorothy's slight weight as they made their way back along the arm, through the hall and a library and into another wing. The footman opened a door into a warm, modestly sized bedroom.

"Take away our luggage," Jancy instructed, "and find

Lady Austrey's maid. Send tea and light food here." She thought quickly. "And tell the housekeeper I wish to see her in the library. And I'll want a tea tray there, too."

At least she knew where that library was, and she didn't intend to return to the other wing if she could help it. Should she order refreshments to be sent to Simon and his father? She had no idea where they were, and if they wanted food, they should be up to the task of ordering it themselves.

"Very good, ma'am." He picked up their valises and left.

Jancy sat the widow in a chair and found a blanket to tuck around her, amazed at how she was taking command. Perhaps her various trials had toughened her. His rock, Simon had said. She would be that if she could.

The brief visit to Long Chart had been a blessing in preparation for this. If she'd come here with only Brideswell for experience, she might be as staggered as the widow.

In moments the maid appeared, the one who'd been with Cousin Dorothy before. She was swollen-eyed but anxious to do anything necessary. Possibly she was protective of her place at the widow's side. Jancy could understand that, but not how the woman had failed to take care of her mistress by making her eat and sleep.

She wanted to get Cousin Dorothy to bed but thought she might not want a stranger helping her to undress. So she waited only until the tea arrived and the widow had drunk one well-sugared cup.

"Persuade your mistress to go to bed," she instructed the maid and left.

She followed the arm back to the main house, grateful that the geography of Marlowe was simple. No rambling corridors here. Instead an arrangement of neat cubes. In the library, a somber, white-haired lady awaited her, and a tea tray sat on a small table beside a chair in front of the fire.

The housekeeper curtsied and introduced herself as Mrs. Quincey, housekeeper at Marlowe for over thirty years and employed here all her life. It sounded like a challenge.

Jancy's confidence wavered. Did it seem as if she were rushing in gleefully to take possession before one master was buried or the other even dead?

Rock, she reminded herself and sat by the tea tray. "Please sit, Mrs. Quincey, so we can discuss how to go on."

The woman did so, but stiffly upright.

Oh, Lord, she probably shouldn't have invited her to sit, but she could hardly keep such an elderly lady standing. Impatience came to her rescue. Be it right or wrong, she had no time for games at a time like this.

"Mrs. Quincey, I look to you for advice. I am young and have no experience with a house like Marlowe, but clearly Lady Austrey must not be asked to manage here for a while, so together, we must do our best."

Astonishingly, honesty worked.

The woman relaxed, accepted a cup of tea, and began to talk—but she, too, wanted to talk about the deceased. Apparently she'd known him from the cradle and truly grieved his death and the manner of it.

"His brother died in the war," she said. "Crushed at some siege. It seemed so tragic a fate then, but it was mercifully quick. It's a sorry business to be so long a-dying." She put down her cup. "But it's the living that needs us, isn't it, ma'am. So what do you require?"

"Everything. Explain how the house is managed, please."

Jancy soon understood the basics, in theory, at least. Stewards, butlers, underbutlers, senior footmen, junior footmen. Mrs. Quincey had an assistant housekeeper and a maid who acted as her servant. Jancy would have been in a panic if it wasn't clear that the house almost ran on the wheels of its own routines. Here, she clearly would not have to go to the kitchens to help prepare food for the funeral guests, even though Mrs. Quincey apologized for the lack of a chef.

"We couldn't keep one, ma'am, with no call on his skills. Mrs. Renishaw does well enough for sickrooms and servants, but . . ."

"I'm sure she will be adequate for some time."

The woman's eyes turned anxious. "Will . . . When the time comes," she said, "will the new earl wish to live here?"

Clearly the household understood the situation and were fearful.

Jancy fell back on honesty again. "It hasn't been discussed."

The old woman sighed. "Very well, ma'am. You and the gentlemen will wish dinner. At five?"

Jancy agreed to that.

"There is the question of *where* dinner should be served, ma'am."

"Why?"

"The grand dining room is in the main house, ma'am, but generally only used for large gatherings. The family dining room is in the west wing."

In other words, near the dead body. Jancy remembered she and Simon going to the kitchen to eat because Isaiah's body was laid out in the dining room. At the end, great and small, death was much the same, but here, the kitchen was not an option.

Feeling as if she stepped onto difficult ground, Jancy asked, "Should Lord Austrey be elsewhere, perhaps? What has happened in the past?"

"It's forty-two years since the death of the earl's father, ma'am, but I believe he lay in the chapel."

"There's a chapel?"

"Oh, yes, ma'am. Off the great hall."

"Right. How do we do it?"

In half an hour, a procession was arranged. Simon and his father led the way and Lord Austrey's sorrowful valet followed the bier on which the dead viscount was carried by six footmen. They made their slow way out of the west wing and into a tiny, pale marble chapel.

Jancy observed only to be sure nothing went wrong and then hurried to order the bedroom stripped and cleaned. It was more as ritual than necessity, though when the cause of the sickness was unknown, a thorough cleaning was always a wise precaution.

She certainly had no intention of sleeping in there, for a whole host of reasons. There were two other bedrooms in this wing, however, as well as the small dining room and drawing room. It was almost a little house save for kitchens and other such offices.

The guest wing apparently was almost identical, but lacking its own dining room. The other two wings, the ones at the back, though as elegant on the outside, were utilitarian. One housed the kitchens, the other the stables.

She gave orders for another guest wing room to be prepared for Simon and herself and looked in on Cousin Dorothy. She was sound asleep. After a mental check for anything left undone, she summoned a maid to help tidy her and then found Simon and his father to ask if they were ready to eat.

They were, and the light meal was perfectly adequate. They all ate hungrily while discussing plans for the funeral. In view of the earl's state, it would be a simple affair with only local mourners.

The financial administration of the estate was more complex. During the earl's long illness, Austrey had run everything. During Austrey's illness Dorothy and advisers had carried out his wishes. Now she had tossed it into the hands of Simon's father, but he didn't have authority until the earl recovered enough to authorize it. Which seemed unlikely. The family solicitor would arrive tomorrow to sort that out.

After the meal, Jancy took a moment with Simon. "I know how little you relish this kind of administration."

He smiled. "And this time, there's no Jancy to guide me."

"I'm sure the earldom's officers are much more capable that I."

His eyes danced wickedly. "Only in certain dry respects."

"Don't be naughty."

"I wish I had time to be. Later," he said and kissed her.

Jancy wasted a moment wishing she could take all burdens from his shoulders and then summoned Mrs. Quincey for a tour of the house.

She looked into a number of splendid chambers in the main house, passing by only one—the State Bedchamber, which opened off the main hall, where the Earl of Marlowe drifted with extreme slowness toward death, apparently attended at all times by three servants and a doctor.

She took a quick tour of complex kitchens and stables about which she knew nothing. The basement of the main house held laundries, stillrooms, storehouses and wine cellars, and accommodations for the male servants. Here, there were all the mazelike corridors anyone could wish but, as Simon had said, briskly clean.

The female servants apparently had rooms in the attics on either side of the great skylight. Jancy wondered how warm they were in winter but reminded herself it really wasn't her business.

By the time Jancy settled into bed that night, her head was aching and she wanted Simon. She hadn't seen him for hours. She lay there realizing that she'd slept in a different bed for five nights in a row and raced about in between. No wonder the earth seemed to whirl around her.

Simon came at last, clearly as worn out as she. As soon as he joined her in bed, they tucked into each other's arms. "You've been remarkable here, Jancy St.

Bride. I know how uncomfortable this place must be for you."

"I had my moments of terror. But poor Dorothy needed help, and managing this place is not so different from Trewitt House when it comes to beds, dinner, and a cup of tea."

"I wish the estate and finances were as simple as Isaiah's."

He told her of his day. His experience had been much like hers. Leaving aside the legal complications, the estate was well managed and could sail along with little help.

"Can't it be left to do so?" she asked. "I can't imagine how your family is going to move here happily."

"I know. But a great house is like a ship. Even in fine weather, someone has to be constantly in command."

"The servants seem excellent."

"That never serves for long. And what point in having servants with no one to serve?"

Jancy thought of the impossibility of keeping a chef here and sighed. Perhaps they sighed together.

"But doesn't the same thing apply to Brideswell?" she asked. "It shouldn't be left empty, either."

"I'll be expected to make it my principal home."

Given his love for his home, she was surprised to hear resignation rather than pleasure.

"You wouldn't like that?" she asked, feeling her way.

"Agriculture bores me. It must be Black Ademar's hair. And anyway, it wouldn't be the same place."

A death, as she'd thought. "The children and old people could stay. . . ." But it wasn't a solution. She became aware of something strained in the silence. "Simon, what is it?"

Dacre? *Hasketts?*

He gently rubbed his knuckles down her cheek. "Nothing terrible, love. Depending on how you look at it, I suppose. Do you hate this place?"

"Hate? No. Why should I?"

"Do you like it, then?"

She couldn't see where he was going. "It's beautiful. But cold."

"Yes."

"Simon? Just tell me what's bothering you. Please."

He sighed and looked into her eyes. "I don't want to impose something on you. But . . . I want to take this burden from my father before it breaks his heart."

"The earldom? You can do that?"

"No. But I can offer to live here. To make this my principal residence and take over the management of it. As earl, he'd visit, of course, but he and the rest of the family can carry on as usual at Brideswell."

Live *here*?

"But you love Brideswell," she protested.

"Yes, but as a place to visit. I never expected to make it my home until Father died, and as I said, the business of Brideswell—tending the land and tenants—isn't the life I'd choose. I want Parliament, a small house in town, and Brideswell for country visits."

"But if you take over Marlowe . . ."

But he understood the implications. She wanted to protest against such a sacrifice, but it was in Simon's nature and part of why she loved him so much.

"It won't be the same here," he said. "My father and my father's father, and probably all their fathers, have actually run the Brideswell estates and been closely involved with everything in our part of Lincolnshire. St. Bride tendrils run through every field and into every home, though in a benign way. Marlowe is more . . . distant."

"More like a machine?" she suggested.

"Yes. After all, in his young years Marlowe hardly lived a rural existence. He inhabited London and court and even Paris before the revolution."

"So you'll still be able to stand for the House of Commons? Until you become Lord Austrey, at least."

"Even then. Austrey's a courtesy title. I won't get a seat in the House of Lords until I'm Marlowe. It won't be so bad, Jancy. We can still have the house in town. In fact the earldom owns one."

Doubtless not the small, cozy house they'd talked about, but she didn't say that. He sounded as if he was persuading her, but she knew he was trying to persuade himself.

She had to make sure he was thinking clearly. "You'll have to spend quite a bit of time here. We will, I mean."

"It seems a small price to pay for Brideswell."

"What do you mean?"

"If we do this, Brideswell will still exist. It will be there, ready to embrace us and our children whenever we care to go."

"I see," she said, and indeed she did. "Then we'll do it."

He rested his head against hers. "You don't mind?"

She hugged him close. "I value Brideswell, too. And I was worrying about the children in this chilly space."

And I'll find a way for this not to freeze your heart and quench your spirit.

"We will have children of our own, I hope," he said.

"Then we'll find a way for them to be comfortable here. We could always give the marble hall a coat of pink paint."

"Sacrilege," he said, laughing into her neck. "But you know, the walls there are only painted to look like marble. So why not? Not pink, perhaps, but color of some sort." His lips found hers. "Thank God for you, Jancy."

She kissed him back, rolling him so she could drive away his worries for a little while.

Jancy woke the next morning and had to sort out her mind to discover where she was. When she remembered, she realized that she'd been confused by the modest size of the bedroom and even, perhaps, by the sense of being in a small building. As she'd thought, these villas were like small houses.

When Simon woke, he smiled at her, but she saw the hint of burden in them.

"I've been thinking," she said.

"Oh, woe is me." But his eyes smiled.

"Simon, why can't we think of the family wing as our home? I believe we could even make an outside entrance. Then we can look after this place without having to live in it most of the time."

He rolled onto his front, head pillowed on his arms, smiling brilliantly at her. "We could, couldn't we? Add in the occasional grand house party to keep the place alive, and duty is served."

"Perhaps a party for all the Rogues."

"Now there's a thought. My angel bride."

"You'd have thought of it. I just have less to worry about right now."

"All's right with the world when my Jancy is in it." He rolled out of bed. "I feel poetry coming on. All's right with the world when my Jancy is in it. She has lovely hair but then she will up pin it. . . ."

She pulled a laughing face at him.

"She conquers all problems . . . and sings like a linnet."

"Idiot!"

"I love her, adore her, and there's the full truth in it." He blew her a kiss and went into the small dressing room next door.

Jancy sat there, hugging her knees, grinning like the idiot she'd called him.

She did as she ought and rang for a maid to assist her. She had no choice if she wanted to wear Lady Thea's dark dress. She supposed more mourning clothes were an urgent necessity but had no idea how to go about that right now.

They crossed the house to the family dining room, where Simon's father was already at the table. Once they were served, Simon dismissed the footman and made his suggestion.

His father stared. "What? No, no, Simon, I won't place such a burden on you. You want Parliament, and I'm sure you'll serve the nation well."

"I hope so," Simon said with skillful carelessness. "But a country house is no bad thing for a politician, Father. And I'm hoping for free use of the town house."

"But you can have that without taking on this place. Don't try to tell me that estate management is suddenly to your taste, because I know it's not."

He cut his beef as if that was the end of the matter.

"Of course it isn't," Simon said, "but this place almost runs itself. Admit it, Father, apart from all the other problems, you'd be bored here. It's a perfect jewel. There's no building to be done. The park defies the notion of more improvement. And as the tenants and local businesses are used to a cool and distant hand, you'd probably drive them to rebellion by trying to improve their lot."

Mr. St. Bride glared at him, but his mouth worked and Jancy thought a tear might be forming.

"What's more," Simon said, "Jancy points out that we can live in this wing very cozily while having a grand house for entertaining. Truly, Father, there's nothing we want more."

Though Simon's words were true in context, Jancy didn't think his father was fooled. But that tear escaped, to be dabbed with a handkerchief. "Thank you, thank you, my dearest son. Would have broken your mother's heart to leave Brideswell, you know."

"I know," Simon said, smiling. "And we couldn't have that."

Chapter Thirty-Five

*J*ancy left Simon with his father, happy overall with the way things were turning out. She'd never have chosen to live in a place like this, but she could and would make a home here.

She visited Cousin Dorothy and found her still worn down and grieving, but she appeared to want to take up management of the house. Occupation would doubtless be good for her, so Jancy expressed gratitude but was left at a loose end.

She wandered the house again, enjoying it as a guest. It truly was beautiful in its proportions, and the bas-relief classical figures, lovely plasterwork, and works of art were a wonder to her. She simply couldn't understand why anyone would create a house for show, however, especially when they then mostly lived in an annex. Marlowe wasn't even particularly accessible to people who might want to come and admire.

She wondered if it would be scandalous to have true public days when everyone, even the Hasketts of the world, could come and gawk at it.

The family portraits interested her, but if any of this branch of the St. Brides had been inflicted with Black Ademar's hair, it hadn't been recorded. Of course, for the past century or more, men had often worn wigs.

Restless, she put on a cloak and went for a walk to assess the place from the outside. She left by the terrace at the back, which led down to formal gardens clearly as meticulously cared for as the house. No moss grew on paths, and there was scarcely even a fallen leaf on the ground.

She encountered a few gardeners but suspected there must be many more, carefully keeping out of her way. She'd rather be aware of them. The sense of being alone in a vast empty countryside was unsettling. They could certainly open the garden to visitors. The gardens, like the house, had been created for show.

But she wanted an ordinary garden, like the ones in Carlisle and York—for fruits, vegetables, and perfumed flowers. She pulled a face at the shock she'd cause by planting her own beans.

She sat on the rim of a still fountain where big stone fish would spout water in summer, considering where such a little garden could be made. Horrendous, she supposed, to put it right by their villa home. She swiveled to take in the view away from the house, which included miniature temples and even some broken pillars suggesting that a Roman house had once stood there. It almost certainly hadn't.

In the distance a large stone house reminded her that she and Simon would have wealthy neighbors. Worries crept back like damp. Living here would mean becoming part of an elite county society. She'd have to host dinners and balls, perhaps for people like Mrs. Ransome-Brown.

Hasketts were good mimics, she reminded herself. Look how she'd put on the Grand Panjandrum for the maid at Long Chart. But thought of Dacre and the picture fretted her. If Hal had failed to deal with the man, what would he want?

Money? In this world that might not be a problem, though she'd hate to give him a penny.

Influence? Again, she'd not wish to favor anyone on those terms, but he seemed intelligent and hardworking, so perhaps it wouldn't be too corrupt.

But she and Simon would live under an ax of exposure, subject to infinite demands. That would be intolerable, and now, with Simon taking charge of Marlowe and soon to become Lord Austrey, her origins would be a horrible scandal. She'd probably be banned from good society, which would be unbearable for him. . . .

She couldn't imagine how she'd let him soothe her. They'd not dealt with the fact that her switched identity threatened the validity of her marriage. She remembered hearing about a case of an heir denied his father's title and estates because the courts decided his father hadn't been properly married to his mother at the time of his birth. A man could will his property where he wished, but a title had to go to his oldest legitimate son.

What if Dacre was clever enough to bide his time until after she and Simon had a son? Then he'd have a horrible hold over them. Now was not the time to make Simon face these things, but she would have to.

And behind it all, Hasketts lurked. What if Dacre went checking on her parentage? Had Martha told her secrets to anyone other than Isaiah?

She saw a movement to the side and turned, expecting another gardener. Then she rose to her feet. "Captain Norton! What are you doing here?" Feeling ungracious, she smiled. "You find an unhappy house, but welcome. The *Eweretta* made smooth passage to London?"

"Very smooth. We disembarked days ago. I've been traveling."

She couldn't imagine why he was here.

"And heard Simon was here? Please, come up to the house."

He strolled beside her. "A very fine property. And all to be Simon's one day, I gather, on top of Brideswell. Some people are blessedly born, aren't they?"

She could have told him what they thought of this blessing, but there was no point. "Do you have family in this area?" she asked, wondering where to put him if he wanted to stay.

"No, I came to see you—Nan St. Bride."

She stopped and turned slowly to face him. "But you were Simon's second!"

He shrugged, at ease and slightly amused, like a cat with a trapped mouse.

"I didn't realize quickly enough what was afoot. You're looking very fine, Nan. Quite the grand lady now. But I think, if you came face to face with your old neighbor Mrs. Entwistle, she would know the truth."

Jancy fought to hide a pounding heart and dry mouth. "What do you want?"

He smiled. "So quick. I always did admire your wits. Why did you do it? To get your cousin's inheritance, I suppose, so don't look down your nose at me. Then you worked your wiles on Trewitt to get his money, and now this on top. I do so admire success."

Fury threatened to overwhelm her, but she clung to calm. "What do you want?" she repeated.

"Straight to business, but then, you're used to the shop, aren't you? The future Countess of Marlowe, working in a shop. What will the world say?"

She simply met his eyes, refusing to be baited.

"Very well, it's nothing too difficult. Some of Simon's papers could blight my prospects. Bring them to me and no one will learn of your deception, not even St. Bride. From me, at least."

She fought to hide her surprise and rapid thought.

He didn't know Simon knew the truth.

He didn't know the papers were elsewhere.

"If I give you the papers, you'll never tell anyone?" she asked, trying to appear anxious to appease him.

"Why would I? It would not benefit me."

But you'll be back for more, you cur.

"What papers are they? How will I know? You can't be named or Simon would have realized."

"Bring them all to me"—he glanced around—"by the fountain. I'll find the crucial ones, and that will be that."

His calm certainty that she would do as he demanded

made her want to kill him. Hoping he took her tension for fear, she said, "Very well," and turned to hurry back to the house.

Fury burned fiercest, but beneath ran choking terror. Short of killing him, how could he be stopped? Simon. She needed Simon. She ran up the wide steps but made herself slow before entering the house and hurrying toward the estate offices.

Only servants were there, and they didn't know where Simon was. She ran back into the main house. Her head was buzzing so she could hardly think, but she made for the guest wing—and almost collided with Simon.

He caught her hands. "I was looking for you. Marlowe's gone."

The shock of that made her sway.

He caught her and carried her to a marble bench. "I shouldn't have broken the news like that."

"It's not that. Or partly that." This place almost echoed, and heaven knew who could hear them. She grabbed his hand and towed him out through the front doors—at the opposite side of the house to where Norton waited.

"Jancy, what's the matter?"

As soon as they were down the steps, she breathlessly explained. "Norton's here. He took the drawing. Took it to Carlisle. He *knows*, Simon, and he wants your papers for his silence! What do we do?"

"Where is he?"

"Near a fountain with big fish."

He strode in that direction. She ran after. "What are we going to *do*?"

"I'm going to murder him." He began to run. She pursued, but it was hopeless. She couldn't keep up.

From a distance she saw Simon grab Norton by the lapels and knock him down, falling on him, pounding. By the time she reached them, Norton was begging for mercy.

Jancy flung herself at Simon and grabbed his arm. "Stop! Stop!"

She could feel the rock hard tension throughout his body, but then he surged to his feet. "Get up," he snapped.

Captain Norton was half sobbing, a hand to his probably broken nose, but he struggled up. "All I wanted was some papers!"

"You frightened my wife. You *threatened* my wife. What did you do with the drawing you stole?"

Jancy swallowed. If Simon had asked anything of her in that tone, she'd have confessed in an instant.

Norton babbled, "Took it to Carlisle. To her neighbors."

"To *Lady Austrey*'s neighbors," Simon corrected.

Norton's eyes showed white. "I didn't tell them anything! Pretended it was a bequest. Said it was Martha Otterburn and her daughter. They said no, it was the niece, but thank you very much. Nice to be remembered. That's all. I swear it!"

"Which you will completely forget." The words were like chips of ice.

Norton looked as if he'd protest, but then he mumbled, "Yes, of course."

"My lord."

"My lord!"

Simon eyed him, rubbing his knuckles. "I presume you are the 'coin' noted by McArthur as being very useful to him. Clever to use your rank as an initial and add a letter. Captain Oliver Norton. That'll probably help us identify 'land,' as well. Yes, I can see that once someone worked out who 'coin' was, it would blight your prospects."

"I never meant to do any harm! Just wanted to get ahead. Everyone was doing it. . . ."

"Pay attention," Simon said flatly. "I will extract the revealing papers and keep them safe. As long as you hold your tongue, you may carry on your miserable way—but if you're wise, your way will never intersect with mine. If you make any trouble ever, I will crush you. Now leave."

Jancy thought that Norton would flare up at the cold, dismissive tone, but perhaps he realized that in a way, he had what he'd come for. He turned and stumbled away.

Belatedly Jancy looked around, worried about servants. This was an open spot and deserted, so perhaps no one had overheard what was said.

But someone might have seen.

They'd have seen only a fight.

All the same, she felt as if Pandora's box had opened. The truth was out, and despite Simon's threat, it could never be locked up again.

Simon turned to her. "He won't talk."

"But it feels as if the ground has dropped from beneath my feet. Simon, who will it be next, and what will *they* want?"

"No one. If someone denounces you as Nan, not Jane, we tell them to go to hell."

"But I probably broke the law!"

"I doubt it, but if so, I know excellent lawyers."

A residue of fury and violence hung around him, making her quake. She couldn't persist, not now at least, when he was dealing with the earl's death, plunged into a new, unwanted position. She took his bruised hands. "I'm so sorry, love. About the earl."

He shrugged. "It was expected."

"I'm truly Lady Austrey now?"

"I exaggerated for effect. The law requires that we wait to be absolutely certain that Dorothy doesn't produce a son. Even though she's certain it's impossible, we'll have to wait a little while."

"So what happens in the meantime?"

"The estate is administered by trustees, but in practice, we'll have the handling of it. In due course, Father will become Earl of Marlowe and I will become Austrey.

Our oldest son, if we have one, will be Lord Bruxlow, poor mite." He took her shoulders, tension gone. "Are you all right? I'm sorry he frightened you."

"Yes."

She couldn't tell him he had frightened her more. He'd frightened her with his violence, but also because he truly seemed ready to face the next accuser with the truth. She couldn't imagine all the repercussions of that, but one stood shockingly in her mind.

She licked her lips. "Simon, we can't admit that I'm Nan, not Jane."

"Why not? It's not ideal, I grant, but you made a mistake in a time of stress. It's certainly better than letting worms like Norton blackmail us."

"I lied to people over and over about it."

"We can deal with that." An edge of impatience told her this was a terrible time for this, but what could she do? She *couldn't* let him proceed this way. She wanted to wail with the pain of what he was forcing her to do.

"We can't admit it, because it could expose things you would never want exposed."

His eyes fixed on hers, suddenly sharp. "Are you married? I mean to someone else?"

"No!"

"Then what could possibly matter?"

Chapter Thirty-Six

S he was going to have to tell him. "When I went to live with Martha Otterburn, I wasn't sent by Scottish relatives. I've never been in Scotland in my life."

He waited.

"I was taken there by my mother. I was, am, Archibald Otterburn's daughter—I never lied about that—but by a woman called Tillie Haskett. He sinned with her when Martha was carrying Jane."

"I see."

She waited, despairing, for judgment.

"That's it?"

"I'm a *bastard*!"

"So was William the Conqueror, and the first Duke of Richmond, and Queen Elizabeth, depending on how you look at it. It's unfortunate, but you won't be the first unblessed child to marry into the nobility."

She gave a short laugh. "I'll be the first *Haskett*. Simon—the Hasketts are vagrants and wastrels. I have relatives who've been jailed, even transported! And I carry their blood. When we were clearing Uncle Isaiah's room, I ran off with Martha's letters because I feared what might be in them, and I was right. Martha told him what she'd done. She described my dirty Haskett mother and my *contaminated* Haskett blood."

"Haskett," he said, frowning slightly. "I suppose there was no friend Jane who drowned in the river."

She felt sick. "No. I'm sorry. I never wanted to lie to you."

He turned to stare out at the countryside, and she wondered if she should just creep away.

Then he looked at her. "So you invented those Haskett men who tried to help. They didn't sound so bad."

"But they're by no stretch of the imagination decent, upright Christians."

"Nor are half the aristocracy."

She sighed, feeling weary to death. "Simon, you trace your hair and your temperament to one ancestor, and your attachment to causes to another. You don't want a future Earl of Marlowe to have the characteristics of the Hasketts."

He stood like a statue, face set and somber in the cold November light, a breeze stirring his fire-touched hair. Each breath Jancy took hurt. This was the end.

Then he said, "I want future Earls of Marlowe to have your characteristics. Knowing you, my love, has taught me that what we *are* matters. Whatever your origins, Jancy, you are pure gold."

"Simon . . ."

"Hush. The British aristocracy is riddled with thieves and murderers. We have a pirate a few generations back."

"But, Simon, what if anyone finds out? Perhaps you don't understand. . . ."

"Oh, I think I do. We have Hasketts around Brideswell. The Cockertons for one, and the Strubbs family. Yes, it would be simpler if the world never knows who your mother is, but if it comes out, we stare them down."

"You'll be ostracized. I'll never be accepted anywhere."

"I assure you, the Rogues will embrace us, and I doubt the *ton* will turn its back then."

Jancy didn't know what to make of this. He spoke of

his world, so he should know, but she didn't believe it. He wanted it to be this way, but she didn't believe it.

She said as much.

He tucked her arm in his. "Come on back to the house. We need to talk about it, but I will not lose you, Jancy. I will not." As they approached the terrace, he asked, "Who else knows who your mother was? These neighbors?"

"I doubt Martha told anyone but Isaiah. She found it shameful."

He ignored that. "Thus most of the problems are solved."

"But what of the Otterburns? They have to know I don't belong."

They climbed the shallow stone steps. "Families are often wildly scattered. I met a St. Bride in Canada who'd never heard of Brideswell. We traced the connection back to a point round about the Wars of the Roses. But don't you see, it doesn't matter. If the subject ever comes up, we admit that Martha Otterburn made up the Scottish story to cover her husband's indiscretion. The beauty of truth."

She went with him into the house, wondering with hope and disbelief if he truly could waft all the problems away. He took her to their bedroom and assisted her off with her cloak. But then he turned stern eyes on her. "If there are any more secrets, Jancy, of your mercy, tell me now."

She blinked away tears. "No, none. I promise. I'm sorry, Simon. I meant to tell you everything in Poole, but I lost courage. And I wanted to be with you too much."

He brushed the tears away. "There is no such thing as too much in that respect. And I doubt your wanting can be greater than mine. You are my life, Jancy. Without you, I die."

She felt the same way, and they kissed as if they were each other's breath and blood. But then he pulled free. He sat her on the small sofa, taking the seat beside her.

"To do this, we need to be prepared. What else can rise to bite us?"

She shivered at that image. "The Hasketts. They have to know." But then she considered. "I wonder. I don't remember any of them ever mentioning my father." She felt her cheeks heat. "My mother . . . no one questioned who fathered her children."

His brows rose and he said, "I see," but he seemed more amused than shocked. "So it's possible your mother never told her family who your father was?"

"Yes." It still embarrassed her, but she said, "She might not have known herself if I hadn't ended up looking so very like him."

"So just your mother. Is she likely to tell?"

Jancy stared into the fire, struggling with that. "It's so long since I knew her, and I was a child." She looked at him. "I loved her in a way. She took good care of us in her careless fashion."

"How many brothers and sisters have you?"

"Four—then. As she said, babbies are easy enough to come by."

She realized she'd slipped into an accent and flushed.

When she glanced at him, he was smiling. "I'm finally realizing where my wicked, saucy Jancy comes from."

"Don't!"

"But I like my wicked, saucy Jancy. I can't wait to meet your mother."

"Don't get any romantical imaginings," she said grimly. "I saw her once in the street, about three years after she left me at Martha's. She was dirty, rough, ragged, and drunk. My only feeling then was terror that she might change her mind and drag me away."

"But she didn't. I assume you learned fortune-telling from her."

"That was Aunt Sadie."

"And the maggots?"

"Granny Haskett."

"Blessed Granny Haskett. I owe her a debt, and your mother a debt for you, so perhaps I should pay them."

"They'll take money, that's for sure. But then they'll only want more."

"Excellent. My love, only consider—it's my duty to take care of your mother and her family."

"Simon, what are you plotting?"

He slid down in his seat, looking very pleased with himself. "Where do they live?"

"On the roads," she said but then sighed. "They travel spring to autumn, doing casual work, some horse-trading, some begging. Thieving and poaching if they can get away with it. Winter, they have a place on the fells. A farm, but it's ramshackle and the land's too harsh so they don't bother with it."

"So if I found them a good farm, they'd not work it?"

"I doubt it. I was a child," she repeated, "but I think they *like* their life. I liked it well enough except for the harshest times of winter and when someone got in trouble with the law. To begin with in Abbey Street, I hated being stuck inside, always in the same place."

Simon contemplated the ceiling and then looked at her. "I'm willing to gamble that your mother has your best interests at heart. She found you a good home, and she never made trouble, did she? Coming around to beg, trying to get you to steal things?"

"No, never. She never contacted me at all. I think she took me to Martha because she was worried. I stood out among the Hasketts because of my coloring, and that drew attention. People thought I might be stolen. It made Tillie laugh, babbies being easy enough to come by, but Hasketts don't like to attract too much attention. And then there was Uncle Lemuel, who was treating me in a strange way." She looked at him. "You know what I mean?"

"Yes. I am prepared to like your mother."

She just shook her head. If he insisted on this unlikely

meeting, he'd learn the truth. But she no longer feared that he'd reject her for it.

She remembered him describing her as pure gold.

Perhaps she should fight his insanity, but she wouldn't.

"Does that make us safe, then?" she asked. "It seems so strange."

"Assuming we're right about your mother, the possibility of anyone discovering you were born a Haskett is remote. Your being a bastard is simply unfortunate. Warm acceptance by many people of importance will render it toothless."

"What about my being a hardened liar? I lived in York as Isaiah Trewitt's niece."

"And here you have a Cousin Dorothy who is no cousin even of mine. I have two relatives I call aunt and uncle who are not blood relatives."

"I'm sure I must have referred to Martha as my mother."

"She was your foster mother."

"On the ship, on the *Wallace*," she threw at him, "I told them Nan was dead."

"A misunderstanding due to your grief and frailty."

"Then what about the *Eweretta*?"

"You were Jane St. Bride," he pointed out.

"But daughter of Archibald Otterburn and his wife."

Strange to feel triumphant at scoring a blow that shattered her own heart.

But then Simon said, "I don't remember you claiming to be Martha's daughter. Unless you did so in a private conversation."

"I must have. When Dacre realized I was supposedly the little girl at Otterburn's Academy."

"Can you be sure?"

She frowned over it. "No."

"Then how can he be? That's the beauty of this, you see. How many people can swear to the details of an idle conversation? People assume things, but that's not the same, and if they are firmly told they misunderstood, they will accept that. Thank heaven there are no angels recording everything we do and say."

"I thought there were," she said.

He smiled. "If so, they do not seem to read them back in this life."

"What about the drawings?" she asked.

"Signed by Jane Anne Otterburn. Why would anyone think you said you were Jane, when you denied being able to draw?"

She pressed her fingers to her head. "This can't work!"

He pulled her hands down. "Trust me, it will. By great good chance, we haven't even had time to give my family any details that need correction or explanation. And don't forget the ace we hold. Who is going to make trouble for Lady Austrey, wife of the future Earl of Marlowe?"

"Blackmail," she shot back at him.

"You see how I deal with blackmail."

"You can be remarkably formidable."

"Then trust me to make this work."

"I don't feel worthy of this. I did lie, Simon. To so many people, including you."

He kissed away further protests. "Trust me, Jancy. We make no issue of it but proceed from now with you as the former Nan Otterburn, Archibald Otterburn's peccadillo."

She stared at him, this man she loved beyond sanity. "Very well. I will trust that you're right. Oh, but there's one thing. . . ." At his expression, she quickly went on. "Not a secret! But our wedding, Simon. I worry there might be something irregular about it. I truly believed I could set you free because you'd thought you were marrying someone else."

"Fraud certainly is cause, but of course in the eyes of the world I knew the truth as much as Isaiah did. The only person I might have said otherwise to is Hal, and we can trust him." But then he raised her hands to brush his lips across her knuckles. "My dearest darling Jancy, will you marry me?"

She wrinkled her brows at him.

He smiled. "I know of no law that says we can't go through the ceremony twice, and my mother will delight in throwing a Brideswell wedding. Not immediately, but I think even in a month it will not shock. Well, my love?"

She looked up into his smiling eyes. "Yes, my most wonderful Simon, I will marry you, again and for all time."

Chapter Thirty-Seven

*T*he sun shone for the wedding, which was a bit of a miracle in early December. Jancy looked out of the window of her bedroom, in which she'd slept alone for this one night, cradling the box that held the polished heart, smiling at the sea.

She and Simon had traveled north after the funerals to tidy all the details of her situation. The Entwistles and Cubhouses had been distressed to discover that there'd been a mistake—that Jane was dead, not Nan—but that didn't mean they were sad to see her alive. Her handsome, important husband had been a nine days' wonder.

Jancy had done as she'd thought she'd never be able to do and shown Simon their house, the places she and Jane had played, and Martha's grave. There they'd arranged for a headstone in memory of Jane Otterburn, who had in her charity drawn likenesses at the summer fair in 1815, and thus raised money but also created treasured images.

Using a solicitor as an intermediary, they'd made contact with Tillie. Jancy thought Simon had been a bit shocked by the rough, grubby woman who'd obviously dressed her best in a worn velvet cloak and high bonnet with broken straw and too many flowers, but she herself had been overtaken by a kind of fondness.

She wasn't sure she even thought of Tillie as her

mother anymore, but there were good memories and they'd smiled at each other, almost as old friends.

Tillie had been cock-a-hoop at the thought of her daughter marrying so grandly and had promptly extorted money. Of course Simon had come prepared to pay, and Jancy knew that the fifty pounds Tillie demanded was nothing to him, but still she was both horrified and amused.

"You are my wife's mother," Simon had said, "so we both want you to be comfortable. Indefinitely."

Tillie had changed then, in the way Jancy remembered from the day she'd taken her to Martha's. A sharp directness had come into her eyes, and a smile, too.

"You're a good 'un. We don't want me family to be asking too many questions, though, so you'll have to make it like an old admirer 'as left me a bit every month. A nootie, don't they call it?"

"An annuity, yes."

"Enough to buy me a bit of finery and medicines when anyone needs 'em. And coals and food in the winter. Terrible hard on the bairns and elders, winter is." The beggar's whine had returned. "Ten pounds a month? House needs a new roof. Let's say ten extra now for that."

Ten pounds a month was a fortune to a Haskett.

"He was a most devoted admirer," Simon had said, "which isn't at all surprising. We'll make it twenty, and you'll probably receive gifts now and then."

For once, Tillie had looked at a loss, but she'd recovered quickly. "Should 'ave asked for more, should I?" She looked at Jancy. "You don't need to worry I'll bother you, our Jancy, but it pleases me fine what's become of you."

"Because of you."

"Then come north now and then and let me see yer." She'd stood and twitched her outrageous bonnet. "And don't forget those presents!"

Jancy had already sent an anonymous present of a warm cloak, flannel petticoats, and a gaudy brooch she knew Tillie would love, and another of a basket of oranges.

"Thank you, Tillie," she said softly, and turned to prepare for her wedding.

Soon she would walk on Simon's arm though a crisp, golden morning to the church in Monkton St. Bride, surrounded by his family and friends. Hal had come, Mrs. Beaumont proudly on his arm. Prepared by Simon, the St. Brides had welcomed the couple without restraint, but it would not be that way everywhere. Jancy had seen worry in Blanche's eyes. Fear that she brought pain to the man she loved.

Then there was a cheerful Irishman called Miles Cavanagh, with a dark-haired Irish wife. They'd brought two fine Irish horses, a mare and stallion—he'd made a risqué joke—as a bridal gift. Lord Darius was also here, and Mara St. Bride seemed to have appointed herself his guardian angel. He was still unwell and would benefit from Brideswell warmth, but she wasn't sure he had enough to offer Mara in return.

Gifts and congratulatory messages had arrived from all the other Rogues. Nicholas Delaney had sent a startlingly beautiful set of dueling pistols, with stocks of pearl set with jewels. The letter had said: *I hope you'll note that these are too ornate to ever actually be used.*

Simon had laughed and said, "I've been sharply chastised."

Jancy had a new gown of dark blue made in the latest style and a matching Scottish cap that showed off the curls around her face. For this occasion, she'd added a rather large round button atop. When she went downstairs and Simon saw it, he laughed aloud and insisted that they recite the piece then and there. Everyone joined in.

Because of the deaths this was officially a quiet affair, but nothing seemed to be quiet where Brideswell was concerned. Villagers lined the winding street to wish Mr. Simon and his lady well.

Near the church, they stopped at the Bride's Well. Simon followed tradition and dipped some water for Jancy. She gave him a look but drank as a virtuous bride was supposed to. When she didn't drop dead, everyone applauded, and they could enter the church.

This time they had a license and every detail was precise. Simon slid a new golden ring onto her finger and then a diamond hoop above it, to guard it, as the tradition went. Jancy had the other wedding ring on a chain around her neck, for it would always have special meaning for her.

They left the church to ringing bells, to be showered with grain and good wishes, and walked back to Brideswell, tossing coins and trinkets. They left in an hour, however, to spend their wedding night at Marlowe.

A new beginning, and a beginning of making the great house their own. The family wing had been redecorated and a new entrance had been built at one side, so that when they arrived they could slip directly into their home. Time enough tomorrow to receive the formal congratulations of Marlowe.

Jancy had a maid now, and Simon a valet, but they dispensed with them, too, as they hurried to their bedroom.

But there, Simon said, "Wait."

"Why?" she demanded, taking off her cloak and hat.

"I have a surprise for you. Now why, my love, would you look suspicious?"

She frowned, trying to hide laughter. "I don't want a surprise."

"I thought you might be eager to improve your knowledge of matters aristocratic."

"Now?"

"Certainly." He picked her up and sat her on the bed. "I hope you remember dukes to baronets."

She grinned. "Perfectly."

He raised her foot and pushed her skirts back. "Thus we come to the Order of the Garter, a most select and ancient honor." He tugged her garter loose and began to slip down her pink silk stocking. "The motto is, *Honi soit qui mal y pense.*"

"I know that one. Shame to him who thinks wicked thoughts. Like you, sir, I believe."

"You're taking liberties with the translation."

"You're taking liberties with my leg." She leaned forward and worked at his waistcoat buttons.

"I see you're an apt student. We must now undress." He stepped back and completed the unfastening of his buttons.

Laughing, Jancy watched for a moment but then slid off the bed to strip. She needed help with her fashionable gown and corset. "There's an order of nakedness?"

"I'm sure there would be if a monarch had thought of it." He lifted off her shift and unpinned her hair. Then he took her hand and led her toward their small dressing room. "There is, however, an Order of the Bath."

The center of the room was now taken up by an enormous bath tub—a glorious thing of deep blue, painted with fishes, big enough for two, and already steaming with hot water.

"How did you *do* this?" she exclaimed, running over to admire it.

"Pure brilliance." He handed her up the steps and into it and quickly followed her into warm, perfumed water.

"Oh, Simon, this is heavenly!"

He was already soaping his hands. He slid them over her torso and up to her breasts. "I believe we can improve even on heaven. The motto of the Bath is, '*I serve. . . .*'"

Author's Note

*T*his is the first book I've written using a Canadian setting, but I must have subconsciously intended it back in 1977, when I wrote the first draft of the book that became *An Arranged Marriage*, and said that Simon was in Canada. My family had just arrived in Canada then, which was probably the reason.

Simon didn't get much of a mention from then on. I think he was hiding from me, and very sensible, too. What happened when I found him? A duel, a death, and a forced marriage. But as I keep telling my characters, it's all worth it in the end.

I enjoyed doing research for this, but the early days of Upper Canada are so full of wonderful stories it was hard not to try to slip some of them in. The relevant one, however, lurked in a blind spot. For a long time in the writing of this book, Lancelot McArthur survived the second duel, but that left a trailing thread that I was never happy with. Suddenly, very late in the creative process, I remembered the Ridout duel, and knew what should happen.

In the acknowledgments at the front of this book I noted The Ridout Letters, which provided me with a vivid sense of life in York, now Toronto, in the early nineteenth century. Those letters end before the tragic duel, though it is mentioned as an aside in the accompanying text.

John Ridout did well during the War of 1812, taking an active part in the defense of his country at only age fourteen. His brief life is laid out on his gravestone, which was erected in the graveyard of St. James's Church, the same one where Isaiah Trewitt was buried, and which Jancy and Simon attended. The memorial is now preserved in the porch of St. James's Cathedral, which was built on the same site.

"In Memory of John Ridout. Son of Thomas Ridout, Surveyor General.

His filial affection, engaging manners, and nobleness of mind gave early promise of future excellence. This promise he gallantly fulfilled by his brave, active, and enterprising conduct which gained the praise of his superiors while serving as midshipman in the Provincial Navy during the late War. At the return of peace he commenced with ardour the study of law, and with the fairest prospects, but a Blight came, and he was consigned to an early grave on July 12, 1817, aged 18."

The "blight" was Samuel Peter Jarvis, a York businessman who had previously been on friendly terms with the Ridout family. Business led to some disagreements and somehow it ended up on July 12, 1817, in a duel at dawn at Elmsley's Farm.

All was conducted according to the code but for some reason on the count of "two" Ridout fired, missed, and began to walk away. One hypothesis is that Ridout, who had issued the challenge, thought a symbolic shot would show he regretted the affair and end the matter. It was, however, a shocking act that could have been meant to cheat and murder.

He was brought back and after a conference it was decided that the duel must go on. At first the intention was to start from scratch by reloading Ridout's pistol but Sam Jarvis claimed his shot, so Ridout took his stance to await it. Perhaps it was reasonable that Jarvis not expose himself to danger, but what possessed him to shoot to kill, no one ever knew. In moments, young John Ridout was dead.

Jarvis was arrested and tried, but acquitted on the grounds that his action was within the dueling code. The seconds were also tried many years later, and also acquitted.

As I said, it finally dawned on me that I could use the Ridout duel as a template for the one between Simon and McArthur, with McArthur trying, much more sneakily, to steal an early shot and in the second instance, Simon claiming his shot and killing him. Of course I didn't want Simon stuck in York for a trial, so I used the fact that Lt. Gov. Gore would want him out of there to slide over that. If tried, he would certainly have been acquitted.

For the record, Sam Jarvis ended up as Superintendent of Indian Affairs and died in 1857.

The use of maggots here is all true, both that they work and that the medical community ignored their benefits. A doctor with the French army had already reported that soldiers whose wounds had been neglected and become infested with maggots did better, but the idea wasn't pursued, perhaps because it seemed unpleasant. This attitude persists. Maggots are used in hospitals today to treat stubbornly infected wounds, but apparently some patients refuse the treatment, even though it might be their last chance to save a limb.

I was puzzling about how Jancy would get instant maggots, and also about how to be sure they were the right sort. That turned out to be easy—eventually. My husband suggested that I check out angling, and sure enough. Anglers know all about maggots, the gathering and care thereof. The best source of them is hanging game. The maggots there are sure to be the right sort.

In this research I learned about one interesting trick. Apparently poachers would hang a dead rabbit over a stream. The sated maggots would fall in the stream and fish would gather there to feast. The poacher came back and scooped up the fish.

I was fascinated to learn that sewing wounds wasn't recommended before the days of antibiotics. It was much more important to keep the wound open so that any toxins could drain. Doctors frequently used bits of metal or wood to do just that. So much for my scene in *Lord of My Heart* where Madeleine sews up Aimery's arm.

We writers do our best, but we're always learning.

The next book will be Dare's, opium addiction and all, and if you saw a hint that Mara St. Bride will play a part, you were right. I do have a medieval simmering about that infamous ancestor, Ademar de Braque, set in the Baron's War of the thirteenth century.

In 2006, a fantasy-romance collection, *Irresistible Forces,* is out in paperback. My story in there won the Sapphire Award as best short SF-Romance of 2004.

If you enjoy audio books, many of my novels are being produced by Recorded Books.

If you want to hear about new and reissued books, join my e-mail list. I don't share addresses with anyone. E-mail me at jo@jobev.com, or use the link on my Web page: www.jobev.com. If you prefer, you can use the paper post. Write to me c/o Margaret Ruley, The Rotrosen Agency, 318 East 51st Street, New York, NY 10022.

Share the joy of reading. Give books as presents.

All best wishes, Jo

Dear Reader:

I hope you've enjoyed reading this adventure of the Company of Rogues.

I love these men, and I've had fun writing about them over the past thirty years. (Yes, really! My first Rogues novel was the first book I ever finished. It just took a while to get it right and sell it.)

The adventure started for them when they were schoolboys at Harrow. Boys' schools were rough places in those days and an enterprising lad called Nicholas Delaney gathered a group for mutual support—one for all and all for one—forging a bond that lasted into adulthood.

They're a mixed bunch because Nicholas chose the outsiders, the unusual, and the ones who needed protection most. For example, we have Miles Cavanagh, an Irish rebel, and Lucien de Vaux, Marquess of Arden, haughty heir to a dukedom. Leander Knollis was the suave son of a diplomat, who scarcely knew England at all, and quiet Francis Haile, Viscount Middlethrope, arrived at school grieving his recently dead father. Despite their variety, the Rogues are consistent in honor. Whatever their natures, they serve their country in Parliament, on the battlefield, or by tending the land, because that's what heroes do.

For me as an author, their differences have been a joy, because each Rogue has fallen into a different kind of adventure. Or perhaps I should say, they have run into a different kind of woman, seemingly designed to test their limits. A tempestuous ward. A Regency-era feminist. A woman trained in the erotic arts. A poet's widow who's fed up with being seen as the perfect "angel bride." (Want to guess which Rogue above gets which?)

All things come to an end, however, and they are nearly all settled in matrimony. *The Rogue's Return* will be followed by Lord Darius Debenham's story in 2007, completing the series.

However, there will be books about friends and relatives, all in the same "world." The Company of Rogues series (including some spin-offs*) is as follows: *An Arranged Marriage* (Nicholas), *An Unwilling Bride* (Lucien), *Christmas Angel* (Leander), *Forbidden* (Francis), *Dangerous Joy* (Miles), *The Dragon's Bride* (Con), *The Devil's Heiress*, *Hazard*, *St. Raven*, *Skylark* (Stephen), *The Rogue's Return* (Simon).

I hope you enjoy them all.

All best wishes,
Jo

DON'T MISS THE OTHER
PASSIONATE HISTORICAL ROMANCES
IN JO BEVERLEY'S
COMPANY OF ROGUES SERIES

The Dragon's Bride
May 2001

Con Somerford, the new Earl of Wyvern, arrives at his fortress on the cliffs of Devon to find a woman from his past waiting for him—pistol in hand. Once, he and Susan Kerslake shared a magic that was destroyed by youthful arrogance and innocence. Can time teach them both to surrender to the desire that comes along only once—or twice—in a lifetime?

"Vintage Jo Beverley. Fast pacing, strong characters, sensuality, and a poignant love story make this a tale to cherish time and time again."
—*Romantic Times* (Top Pick)

"For those who enjoy a Regency setting and an intelligent, sensual plot, *The Dragon's Bride* is a must read."
—*Affaire de Coeur*

The Devil's Heiress
August 2001

Clarissa Greystone is called the Devil's Heiress. Burdened with the wealth of a man she despised, she is a fortune's hunter's dream. And no one needs that fortune more than Major George Hawkinville . . . but how will he ignore the hunger in his heart when Clarissa boldly steps into his trap?

"[A] deftly woven tale of romantic intrigue . . . Head and shoulders above the usual Regency fare, this novl's sensitive prose, charismatic characters and expert plotting will keep readers enthralled from first page to last."
—*Publishers Weekly*

"With her talent for writing powerful love stories and masterful plotting, Ms. Beverley cleverly brings together this dynamic duo. Her altest captivating romance . . . is easily a 'keeper'!" —*Romantic Times* (Top Pick)

Hazard
May 2002

The sheltered daughter of a duke, Lady Anne Peckworth has always been a perfect lady, even when jilted. Twice. Now, however, she's angry, and she's angry at the single most reckless, most irresponsible, most irresistible man she's ever known, Race de Vere. Race has invaded her orderly world like a pirate, tempting her to the edge and beyond. He leads her into impropriety, into wickedness, and then into the most dangerous step of all—the adventure that could win or lose her everything in one hazardous night.

"Engaging. . . . Fans will appreciate the spicy chemistry between [Anne] and Race."   —*Publishers Weekly*

"Fans of Jo Beverley's Company of Rogues series will truly enjoy this delightful adventure."   —*Booklist*

St. Raven
February 2003

Cressida Mandeville agrees to Lord Crofton's vile proposal, but secretly she has other plans. She will trick the loathsome man, find her father's hidden wealth, and save the family from ruin. All goes well, until a daring highwayman, Tristan Tregallows, Duke of St. Raven, stops their carriage, whirls Cressida up onto his dark horse, and demands a kiss. When St. Raven discovers Cressida is on a quest, he knows he must become her partner and protector. But he doesn't expect the dangers to his heart.

"Beverley's delicious, well-crafted, and wickedly captivating romance is a surefire winner." —*Romantic Times*

"A well-crafted story and an ultimately very satisfying romance."   —*The Romance Reader*

Skylark
May 2004

Once she was Mrs. Hal Gardeyne, the darling Lady Skylark of London society, but now she's a terrified mother. Hal's death has made young Harry heir to her father-in-law's title and estates, and she fears Harry's uncle wants those prizes enough to commit murder. Then a mysterious letter that could change everything arrives. Is there a long-lost heir to the Caldford estate? Laura must uncover the answers even if it means turning to Sir Stephen Ball—a man whose heart she broke years before. Together, Stephen and Laura must discover the truth despite the dangerous obstacles in their path. Will they be able to overcome their enemies before the passion that has reignited between them sweeps them both away?

"Beverley is a master who sets the tone for a wickedly sensual romance."
—*Romantic Times*

"The story is told with charm and wit, with narrative limited to the pertinent, and plenty of lively and meaningful dialogue."
—Romance Reviews Today

JO BEVERLEY

TO RESCUE A ROGUE

Now, in a special treat, the *New York Times* bestselling
author brings all twelve Rogues together to guarantee a
splendid series finale for the last bachelor in
their Company

Lady Mara St. Bride has never backed down from a
good adventure, which was how she wound up
roaming the streets of London in the middle of the
night, wearing nothing but a shift and corset
beneath an old blanket. Luckily, her brother's
oldest friend, the devilishly sexy Lord Darius
Debenham, answered her plea for help. Now she
intends to repay the favor...

Before he was wounded at Waterloo, Dare had
embraced everything life had to offer. Forever
changed by the war, he now believes nothing—not
even the interference of a lovely young minx like
Mara—can rescue him from his demons. But Mara
is determined to reignite his warm smile, and
enlists the help of all the Rogues to offer Dare a
temptation he cannot resist...

**Available wherever books are sold or at
penguin.com**